ELUTHIENN
A TALE OF THE FROMRYR

BOOK 1

Sam Middleton

Darkenheit Publishing

Eluthienn: A Tale of the Fromryr

Cover design by Charles Utting
Editing by Brett Savory
ISBN: 978-1-7393742-3-5
First edition: March 2024

Special thanks…

…to Charles Utting, who turned my mad science-fiction fantasy blend into one hell of a cover, Luan Bittencourt, who created masterpieces from my rough sketches, and Katie, who went above and beyond in providing feedback for this book.

A note to the reader

There's a glossary in the back – you're probably going to need it. It **does not** contain spoilers.

Pronunciation:
Aetraya: *EE - tray - uh*
Aeturnum: *EE - turn - uhm*
Formaria: *For - mare - ee - uh*
Fromryr: *Fruhm - rear*
Gyre: *Jy - er*

Other stories set in the world of the Fromryr can be found in the short story collections, Of Strange Worlds and Stranger Tales.

If you like the world of Aetraya, you can find out more at www.sammiddletonbooks.com

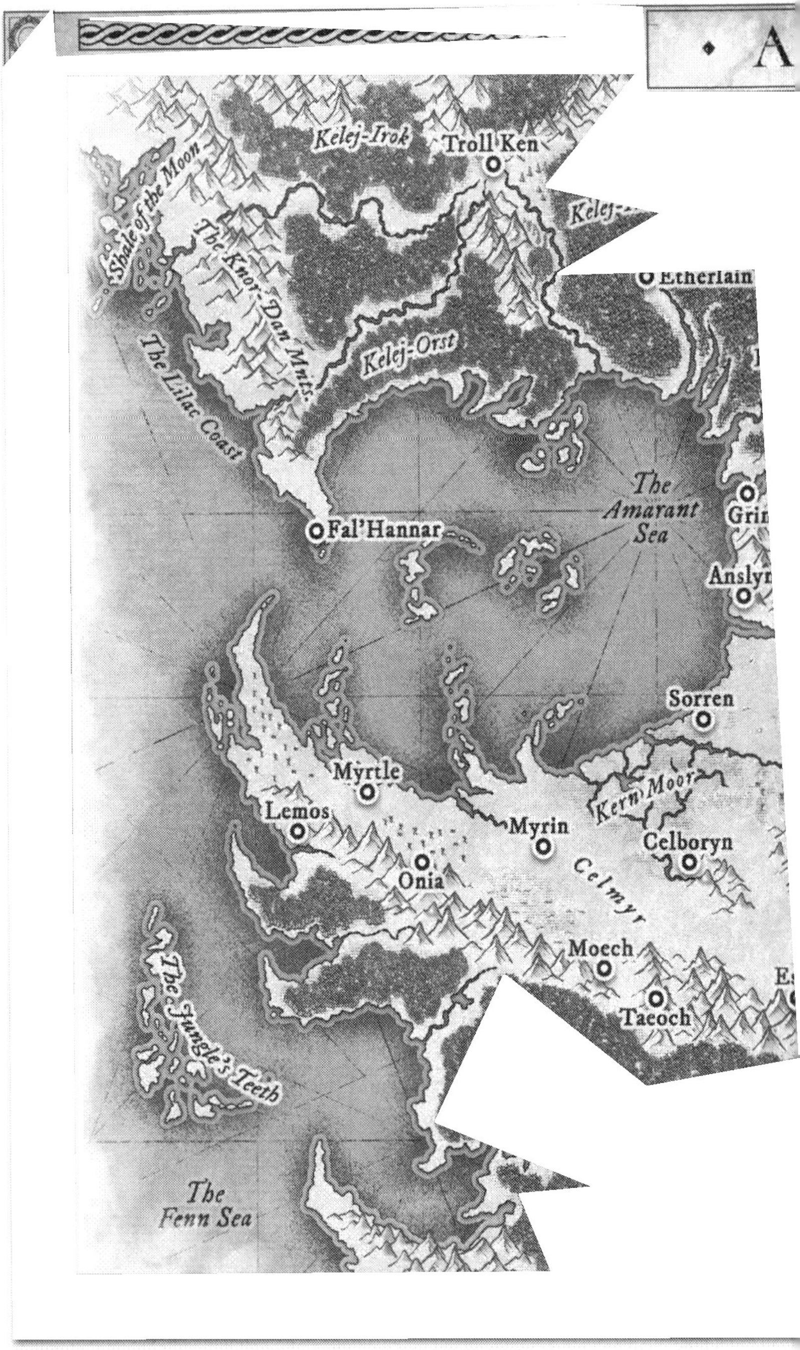
Kelej-Irok
Troll Ken
Shale of the Moon
The Knor-Dan Mnts.
Etherlain
The Lilac Coast
Kelej-Orst
The Amarant Sea
Fal'Hannar
Sorren
Myrtle
Lemos
Kern Moor
Myrin
Celboryn
Onia
Celmyr
Moech
Taeoch
The Jungle's Teeth
The Fenn Sea

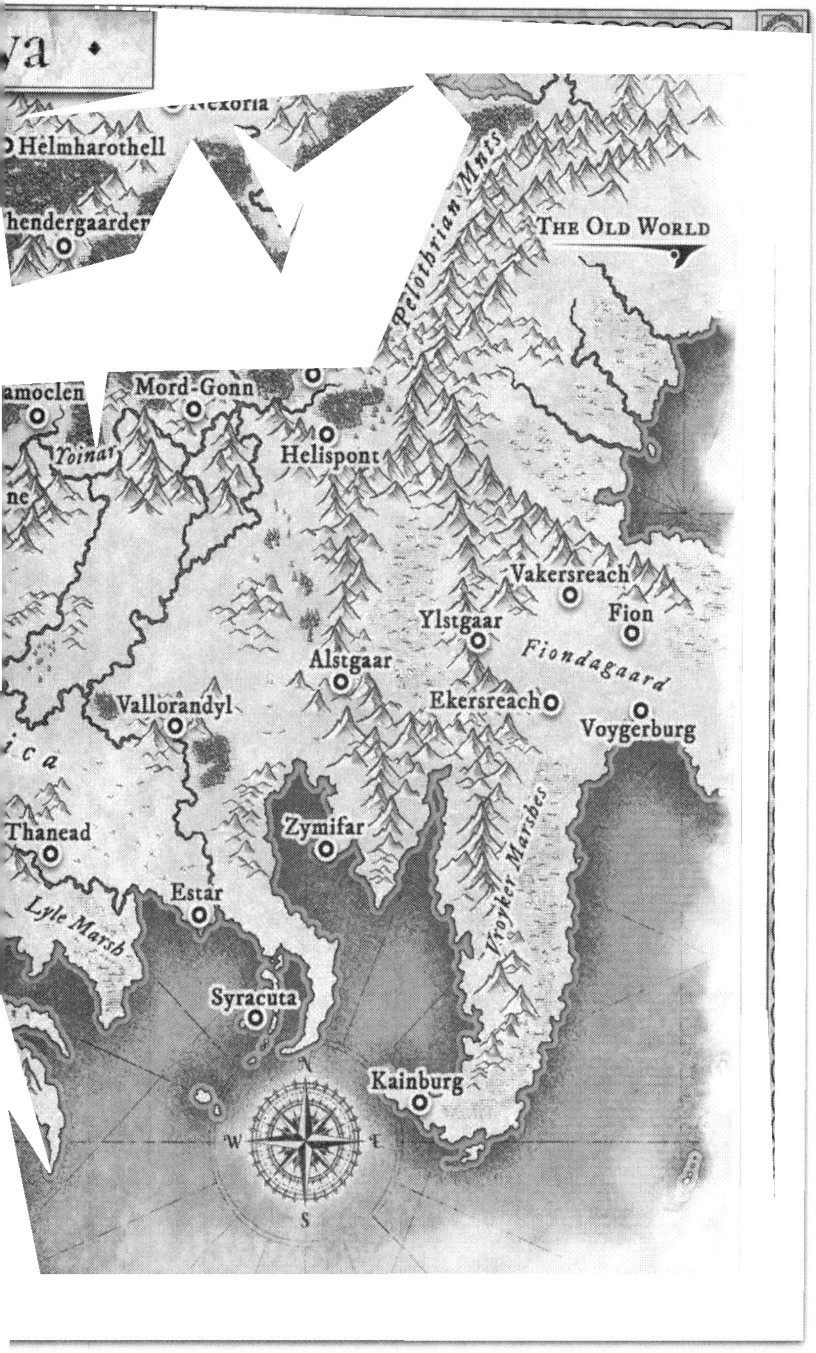

va
Nexoria
Helmharothell
hendergaarden
Pelotbrian Mnts
THE OLD WORLD
amoclen
Mord-Gonn
Toinar
Helispont
ne
Vakersreach
Fion
Ylstgaar
Fiondagaard
Alstgaar
Vallorandyl
Ekersreach
Voygerburg
ica
Zymifar
Thanead
Vroyker Marshes
Estar
Lyle Marsh
Syracuta
Kainburg
N
W
E
S

Lucretia
Omega
Xeron
Ilantia
Maylanese Gulf
Thela
Kyor
Seph
Vypora
Calanthis Major
Asteron
Grindle
Calaxis
Everaux
Veraxi
Map Key
Maw
Vault
Cauldron
Spire
Cradle
Cove
Calanthis Minor
Vox
Ersana
Siad

FORMARIA
Kronos
Talon
Acheron
Maledus
Teuron
Taranis
Talisor
Reantha
KLIOXIES
Theselan
Baron
Pheobe
Hyralian Gulf
Tia
Pontifax
Damoclen
Helispont

Epistolar message
Vallorandyl to Fion

A telling in Fion.

The teller is Vermillies Sidtch, Lord Regent of Ravinica and Absolver General.

The witness is Emries von Cadst, Duke of Ylstgaar, Adjutant to the Fion Throne, and Marshal of the Western Front.

The telling is of a stranger who came before the Ravinican throne. A cripple, bent and broken, he emerged from the recesses – from the very shadows themselves, for it was the hour of the wolf, and I neither saw nor heard him approach. Already, I loathed the wretch and how he crept toward me. His hobbled gait, his contorted frame, and most of all his exaggerated limp – as if he wanted me to believe it was a wound earned in some heroic fight. All of it, I was sure, was a performance, and still believe to be a deceit to elicit my compassion. Like a beggar expecting me to take pity, and so trust him not to spend my charity on drink. I can tell you, My Duke, such an outcome was impossible, for with every painstaking step he took, my repulsion grew; he dragged one foot across the hard tiles, and with the other, limped pathetically – a grotesque show akin to watching a snake trying to mimic a man. All the while he was hooded and cloaked in a tattered black rag, concealing his form and features. But even concealed, I was certain he derived delight from my disgust at his decaying form.

Alone with this thing, I said: "Show yourself, creature, and explain to me how you were able to pass the guards unseen."

He didn't remove his hood. Instead, he released a wheezing breath, rancid and smelling of death, and said: "I know of whom you seek." It was as if a corpse spoke – its vocal cords butchered in life by a blade. "I know where you can find Eluthienn Leonette."

At that, my first thought was: *He will now lie with every word.*

"Who are you?" I said. "Why won't you reveal yourself?"

"Of that, I'm not even sure," he said, and I thought I could hear the words spoken through a smile. Of course, I was angry now, sure this thing intended to trick me.

"Then what would make me believe a single thing to escape your wretched mouth?" I said.

He said back: "All the long years you've searched in vain. All the answers you've never had. All the fear you hold at his return."

"The prince is gone," I said. "Not a shred of his whereabouts have ever been found. What could you know that Ravinica's spies do not?"

"I know his tale."

At this I was confused, and could only believe it was all deception, so I asked: "What tale?"

"From the moment you deposed him to the hour in which we speak now, I know what happened to the prince."

"And what do you want for this information? Gold? Land? Titles?"

But he wanted none, and so I am sure what I am about to tell you is all a lie, for he said: "I would have you listen." And I could now, with certainty, hear his smile. "Each night I will return at this hour," he said. "And each night I will tell Eluthienn's tale. And I want you to listen until his tale his done."

And so I listened, and later committed to parchment the first part of the stranger's tale of Eluthienn. I recount this for you now, My Duke, for – and I am sure you will agree – whatever its ending, it will be of consequence to our plans.

ONE

LYANDER

Morning's pale shadow crept over the treetops, and Kalbrayeth Lyander stood baffled at the prospect of someone surviving long enough to build the house in front of him.

They're either lucky, or up to their neck in the blackest magic possible, he thought. Though he knew both options were as unlikely as the other.

The good people of Vergraine – his reason for being here – believed the house's owner a conjuror of Immurati. Specifically, a demonic spectre haunting them all in the night. It would go some way in accounting for the owner's choice of location. The problem was, the good people of Vergraine – along with the rest of the Pontivar valley, for that matter – liked to tell tall tales about the "evil" living on their doorstep. Really tall tales.

On the other hand, the idea this new resident

was simply lucky, was even less believable. “Yeggardania,” the forest in which the house had been built, and “lucky” were not two words ever used in the same sentence. Although, someone more meticulous than him might say the house wasn’t actually *in* the Yeggardanian forest.

They might also say, it’s not much of a house.

Its twisted dark beams propped up a roof sagging under its own weight, which slanted away from the chimney, a cobbling of white stone and grey slate. The door, which clung to its hinges, looked like it had been built from whatever was leftover from constructing the walls and roof, while the window, crooked and poorly set, gave the impression the whole thing was slowly sinking to one side.

It sat there, like a bear’s decaying carcass, on the *border* of the Yeggardanian forest, where the Pontivar’s beech and maple became indistinguishable from the larger arborealis, their slimmer cousins, the aranthie, and their distant relation, the sicathorn; where the smooth grey and furrowed grey-brown gave way to darker, thicker trunks; and where notched bark turned to coiling vines, and winding roots became feeler-like limbs, spearing the hapless ground around them.

Where the known, the (relatively) safe, gave way to the unknown, and almost certain death.

Holding the reins of his horse – who clearly wasn’t having the same internal dilemma he was – Lyander tried to recall what the baron had told him two nights past. That in itself was difficult because the baron had been several jugs deep into what passed for wine in the Pontivar valley.

“Unnatural,” Lyander seemed to remember the baron slurring at him. That was it; he’d said it was “unnatural for a man to live out there on his own for so long.”

They'd been sat in the baron's chambers, a room of soot-stained timber and creaking beams overlooking most of Vergraine. Taking up one entire side was a table that could seat sixteen and adorned with a scattering of silverware. Behind where they sat at the baron's desk were two couches facing one another in front of a hearth crackling softly. The light of the fire had turned their rouge colouring a blood red, and their grey creases into black arteries.

Draped on the wall above them, the green and white flag of house Angelaux. Every now and then it trembled in the town's summer breeze, wafting in to mingle with the lingering aroma of wood smoke and old wine. For Vergraine, the contents of the room bordered on extravagant, but Lyander hadn't thought the baron particularly wealthy. If he'd had to guess, the man had been "promoted" into the position as a punishment, or because he lacked the talent to govern anything bigger than a fishing village. That might have been unfair, but it was hard to think anything else when looking into a face resembling kneaded dough.

"Bolton Forth is his name – used to be a farmer," the baron had said. "Or that's what he told us, anyway. Come here six months ago from some town in Ravinica. Braega, I think he called it, though I never heard of it myself. Well, this farmer wanted a quiet place to retire and bury his daughter. She'd died the year before of the pox, you see – along with half the farms north of the Harinor, and he didn't want her in some mass grave. Which was a fair thing, as I saw it." He'd knocked back what was left in his cup and poured himself some more wine from one of the jugs left between them. "Sickle skin. Bad way to go. And worse to watch it happen to a child of your own. Doesn't affect adults, of course, but a stranger appearing with a box of bones in our midst – folk didn't like it. Not one bit."

He'd leant forward then, as if to a co-conspirator, saying: "Suspicious lot they are, these Vergrainians. Very suspicious."

Lyander couldn't have agreed more.

Another swig followed. "Well, he said he'd find a place outside the town. Wouldn't cause any trouble. Would hardly see him, in fact. He just wanted a place to bury his daughter and live out the rest of his days in peace."

Lyander had thought moving to the most dangerous forest in the known world a poor retirement plan, but he let the baron continue uninterrupted.

"When he told us where he was planning on settling, everyone thought he was mad. But when they saw he was serious, well, they weren't having any of it. That's until I stepped in and told them they should find it in their hearts to have a kindness. See, I'm the sort of man who likes to give people the benefit of the doubt. Guilty when proven and not before, and all that."

I'd guess you're also the "avoid conflict at all costs" type of man, Lyander remembered thinking at the time.

"At any rate, he wouldn't last two months out there, I said to them when the stranger had gone. And then they could all go back to being suspicious of each other. Of course, last he did. And odd things started happening a month or so after he'd settled in and built that house. Noises in the night when the patrols were out past the river. A wailing, some described it. A screeching, said others. And many have gone west, by way of the Yoinar, and seen some ghostly apparition they swore took the shape of a little girl."

The baron had patted the air with his hands then, and said: "Now, I didn't believe it. On account of all manner of things being in that forest, creating all manner of disturbances. Being so close to Yeggardania, you understand, odd things is wont to happen on our doorstep."

An understatement if ever there was one, Lyander had thought. *But he's right: There were usually far more corporeal explanations than the spirits of dead children.*

He remembered taking his first drink of wine then, wishing he hadn't, then saying: "So you went out there with them and proved it was all their imagination?"

The baron had been just sober enough to look abashed. "Well now, you see, I'm more of an administrator," he'd said, the last word sounding like he was talking through a mouth full of snow.

"And it would've done little good trying to convince them they hadn't seen what they all said they'd seen. By then, half the town was at my door demanding I send for a witch-hunter. And all the while we've got those *ambassadors* from Ravinica going up the Pontivar, asking about their missing prince. People thought it was all bad tidings. I had to do something, just to keep them all from panicking."

"But instead of calling a witch-hunter, you called me," Lyander had said.

"These river folk might be a tough breed, but some of them couldn't tell the difference between a Morlett and one of their neighbour's children, let alone a demon and a witch."

"But you can?" Lyander had asked, thinking he might need to reassess his opinion of the baron.

"Well, being a man of my position, you come to know certain things about the world. So I know a witch isn't the sort of problem I have here," he'd said, jabbing a finger at the desk, oblivious to what must have been a sceptical look on Lyander's face. "This thing. This spirit of the dead. That needs one of you fellows. It needs an exorcist."

Lyander had said nothing, considering the request as the baron's watery blue eyes blinked at him, expectantly.

"If you follow the Yoinar west and come off where the river forks, you'll find him. His name's Bolton Forth," the baron had pressed. "I'll pay, of course. Will pay well for your services."

"That won't be necessary," Lyander had finally said. "The Ecclessius will pay me. If this is, indeed, a problem for the Church."

Looking at the house, he still wasn't convinced it would be. *But it's been months since you collected a bounty*; *it's not as if you can afford to be picky about the jobs you take. Not*, he reminded himself, *that you've ever been able to be picky about the jobs you take.*

So he pulled back the hood of his cloak, tied his horse's reins to the nearest tree branch, and started for the door. He gave it three hard raps, causing it to shake in its frame.

No response.

He waited, then knocked again. Still no response. Looking down at the handle – a spit of black iron – he shrugged to himself, and pulled the latch on the off chance the door was unlocked.

To his surprise, it was.

I suppose when most things in the immediate vicinity can rip a door from its hinges, there's no point bothering with locks.

He pulled back his cloak and unsheathed his sword, slowly pushing the door open and stepping inside.

His eyes took a moment to adjust to the semi-darkness but when they did, he decided his earlier assessment of the house not being much of a house was fair. Whoever Bolton Forth was, he lived a simple existence. Most of the room was taken up by a round table, under which sat a single wooden stool. Behind that was a hearth built into the wall and the bare earth floor. Hanging over it on a spit was a mottled clay pot that looked like it could have belonged to one of Bolton's ancestors. And on the other side of the room was a cot and a makeshift workbench, above which hung an axe and woodcutting tools. Next to them, another stool positioned outside a door leading into another room. The whole place smelled of firewood, old leather, and what he thought could be mushrooms but might just be damp earth.

"Let's see what you're hiding," he said to the empty room. He pulled out a small hourglass from his breast pocket and set it on top of the workbench, watching it carefully. The sand, which was as black as mined coal, drifted peacefully from top to bottom, just like the sand in any hourglass would. *Never that easy. Looks like I'm doing this the hard way.*

Picking the hearth first, he looked inside the pot and, using a ladle hung on the beam above it, scooped up some of the liquid. It looked like water. He sniffed it to be certain, or as certain as he could be without tasting it, which he wasn't about to do, and decided it was water.

He returned the ladle to its hook and walked around the table. On the floor was a battered-looking chest with a rusted iron rim, the wood so worn it looked like it had been carried the length of the Pontivar twice over. It didn't have a lock, so Lyander used the toe of his boot to push the lid open.

It contained clothing and linen. Sifting through it with the tip of his sword, he found shirts and what looked like bedding for the cot. He dropped the lid and moved over to the other door, eyeing the hourglass for even the slightest discrepancy in the flow of sand. It fell as smoothly as a summer snow drift. So far, Bolton wasn't hiding anything.

Assuming that, like everything else in the house, this door would be unlocked, Lyander reached out and turned the handle, hearing the lock rattle on the other side.

Why lock a room in your house if you weren't also going to lock the front door?

With no answer for the question, he thought about breaking the door down with the axe, but decided against it. Peculiar as this was, there was still an overwhelmingly good chance Bolton Forth had nothing to do with what the Vergrainian patrols claimed to have seen. And Lyander didn't want to smash up a potentially innocent man's home. Turning, he gave the room another sweep, knowing that if there was anything incriminating, he would have found it already.

Sheathing his sword, he sat in the chair next to the workbench and just for something to do, flipped the hourglass. Like before, the sand flowed quite ordinarily to form a neat pile in the lower bulb.

Looks like I'll have to wait.

He wasn't waiting long. After flipping the hour glass for the fifth time, he heard footsteps from around the back of the house.

They stopped momentarily when they neared the open door, and a second later, a man stepped into the doorway. Heavyset with a thick chest and arms taking up most of the frame, he cast a long shadow into the room. He wore a dark shirt that looked like it belonged to a much smaller man and tan pants stained with mud. Apart from a dark ring of stubble, he was completely bald.

He looks like he's spent most of his life carrying rocks out of mines, Lyander thought, *not sowing barley in a field.*

Two beady eyes, like beetles burrowing out of sand, fixed on Lyander, then the man walked over to the pot. Taking the ladle, he poured the liquid into a nearby cup and drank long, deep gulps.

Definitely water, then.

Lyander watched him finish, then spoke: "I hope you don't mind the intrusion. The door was unlocked."

Bolton poured himself more water. "Don't mind," he said without looking at him. "Don't get many people coming this way." His voice was muted and coarse, like a whetstone drawn down a rough edge.

"Is that why you don't lock your front door?" Lyander asked.

"It's part of the reason."

"What's the other part?"

"Didn't have another lock."

Lyander didn't think Bolton was trying to be funny.

"What's behind the door you did lock?"

Bolton paused. The way his eyes seemed to nestle in his face made it look like he was thinking, although it was hard to tell. "You a mercenary?" he asked eventually.

"No, I'm not a mercenary," Lyander replied.

"But the baron hired you?"

"He told me where to find you."

"Must have filled your pockets to convince you to come out here."

"I only take payment from the Church."

At that, Bolton's eyes flicked to the hourglass and back up to meet Lyander's.

"Helps me tell if something maligned or abhorrent is being hidden from me," Lyander said, nodding at the hourglass. "Called a fulcrum." He paused, then asked: "Are you Bolton Forth?"

"I'm a woodsman," Bolton said.

Lyander glanced at the hourglass: no change.

"Can't be much money in that, seeing as the nearest town is *in* a wood."

"I harvest mirror caps. They grow on the borders of Yeggardania. Most people are too scared to go in deep enough to find them," he said, and the way he said it, it didn't sound like a boast.

"But you're not," Lyander said, making it a statement, not a question.

Bolton stared at him: two immutable black beetles shining back at him.

Lyander tried a different tact: "You don't get any trouble living out here? No Phractii? Or Morletts?"

Bolton shook his head. "Don't get any Phractii. Don't know what a Morlett is."

"Bit like a goblin. About yay high." Lyander gestured with his hand at around the waist height of a grown man. "Skin like ash. Red eyes. They eat poison toadstools when they can't get human."

"Never seen one."

"I'm finding that hard to believe, Mr Forth," Lyander said. "A man out here all on his own would get picked off by something eventually. That's why everyone who lives in the Pontivar valley lives in a town. And they build high walls around those towns. And they also lock their front doors."

Bolton snorted. "And at night they all sit around their fires telling each other ghost stories about the things that go bump in the forest and the strange noises they hear when the moon is low in the sky," he said.

He's not wrong, but it still doesn't explain how he's managed to survive out here.

"You're not from the Pontivar, are you?" Lyander said. "Out here, the things that go bump and make strange noises are very real, so I'm a bit confused as to how you've managed to live this long."

"Guess I'm lucky," Bolton said.

"No one's lucky out here." Lyander nodded at the door next to him. "Want to show me what's behind this?" he said.

Bolton contemplated the contents of his mug before looking over at the door. *Is that anger in those beady black eyes? Or resignation? Either way, about now is when I can expect Bolton to call time on the pleasantries and start causing problems.* In anticipation of those problems, Lyander rose to his feet and rested a purposeful hand on his sword's pommel. With the other, he turned the hourglass on its head and waited for Bolton to move.

With the look of a man asked to hand over his most treasured possession, Bolton set down his mug, took a key from a small pouch in his belt and walked over to the door. He hesitated for only a second, then slotted the key into the lock and turned. Pushing the door open, he stood back and gave Lyander a hard look, their eyes level.

There was no chance he was letting Bolton walk in behind him, so pointing at the room with his chin, he said: "After you."

Bolton complied.

A large cot with a patchwork quilt made from faded and fraying squares took up most of the room. In the corner, a lamp sat on a wooden stool, and from the look of the glass, it had either been thoroughly cleaned of stains or never used. The single window above the bed was shuttered and closed; dust, nearly an inch thick, lined its lower lip.

Careful to keep a healthy distance from Bolton, Lyander glanced back at the hourglass. The sand fell as normal: no sorcery detected; no maligned or abhorrent intent; and nothing concealed from him that he couldn't see with his own eyes. Unless there was another child the baron had failed to mention, Bolton had built a room for his dead daughter.

Lyander's face must have given away what he

was thinking because Bolton said: "A man can do what he wants with his own house." His eyes were wet, and whatever emotions Lyander saw in them before were replaced with the look of complete sadness.

"Her remains, where are they?" he asked, not unkindly.

Bolton turned to look at the bed, not taking his eyes from the quilt. "There's a glade beyond the house. I buried her there," he said.

"Mind if I take a look?"

Lyander would, anyway, but he felt the need to be respectful while standing in what could only be some sort of shrine to the man's dead child. He'd seen people deal with loss in many different ways. This was far from the strangest.

"Out round the back there's a path of sorts. It heads northwest."

Lyander nodded but Bolton didn't seem to notice. He turned and walked out of the room, picking up the hourglass as he went, leaving Bolton standing next to the bed he'd made for a child that would never sleep in it.

As if it were an afterthought, Bolton called after him: "Don't they give you names in that Church of yours?"

"My name's Lyander," he said, turning to look at Bolton. "And it's not my Church."

#

Bolton's idea of a path was, at best, the occasional muddy boot print next to some disturbed leaves. Lyander followed it all the same as it wound round the back of the house and into the forest. And not that he would forget it, deeper into Yeggardania.

The only thing troubling him about Bolton's

story (aside from the fact he was living out here in the first place) was he buried his daughter's body, and that it stayed buried. He could count on two hands the number of creatures that would make use of a rotting corpse.

Morletts, which were known for raiding cemeteries and burial mounds, viewed them as a particular delicacy. Phractii liked to raise young within a corpse's bowels, the guts becoming an immediate food source for the hatchlings. While Araknors spun them in their webs, and left them hanging from trees, presumably to "save them for later." It was why most of the Pontivar valley committed their dead to funeral pyres.

He could only assume if Bolton had remained out here unscathed, this part of the forest was, for some reason, less frequented by its typical denizens. Lyander didn't really believe it, though. His sword held ready at his side, he peered round every arborealis and aranthie he passed, an unsettled feeling creeping up the back of his mind.

The path became steeper and the landscape more crowded, forcing him to pull himself around trees, over ditches, and past large jutting boulders. His undershirt stuck to his lower back, then his chest, then most of his body. He wished he'd left his cloak with his horse and thought about leaving it next to the path, then decided that was about as smart as rubbing his sweat on the nearest tree. The air thinned, then the light turned a yellow-brown before becoming various green hues, and the creaking trees and his heavy breathing seemed far too loud in a mostly silent forest.

Soon the path angled round, becoming level, and heading west. If he walked straight in this direction for two months, he would soon find himself near Etherlain and on the shores of the Amarant Sea.

It's just a shame there's half a continent's worth of forest between here and there that would try to kill me every step of the way.

Ahead, the boot prints stopped at an aranthie root thick as a horse and growing at an angle across the path. He grabbed a vine tangling itself around the tree, and was about to hoist himself over and onto the other side when something shook violently in his chest.

Instinctively, he pulled up his hand, expecting to find the crossbow bolt's shaft protruding from his ribs. Only when he looked down, not finding one, did he realise it was the hourglass causing him to shake.

Well, thank the endless abyss, he thought, knowing a bolt there would have been his death. Then he remembered what a vibrating fulcrum meant, and he forgot all about his thanks. Heart speeding up, panic warring with a burst of adrenaline, he brought his sword up and turned quickly on the spot, scanning the gaps between the trees to locate the source of the fulcrum's activation.

There was nothing: no sounds or strange smells. Just the mass of twisted Yeggardanian trees and the tinted noon sun doing its best to breach the canopy. Yet the fulcrum continued to vibrate, buzzing under his cloak like a trapped hornet.

He stared into the forest for another tense minute, keeping his breathing shallow, trying not think about how loud his thudding heart sounded. But as it became apparent nothing was going to make itself known, he took the fulcrum from his pocket and held it to his face. The sand, which before was a calm stream, swirled angrily, buffeting the glass and refusing to settle. Keeping his sword level and his eyes on the surrounding trees, he took a tentative step back from the giant root. The vibrating subsided.

He moved off to the side and away from the path, but nothing changed, the sand eddying at little more than a strong breeze. But when he walked toward the root crossing the path, the vibration grew once more.

Either there's a gyranic entity ahead of me on this path, or Bolton hasn't been entirely honest with me. Given what must now be close proximity to his daughter's grave, Lyander was betting on the latter. Pulling himself up and over the root, he followed the path as it continued to climb. Rounding a corner, he came upon a wall of boulders, their blue-grey faces covered in moss, the dark brown roots winding through them like tangled hair.

He searched for a way around but the path was too steep on either side. He would need to scale them and hope that whatever the fulcrum was reacting to wasn't lying in wait at the top. Listening first, he heard only the hourglass's buzz, which vibrated in what felt like panicked desperation to be free of his hand.

Whatever's up there has a mean advantage, he thought, sheathing his sword as quietly as he could. *Let's hope it has terrible hearing*. Using the roots to pull himself up with his free hand, he climbed, neared the top, and threw himself over the cleft and drew his sword again, intending as best he could to defend himself from whatever he was about to meet.

Which was a mostly empty glade.

Here, the sun found a place to breach the canopy, and bask the tree trunks in its golden light, turning the knee-high grass a shimmering, almost emerald green. Toward the centre, white flowers he didn't know the name of surrounded a pale headstone. It was beautiful and utterly serene, like the glade knew it held the dead and made an effort to be perfectly calm. For a moment, Lyander simply stared.

Then the fulcrum exploded.

He jumped, more out of surprise than pain and looked down at his hand. It was covered in smoking black powder and shattered glass. Something acetic, like spoiled wine, and the pungency of burning matches rose through his sinuses, causing a headache behind his eyes. He coughed, shook his head, and took a step back, as a burning crept into his fingers, then his palm. Eyes watering, he ripped off his glove and threw it to one side, revealing faint white blotches.

As far as he could recall, there were no recorded cases of fulcrums exploding from the very thing they were designed to detect. But looking around at the broken remnants, it was clear they could. Stunned, he shook the pain from his hand, and eyed the glade. *Well, there's only one place that amount of sorcery could come from*, he thought. With his palm and fingers still stinging, he pushed through the grass and stood before the grave, reading the inscription aloud: "Here lies Ameria Forth. Daughter of Bolton and Kaylin Forth. The light she brought to this world will be remembered by those who loved her."

With the lettering uneven in places, the "y" too long, the "r" in daughter slanting sideways, Lyander suspected it was Bolton's doing, rather than a mason's. If he didn't now strongly suspect Bolton of deception, he might feel guilty at what he was about to do. He stared at the hardpacked earth, thinking about how he could dig up a grave without a shovel – perhaps using his sword to cut at the dry ground, then pull the softer earth away with his hands.

But all thoughts of digging disappeared with the quick, methodical sound of someone coming up behind him.

In a single movement, he spun on the spot and brought his sword up and across his body in a defensive parry just in time to catch the axe swinging for his head. The glade rung as steel met steel, and he was given just enough time to look into Bolton's murderous black eyes before he needed to parry another attack. It forced him back, nearly causing him to stumble over the headstone. Lyander manoeuvred around it awkwardly and into the open glade but at the cost of giving Bolton time to once again bring the axe up and down upon him. It was the sort of blow capable of shattering his collar bone and burying itself deep in his neck if Lyander hadn't turned and brought his sword up to meet it.

Four swings in and it was clear Bolton was a trained fighter. He dealt precise cuts aimed at Lyander's neck, his elbows and his wrists, driving Lyander back with practiced footwork. *So much for being a farmer*, he thought, breathing heavily, his arm growing numb from the parries.

But while the blows were well-placed, they were delivered with reckless anger, each one made with the animalistic grunts of a man eager to kill his foe quickly.

Deflecting the blows to his left and right, Lyander allowed himself to be pushed back, regaining control of the fight. With each step, he gave just a little more ground, forcing Bolton to reach just a little farther with every cut. Bolton hewed savagely as they neared the glade's edge, and Lyander could see the early blooms of triumph in the eyes of a man who believed he was gaining the upper hand in a fight he hadn't been sure he was going to win.

Desperate to capitalise on the gains Lyander had given him, Bolton brought the axe down in one wild cut to end it all. But Lyander stepped aside, the axe head flying inches from his face and into the space he'd been only a moment ago, causing Bolton to overstep. As he did so, Lyander brought his sword up, thrusting into Bolton's throat, and out the other side. The spinal cord separated with a wet crunch and Bolton's head jerked forward, blood streaming from the wound in his neck. He hung from the end of Lyander's sword, eyes filled with astonishment as if struggling to accept his death, before Lyander withdrew the blade. The body collapsed onto the grass, hands still gripping the axe.

Lyander took a breath, steadying himself from the shock of the unexpected duel, and looked down at the human-shaped boulder that was Bolton's corpse.

As liable as they are to embellish a story, he thought, *I think the good people of Vergraine might have been onto something when it came to Bolton Forth.*

But with his death, the only truth would be found in his daughter's grave, and he needed to move quickly. If there were two things guaranteeing an unfriendly encounter in Yeggardania, it was the sound of ringing steel and the smell of fresh blood on the air.

Lyander pried the axe from Bolton's hands, stepped around the headstone and hacked at the earth, drawing it away in short sweeps. Breaking the hard soil, he dropped to his knees and resorted to his earlier plan of dragging out armfuls. Every now and then, he looked up, scanned the glade, and in between his own laboured breaths, tried to listen for something approaching.

Still, there was nothing.

The coffin, when he finally reached it, was all of four feet in length, its wood a deep, burnished red.

He leant into the grave and dragged the coffin onto the grass. Only when he stood up did he notice the heavy padlock bolting the lid shut.

Now, is that to stop something from getting out or from getting in?

With no time to mull it over, Lyander picked up the axe, brought it above his head, and was about to swing it down upon the lock, when a better idea occurred to him. Pushing Bolton's body over so he could get at the pouch on the side of the dead man's belt, he unbuttoned it, and fished inside, finding two keys: the one Bolton used to open the door to his daughter's room and, presumably, the one that would open her coffin; he took the one that was the same dirty silver as the padlock.

Crouching down, he slid the key into the lock, turned it, and before the padlock hit the earth, he was a sword's length away, his blade raised for whatever was about to spring out.

But the glade was silent, and so was the coffin.

With extreme caution, expecting at any moment some half-dead spectre to vault out of the coffin, he edged forward and kicked the lid with his foot.

It fell to the side.

There, with her arms folded across her body and draped in a white blouse turning grey with filth, was a young girl's decaying body: her skin, black and dry as parchment; her eyes sunken in their sockets, only single strands of pale hair clinging to her mottled scalp. Despite her appearance, the smell of grave rot was faint.

Caught between wariness and the desire to leave the glade as quickly as possible, Lyander forced himself to inspect the corpse. Kneeling, he looked for brands, stitches, skin growths, or distorted limbs – the tell-tale signs of corruption. When he found nothing on her front, he reached in and turned her over as carefully as if she were still alive. There was no indication of tampering, no signs of malignance or abhorrence, no artefacts hidden around or beneath her.

Which didn't add up. Neither her body nor anything in the grave produced even a hint of sorcery, and certainly nowhere near enough to cause a fulcrum to explode.

Confused, he felt the early prickling disquiet of foreboding. But knowing he couldn't sit around Yeggardania trying to figure it out, he clamped down on those emotions and decided his next moves.

He would need to take the body to the nearest spire. Damoclen was the closest with its own sanctum, and he knew the exhumarian stationed there, who could analyse the corpse.

He closed the lid, locked it shut, and was about to hoist it onto his shoulder when his gaze fell on Bolton's corpse. It would attract pretty much anything in the forest that drew breath (and a lot of things that didn't).

Wanting to leave immediately but knowing he'd feel guilty if he did, he gave his surroundings another quick glance, then picked up the axe and made the grave twice as long. Even if Bolton had tried to murder him, Lyander wasn't prepared to let his corpse become a Phractii nesting ground.

There were just some things no one deserved to happen to them.

Once it was large enough, he dragged Bolton's body into the grave and pushed the earth on top. It was a poor job, but it might keep the smell off the wind long enough for Vergraine's scouts to come and burn the corpse.

Taking one last look around him, he hoisted the coffin onto his shoulder and set off down the path, leaving the glade, and the dead, in silence.

Two

Brazier

Brazier Veranquis squatted in the wet grass of the Yeggardanian forest, trying not to feel queasy as he watched a fleshy, pore-pocked larva struggle to crawl up the flank of an arborealis tree. The larva was roughly the length of his forearm and moved in an undulating slither that looked like it took a lot of effort for what little ground it gained.

The pores lining its invertebrate body were the colour of infected sores and leaked a watery brown fluid, oozing a silky trail down the tree. When it crawled its way level with his eye line, the translucent white form of a nursery Araknor scuttled up the tree and stopped just short of the larva. The dire spider's whole body tensed, rocking back and forth on all eight of its segmented limbs, as if entering into some kind of hypnotic paralysis.

Then, in the time it took Brazier to blink, the

Araknor extended two bone-white mandibles and pounced on the larva. But instead of ripping into the soft flesh beneath it, the spider went completely still. A thin grey spine protruded from the centre of its body. It released a short, high-pitched squeal, quivered and scrunched up its legs into a tight embrace. A second later, the spine retracted into the pore, and the Araknor went still again. The larva slunk out from underneath its would-be murderer and continued its journey up the tree, as if something hadn't just tried to eat it.

The Araknor, which was now a sickly grey colour so opaque Brazier could see the bark beneath it, began to follow the larva with graceful serenity. All the skittishness of its previous life expunged for making a bad decision about lunch.

"Animus Captionem," a female voice said, causing Brazier to jump.

He turned to find the slender form of operations officer Freyen Fortigris standing in the grass next him. Leaning on one leg, she cradled a crossbow in her arms. Her shoulder-length hair fell in dark ringlets and the faint outline of amusement played across her angular features. Every gnome Brazier knew had the uncanny ability to move without making a sound, and he was fairly certain Freyen did just that to see if she could sneak up on him. He made a mental note to not let himself get distracted while on duty in the future. She'd only been with the crew for six weeks and he didn't want her to get the impression the first officer was *skittish*.

"Secretes a mucus that's mixed with its own blood," she said. "Makes a predator think the larva is wounded. Then when it gets close enough, it drains and binds the predator's gyranic signal to itself. Larva gets a food source and a bodyguard all in one."

Brazier did not know why she would know this, given the script on her background described an entire career moving food stuffs from Everaux to Formaria's northern border.

"This thing eats souls?" was all he could think to say.

"Pretty much."

"This is why I hate Yeggardania."

Freyen laughed. It was light and carefree, almost musical. It was not what Brazier expected from someone who spent her days ordering around a crew of fifty miners.

"Last hauls in," she said, shouldering the crossbow. "We're packing up the toys. Want me to give the order to move out? Or do you need some more quality time with our friend here?"

"No," Brazier said, shaking his head. "We've spent as much time together as I'm comfortable with. Pull in the perimeter and let's get out this place."

"Yes, sir," she said, still smiling.

Brazier watched her stalk toward the cave mouth, her lithe form cutting the thinnest of trails through the long grass. She signalled to the two dwarves standing outside and they marched off in different directions around the clearing.

Four dwarves and six gnomes streamed in from its edges where they'd been standing in positions similar to his own. They all carried crossbows, battle axes, or both, every one of them opting for chain vests over their armoured mining gambesons. He could hear the clink of mail links as they passed. The combination meant carrying a lot of extra weight, but given the choice between more armour or more speed, most miners on perimeter duty would choose the armour. Only Freyen seemed content with a leather cuirass over her dark green uniform. He thought it was a bold choice, even if she did look handy with that crossbow.

The last light of the evening sun began to fall

over the clearing, warming the dew of the previous morning's rain. Droplets sparkled on the leaves and blades of grass, the air smelt crisp and timeless, and the amber glow seemed to evaporate shadows before his very eyes. A veneer of calm settled on Yeggardania and Brazier found it totally unconvincing.

He gave the larva and its spectral companion one last look and headed to the perimeter team at the cave's mouth. They were kneeling in a loose formation, their eyes darting between him and the forest behind him. *I'm not the only one who doesn't like going topside.*

"Axelock, take point. We'll follow you in," he said to a dwarf with greying dreadlocks and neck muscles like bunches of taut rope. He wore padded maroon trousers and a dirty beige gambeson beneath his chain mail. Lined with iron rings and gated rock locks along the arms, it performed the dual function of combat armour and mining gear. Axelock peeled off, and Brazier and his team fell in behind with practiced co-ordination.

Lit by potholes in its roof, and with a turquoise-coloured lake running its length, the cave held a damp warmth common to every system leading into the underground. It was also carpeted with the purple-grey corpses of a fully-fledged nest of Phractii.

When alive, the creatures were the size of large dogs. But that was where the similarities ended.

Their heads were oval shells; their mouths gaping maws; their two forelimbs and two hind limbs ended in talons; and four feeler-like appendages extended up to six feet from their bellies. And if that wasn't enough, they could fly. Freyen called them tentacles with wings, and he had to stop himself from pointing out that was a wholly inadequate description.

It took the entire team three hours to hunt down and kill every one of them, none of which gave up easily. Before the night was done, Jaren's shoulder blade down to his buttocks ran with lacerations, and Liza's left arm was swollen with welts that turned white, then purple, then blue, then back to white before dissolving into pasty rings of green puss. Brazier watched Liza walk out of the cave but knew the dwarf would be lucky to keep her arm.

There was also a lot of armour to replace, and their supply of dressings and thread was empty. Now, the Phractii lay in solitary death poses and gave off a putrid smell somewhere between vomit and the coppery taste of iron. Depending on which member of the team had found them first, they were either studded with bolts or heaped in bloody piles like chopped fish meat. With the efficiency of a professional, Axelock took the cleanest route through the cave he could find. Brazier only stepped in guts twice.

Before them, was a cluster of scattered boulders and stalagmites, behind which was a fissure cut through the wall of the cave like a lightning strike frozen in time. Coming from within was the harsh sweetness of raw gyre ice, the smell both pleasantly warm and creating a nauseating bite at the back of Brazier's throat.

The team formed a defensive line within the rock formations, then one by one, began moving down the fissure. It opened into a much larger cavern, through which ran the deep scar of a recently excavated ravine. Brazier crested a lip of rock just outside the passage and surveyed the remains of what had been a small but bountiful vein of gyre ice. Thirty miners strapped into winches and armed with pickaxes and climbing spikes took a single day to reduce a half-mile-long, sixty-tonne wall of hard packed magical blue ice into more manageable chunks. All that remained was the occasional blue streak and specks of silvery-white particles drifting lazily in the air. They lit the ravine like celestial fireflies.

At the end, where the ravine opened out into the black nothingness of one of Formaria's countless tunnels, floated the *Chalice of Amaranth* in all her unassuming glory.

A fifth of a mile long – and once described to him as an upside down whale – the *Chalice* was a cauldron-class miner perfect for the slow and ponderous life of ice haulage. Almost entirely a dirty bronze-gold, she was all smooth curves and flowing contours. Despite her 'bulk', the *Chalice*, like so many gyre ships, possessed a streamline elegance – like a celestial organism, at once defying and completely at home in a darkness so absolute, so unremitting, it seemed possible to drown in it. Lining her flanks were sixteen gyre thrusters, their discs ringed with blue flame and set on limb-like extensions. Brazier saw the four toward the bow and the four toward the stern were already lit and ablaze with gyre light.

Which meant his brother was in a hurry to leave.

"Zee," a voice called out to him from the ridgeline of the ravine. Erin's blonde hair, flecked with a growing amount of white, made it look like it was snowing.

He ran his fingers through his own red mane and felt them come away with wet flakes.

"Cap's calling double time," Erin shouted up to him. "Wants everyone to shift ass and lock in."

Not a good sign, he thought, trying not to list all the reasons his brother would have for making a swift exit.

"How long?" he called back to her.

"We're on the float in ten."

"On my way."

He snaked his way along the ridgeline, catching up with Erin and the rest of the team, attaching climbing locks to their gambesons and threading thick lengths of rope through the heavy chain links. Moving quickly, they lowered themselves down rope lines secured to the ravine wall the previous night. When it was Freyen's turn, she practically skipped over the edge and sailed backward down its jagged face. He expected his own descent would be conspicuously less elegant in comparison.

Slotting his axe into a holster in his belt, he began strapping himself up, attached his gambeson to one of the rock locks hammered into the floor and walked backward over the edge. Climbing down, he untied the line at each lock he passed. He hit the bottom, they gathered the rope, and headed toward the end of the ravine.

Half of the *Chalice*'s thrusters span up grey dust clouds, painting the rock floor in cones of luminous blue light. They generated a soft thrum that was the sort of sound Brazier imagined a sleeping lion might make, if that lion was the size of a small fortress and weighed over twenty thousand tonnes.

Dwarves and gnomes laden with mining gear moved beneath the ship, lining up carts packed with ice to be loaded onto the ship's ground platform. It was lowered to the tunnel floor from inside the ship's feranium bay by chain belts and surrounded in a loose semi-circle by another team of dwarves. Their stances wide and postures tense, each one held a crossbow with an underslung gyre torch blazing a thin blue line into the tunnel's darkness.

A muscle-bound female dwarf with hair the colour of black malt beer and a face caught permanently between a scowl and a smirk coordinated the whole thing. She wore a sleeveless grey shirt under her faded black coveralls. The leather belt around her waist carried what Brazier thought was about three times as many tools as she could ever reasonably need. But there was only one feature he, or anyone else, really paid attention to: the bronzite mechanical augmentation connected to her collar bone, replacing her entire right arm.

Gyranic enginator Daniela Gundrisson told everyone she had been awarded the augment for extreme valour while replacing a vault-class destroyer's contaminated gyre core. None other than the Lord Admiral of the Navarch himself presented the enginator with the limb replacement. And with an arm that could punch a hole through a ship's hull, no one was going to call bullshit on that story, even if they thought it was.

She used the bronzite limb, along with some tersely delivered commands, to direct the flow of mining carts. As far as Brazier could tell, no one had a problem with her doing that.

"You trying to put me out of a job, Switch?" Freyen said, as they walked up to the enginator, the rest of their team fanning out to join the others surrounding the platform.

Switch was the enginator's preferred name. Brazier had called her Daniela once – she was new and he was drunk. She smiled at him in exactly the sort of way wolves smile before they eat and proceeded to tell him that if he ever called her Daniela again, he'd find out what pure bronzite tasted like. Having enough sense not to point out that such an act would get her thrown off the crew, he instead smiled back, saying: "Switch it is."

Looking at Freyen, the enginator held up both her real and mechanical hands. "Just trying to move to the cap's accelerated timetable," she said. Then she turned her coal-coloured eyes on Brazier and pointed at him accusingly. "He's got me burning raw ice, Zee, and it's killing my engines. The synths are all cooked and most of the reductors will need replacing if he wants us to fly without dragging our ass."

Somehow, his brother's decisions often became his problems.

"But because you're the best enginator we could afford, you can make it all work, anyway," he said.

She actually laughed. "Well, you got most of that right. I can get her on the float, but manoeuvring isn't going to be a lot of fun. And I wouldn't advise anything above four twelfths of a sprawl."

"I'll let the captain know," Brazier said. "Fly straight and slow so we don't break anything."

"Hey, Switch," a dwarf with a young face, large nose, and short, rust-coloured hair called out from beneath the ship. Colt stood on the platform, an arm resting lazily on one of the carts, half his body lit up by the glowing ice. Brazier could make out the individual hairs on his wrist and hand. "Davrin just called from engineering; we've got three coils out of place and another reductor just blew."

Switch swore and Brazier watched her scowl move into its full ascendency. "Tell him not to touch anything until I get there," she shouted back. Then to Brazier: "There's only so much I can do before this thing falls out the air, Zee."

"I heard you," he said. "Straight and slow."

Looking unconvinced, she turned to Freyen: "You can have your job back now."

Freyen's eyebrows crawled toward her hairline. "Thanks," she said, but Switch was already ambling off to join Colt and the rest of the carts on the platform. She shouted for the controller to pull them up, and the platform ascended into the *Chalice*, iron links clicking softly as it rose.

The platform shut above them, leaving only the thruster's background thrum and their whirling grey clouds. A minute later, an empty platform descended, creating tiny waves of dust and a clank as it hit the tunnel floor.

Brazier and the remainder of the crew stepped onto it and he shouted for them to be pulled up.

"Easy haul," said a dwarf with short blond hair, a purple scar running from his left eye to his ear, and what seemed like a permanent grin taking up half his face. Dalfin, nearly a head taller than most of his kind, held up his forearm for Erin to slam her own against it.

"Just another *Chalice* crew hack and grab," she said.

"In and out before anything even knew we were there." Dalfin grinned back at her.

"Sounds like a night in the sack with you, Dalfin," a red-headed dwarf named Jazrien said so everyone could hear.

"No need to get all hot and bothered with me, Jaz," Dalfin replied. "If you want round two, all you got to do is ask."

Some of the team whistled.

"Not for all the ice in Formaria, baba'te," Jazrien said, using the Thendergaarden slang for "lover." More whistles followed.

After thirty hours without sleep, Brazier wanted nothing more than to join in. But he couldn't shake the sense of foreboding since his brother's order to return to the ship.

"We can publicly debate Dalfin's stamina later," he said. "I want everyone at their stations. Cap's called double-time for a reason, and it probably isn't a good one." Then as an afterthought: "And try not to get in Switch's way. She looks more pissed than usual."

A chorus of "yes, sirs," rang out as the platform came to a stop with a metallic thud, followed by the sound of locks slotting into place.

Around them, the feranium could have been a forge in one of Formaria's cauldron cities. Twelve circular pits – each one the diameter of a gyre thruster – ran in two rows down either side of the bay. Roughly three feet deep, they bottomed out at solid bronzite slabs lined with hairline fractures, as if hit by hammer blows. Above them, suspended from the ceiling, were twelve matching drums, which clamped down over the pits every time they were fed a cartload of ice. They thrummed, then hissed, then smoke shot from between the fastenings before the drums retracted, leaving nothing but the cracked surfaces.

Ice that wasn't used to fuel the ship was wheeled to the south end of the bay. Once there, the carts were fastened, then covered with solid bronzite lids, which took two dwarves to lift into place.

And above them, a deep blue conduit, like an upside down canal, ran from one end of the bay to the other. Its soft glow permeated the gloom, making the furnaces and neat rows of carts look like an underwater city.

Brazier let his team disperse, then headed to the opposite end of the bay. There, entrenched in the bay's wall from floor to ceiling, was one of the ship's internal lifts: one long, octagonal column the same smudged-gold colour as everything else. A chest-high terminal that looked like a cross between a lectern and some sort of runic ward stone sat to its right. Brazier stepped up to it.

At the terminal's centre was a hexagonal depression ringed in blue light with two blue lines shooting off from either side. It contained what looked like black sand mixed with silver filaments. The composite was known as hex reduction: two parts refined gyre ice to three parts magmaralis, a jet-black compound more commonly referred to as voidstone.

Removing his glove, he sunk his hand into the hexagon. At first, the filaments shifted away from its presence, and then in unison curled around his fingers, creating a bed for his hand as soft as deer's hide. He felt something click in his mind and the immediate sense of clarity was like waking from a dream. *Navigorum,* he thought. The sand vibrated and sent a crystal pulse down the two adjacent channels. He pulled his hand from its silken embrace and doors parted on one of the octagon's faces, revealing a platform large enough for eight carts. He stepped onto it, was given one final glimpse of blue-tinged gasses expelling into the air, then the doors closed. The lift soared upward.

He felt a brief sense of weightlessness before it slowed to a gradual stop. Then, as if contemplating which direction it would take, it moved horizontally, giving the impression of being propelled through the air. He was, in fact, travelling along the spine of the ship, past the galley, the crew quarters, and the second and third feraniums.

It slowed again, climbed briefly, then stopped. The feeling of hitting solid ground, then the doors parted to reveal a long corridor, from the end of which came the low, clipped tones of a serious conversation.

One of the voices was his brother's.

The navigorum, or nav deck, was an octagonal compartment twice the size of his own quarters and only slightly bigger than the ship's internal lift. The air smelt faintly of someone's Charok tea, and the infusion was failing spectacularly to cover the odour of warm bodies. Toward the end of the deck and taking up half the space was an entire pit of hex reduction. Kneeling in it with his arms stretched out to his sides, his palms facing outward as if in some sort of meditative trance, was the ship's navigator.

Jandrice Karmoon was one of the few humans on board the *Chalice,* and he stuck out like a dwarf at a goblin blood feast. His dark hair was a mess, his bare feet were black with dirt, his trousers frayed all the way up to the shin, and his shirt, which was yellow with perspiration, hung from him like a shroud. Brazier couldn't help but think of a religious penitent whenever he looked at the man.

Surrounding *the pit* was a long terminal stretching around it in a semi-hexagon. Wells of hex were embedded across its surface, the filaments formed into floating sculpts of the *Chalice*, the adjacent tunnel system, and a small craft that looked like the abdomen of a wasp combined with the head of a bird of prey.

His brother leant over the terminal, inspecting the unknown ship.

Torquen Veranquis was thirty years older than Brazier, age lines running down both his cheeks and a dusting of ginger hair he never grew longer than stubble. His beard, the colour of late summer sun, was the sort of facial hair most dwarves aspired to grow, and his blue eyes were hard but not unkind. That description also summed up his captaincy of the ship; the crew didn't always like him, but they always respected him.

"She's floating dark," Torquen said without looking at him. His voice, filled with intention, layered with severity, was like broken iron dragged across a dungeon floor. "Got a distress signal twenty minutes ago and it's been going off every three minutes since."

"The crew?" Brazier asked.

"Jan's not picking up any lifeforms. Friendly or otherwise."

"What do we know about the ship?"

"Spire-class. Light craft. Large crew quarters. Small storage. Probably a troop carrier."

"And she's still running?"

"Tell him what you told me, Jan," Torquen said.

The navigator knelt without responding, the man's shoulder's rising and falling with each breath.

"Jan," Torquen said, raising his voice. The navigator jerked as if woken from a light sleep. "Tell Brazier what's going on with that ship."

"Engine core and thrusters are operational. Hex network is secure and operational," Jan said, his voice so soft, Brazier found himself leaning over the terminal just to hear him. "But there's no signature."

Like living creatures, a ship's engine core blazed like a torch in the swirling maelstrom lying just behind the material realm and was only visible to beings with magical abilities. A ship's signature could only be destroyed if the core was destroyed. Having one without the other wasn't possible.

"That's not possible," Brazier said.

"Apparently it is now," Torquen replied.

"What did Jan say about it?"

"Nothing more than what he just told you."

Brazier considered for a moment, then said, "Ask Switch?"

His brother nodded. "Jan, tether us to Switch's location," he said.

"Tethering."

One of the wells not generating a sculpture pulsed like the surface of a pond.

"I'm a little busy here, Captain," Switch's voice rang with perfect clarity from within the well.

"I only need a minute," Torquen said. "Can an engine core's gyre signature malfunction or become compromised?"

"Err, not that I've ever heard of. It's about the only part of the ship I don't need to worry about," Switch said.

"Can they be destroyed by sorcery?" Torquen asked.

"The core is basically a fulcrum," Switch said. When he didn't understand something, his brother had a tendency to squint.

"That means no, it can't," Brazier said to him.

Torquen grunted his thanks.

"If you found a ship with an operational core but no signature, what would you think?" Torquen said to the well.

There was a pause before Switch replied. "Either the reading's wrong or something's blocking the signal. But I don't know anything that can do that."

"Thank you, Switch," Torquen said.

Jan dropped the tether and the filaments went still.

His brother looked into his eyes and Brazier knew they were both thinking the same thing. The law of the underground was simple. In a world where every ounce of industrial output revolved around keeping the enemies of Formaria at bay, abandoning ships was a criminal act. They were just too valuable to let fall into enemy hands.

But something about this felt like a trap, and even on a good day, the *Chalice* was not a ship to take into a fight. And today was not a good day. With the engines in their current state, any quick getaways would be like moving through treacle. And they were carrying three full feraniums of ice. If they were boarded by a sorcerer and the attackers managed to open just a handful of crates, the ship became a tinderbox of untapped power.

The smarter choice would be to ignore the distress beacon and sprawl like black hell in the opposite direction, have Jan wipe it from the ship's hex network, then explain it as tunnel interference to any Navarch dock official who asked. Neither of them said it but they both knew that was why Torquen was firing up the engines with unprocessed ice – so at the very least, there was the option of turning tail and getting as far away from whatever attacked the unknown ship as possible.

For Brazier, it was an ugly option.

"We're not the type to just float on by," he said.

"We have fifty souls on board. And that looks like an ambush." His brother pointed an accusing finger at the ship.

"How far out is she?"

"Three hours if we sprawl hard."

"What's the access like?"

His brother gave him a hard look before turning to the navigator. "Jan, give me a layout of the tunnels around that ship."

The back of Jan's head twitched, the hex sculpt of the unknown ship dissolving and reforming into a long tunnel. Connected to it at right angles were two smaller shafts about two thirds of the way along. A tiny cluster of hex – no more than six or seven filaments – floated in the main tunnel. It took Brazier a moment before he realised they represented the unknown ship.

"Primary shaft is one-point-four leagues long, running a northeasterly course from our position. There're two secondary lines perpendicular one-point-two leagues from the south access. Unknown vessel is a league from the south access," Jan said.

"That gives us a solid window," Brazier said. "If Jan's not picking up any readings from the tunnel or those secondaries, we can get there and get out before whatever did this to her shows up again."

Torquen sighed and ran a hand over his bristled head. "I thought this sort of thing was long behind me." He looked straight at Brazier; two piercing blue lagoons among his eyelid's tired crags.

"We're not the type to float on by," Brazier said again, and his brother's smile was exhaustion, resignation, and maybe the barest hint of pride all rolled into one.

"Prep a landing team," Torquen said. "A small one. And take Switch. If there's anyone who can tell us why that ship is behaving the way it is, it's her." Then, with all the tiredness gone from his brother's voice: "If that tunnel so much as smells funny, you will double-time it back here immediately."

"Got it," Brazier said.

"Jan, get us within point-three of a league of that ship. At a league out, go dark and float us in ass backward. I want a straight line out of there if we need to make a run for it. And give me ship-wide."

Like before, Torquen spoke into the well.

"We are on intercept course. Prepare the ship for hard sprawl."

THREE

LYANDER

By the time he reached Bolton's house, he was sweating with the effort of carrying the coffin. He put it down in front of his horse, which was thankfully still tied to the tree.

"It's your turn to carry this," he said to her.

She looked at him blankly.

"Great. I didn't think you'd mind, either."

He took a length of rope he carried on his saddle and used it to tie the coffin in place. It sat awkwardly on top of her and she snorted a mild protest, but it would do until they reached Vergraine.

Taking the reins, he led her away from the house and down the track connecting them with the Yoinar. Why Bolton chose to settle in this particular part of the forest, he would likely never know. The track to the river was long, winding, and difficult. And that was without leading a horse down it. He could only guess Bolton had wanted to discourage any visitors who might happen upon him – not that it would ever have been a problem. This part of the Yoinar was connected by a raft crossing that looked like it had been built in a previous age; the only people who were ever likely to use it were the Vergrainian patrols that ranged north. But even they would only come this far out if they really needed to. In the Pontivar valley, patrolling in sight of your own walls was hard enough.

At the platform, he untied the coffin from the saddle and set it next to her on one of the rafts. Here, the river was narrow enough to be poled but he didn't want to risk unsteadying her with the extra weight. Even on the way over, she hadn't exactly seemed thrilled by the idea of travelling across a body of moving water.

When they reached the other side, it took another two hours before he finally found the Pontivar merchant track, a wide, well-maintained road running the length of the Yoinar and going through every village, town, and city in the valley. As far as trading routes went, a merchant wagon accompanied by a complement of armed guards could feel relatively confident they would make it from one town to the next unscathed. He made do with a drawn sword, hoping the glint of cold steel put off anything that might consider him a meal.

Luckily for him, it did – right to Vergraine's gates, which they arrived at by late evening. The forest was so thick and the canopy so dense, it appeared before him as a ball of orange light bobbing in a sea of inky blackness. If he didn't know there was a settlement ahead of him, he would have mistaken it for a campfire.

The orange ball soon joined others, and they moved from right to left across his horizon. Some flickered in and out of existence, revealing the outline of a tree or a branch they were momentarily expunged by.

The first ball of light, however, remained fixed

squarely ahead of him. As he drew closer, it unveiled for him the faint semi-circle of a gatehouse, the teeth of its portcullis, then its two flanking towers. It looked like a portal to another world.

The light eventually materialised into a torch held by the baron, standing behind the gate alongside several guards. They wore dark leather tunics and carried a type of polearm adapted for groups of hunters to fight and trap large monsters. Their wedged shields bore the combined coat of arms of their town and its ruling house: Vergraine's horned river serpent on a field of azure, and Angelaux's white doves on a field of green.

"Was it him, then?" the baron asked eagerly, sweat at his temples despite the cool air. "Was it Bolton?"

Just outside the town, a breeze rocked the galleys in their berths, then caught the baron's torch, and as the light flickered off the shields surrounding him, it made the serpents dance on their painted rivers. Tired from events he didn't fully understand, Lyander imagined them hissing at him.

He pushed the thought aside and focused on the baron, watching the man's jowls quiver under the dancing torchlight.

"It's possible," Lyander said simply, thinking about how to recount his very strange day into something that made sense. If he couldn't understand what happened, he decided, there was little point in trying to explain it to the baron, so he gave as brief a summary as he could: "Bolton started swinging an axe at me when I found his daughter's grave, so I put him down and buried him in the same place – fifteen minutes along the path behind his house. It's in a glade, and you should do something about the body. There's also a chance his daughter's remains are corrupted but I'll need the Order to inspect them to be certain, so if you can have a ship ready, I'll take them to Damoclen at first light. Oh, and I'll need another night's board at that inn, if you don't mind."

When Lyander mentioned the remains, the baron held up his torch, putting a hand to his mouth as he caught sight of the coffin. His guard seemed to shrink back, like they were afraid of being caught in the light.

"Begging your pardon," the baron said, shifting on his feet, "but I'll be needing to ask you to leave at once – on account of what you say you bring with you, you understand. Best if it don't stay here any longer than needs be. We can have a ship ready for you in the hour. And a fresh horse."

Lyander rubbed his temples. Trying to convince some of the most suspicious people in all of Aetraya there was nothing to fear from a coffin full of . . . well, even he didn't know what, would get him nowhere. Plus, he could sleep just as well on a river galley as he could at an inn.

"Keep the horse. I like the one I've got. Just make sure you have food and a warm bed on that ship."

The baron looked relieved Lyander wasn't going to demand to stay the night in his town. Turning to the man next to him, he said: "Wake Captain Arryan and have him prepare his ship to make for Damoclen. If he refuses, tell him he'll be paid for the trouble."

The guard gave a hasty "yessir," and left down a street, heading into the centre of Vergraine. "Banor," the baron said to a fair-haired man with a wisp of a moustache. "At first light, take five men, or as many as you think you need, and dispose of Bolton's body. The rest of you can go back to your duties."

Banor looked like he'd just been asked to lead a patrol into the heart of Yeggardanian itself, but the baron gave him no chance to respond. He turned back to Lyander. "If you would follow me to the docks," he said, and without waiting to see if Lyander was following him or not, the baron set off, clearly wanting to keep a sizeable distance between himself and the coffin.

Vergraine was like any other town in the Pontivar valley – a chaotic assortment of timber buildings grown up around a river that was the mainstay of its economy. Like so many of the Pontivar's towns, it had been settled by some unknown tribal leader following the Fennian war. Whoever they were, they'd lacked the foresight to settle on one of the Yoinar's many forks, which flowed south into Ravinica. As a result, Vergraine didn't benefit from the taxes levied on imported foods or the southern merchant vessels bringing coin and commerce to any town they visited. As he followed the baron through the town, Lyander thought it showed.

The docks, built outside Vergraine's walls, occupied a narrow stretch of the river. On the opposite bank, he could make out the fortified watchtowers and wooden palisade guarding the crossing used by patrols roaming north. Other than the boats swaying gently in their moorings and the occasional swish of a river eel across the surface, the docks were silent.

There were eight galleys at berth and the baron stopped in front of the smallest – a weather-beaten cog with a mermaid at its bow. Her naked breasts and scaled fin were worn to the bare timber, and the paint and oiled coating on her face was cracked and peeling. She smiled malevolently at them through her colourless eyes.

"You said it's *possible* Bolton was behind this?" the baron said. Lyander could smell wine on his breath. "Am I to assume the problem here has gone away, then? That we won't be seeing anymore of the . . ." He trailed off, nervous eyes trying to look everywhere but the coffin.

"I'll know more when I get to Damoclen,"

Lyander replied.

"And what am I supposed to tell the town until then?"

Lyander stopped himself from rubbing his temples again. Helping ill-suited rulers govern their populace wasn't what he'd expected when he became an exorcist. *Not that you ever expected to become an exorcist.*

"Tell them whatever you want," he said. But then he remembered the exploding fulcrum and Bolton's near-animalistic rage. "Just make sure you burn Bolton's body tonight. Don't wait until morning," he said.

Before the baron could reply, the sound of footsteps clopping along the jetty came up behind them. They turned to see ten men approaching, one clearly leading them, all wearing an assortment of loose tunics and beige or brown breeches. Several carried crates and all were armed with short swords or hatchets slung into their leather belts.

"Man just came to my door, telling me I had to sail for Damoclen within the hour," the lead man said. "By the baron's orders, he said. Refused to tell me why I was going or who I was taking, but promised me and my men would be paid for the trouble." The man who Lyander could only now assume was Captain Arryan was squat and bowlegged with enough creases in his face to look like crumpled parchment. He wore a black cap sporting a red feather and a navy blue long coat. Both looked about as old as he was.

"I need you to see this man and his cargo to Damoclen," the baron said. "You'll be paid a regular haulage fee, plus compensation for the short notice."

The captain shot a glance at Lyander's horse the moment the baron mentioned the word "cargo."

"Finally decided to do something about that little problem, eh?" Arryan said, pointing at the coffin. "If that's what I think it is, you can pay double. Plus compensation for the short notice *and* travelling by night."

The baron's face creased into lumpy concentration, his eyes hard on Arryan's face – calculating, Lyander supposed, whether his fear of the coffin was worth that much.

Apparently it was. "Fine," the baron said, shaking his head as if he'd been given no choice. "Fine. Fine. Double pay, plus additional fees."

He turned to Lyander, opened his mouth to ask something but then seemed to reconsidered, before saying hastily: "Vergraine thanks you for your service." Then he was gone, his heavy plods echoing along the jetty.

Lyander followed the captain and his crew onto their ship.

#

Damoclen was a two-day sail upriver and the way Captain Arryan's men rowed gave Lyander the distinct impression they wanted him there as quickly as possible. He didn't blame them. The average person viewed his profession with something between awe and outright horror. Adding a coffin was never going to help that.

It was a view Arryan also appeared to share. Although the captain made sure he had his own cabin, three square meals a day, and feed for his horse, he made as little conversation with Lyander as he could. Which left Lyander with plenty of time to chew on the events leading up to Bolton's death.

His one and only theory was Bolton's daughter's decaying body had been reanimated by a previously unknown kind of sorcery, detectable only by fulcrums. In this theory, Bolton needed to be completely unaware of what was happening to his daughter's remains and was simply a father so heartbroken he couldn't bear the thought of someone digging around his dead child's grave.

The alternative, and simpler theory, would be Bolton knew something and was trying to hide it. But if that were the case, the fulcrum would have picked up on any deception associated with the sorcery surrounding the girl's remains while Lyander had been in his house. So, Bolton had to be a grieving father, ignorant of the mystery surrounding Ameria Forth.

Still, it was a theory leaving Lyander with more questions than answers. The most puzzling of which was: *How has Bolton survived on the border of Yeggardania for two months without being eaten?*

He hoped the exhumarian could provide some sort of explanation. If only so he had a credible story to offer the Ecclessius as to why an ancient and irreplaceable Formarian device had been destroyed.

Captain Arryan's ship followed a channel forking off from the Yoinar proper and quickly bent round to head north. The river flowed faster here and the forest took on a noticeably denser quality. Now and then, a Morlett's feasting cry or an Araknor's scuttling climb caused the men to look up from their posts, and made Captain Arryan finger his silver cutlass, but nothing made itself known to them.

A tacit understanding existed between the monsters of the forest and those who travelled the valley regularly. Something akin to a natural law stating: If you look scarier and stronger than me, I'll leave you alone. It was why the captain had twice the number of sailors he needed to row Lyander upstream. Thirteen men in a moving ship was a little too much for the denizens of the Yoinar's northern bank. Most of them, anyway.

The canopy began to hem them in, and within a

matter of minutes the main body of the Yoinar was lost behind the tangled mass of arborealis. Damoclen appeared to them in the same fashion. One minute they were surrounded by impenetrable forest, the next they sailed into the shadow of its twined spire. Completely uniform in design, it looked like an elongated spear tip. Roughly thirty feet in height, it was slit down the middle like a sword cut lengthways, ending in two flat peaks.

The base, which it sat on, was a sort of half-moon – a fortified platform easily four times the size of Arryan's ship. The whole thing was an intricate layering of a grey compound unique to all Formarian architecture, and which reflected stormy grey blues and various light purple hues. To Lyander, it looked a bit like a bird with a particularly large beak opening its mouth, waiting to be fed. For someone unfamiliar with Yeggardania, it would seem like a small fortress, but as far as spires went, it was small.

There were hundreds of installations like it scattered throughout Yeggardania and the underground world of Formaria. Some – mainly those on the northern border – were as large as small cities. What actually gave a spire its name wasn't the visible structure above ground but the large spire-shaped complex running for leagues directly beneath it and connecting the Formarian tunnel kingdoms with the outside world.

Who the Formarians were and why they built the fortified structures was a mystery, but it was clear Damoclen had not been intended as a port for river vessels. The dock, which ran along the northern bank, was built from hewn stone rather than the spire's grey slabs.

As the ship pulled up to it, three of Arryan's men jumped onto the stone pier and towed them into a berth. They attached a boarding plank and Lyander led his horse and the coffin she carried off the ship. Captain

Arryan followed him over.

"Thanks for the ride, Captain," Lyander said, holding out his hand.

Arryan eyed it, then said: "Don't thank me. I wouldn't have sailed you here unless the baron was going to make it worth my while. Not with that thing you're carrying."

Lyander dropped his hand: "Well, my thanks all the same. It was better than walking."

Arryan grunted, nodded, then called his men to set sail.

Don't think I've made a friend there.

He watched the sailors push off and the river carry the galley and its smiling mermaid back to Vergraine. It rounded the bend, and Lyander heard the sound of mail and steel-capped boots coming from the other end of the pier. Three squat forms walked toward him. Two clad head to toe in plate and mail over maroon gambesons, and carrying the sort of crossbows capable of slaying an adolescent griffon from twelve hundred feet. They flanked the one in the middle who wore only a gambeson and carried no weapons. All three dwarves sported long black beards and shaved heads.

"Well now," the one in the middle called out to Lyander. "What's the Yoinar washed up this time? A grave robber, it looks like? Exorcist not all it's cracked up to be, eh?"

"Turns out they're often one and the same," Lyander replied to the dwarf. "It's good to see you again, Folgar."

The dwarf embraced him – something Lyander always found odd. Not that he minded the show of emotion. It was just that a hug from a Dwen'hiema felt like being crushed by an abnormally strong child.

"From where have you come? Who brought you and what are you doing here?" Folgar asked, steering him in the direction of the spire. “The lot, deartháir. I want to know everything. I haven’t seen you in an age.”

“I came from Vergraine,” Lyander told him as they walked.

“Charming town,” Folgar said.

“Captain Arryan provided the passage.”

“Lovely man.”

“And I need the Ecclessius to inspect a rotting and possibly possessed corpse.”

“You always bring the best presents, Lyander.”

He couldn’t help but laugh.

Folgar grinned and said: “Finish your business with the Church, and I expect you back up to the surface on the double. This side of the forest is a bore.”

The exit from the pier led almost straight to the spire’s entrance, a gateway at the base of the platform wide enough to fit two fully laden carts. Solid grey doors slid apart as they approached, presenting a set of steps leading up to the half-moon. Once they were through and climbing the steps, he heard a soft shunt as the doors closed behind them.

“Odd one this, Folgar. Don’t know how long I’ll be,” Lyander said.

“I won’t be going anywhere. Always topside, me.”

“I’ll know where to find you, then.”

The half-moon arched high above them. This close, Lyander could see the perfectly stratiform lines of construction; in between the grey plating were faint blue channels, almost invisible from a distance.

He patted his horse on the flank. “Can I leave her with you?”

“Safe hands up here,” Folgar replied. “Want these here to help you with the coffin?”

Lyander unstrapped the wooden box and hefted it onto his shoulders. “Thanks, but I’ll manage,” he said.

A large octagonal ring was cut into the centre of the floor. Beyond it, a dwarf stood behind a sort of counter stretching around him, made from the same light grey material as the spire. It looked a bit like the stone version of a spice merchant's stall, but Lyander knew on the other side there was a hex system that would send the octagon shooting through the installation.

Lyander walked onto it and turned to face Folgar, now holding his horse's reins. Behind him, the contingent of Dwen'hiema regulars were scattered across the platform, all wearing the same plate and mail as the two flanking Folgar. They carried either heavy crossbows or twin-headed axes looking too big to be held by something that only came up to his own waist.

In the west, the sun began to set and cast its amber glow across the skyline. It lit up the land below, and from his vantage, Lyander could see the Pontivar's rolling forests and its distant mountain range, behind which lay Ravinica.

"You should know, dearthâir: The praefector here, he's about as friendly as your Captain Arryan," Folgar said, and waved at the coffin. "Don't think he's going to appreciate the little gift you've brought."

"That's a shame," Lyander replied. "Everyone else I meet gives me such warm welcomes."

It was Folgar's turn to laugh.

Lyander signalled to the operator behind him. There was another soft shunt accompanied by the sound of escaping air. The floor gave way around him and his horizon rose up before him. Folgar gave a wave, then grey and purple walls replaced him. They glimmered like dark crystal mirrors as he descended.

#

The light grew to the size of his fingernail, then a

subterranean cavern replaced the tunnel walls, and the light was everywhere. Luminous sapphire ran between the geometric tiling, reflected everywhere and turning the hard grey the colour of wet steel.

A product of Formarian innovation, underground installations like Damoclen were built directly on top of gyre deposits to channel the raw power. It was a method known as *harnessing,* and just like every other technology left behind by the Formarians, no one really knew how it worked.

He drifted down, the lift connected with a raised platform, and four entrances leading into low-ceilinged corridors faced him on all sides. He shifted the coffin into a more comfortable position, stepped off the landing and took the one directly in front of him. Perfectly linear patterns lined the walls, and overhead, a blue vein ran like a river into the underworld.

It led him onto a wide concourse, which dropped away on either side into the darkness of a chasm. At the end, an octagonal grey chute ran up into the dark brown rock of the cavern's roof; outside its doors was a terminal a third the size of the one at the spire's mouth. Lyander headed toward it, his footsteps echoing off the concourse and into the depths beneath him.

Most other spires would be a hive of activity, but only a fraction of Formaria's military might was ever committed to the southern border. Although he knew it wasn't, the spire felt empty – like it was just him walking through the timeless relic of a forgotten race.

Well, you and whatever in the black hell you're carrying on your shoulder.

At the lift, the terminal's hexagonal node – skirted with blue and filled with the voidstone-gyre ice blend – looked up at him like the eye of some giant mechanical insect. He pressed a hand into its centre. The filaments moved around his fingers sluggishly, like a nest of mites slowly waking up and trying to get out of his reach. Then, as one, they curled lightly around his hand. He felt an uncomfortable tap at the base of his skull, followed by the familiar rushing awareness. In his mind, he pictured his destination, silently voicing *sanctum*.

Underneath his hand, the hex trembled before sending a pulse down the two offshoots. The filaments loosened, and the lift's doors opened to reveal a base identical to the one from the surface. He stepped onto it and it shot downward.

Formaria was a land beset by war. Facing an onslaught from every quarter by enemies too numerous to truly know their number, it had fought hundreds of battles daily for the past thousand years. Enduring in this perpetual state for such a length of time was not due to military might alone – although that was considerable – but because of the little pockets of sliver-tinged black compound he'd sunk his hand into, and the thousands of others just like it. They made assaulting structures like Damoclen a tactical nightmare.

Attackers could be cut off from one another – forces ten times the number of those under siege reduced to small groups, hemmed into killing grounds. And the whole time, the defenders used a form of communication keeping them one step ahead of their enemy. All because of a technology some dwarf probably figured out by sticking his hand into, just to see what would happen. It made Lyander a little sad to think they only prevailed for this long because the wheels of chance and fate had seen the Fromryr settle upon the ruins of a race more capable than its own.

The octagon stopped in the middle of a spherical chamber bouncing silver shadows around its curved features. Three passages ran off from it in opposite directions. He turned to face the one on his left, giving a view of the room beyond: a large hall littered with triangular blocks looking like squat angular thrones. Icy channels ran up the thrones in streams and lit the space around them. From above, mechanical arms dropped down like giant spiders' legs.

He was looking into one of the Formarian repair shops, where their humanoid but definitely not human left-behinds could be reconstructed, regenerated and, when needed – which it often was – brought back from the brink of annihilation. Lyander thought it looked like a tomb.

Turning away, he took the passage to his right, following a flight of steps spiralling down. When he reached the bottom, he faced a poorly lit corridor, from the end of which came a glowing white light. He walked toward it.

The sanctum, a large octagonal chamber, rose to a perfect orthogonal peak. Eight freestanding pillars surrounded a small section in the centre. They looked like miniature spires and ended in claw-like tips. Each one generated a beam of light running up to the room's vaulted ceiling. The effect resulted in a white-gold translucent barrier in between each pillar and made the whole thing look like a very expensive prison cell.

"Please refrain from coming any closer," a soft, almost musical voice said from inside the prison of light. "Our friend here is perfectly harmless. But you can never be too sure about what might linger when it comes to the maligned."

Lyander, walking toward the pillars, stopped. Peering around them, he could see a wiry figure with its back turned to him and hunched over a rectangular block looking like the tomb of some ancient king, except it was a shiny black rather than dull stone. The figure wore a dark gown with an exhumarian's leather amice draped over his shoulders. His name was Dracht, and Lyander didn't know anyone better at solving mysteries by digging around in the bowels of dead things.

"Tricksy when they want to be," Dracht continued. "Tricksy, tricksy, tricksy," he chimed, and then added, "although this fellow has been a little obvious."

A soldier's body lay on the block. From what Lyander could see, he still wore plate armour over his legs, but his torso was completely bare. Where his right arm should have been was a thick pinkish green tendril draped over the side of the block. A horn grew out of the soldier's forehead, crushing the left socket beneath it. The warped eye looked straight at Lyander.

Trying not think about how the soldier had met such a gruesome fate, he said: "Perhaps I can offer you something more interesting?"

"Ahh, a puzzle, is it?" Dracht said, still hunched over the block. "The praefector didn't mention a new sanction."

"I thought I'd find out what it is I needed to sanction first."

At that, Dracht half-turned, glancing at him out of the corner of his eye before returning to his work. He made a tutting sound. "Always breaking the rules, aren't we, Lyander. What have you brought me, then?"

"A corpse," Lyander replied.

"I have plenty of those already."

"This one caused a fulcrum to explode," Lyander said, adding: "I think."

"You were there when this happened?"

"I was holding the fulcrum."

Lyander heard something sounding like metal implements scraping together, then Dracht said: "But you're not sure?"

"There wasn't a trace of sorcery in the area," Lyander replied.

"And the corpse. Is their malignance or abhorrence?" Dracht asked.

"Neither. Not that I could find."

Dracht paused whatever he was doing to the infected soldier, then said: "You're right. You have brought me something very interesting." He pulled off his black leather gloves and placed them at the end of the block. They were slick with a dark orange gore.

Turning to the pillar behind him, he pressed his hand to the small console attached to it. A *hum* echoed around the chamber and little silvery black filaments on the surface of the block began climbing the malformed body and drawing it down like living quicksand.

Dracht smiled at Lyander, his teeth yellowed, his skin the colour of milk. It pulled across his face and bald head like a hide stretched for tanning. He looked like a man half starved to death, but Lyander knew it was just a side effect of extended time undergoing liturgical purification. Constant exposure to malignance came with consequences, and for once, Lyander was thankful he wasn't a very good exorcist. If he was, he might need the same regularity of *purification* as Dracht.

"If you wouldn't mind," the exhumarian said, gesturing at the examination block, which had now completely swallowed the corrupted body.

Lyander stepped past the pillars, the translucent barrier feeling like a wall of cold mist. He set the coffin on the floor, unlocked it, and opened the lid. There was no change to the girl's body – the skin still a blotchy black and grey, and what remained of her hair fell like pieces of string across her sunken face. Carefully, he scooped up the corpse and laid it on the now solid surface.

"You performed the rites on her?" Dracht asked, looking down at her from the block's opposite end.

"That doesn't do anything, and you know it,

Dracht," Lyander said. "And anyway, I don't carry a cross."

"Still the unbeliever," Dracht said, rolling his eyes. "An exorcist who doesn't carry out exorcisms. One day you will tell me how that works." He reached under his amice and untied a necklace from around his neck. It held a small cross made from arborealis wood. The twisted icon looked more like vines tangled around each other than something carved from a tree. Dracht handed it to him; Lyander simply stared at it.

"You know as well as I do, they only work inside the Immuratum," he said.

"And as one of the few people in all of Formaria likely to enter the chaos realm, don't you think you should wear one?"

"I'm not getting those kinds of bounties, and you know it," Lyander said, but took the cross to appease his friend. He held it in his hand, resolving to find a *safe place* for it once he was done with Dracht.

The exhumarian smiled sadly at Lyander, then moved around the block to inspect the girl's arms and face. The gilded cage shimmered behind him, making his pale features radiant, almost angelic.

Dracht made a *hmm* sound every time he inspected a new body part. "While the smell is faint, it is clear she has been dead some time," he said. "But the corpse is too well preserved, which would suggest sorcery of some form. But as you say, there is no Immuratic or Aeturnic forces present. Nor even that of the gyre, for that matter."

"Know anything that can do that?"

"I have my suspicions, but the chamber will know for certain. I will stimulate the body just enough to reveal whatever has a hold over it."

He must have seen a look on Lyander's face because he nodded up at the light converging in the centre of the ceiling and added: "We are protected. The sanctum will see to that."

Although he trusted the exhumarian, Lyander had never actually been around for this part – the idea of animating the dead left him on edge.

Dracht stepped over to the terminal, pressing his hand to it and mouthing the words, *vitae exhorium*. The block's filaments shifted and formed into slow-moving circles. They looked like tiny black whirlpools swirling under the corpse and gave the false impression the body was moving, as if the girl was waking from a very deep sleep.

Then Lyander saw her jaw move. Just a twitch. Barely perceptible. But it was enough to make him reach for his sword.

"The sanctum," Dracht said, quickly, "replicates just a fraction of whatever sorcery is present so that we may glimpse the truth." He nodded at Lyander's hand, which he realised was clutching the hilt of his sword. "So you won't need that."

Feeling a little foolish, he said: "Her mouth moved."

"I would hope something happened."

Dracht picked up a scalpel from the end of the block, using it to gently pry apart the girl's mouth. On the top row of her teeth – where there definitely hadn't been one before because Lyander had checked – was a long, curling, bone-white fang.

Dracht made another *hmm* sound, let the girl's upper lip drop and moved down to inspect her arms and wrists, feeling along them like he was checking for a pulse. He got to her hands and Lyander could see her nails forming into jagged claws, like tiny yellow stalactites.

"I'm afraid this is no demon host, Lyander," Dracht said, still peering at her hands. "She is of the

Aeturnum."

"And how," Lyander asked, hearing the irritation in his voice, "are you coming to that conclusion?" If Dracht was right – which he generally was – he wasn't getting paid. He would be forced to hand the investigation over to a witch-hunter who, after doing none of the work, would claim the bounty instead.

Dracht made a shallow incision in her wrist and black liquid pooled in the slit. There was the faintest blue tint to it – the exact colour that would not be in the blood of someone hosting a demon.

"Even if this was an Aeturni, I would have known," Lyander said, but wasn't entirely convinced by his own words. "Especially one powerful enough to break a fulcrum."

"While she is *of* the Aeturnum, I don't think she is a true Aeturni," Dracht said, laying her hand down and looking at Lyander. "I believe she is Lamian; she is a vampire."

Lyander started laughing, then stopped when he saw the exhumarian's face; it held the look of good-humoured patience, as if he was waiting for a child to stop misbehaving.

"Dracht," Lyander said, with gentle reproach. "Vampires are a bit like dragons – a scholar can achieve an unremarkable career writing about them, and they make for good fireside tales, but there's no evidence they ever existed."

"Insights from a well-read scholar, I don't doubt," Dracht said, and if Lyander didn't know it was a joke, he might have blushed. "Your fulcrum detected this being because its presence burns like a torch in the gyre," Dracht continued, "but even though there is clearly sorcery of some kind, it doesn't create a magical aura in the material realm because it is older than the material realm. They may even be older that the

Formarians themselves."

"And you know this how?"

"Because it is my job to know these things," Dracht said, indicating the chamber around them. "In case it had escaped your notice."

"So you're telling me that this little girl is a lost ancient undead some farmer has been hiding in his back garden?"

"More likely she was *turned* by a lost ancient undead. Why you found her where you did, I cannot say."

"Which lost ancient undead?" Lyander asked, hoping this wasn't about to spiral into the realms of the unbelievable. At some point, he would need to explain all of this to the Ecclessius who, as he well knew, were not the most understanding of institutions.

"It's more likely such a being existed than didn't exist, Lyander," Dracht said, dashing his hopes.

"And how do you think the Ecclessius is going to respond when I tell them I found a little girl turned by a Lord of the Eternal Hunt – beings most sane people in Formaria believe are myths?"

"With incredulity and quite severe misgivings, I should expect," the exhumarian said, a sad smile touching the corners of his pale lips; Dracht was well aware of his relationship with the Church. Or lack thererof. "I can submit my own report," he added, "but I'm afraid the Ecclessius will probably want to see this poor girl for themselves."

Lyander shook his head – that was several steps ahead, and he still had questions. "The Lord of Undead . . ." he said, trying to recall the stories he'd been told as a child.

"Its name is Lokul," Dracht said.

"Lokul – why would Lokul turn a little girl and leave her in a coffin on the edge of Formaria?"

Something else struck Lyander – something more significant. “Wasn’t Lokul destroyed? Isn’t that his story. He was killed by one of Redcrosse’s scions?”

“By Leoncoure Leonette,” Dracht said. “But whether Lokul turned the girl, or another one of its offspring did, I cannot say. Perhaps Lokul is truly destroyed. Perhaps one of its more powerful creations survived the aeons and carried out this deed.” Dracht shrugged, smiling apologetically.

Lyander gave his temples a massage. The idea of the Lords of the Eternal Hunt truly existing – creatures most myths described as some type of demi-gods of the Aeturnum set on conquering the material realm – managed to bother him less than the thought of explaining all this to the Church. Also, he wasn’t getting paid.

“Tell me everything you can about this vampire,” Lyander said.

Dracht’s smile said nothing would please him more. “Of course. You may wish to take a seat.” He pointed at a stool pushed up against one of the pillars behind Lyander. “I expect this will take some time.”

Lyander nodded and turned to take the seat.

But as he did so, he heard something that sounded very much like the wet snapping of joints and a long slow wheeze. Like air escaping an underground fissure.

He spun on the spot, nearly falling backward at the image in front of him. The vampire was sitting upright, its arm outstretched like it was trying to grasp at some unseen thing in the air. It would have looked comical if Lyander hadn’t seen the unadulterated panic written across Dracht’s previously calm features as he fumbled desperately at the console, repeating over and over the words, *“terminus est.”*

Then the vampire screamed.

A gut-wrenching sound filled with pain and hate. A sound that did not belong to a creature of this world and felt innately wrong to Lyander's human experience. He staggered where he stood. A headache bloomed behind his eyes and his vision swam, causing the golden beams of light to multiply around him.

He heard another scream – a human scream. Dracht's scream. He watched through the bright haze overlaying his vision as his friend clawed at his eyes and fell backward against the pillar, liquid spilling through his fingers. Then, with inhuman speed, the vampire jumped off the block and faced Lyander.

Without thinking, Lyander held up the cross still clutched in his hand. The vampire gave a muted shriek and spun away from him. It made for the gap between two of the pillars but pulled back from the translucent barrier as if burned.

It turned, facing him again, hunched like an animal spoiling for a fight. Then, in a voice ugly and broken, through vocal cords eaten away by maggots and defiled by grave rot, it said a single word:

"Eluthienn."

His vision still reeling, Lyander held the cross higher. The vampire screamed, and he felt a force cascade around him as if he were a headland upon which waves were breaking.

The vampire – a hazy black shape now – sprung toward him, its arm slashing outward. Blood drenched the block and he felt his entire wrist go limp, the fingers unresponsive to what he wanted them to do. The cross slipped from the wreckage of his hand.

"Eluthienn!" the vampire screamed again. "Grindlepeake. Ducima ad Grindlepeake."

Somewhere between the vampire waking up and it tearing into his hand, Lyander had drawn his sword. With no recollection of doing so, he gave a prayer of eternal thanks for whatever unconscious reflexes had been drilled into him decades ago. It lasted little more than a second before he brought the blade down in a single, brutal arc. The cut would have felled most creatures five times the size of what he was currently facing. As it was, the four-foot being in front of him pretty much exploded.

Lyander sank to his knees and was forced to use his sword to prop himself up. The blinding headache was gone but was quickly being replaced by an unholy amount of pain in his left hand. What remained of the vampire lay before him: jaw shattered, and everything from the clavicle down to the hip bone a total mess. Blackish blue blood pooled on the floor.

He stared at the body for several heartbeats, decided it wasn't getting back up, then pushed himself to his feet, legs trembling like he was balancing on stilts.

The rational part of Lyander's brain knew Dracht was dead, but something in his mind wouldn't let him believe it until he saw a body. He forced himself to walk around the block.

The exhumarian was slumped against a pillar, head drooping forward, hands in his lap, palms facing the ceiling. They were covered in a watery brown liquid still oozing from his nose and the fleshy pits where his eyes had been. He was dead. Moments ago, the man had been standing before him and now his brains were spilling between his fingers.

Lyander's own head dropped to his chest, his shoulders curling in on himself. He grit his teeth – not against the pain in his hand or head but against the ache in his chest and the memory it brought with it: the howls of hundreds of soldiers dying, cold rock beneath his knees, above him the impregnable darkness lit by columns of blue fire, higher than any mountain, more terrible than any storm. His aching chest felt like a vice clamped over his heart.

From far away, he heard armoured boots pounding down the corridor outside the sanctum, then three Ecclessius knights appeared before the translucent cage. They wore chain vests under white surcoats, emblazoned with a red cross. Behind the gilded barrier, the steel of their drawn swords glinted like polished silver.

The one with a shock of ginger hair sticking out from both his head and his chin stepped forward, pale blue eyes darting from Lyander to Dracht to the vampire, then back to Lyander.

"What happened here, exorcist?"

Lyander cradled his bloody hand to his chest, letting the pain radiate through him, releasing him from the memory's hold.

"The sanctum failed to sedate the creature," he growled through the pain. "I destroyed it but not before it . . ." he faltered on the word, then said, "before it killed the exhumarian."

Surprise shot across the knight's face. "What creature could overcome the sanctum?"

"A vampire."

"I see," he said, but it didn't look like he did; he just looked more concerned. "Your hand, we'll take you to the vulnerum."

Lyander shuffled back around the block and his foot struck something on the floor. He looked down and saw the cross. Leaning his sword against the block, he bent down and picked it up by its leather thong. The wood, black and charred on one side, could have been pulled from hot coals.

"I can take myself," he said, gazing at the thing he was pretty certain had just saved his life.

Four

Brazier

Brazier sat in the armoury watching Switch test the weight and sights of different crossbows. There were four variants on board and she finally settled on a medium-range repeater with a stubby nose, a long shoulder stock, and a burnished gold casing. Held in her mechanical hand, it was hard to tell where the augment ended and the crossbow began.

"So when we find this ship," she said, winding the fist-sized firing wheel, the teeth clicking as it became taut, "and we find it's not flyable, what does the captain intend to do then?"

The rest of the landing team – Freyen, Axelock, and Dalfin – stopped what they were doing and looked at Brazier expectantly. Of the four, only Dalfin appeared unconcerned by the prospect of boarding the mystery ship.

"Send up a flare and wait for the Navarch or

stick it in the hangar bay and take it with us," Brazier ventured. He and Torquen hadn't got much further than 'find out what's going on with the ship.'

"You see, I thought we might run into a problem here," Switch said, picking a magazine from a chest and jamming it into the crossbow. "We're carrying three hundred tonnes of ice. Even without that weight, our engine core – which the cap has been running ragged for the past six hours – would be liable to drop out our ass. We can't add another ship into the equation."

"I thought you said the core was the one part of the ship you didn't need to worry about?" Brazier said.

"I said the signature was the one part of the ship I didn't need to worry about – which is housed in a fulcrum, within the scalopractic chamber that sits within the core."

To Brazier, little of that made sense. He nodded slowly, pretending it did.

"By law," Freyen said, an eyebrow cocked in his direction, "we need to stop, render aid, and report the location of the ship." She slotted two long knives into the scabbards on her hips, then tightened the crossbow strap across her chest. When she next spoke, her voice was noticeably cooler: "We are not obliged to take it with us if it risks the *Chalice*. She's a far more valuable ship."

Switch pointed a bronzite finger at Freyen: "What she said."

"Do we know what did her in?" Axelock asked, a crossbow slung across his back, his forearm resting atop the head of a giant twin-headed axe. Somehow, he managed to make it look small.

"Got to be a goblin tunnel gang, or surface crawlers," Dalfin said before Brazier could reply. "No way it's Mirrovinjin this far south."

"Tunnel gang would've stripped the ship to its

frame and left a floating skeleton," Freyen said. "Brazier just said the ship was in one piece." She turned to him as she said it: "Right?"

"Right," he said. "We don't know what attacked her, but we know they didn't hang around. Jan's not picking up any lifeforms in the primary tunnel or the secondary shafts."

"Doesn't mean there's not something waiting for us," Switch said. "Plenty of ways to hide from navigators."

"Jan might be the weirdest navigator I've ever met, which is saying something, as they're all exceptionally out of their minds," Axelock said. "But he's never wrong about this shit."

"Agreed," Freyen said. "He's wasted on this crew."

"Whatever's out there," Dalfin said, swinging a body-mounted bolt thrower from his hip, "it's welcome to eat my repeater."

"Dwen'hiema!" Axelock said, holding his forearm up for Dalfin to crash his own against.

"It's not going to come to that," Brazier said in a tone he hoped conveyed *you will do exactly as ordered.* "We see anything that looks unfriendly and we are straight back to the *Chalice*."

Dalfin, looking disappointed, stopped striking martial poses, and said, "You got it, boss."

To his right, the armoury's hex terminal came to life in tremulous pulses. It was Torquen's voice: "Brazier, we're five minutes from the drop point."

He got up and stood next to the terminal. "We'll be at the aft access ramp in two," he said.

"Jan thinks there's a hatch on her starboard side. Shouldn't be too hard to get in through there."

"We'll find it."

The connection cut out and he turned to the

others. "Jan's dropping us point-three of a league from the ship," he said. "Aft beam should light up a quarter of that, but we'll need torches for the rest. Take a couple each."

Switch began pulling torches from mounts on the armoury wall and handed them out. The little devices looked like bronze cylinders packed with shards of unrefined gyre ice. Twisting the cap at the bottom of the torch set in motion thirty small axle joints that hit an ignition wheel and caused the shard to blaze into a blue cone until it eventually evaporated into smoke. At the Navarch Academy, he and all the other officers were made to take the devices apart and put them back together until they could do it with their eyes closed. He could name every cog and gear based on touch alone. But not even the Lord Enginator of the Artificium would be able to explain how they actually worked.

He slotted one into the underslung mount on his crossbow and the other into a clip on his gambeson. Then he called for the lift to take them to the hangar bay.

They shot through the belly of the ship before descending several decks. At the hangar bay, the doors opened onto two hundred square feet of mainly empty space with an access ramp half as long and cut into the floor. There was a single terminal in the centre of the bay, but Brazier ignored it and led his team to the edge of the ramp. He heard the rear thrusters kick in, then there was a gentle shudder beneath his feet. When the ship stilled, the ramp opened with a deep shunt and a gust of cool air. Before them, the blackness of Formaria, punctured by the high-intensity beam of the ship's aft searchlight, yawned into view.

Brazier pulled his crossbow into his shoulder and walked into the tunnel, the others two steps behind.

Hundreds of thousands of years ago, the Formarians built a continent-wide tunnel system so deep and complex, new shafts were still being found to this day. The technology, or sorcery, used to achieve such a feat was anyone's guess. But whatever the method, it did not make the tunnels immune to the effects of time. Stalagmites and stalactites – some of which were fifteen feet in length – grew across every inch of this part of the system, creating an entirely new world. Lit up by the *Chalice*'s ghostly beacon, they took on an ashen hue making Brazier feel like he was weaving his way through a pantheon of ancient shrines.

It made for slow going, and it was sometime before they reached the searchlight's extent – a wall of darkness so black, it could have led off the edge of a ravine and he would have been none the wiser.

"Torches," he called behind him, the echo repeating just twice before being swallowed by the black.

Brazier heard five clicks and blue beams shot in different directions. He lit his own and moved forward. Apart from their footfalls and the clank of weapons knocking against a gambeson's rock locks, they made no sound. He was about to swing round a particularly stumpy-looking rock deposit when the sound of Axelock swearing and boots skidding along the floor brought him to a halt. He spun on the spot and saw the dwarf franticly scanning back and forth with the gyre torch, his axe held menacingly in his other hand. Brazier instinctively brought up his own torch in the direction Axelock was pointing his.

"What is it?" he said, trying to keep the panic from his voice. The others came to a stop and three more beams added to Axelock's and his own. Trying to look everywhere at once, he saw nothing but dancing blue light and the occasional flash of grey stalagmite.

"Axelock, do you have eyes on something?" Brazier asked again.

The burly dwarf took a painfully long time before responding. Then said: "No, boss. Thought I saw movement but must be imagining things."

No one dropped their torch until Brazier said, "Okay, let's keep moving."

In the all-consuming darkness of the Formarian tunnels, smell was often the first sign of something unpleasant coming one's way. Mirrovinjin smelled like corpses. Surface crawlers smelled like swamp. Rakkan, on those rare occasions they made themselves known, smelled like unwashed body. And goblins smelled like rotting food in addition to all of the above. Moving through the tunnel, all Brazier could smell was the mineral earthiness of cold rock but five minutes on from the false alarm, and he still needed to stop himself from sniffing at every new cluster and deposit they past.

When they finally came across the stranded ship, it was the change in temperature that revealed its location. Stagnant cool gave way to a pocket of warmth, and Brazier looked up to see the ship's reddish gold cockpit materialising out of the blackness like it was being summoned from the depths of an ocean.

"We've got her," he called over his shoulder, and began moving round to her starboard side to try and find the access hatch. This close up, the ship looked even more like an insect. The cockpit – a flattened triangle looking a bit like a shark's nose – was connected to a rounded fuselage with overlapping plating along its upper hull. Connected to that was a bulbous stern easily four times the size of the rest of the ship and gave the whole thing a pregnant look. The six thrusters, their discs a quarter the diameter of the *Chalice*'s, sprouted from each segment of the ship on ninety-degree extensions. They looked like Araknor's legs.

"That is one fuck-ugly ship," Switch said. "Just as well we're not taking her with us."

"Got the hatch," Freyen said. "Just under that thruster's arm." She fixed her torch on the fuselage and revealed an oval door with an indented wheel lock.

"Dalfin, set up over there," Brazier said, pointing to a spot behind them. "Try and hit just beneath the thruster joint."

Dalfin knelt and threw a backpack down next him. He began unpacking rope and a pronged grappling head.

Brazier turned to Switch. "Can you open that?" he asked, nodding up at the hatch.

She concentrated on it like she was trying to solve a complex puzzle. "Shouldn't be a problem."

"Ready, boss," Dalfin said from behind them, the grappling head and rope now attached to one of the bolts.

Brazier told him to fire.

The dwarf leant back to absorb the recoil, then released the bolt. It sprang from the weapon, hit the thruster's arm with a soft *thunk* and prongs snapped shut on the grappling head, locking the bolt into place. Leaning back and grinning stupidly, the blond dwarf waved his free arm invitingly at the now taut rope. Out of the corner of his eye, Brazier saw Freyen roll her eyes.

Switch strapped her crossbow tight across her chest and made sure her tool pouches were all buttoned up.

"Drop me, big man," she said, grabbing the line, "and you'll know about it shortly after."

"Wouldn't dream of it," Dalfin said, still grinning.

Switch jumped up, throwing her legs around the rope. For a moment, Brazier thought Dalfin was going to tumble forward but he steadied himself, digging in his heels. Switch pulled herself up the line. When she got to the top, she pulled herself onto the rim of the hatch and flattened herself against it. Reaching round, she undid a pocket, pulled out a cog-like device, and slotted it into the wheel lock.

"This'll crack her open," she said, and began pulling on the device's small handle with what looked like every ounce of strength her mechanical arm could provide. She made a sound somewhere between a grunt and a growl and the lock gave way, the cog turned, and Brazier heard the door's internal locks cycling open. There was a click, Switch pushed on the hatch, and it swung inward.

"Shit in the abyss!" she swore with such vehemence, Dalfin nearly slipped over. "This place smells like a troll mating ground."

Brazier didn't know what a troll mating ground smelled like, but he assumed it was bad.

"Zee, you're going to want to come up and see this."

He didn't wait around. Tightening his crossbow across his front, he jumped onto the rope and began climbing.

The stench hit him before he was halfway up the line, and he breathed through his nose to stop himself from gagging. Apparently, troll mating grounds smelled a lot like death and vomit.

When he reached the thruster arm, Switch made space by stepping into the ship. Brazier perched his leg on the rim of the hatch while holding the shaft of the grappling bolt for balance. Then he swung himself round and jumped in after her.

He splashed into something wet and pointed his torch at his feet, thinking the synthesisers must have leaked and he was standing in refined ice. That would explain the lack of light, but looking down he realised he couldn't be more wrong. The liquid was a dark red, almost brown colour. *Blood.*

He searched for its source, and found himself staring into the lifeless gaze of a young gnome. Face shockingly pale and mouth hung open like he'd been trying to say something in the moment of his death. Brazier brought his torch over the gnome's torso and felt a stab of sorrow – his death hadn't been quick or clean. The entire upper body had been ripped open from sternum to groin, his guts spilling out over the decking. One of his arms was completely missing just above the elbow, the other was shredded by long cuts, down to the bone.

"There're more of them over here," Switch said.

Brazier followed her torch light to the other side of the fuselage. A human male and dwarven female lay face down. It was unclear how the dwarf died but the human's back was lined with gashes so deep, Brazier could see individual vertebrae. Just beyond them, another dwarf was slumped against a low balustrade. He didn't have a head.

From behind him, he heard Freyen jump into the fuselage. Even in the half-light provided by the torches, he could see her face go hard as she took in the sight and smell of the crew.

"I'm going with Mirrovinjin," Switch said. "This looks like their kind of carnage."

Brazier couldn't argue with the observation, but he wasn't convinced. Of all the things that could have done this, the Mirrovinjin were the least likely to leave an operational gyre ship floating around.

"Let's sweep the rest of the ship before we jump to any conclusions," he said. Then remembering his earlier thought: "What's with the lights?"

"Engine core might be running some sort of reduced auxiliary protocol. Will need to look at it to be sure, though," Switch said.

"See if you can get power to the thrusters while you're there. Freyen, take the hold. I'll see what's still working on the nav deck," Brazier said.

Switch circled round the balustrade and descended into the ship. Freyen moved past him and followed her down.

Without the other's torches, it was impossibly dark in the fuselage, so he clicked on his spare and repositioned it on his gambeson. It beamed out from his shoulder.

Using the two light sources, he searched the end of the fuselage and found the hatch leading to the cockpit. It was identical to the one on the hull and hanging wide open. Above it, he saw a small plaque, brown with age and engraved upon it the words *The Solace of Iron*. Brazier thought it was an odd name for a transport ship, but he wasn't going to dwell on it. Right now, the whole situation was odd.

At the hatch, he scanned the room inside. He expected another bloodbath but that didn't stop the hot wave of anger and sadness at what he saw.

Three bodies: two humans – one male, one female – and a male dwarf. The latter, bent awkwardly over the navigation terminal, looked like the ship's captain. Blood from his chest had leaked into one of the hex wells. On the floor next to him was the male human who clearly died fighting, an axe clutched in one of his hands, the head black with drying blood. The female, who was clearly the ship's navigator, was sprawled in the navigation pit. A deep slash ran from her ear, across her neck, and down the opposite collar bone.

It was then he noticed their uniforms. They all wore black gambesons with golden yellow circles on their shoulders and in the centre of their chests. In each circle, a black wyvern curled into a tight ball – the insignia of the Thendergaarden Custodian force. The ship's name suddenly made a lot more sense.

"Brazier, I'm in the hold." Freyen's voice – coming from the hex well without blood in it – made him jump. "Cap said this was a troop transport?"

Brazier stepped onto the deck and set his crossbow on the navigation terminal.

"That's what it looked like on the hex," he said, picking up the ship's captain and placing him carefully on the floor next to his dead crewmate. It was the most immediately respectful thing he could think of doing.

"That's not what it looks like from in here," Freyen said.

"I know. It's a prisoner transport."

"How do you know that?"

"I'm looking at three dead Custodians. What are you looking at?"

"A bunch of personal holding cells with a bunch of dead prisoners in them. Two humans. The rest are dwarves. Looks like they were all killed in their constraints," she said. "Not a nice way to go, even for a criminal."

Brazier pictured rows of grate-locked cells with shackled and slaughtered bodies inside, thinking he'd given Freyen the raw end of the deal by taking the nav deck.

"There's something else," she said. "There's a high security cell at the back of the hold. Another dwarf."

Brazier heard her hesitate, then: "He's still alive."

That was going to complicate things.

"Is he secure?"

"You couldn't make him more secure if you tried. His constraints have constraints. And he's got a mouth clamp. Looks like it's administering some sort of sedative."

Brazier didn't know how dangerous you needed to be before you were body clamped and drugged, but he assumed it put you on a list of individuals the Thendergaarden Custodia would not want to lose.

"Someone very important is going to want him back," Brazier said. "I'll let Torquen know what we've found. Get back to the engines and make sure you lock any hatches behind you."

He waited for the tether to drop, then placed his hand into the well. *Brazier Veranquis, tether from the Solace of Iron to the Chalice of Amaranth. Navigator: Jandrice Karmoon*, he said in his mind. Unlike inter-ship communication, which felt like dipping your brain into a cold lake, tethering outside of a ship felt like throwing yourself into a dense fog. That was until you were picked up by the recipient, and then it was back to the lake.

His head stopped swimming and Jan's soft voice echoed around his skull: *Received, Brazier.*

The feeling of something small and slick swimming around his skull, then Jan's voice: *Auric identification confirmed. Would you like to speak to the captain?*

Brazier pulled his hand out of the well, and said, "Yes, please, Jan."

A moment later, Torquen's voice vibrated across the hex: "Brazier, what's happening out there?"

"We're on a Custodian transport vessel," he said. "It's in one piece, but I can't say the same for the crew or most of the prisoners."

"What do you mean *most* of the prisoners?"

"Freyen's found a live one. High security by the sounds of it."

Torquen swore, causing a tiny string of hex to jump half an inch into the air.

"Is the ship flyable?"

"Switch is working on it."

"Okay, we'll report it now. Theselan is the closest spire but it's still forty leagues out, so we won't get a response for a while. We can bring the *Chalice* in closer, but you're going to have to sit tight for the time being."

"We can do that."

"Switch needs to get those engines working, Brazier," Torquen said. "The *Chalice* can't take the weight of that ship, and the Custodia aren't going to let us leave one of their most wanted floating in the dark. They'll make us wait for them to come and collect."

The implication was as clear as daylight breaking through a tunnel. A relief force from Theselan would take a day to reach them. Being on the float for that long was a risk. Being on the float for that long in a section recently attacked, and you were practically inviting trouble.

"If anyone can make this thing fly, it's Switch," he said. They were words he believed.

"Update me when it happens." The hex went flat.

As if on cue, Switch tethered into the nav deck, her voice coming from an adjacent well to the one through which he'd spoken to Torquen.

"Zee, I'm restarting the engines now," she said. "Going to need to null the core and then restart the harnessing protocol. It might get bumpy. Then again, it might not."

"Erm, okay. Maybe wait for me to get there." His presence would offer little in the way of technical expertise, but if something was going to go wrong, he wanted to be near at hand.

He picked up his crossbow and made his way below deck.

Switch stood with her back to him in the middle

of five bronze pillars. Her crossbow was on the floor and both her torches and Freyen's spare were positioned against it. All three beamed up at a floating metal sphere comprising hexagonal tiles with crystal-like dots in their centres: the engine core.

Brazier moved to get a better view and saw two of the tiles hung open, Switch's augmented arm thrust into the centre. From the way she was moving it around, it looked like she was trying to find something particularly hard to reach.

"Got you," she said, as Brazier moved to stand next to one of the pillars. Freyen was standing on the opposite side, looking over Switch's shoulder and into the metal sphere, a dubious look on her face, which Brazier found himself silently agreeing with. You'd have to pay him a lot of gold to get him to shove his hand into an engine core.

"Alright, boys and girls, hold on to your breeches," Switch said.

She twisted something in the core and a metallic click rang through the room. She pulled her hand free and the hexagonal tiles closed themselves shut. There were five more clicks, all in quick succession, then Brazier felt gravity give way beneath his feet. The ship began tilting to one side, like it had been cut from an invisible anchor.

"This is supposed to be happening, right?" Brazier said, reaching out to a pillar for support.

"She just needs a moment to warm up," Switch said, also reaching out to the pillar next to her. "She'll power up any second now."

The ship continued to tilt so he was now leaning against the pillar. One of the torches began to roll across the decking.

"Any second now," Switch said, as if by voicing the words she could will it to happen.

Something in the bones of the ship creaked, and Brazier felt them drifting toward the tunnel floor.

"Any second now," Switch repeated, staring fixedly at the engine core.

"Switch, I'm no expert, but I don't think the protocol is going to start," Brazier said.

"You're right, Zee. You're not an expert," Switch said. Then she smacked the core with her mechanical fist. The crystals in the middle of the tiles flared into life with blue light. Then they died.

"Come on," Switch said, giving the sphere another smack. The crystals glowed, then flickered, trying desperately to hold on to their light. Instead of drifting smoothly, the ship shuddered. It gave a long, aching groan, then the core lit up like a star burning out of existence. Brazier shielded his eyes, clinging to the pillar and waiting for the blaze to subside.

The ship stopped its juddering decline, righted itself in the air, and the light dimmed. Lines of rich sapphire formed between the core's tiles and flooded into each of its crystals. Above them, channels of the same blue light coursed through the engine room like sluice gates releasing their hold.

"Told you it would start," Switch said. "Just needed some encouragement."

"Good to know you can punch an engine core to make it work," Freyen said. "This how you treat the *Chalice*?"

"Nah. I can have that kitten purring any time I want to. This," she said, pointing a finger at the engine core, "has been tampered with. But I've got no idea how. I still don't know whether it's going to put out a signature or not."

"We can make do without one," Brazier said. "We just need her to –"

A hex terminal in the corner of the room pulsed

with activity. It was Torquen: "Brazier, are you receiving? Brazier, respond."

Something in the tone of his brother's voice made him move very quickly around the pillars.

"Receiving," he said to the hex.

"We've got movement in the tunnel," Torquen said. "A lot of movement."

Five

Lyander

Lyander sat in the vulnerum, his hand wrapped in blood-soaked bandages, the image of Dracht sitting in a puddle of his own brains like a magical imprint burned into his retina. It was there, behind the eyes, before he looked away, lost the image, then it was back again – ghosting his vision, unrelenting in its pursuit.

His thoughts were no better.

It should be you lying on the sanctum floor. You with your brains spilling through your sockets. You whose body should now be held for investigation. But instead, he was here, and Dracht was dead. Dracht – who was kind, who was impossibly good-natured, given his role in life – was dead in his place because being Dracht, he had given Lyander his cross without a second thought.

The hollow, grey, nauseating feeling twisting in Lyander's gut was doing its best to compete with the sharp burning in his hand, which coursed up his arm and into his chest, causing him to breathe heavily, and perspiration to form across his brow.

He couldn't decide which pain he wanted to win.

Damoclen's single war caster, a middle-aged woman with brown hair and creases lining her forehead, was doing her best to make sure it wasn't his hand. A straightforward – if somewhat grisly – flesh wound, it ought to be healed with basic anomancy. But her healing sorcery wasn't really working, and it baffled her. She had done her best to knit the torn ligaments, flayed skin, and broken fingers back together, but something in the vampire's claws – he guessed – was preventing it all from staying together. It meant he was left with a half-stitched, half-magically healed hand that didn't work and wouldn't stop bleeding. To distract himself from it and everything else, he replayed in his mind the vampire's few words.

"Ducima ad Grindlepeake," he said under his breath. It translated to *Lead me to Grindlepeake*. Or maybe *Take me to Grindlepeake*. He wasn't exactly sure. It was an Old World tongue and the last time he'd translated anything like it had been in the Ecclessiarchal monastery. That the vampire spoke a pre-migration language was interesting in itself, but in comparison to what it asked, it barely registered on his now extensive list of questions. Vampires not only now existed – apparently – but one of their number was on the hunt for the most wanted man in Aetraya. Not only that, it also knew where to find him. For the second time in as many days, Lyander wondered if he should have taken the Vergrainian townsfolk more seriously.

"Feeling okay?" the war caster asked, clasping his bandage in place with a pin. When she was done, she wiped her hands on her quartered tunic. In one of the quarters, Angelaux doves flew off toward her shoulder.

Like the rest of her, they were smeared with his blood. The look she gave him said she was less concerned about his wellbeing and more concerned about whether he was going to become a problem for her.

"I'm fine," he said distractedly.

"Good because the praefector wants to see you. And he's pissed. Which is a daily occurrence for him, but whatever you did in the sanctum has managed to transcend him to a whole new state of rage."

"I'll add it to my list of achievements."

"You do that," she said. "Just make sure you go see him. I don't want him in here asking why you left without saying goodbye."

He grunted his assent and got up to leave. "Thanks for this, by the way." He waved his bandaged hand at her.

"Let's not make it a habit."

#

The praefector's office was at the end of a dimly lit corridor shaped like a triangular prism. Where the two sides of the ceiling met, a blue canal glowed, lighting his way and casting silvery shapes along the walls as he walked.

When he got to the end, he pressed his hand into a hexagonal node in the middle of the door and waited to be admitted. Something that felt like the release of tension shifted in his forehead and he removed his hand. The door split into three and each triangle pulled itself apart with a sound like the flat of blades scraping together, and disappeared into the ceiling and floor.

Lyander thought the chamber was unnecessarily large for a single person. Cut into the same prism-like shape as the corridor, he could barely make out where it ended and where it began. A single shaft of white light beamed down from an opening on the side of the ceiling, lighting a jet-black, almost shimmering purple block in the centre of the room. The praefector sat behind it, scribbling furiously on a piece of parchment. He wore the same uniform as the Ecclessius knights, his once blond hair and pale, round complexion turned a ghostly white under the light shining down upon him.

Lyander walked toward the desk, noting the faint smell of lye and bergamot oil.

"I didn't know we'd been graced with the presence of an exorcist," the praefector said, not looking up at him. "There are so few of you to go around these days. But that's because there are so few Immurati left in the world that there's not much point in having many of you, is there? In fact, I'm often surprised the Church still maintains the Order Malignia at all."

The praefector stopped whatever he was writing and looked up at Lyander.

"But, of course, you're not just any exorcist, are you? You're the famed Kalbrayeth Lyander. The only man to have been brought low from the lofty heights of First Champion of the Knights Redcrosse to, well, let's be honest, you're really just a glorified priest now, aren't you. What was it you did again?" He looked up at the ceiling, holding the quill to his lips in mock concentration. "Ahh, that's it. Grievous insubordination. The refusal to carry out orders from a Rosantz royal family member, resulting in the loss of an installation and a notable victory for the Mirrovinjin." He leaned back in his chair. "Costly decisions appear to be a part of your nature, don't they?"

The moment the praefector finished talking, Lyander's wounded hand sent lightning up his arm. Images flashed in front of his eyes: flaming blue columns licking at the cool grey of a spire, the flashes replacing his vision for split seconds, the gyranic blaze rising in his chest as hot-blooded anger. The screams of thousands, so loud they pierced even the abyss, and the face of Ramovand Rosantz, above him, haughty, imperious, just like the praefector's, telling him this was his fault, his decision. A bead of sweat dropped from Lyander's temple, splashing off his thumb, and bringing his mind back to the room. *What in the black void was that?*

Looking down, he realised his hand was gripping his sword handle, wrist trembling, his knuckles white. *It was the wound*, he told himself, *that's why you're letting this pompous ass get to you. It's the pain.* He forced his lungs to work, breathing out one long breath through his nose, then stepped forward, composed but a long way from calm.

"I'd guess we both know a thing or two about that," he said, voice thin. "A man of your age being given command over a southern spire. Either someone doesn't like you or you're also familiar with demotions."

The praefector's mouth thinned to a tight line, his cheeks turning a blotchy red. "You brought an unsecured gyranic entity into my spire without a sanction, resulting in the death of my only exhumarian." His voice was tremulous, the words a snarl. "Before I submit a report to the Ecclessius about your complete lack of judgement and disregard for correct procedure, I think you should tell me what the fuck happened in that sanctum."

Lyander gave him a long stare, taking an embarrassing amount of pleasure from watching the praefector simmer.

"Dracht's analysis led him to the conclusion that the creature was a vampire," Lyander said eventually. "Which is why the sanctum failed to secure it. For some reason it didn't recognise its aura."

"A vampire," the praefector snorted. "You

expect me to believe that thing in there," he pointed over Lyander's shoulder with the hand holding the quill, "is a vampire?"

"I honestly don't care what you believe," Lyander said flatly. "I'm just telling you what happened."

He didn't think it would have been possible but the praefector's cheeks gained several more blotches.

"And did this thing," he said, spittle flying across the desk, "do anything, or say anything to indicate what it was doing wherever you found it? Which was where, can I ask?"

"Buried in a grave on the edge of Yeggardania."

"Of course that's where you found it," the praefector said, his tone making it abundantly clear he didn't believe a word Lyander was telling him. "And did the sanctum reveal to you how it got there? Or what its intentions were?"

Lyander opened his mouth, about to retort with equal venom, but hesitated.

"No," he lied. "The sanctum revealed the nature of the beast and then it awoke almost immediately, killing Dracht before I could get to it. It said nothing."

Knowing the Ecclessius, the truth was not something they would want spread widely. And at any rate, a tale about a baby vampire – and if Dracht was right, the older more dangerous one that turned it – hunting the outlawed prince of Formaria's closest ally would receive nothing but derision from the praefector. And Lyander was doing his best not to punch the man as it was.

"So you know next to nothing about this creature," the praefector replied, lips curling into a smirk. "I would love to be there when you explain that to the Ecclessius."

"Unfortunately for you, you don't hold the

rank," Lyander said through gritted teeth. Then he remembered Dracht, and his eyes pooling in his lap. The praefector might be a shit of a human being, but Lyander was still a member of a holy order with a duty to Formaria. "These beasts use offensive sorcery that is vocally generated and targets a being's gyranic signal. Every person in Damoclen needs to wear a cross."

"I could have figured all of that out from the mess you left in my sanctum," the praefector said. "If that's all you've got, submit yourself for absolution and remove yourself from my spire."

That took Lyander by surprise. "That thing in your sanctum is a being of the Aeturnum. It's not an Immurati," he said.

"We don't know what it is, and until we do, you will ensure you are not maligned." He returned his attention to the piece of parchment, apparently done with the conversation. Which was fine by Lyander.

He was about to step outside the office when the praefector said: "If I find you haven't been absolved, I will have you officially marked as an impurity and advocate the strongest measures of liturgical purification."

It was about the only thing the praefector could threaten him with, so if he wanted Lyander to do it, Lyander didn't have much choice. He also needed to make contact with the Ecclessius using the spire's epistolar and he didn't want the praefector breathing down his neck while he did so.

"Understood," he said, and walked out of the chamber. His shadows danced ahead of him like jesters made from planes of light.

#

Liturgic absolution needed to be undertaken in a

seperium – often small, well-lit chambers referred to as *nests*. Despite what must be infrequent use, almost every installation Lyander knew contained at least one. That alone revealed a lot about the nature of the Immuratic threat Aetraya once faced.

Damoclen's seperium was located at the very bottom of the spire and shaped like a diamond cut in half. The ceiling, like so many other rooms in the installation, met in a peak. Unlike so many other rooms in the installation, the floor was a latticework of concentric triangles lit from below by a deep sun-like yellow. To Lyander, it looked like some ancient architect had tried to recreate a beehive but didn't know that bees built in hexagons, not in triangles.

In the middle of the room and rising out of the floor were two obsidian seats opposite one another. On the one facing Lyander sat a Constructii.

A towering mechanical frame, easily the size of an adolescent giant, sat hunched over like an embalmed king over a Hartafl board. Its limbs, torso, and oval face – all burnished gold or russet copper bronzite alloy – was humanoid where it wasn't protected by the insect-like carapace plating. Where most things had eyes, it had hollow shells that stared blankly into the bright depths beneath it. Until it awoke – then those shells would blaze with gyranic fire.

Lyander pushed aside the unease he often felt around the semi-sentient, not-quite-human creations, and walked over to the chair. As he sat, the Constructii lifted its head and blue suns ignited, boring into his soul.

"Kalbrayeth Lyander. Rank: exorcist. Order: Malignia," it said, metallic vocal cords chiming the words at him. It titled its head to one side in what Lyander could only assume was an attempt to imitate the act of thinking, and said in quick succession: "Most recent bounty: Date AR: 4032. Outcome: successful.

Services rendered: exterminatus. Entity domain: gyranic. Kingdom: Aeturnum. Class: Abhorrentia. Genus: Lamia."

The moment the vampire touched the dais, the sanctum would have fed all it knew about the creature through the spire's gyranic channels to any Constructii present in the installation. Lyander didn't know how it worked and he didn't think anyone else did, either, but he found it mildly comforting to know the sanctum at least recognised the vampiric species, even if it couldn't secure it. It meant he was going up against a known entity. And if it was known, it could be defeated.

"I am afraid, exorcist Kalbrayeth Lyander, that your bounty is Abhorrentia, not Malignia –" the Constructii said but Lyander cut across it. "Yeah, yeah, I know it's some witch-hunter's lucky day," he said, but the Constructii talked over him without missing a beat. "I am unable to pay you for the services rendered to Formaria. Please submit your report and request a witch-hunter to continue the investigation."

"I'll get right on that," Lyander said. "In the meantime, I need absolution."

"That is unnecessary, exorcist Kalbrayeth Lyander. Entity kingdom is Aeturnum not Immuratum. There cannot be malignant presence."

"I know that," Lyander said. "But I need one, anyway."

"I cannot satisfy that request. Absolution is unnecessary for your actions in this bounty."

His hand sent him a painful jab just as he resisted the temptation to rub his temples. "I think I came across a demon while taking a piss in the Yionar three days ago," he said. "Can you please check for malignance."

"Of course I can, exorcist Kalbrayeth Lyander. In future, please be more careful when relieving bodily functions."

"I'll be sure to."

The Constructii lifted its hands from its knees, turning its palms to face the ceiling as if it was making some kind of invisible offering. "Please take my hands and try to relax."

"You need both of them?" Lyander asked, holding up the one wrapped in bandages.

"I do."

Lyander, with utmost care, placed his hands into the machine's and did not relax. He hated this part.

Metallic finders curled around his palms, causing him to wince as they were locked in a firm embrace. A pressure built rapidly at the centre of his brain, and he was forced to swallow just so he didn't retch. It died as quickly as it came and was replaced by a combination of weightlessness and extreme focus. The juxtaposition made him feel like his mind was anchored in place while it floated in a river. Everything around him, save for the torch-like eyes, dimmed so he could look nowhere else.

"For what with my whole world-wide wandering," the Constructii said. Lyander felt compelled to respond; like he was under a spell

"With my whole world-wide wandering," he said, with what he hoped was perfect repetition.

"Whole world-wide wandering," the Constructii said again.

"Whole world-wide wandering," Lyander repeated.

"What with my search drawn out through years."

"My search drawn out through years."

"Drawn out through years."

"Drawn out through years."

"With my whole world-wide wandering."

"With my whole world-wide wandering. Whole world-wide wandering, whole world-wide wandering, whole world-wide wandering," Lyander recited, his mind locked in a concentrated haze, unable to know if he was saying or singing the words.

"You have been absolved," the Constructii said, and let go of Lyander's hands. The fog lifted and the darkness receded from his peripheral vision. "There has been no malignancy detected."

"Make sure the praefector knows," he said, as feeling, and therefore pain, flooded back into his wounded hand. He ground the back of his teeth as the Constructii made the weird tilt gesture. Then it said: "He has been informed."

"That'll be all, then." He stood and the Constructii's head dropped forward with a soft clink, blue eyes winking out.

Lyander's exhalation of relief didn't relieve the tension in his shoulders. Knowing the hard part was still to come, he left the seperium to inform the Church that vampires existed and he knew where to find the heir to the Ravinican throne.

#

Three different lifts took him to somewhere in the spire's upper region. Veering west of the hangar bay and well above the vulnerum and praefector's office, he travelled farther into a pocket of warmth that made his hand itch while it continued to emit its random piercing stabs.

He arrived in the epistolar's anteroom, a spear tip-shaped chamber with a dying indigo light. The ceiling, if there was one, was lost in murky black.

"A visitor," a voice croaked as the lift slotted into place. Lyander turned, facing the shorter side of the chamber and the source of the voice.

The chaplain wore a brown gown split down the middle, its hem threadbare and grubby, the hooded amice a faded red and so large it concealed everything but a wart-ridden chin that looked like it had never known sun or the nurturing glow of gyre ice. For a second, Lyander wondered if the chaplain ever left the antechamber.

"I need to use the epistolar," he said, pulling aside his cloak to reveal the black tunic and its red quartering. "My rank is exorcist, name –"

"I know who you are," the chaplain cut across him. "Few are the exorcists with anything of such importance to necessitate the use of the epistolar."

"Don't I know it," Lyander grumbled, then nodded at the smaller room behind the chaplain: "Is it ready?"

The chaplain held out an arm as if inviting Lyander to sit down for dinner. "It is."

Lyander walked past him and through the opening cut into the wall. Turning, he watched the chaplain place his hand into a hex terminal, and a moment later felt the lift release from its hold. The chaplain sent him skywards.

He emerged into the centre of a hexagonal room, stopping with a shunt that sent jagged lines of silver light chasing each other up the walls and vaulted ceiling. For every side of the hexagon there were two slender pillars, upon which rested small bronze orbs. They reflected the chamber's smooth dark surfaces to create the only sources of light.

Between two of the pillars, steps descended into a pool filled with dark filaments. Unlike the nodes scattered throughout the rest of the spire that were the blended hex reduction, the pool held only grains of pure black voidstone. It looked like the sand dunes of some hellish nightmare captured in a sculpture's impression, but was in fact a small part of what was known as the *Dead Network.* Short of speaking to someone in person, it was the surest way of sending a message within Aetraya without the risk of interception.

Above it protruded a huge bronzite spout big enough for Lyander to climb into and reminded him of the giant crustaceans found at the bottom of the Amarant Sea. He walked over to it and stopped before the pool's rim.

The sound of pressure releasing from mechanical joints. Then, like some chitinous manifestation, a Constructii's face emerged from out of the fountain's depths. The same featureless mask, the same hollow sockets, the same narrow slit for a mouth. But where its cousin's fiery blue eyes exhibited an alien-like intelligence, this one was completely blind.

"Only tales are told," the face said, its metallic voice resonating around the chamber. Whereas most Constructii appeared genderless, those in epistolars seemed to speak with something of a female undertone.

"I understand the requirements," Lyander said.

"Then step forward and tell your story."

Lyander stepped into the pool, sinking slowing into the voidstone, the filaments shifting around him, not like sand, but like a swarm of tiny insects stirring at his intrusion. He waded in up to his waist, careful to keep his wounded hand above the surface, and looked into the Constructii's sightless gaze.

"A telling in Thendergaarden," he said. "The teller is the exorcist Kalbrayeth Lyander. The witnesses are the Ordained Conglomerate of the Ecclessius. The tale is of a creature confirmed to be a vampire, which I discovered on the borders of Yeggardania. There, I found the creature in a grave following spectre-like sightings outside of Vergraine before taking its body for examination here in Damoclen. During examination, it awoke and spoke the words: *Eluthienn, ducima ad Grindlepeake*. While I was forced to destroy it before it could say more, it's my belief that the creature was searching for the outlawed prince of Ravinica, and believed his location to be Ravinica's northern port city, Grindlepeake. I now request clarification on mission parameters and a bounty transfer to the Order Abhorrentia. The teller is Kalbrayeth Lyander. The witnesses are the Ordained Conglomerate of the Ecclessius and no others."

The chamber was silent, the face immutable. Lyander climbed out of the pool, the voidstone falling from him so not a single speck remained on his clothing.

How long it would take for acolytes in Thendergaarden to find and inform members of the Ecclessiarchal leadership of the epistolar request, Lyander couldn't say. But he knew they would need to convene and decide upon a reply. *And they're not going rush for you – you can count on that.*

To pass the time, he flexed the fingers of his ruined hand. The movement sent needling pain all the way to his wrist and left him with a throbbing sensation, but he felt them all respond. To his surprise, he felt cool relief spreading from his chest, acting like a salve for much of the tension he carried. He might be a perennially out of work exorcist, shunned by most ordinary people, disliked by his superiors, and embroiled in circumstances that would once again elicit the Church's ire, but he might still wield a sword in both hands. And, Lyander realised, for a former First Champion of an order dedicated to martial prowess, that mattered.

He left his hand and paced, watching the refracted light ricochet in time to his footsteps, thoughts turning to his immediate situation. Eating, or at least drinking, something before choosing to wait on the

Ecclessius would have been a good idea. They could take hours – longer, perhaps. Deciding the chaplain could inform him of the reply, Lyander reached out a hand for the terminal to see what Folgar could offer him in the way of food, when the face spoke: "Your story is told, exorcist Kalbrayeth Lyander."

That was quick, he thought, stepping back into the pool. *Too quick, surely.*

"A telling at Damoclen spire," the face said, relaying its message. "The teller is Cadarrasta Pulance, Grand Ecclessian of the holy Church of Formaria. The witness is Kalbrayeth Lyander, exorcist. The telling is of the Ordained Conglomerate's gratitude toward the exorcist and how we were so very pleased to hear of his efforts in the name of our Lord, the holy and eternal knight, Redcrosse. The discovery of such a creature is of significant importance to the sanctity of the underground kingdoms, and the exorcist's actions in its retrieval will not go unrewarded.

"For now, as requested, the exorcist's mission parameters are thus: It is Kalbrayeth Lyander's divine task to use the vampire's information and track down Eluthienn Leonette, outlawed prince of Ravinica, with the utmost haste. The exorcist is to discover the connection between the heir to the seat of Vallorandyl and the vampire, and report this information back to the Ordained Conglomerate via the Dead Network. Assigned to his command is a witch-hunter of the Coven, who will join him at Siadon spire and aid him in this mission. The truth of the vampire's intent toward Eluthienn is paramount to Formaria's security – the exorcist will not fail in the task assigned to him. The teller is Cadarrasta Pulance, Grand Ecclessian. The witness is Kalbrayeth Lyander, exorcist, and no others."

Lyander stood in bewildered silence, the black dunes breaking gently against his stomach and sending tiny ripples to die at the edges of the pool. If it hadn't been for their movement, he might have forgotten to keep his hand aloft. He had been expecting, at best, a dressing down for destroying the creature instead of capturing it, followed by orders to return to Thendergaarden – not resounding praise from the head of the Church and the man who severely disliked him (a feeling that was mutual), as well as orders to *go looking* for Ravinica's missing prince.

He could understand the urgency to send someone immediately – the outlawed prince of Formaria's closest ally – on Formaria's borders and hunted by undead beings – presented serious political risks. Not to mention, those undead beings were supposed to be mythical.

What he could not understand was why they were sending *him*. There were any number of Navarch intelligence operatives or Ecclessiarchal agents better suited to this task. In fact, there was every reason *not* to send him. He was the Church's black stain – its mistake; since his "demotion," he was trusted with little more than chasing phantoms across fishing villages. He made an unlikely candidate for a mission that could jeopardise the centuries-long Formryian–Ravinican alliance. Sending him because of his role in discovering the creature or because he was close at hand could hardly be justified.

Something is off, and you know it.

There was something else he knew with complete certainty, something learned through bitter experience at the Church's hands: He was expendable. The connection quickly became evident, and it started to make sense. A humiliated exorcist, with a very public reputation for scorning authority and a history of "ineptitude," sent into Ravinican territory could take the blame for any political fallout. Accompanied by a witch-hunter – probably one of the Church's favourites – and there's someone to testify if anything goes wrong, someone who will say exactly what the Church wants them to.

"A telling in Thendergaarden," he said, wishing the Constructii spoke in more than just colourless, invariable intonations – wishing the face could convey anger. "The teller is the exorcist Kalbrayeth Lyander. The witness is Cadarrasta Pulance, Grand Ecclessian. The telling is of the exorcist's confusion at being the recipient of such instructions from the Grand Ecclessian. Surely there are far more capable" (he almost added 'willing') "servants his *eminence* might consider for such a quest. I would remind the Church that I am not, nor have I ever been, a diplomatic servant. I suggest the Church reconsider my role in this matter. The teller is Kalbrayeth Lyander. The witness is Cadarrasta Pulance, Grand Ecclessian, and no others."

Lyander stood glaring at the face, a seething anger coiling within him, along with a flush of foolishness rising from his chest. Anger at the ease with which the Church could command him. Anger that they could, with a single order, still use him – that they knew *he* knew how he was being used. And foolishness at himself – at the knowledge that his answer was both childish and futile. *When have you ever known the Ecclessius to accommodate or accede to requests, Kalbrayeth? What were you hoping to gain from that little outburst?*

"Your story is told, exorcist, Kalbrayeth Lyander," the face said, the speed of the response telling him all he needed to know about what the Grand Ecclessian thought of his *suggestion*.

"A telling at Damoclen spire," the face said. "The teller is Cadarrasta Pulance, Grand Ecclessian. The witness is the exorcist Kalbrayeth Lyander. In this telling, the holy Church and physical manifestation of Redcrosse's will upon this world sought not the opinions of the exorcist. It impressed upon their servant the severity of the quest to the sacred lands of Formaria and the haste with which the orders would be carried out. It reminded the exorcist that this is the divine interpretation of the supreme will of the One Eternal Lord. And what's more, the Grand Ecclessian was certain the exorcist had not forgotten his place in this world. The orders stand; the exorcist will do his duty. The teller is Cadarrasta Pulance, Grand Ecclessian. The witness is Kalbrayeth Lyander, the exorcist, and no others."

Light danced across the bronzite husk as a familiar feeling settled in Lyander's stomach – raw injustice and a sort of sickly powerlessness, feelings brought on by the words: *his place in this world* – a reminder of whose mercy he was at.

With the anger draining from him, leaving only an empty, passive sort of resignation, he provided the epistolar's requirements for a third time, then said: "The telling is of the exorcist's understanding of the instruction he'd received and how he carried out those instructions as commanded. The teller is Kalbrayeth Lyander and the witness is Cadarrasta Pulance, Grand Ecclessian, and no others."

The face confirmed receipt of the message, and Lyander stepped out of the pool. Absent of any other feelings to compete with, the pain from his hand was free to attack him, riding up his wrist with black delight. Knowing there was no need for the Church to send a reply, he walked to the terminal and threw his good hand into the node, willing the lift to the anteroom. Stepping onto the octagon, he felt the release beneath his feet. As he descended, the face retreated back inside its shell.

Six

Brazier

Brazier ran up the stairs to the fuselage, taking two steps at a time. In the nav deck, he plunged his hand into the command terminal's nearest well, and said, "Tunnel display point five leagues north of the *Chalice of Amaranth*."

The adjacent well produced a sculpt of the tunnel floor and he was given a landscape of jagged spires the size of his index finger.

"Scope out three tenths."

The sand bristled, reforming into what looked like a mouth of broken teeth – moving in between them, a swarm of shadowy figures. Through the black and silver hex reduction, they looked like an army of wraiths moving through a nightmare realm.

"Brazier, are you there?" Torquen's voice came from the well next to it.

"Receiving," he said. "What are we looking at?"

"Jan's counting sixty bodies. They're sitting directly between us."

"How's that possible? We would have run straight into them."

"No idea. Jan said one minute the tunnel was empty, the next it was crawling."

A sinking feeling settled in his gut. "Torquen, we just powered up the engines."

"I know. Jan saw the gyre spike just before he picked up the movement."

The sinking feeling, which felt like bad ale, began to morph into lead rocks.

"Then we just triggered a trap," Brazier said, hoping by speaking the words he would feel calmer about the situation. It didn't work.

His brother was about to reply when he heard Jan's voice in the background: "Fast movers on assault trajectory," the navigator said. "Four minutes to contact."

On the hex display, the figures moved as one, streaming through the tunnel and out of the scope's field of view at an impossible speed. He knew nothing capable of covering a tunnel floor that quickly.

"Jan, set the repeaters to sentience. Maximum cartridge output. No hold on ammunition," Torquen said, with the cool assurance he always fell into whenever they went into battle. It went some way in lessening Brazier's anxiety.

"Repeaters set to sentience. Full expendability protocol issued," Jan replied.

"Give me a second tether. Shipwide," Torquen said.

Brazier heard Jan provide the shipwide connection and Torquen's voice became slightly farther away: "All hands, we have fast-moving hostiles inbound. Battle stations, battle stations. Prepare to repel boarders."

Freyen and Switch entered the nav deck, standing either side of him. He barely noticed them.

"Torquen, we're on our way," Brazier said.

He was about to tell Freyen to fetch Axelock and Dalfin and get them on board the ship when his brother said: "No! Stay put. If we can't fight them off, that ship is our only option."

"Repeaters engaged and firing at full output," Jan said.

Brazier heard himself breathe through his nose, his lips pressed tightly together. "Okay, what do you need us to do?" he said.

"Stay off the hex and let me coordinate this thing. Don't do anything until I give the order."

Brazier stared fixedly at the well before dropping the connection. Even when the sand flattened, he continued to stare, unable to dispel the thought that he should be with the crew; as First Officer, he should be coordinating the repel teams, not watching the battle happen from halfway up the tunnel.

He placed his hand into the well and called up a movement-tracking display a mile out from the *Chalice*. The sand formed into a racing model of the tunnel floor and the unidentifiable beings moving across it.

"By the black abyss, those things are fast," Switch said. "What are they?"

Before Brazier could tell her he didn't know, Torquen's voice broke through one of the wells.

"Brazier, Jan can't identify the enemy. Something about not recognising the gyranic signal. What can you tell me about the crew of that ship?"

What he meant was: *What can you tell me about how they died?*

He pictured the eviscerated gnome in the engine room and looked at the cold body of the navigator in front of him, then down at the captain with his open chest wound. The lacerations were random, unevenly distributed, as if caused by a mix of claws and hard steel.

"Best guess is Mirrovinjin," Brazier said. "But I'm watching them on the hex. Mirrovinjin don't move that fast. And since when can they hide their signal?"

"We'll have to figure that out another time. For now, we'll work under the assumption the Mirrovinjin have a new cloaking technology and they're trying their new toy out on us."

It was as good a guess as any.

"Jan, set a distress beacon and send a message to Theselan: We're under attack by cloaked hostiles, suspected Mirrovinjin."

He heard Jan relay the message. Before he was finished, Torquen gave orders to the crew: "Unidentified enemy forces moving in formation. Repel teams to the starboard bulkheads and the hangar bay."

On the hex, Brazier saw the attackers split into two groups. The larger veered off to the right while the smaller continued straight.

"Repeater batteries at a combined two-thirds load," Jan said. "Enemy count is at forty nine. One minute to contact."

Colt's voice came through the *Chalice's* navigation terminal. Across two hex tethers, it sounded muffled and far away: "Repel teams in the hangar bay."

A moment later, Erin confirmed both her teams were in position along the starboard bulkheads.

"Enemy is under the ship," Jan said. "No targets available for stern repeater."

"Have the keel repeater target the larger group," Torquen said.

"New targets acquired for keel mount –" Jan cut off: "Keel-mounted repeater is unresponsive. It's been disabled. Enemy is cutting through the ship. We're being boarded."

"All hands, prepare to repel boarders!" Then to Jan: "How are they getting through the ship? What equipment do they have?"

Jan hesitated. "They don't, sir. I'm not picking anything up."

"That's not possible," Torquen said.

"Single breach at starboard bulkhead, deck two." It was Erin's voice. "Repel team engaging the enemy. Wait –" she cut off, then said, "Second breach on deck two. Both teams engaged. Shit, they're everywhere!"

"Erin, I need you to identify the enemy!" Torquen said. "What is coming through those breaches?"

Erin's voice became very distant as she moved away from whatever terminal she'd been stood next to. For Brazier, it was like listening to someone yell at him over a canyon: "Karrick! Karrick, behind you!"

"Erin, report!" Torquen shouted.

Brazier could hear the muted thrum of a repeating crossbow, followed by Erin's scream. Then the tether dropped.

"Jan, what's going on down there?" Torquen said.

"Two breaches on deck two. Enemy count is at forty-seven. Twelve crew members deceased."

The information struck Brazier like a hammer blow to the belly. Twelve friends lost in an instant, and he was probably going to lose a lot more. But not seeing it happen, only hearing it over a terminal made it seem unreal somehow. Like it was happening in a dream he expected to wake from.

"Give me a display on the second attack group," Torquen said. "Scope at two thirds."

"Scope at two thirds," Jan confirmed.

There was a moment of silence. When Torquen spoke, he sounded surprised: "Are they climbing the ship?"

"We have eight hostiles moving up the stern," Jan said.

"Track movement," Torquen said.

"Tracking movement. They're nearly at the upper hull."

"Have the bow repeater face south."

"Bow repeater south facing. It's engaging the enemy."

"Status update on the other repel teams."

"Eighteen crew members deceased. Enemy has entered deck three and is moving north."

"They're going for the engines," Torquen said. "Lock down all access hatches and bring the lifts to the roof of the ship."

"Access hatches are locked and lifts are moving to the upper decks."

"Tether to the hangar bay," Torquen said.

"Tethered," Jan confirmed.

"Colt, are you receiving?"

"We're here, Captain."

"The enemy is moving north along deck three. I need your team to cut them off before they reach the engines."

"You got it, sir," Colt said. "We're on our way."

"Jan, drop tether."

"The second attack group has spread out and is moving north along the upper hull," Jan said. "Repeater is struggling to acquire a target."

"How long before they reach the nav deck?"

"Less than a minute."

"Brazier, get out of here."

Brazier was so fixated on the battle, it took him a second to realise his brother was talking to him.

"No," he said flatly. "Tee, there is no way we're leaving you and the crew behind."

"Don't be stupid, Brazier. Whatever's attacking us has slaughtered half the crew in minutes. There's nothing you can do."

Brazier's heartbeat was a rapid thud in his chest. Understanding what his brother was saying, it became a pounding in his ears as rescue scenarios raced through his mind at lighting speed.

"Tee, we can bring the ship around," he said, trying to keep the desperation out of his voice. "Take the lift to the keel access hatch and block all routes behind you. We can get you and Jan out of there."

"We're out of time, Brazier," Torquen said. Brazier could count on one hand the number of times he'd heard his brother sound sad. It came as a shock.

As if to settle the matter, Jan said: "Twenty seconds."

"When they're done here, they'll come for you," Torquen said. "I'm not going to let that hap –"

"I am not leaving you behind, Torquen!" Brazier cut across, only part of him registering the fact he might be shouting.

"Brazier, I'm sorry." In those words, Brazier heard the stalwart composure crack. It wasn't the voice of his captain; it was the voice of his older brother telling him he wouldn't be around anymore. Brazier couldn't speak, he didn't know what to say. Tears welled in his eyes, his throat dry.

"Take that ship and get to Theselan," Torquen said. "That's an order." Then, with calm resolution to the navigator: "Jan, the enemy will not have this ship; is that understood?"

A pause, the sound of thuds somewhere in the background, somewhere on the hull, then Jan's voice, almost serenely: "Overload sequence commenced."

The thuds became louder, turning into a screeching sound, like metal joints being ripped apart.

There was the sound of a sword drawn from its scabbard.

Then nothing. The hex was flat.

Without thinking, Brazier thrust his hand into a well. “Charge thrusters, and set intercept course to the *Chalice of Amaranth*!”

The ship surged as the thrusters whirred into life.

“Switch, tell Axelock and Dalfin to get on board right now. Freyen, you’re copiloting this thing.”

“Brazier,” Freyen said softly, as if the slightest variance in pitch might cause him to erupt with anger. “Jan’s scuttled the ship; the *Chalice* is gone.”

“There’s still time,” he said, refusing to look at her as tears ran down his cheeks.

But there wasn’t. Because in that moment, there was a distant explosive sound, a single violent blast followed by a keening vibration that grew louder until it hit the *Solace* like a storm front. The ship shook furiously, the decking trembling beneath their feet.

It subsided as quickly as it came and the ship grew still again.

Freyen’s hand appeared on his upper arm. “Brazier.” The tenderness in her voice seemed to thaw the wave of adrenaline-fuelled defiance that wouldn’t let him accept a reality in which his brother didn’t exist. “Brazier,” she said again, a note of firmness creeping in. “We need to get out of here now. There might be more of those things out there and if they get to this ship, Torquen will have died for nothing.”

Those last words, his brother’s death spoken out loud, was like a hot knife sunk into his heart. But it still wasn’t real for him; there couldn’t be a reality in which Torquen Veranquis wasn’t alive.

“Brazier,” Freyen said again, desperation filtering into her voice. It acted like an antidote, the red haze diminishing, drawing him to the present. He looked at her, concern and fear in her eyes.

He still had a crew; Freyen, Switch, Axelock, and Dalfin were still his responsibility. And they were waiting on him to get them out of there.

He let out a long, shaky breath and was about to request an emergency course to spire Theselan when a voice came from behind them.

“You know,” its owner said, with such low roughness he could have been gargling stone, “I’d do what the pretty one says.”

All three of them spun on the spot, Freyen and Switch raising their crossbows.

A dwarf, wearing black prisoner’s trousers and a sleeveless black top, stood leaning against the cockpit’s hatch. His skin was the rich black-brown of tilled earth and his eyes were as grey as rain clouds. Around his biceps, thighs, and ankles Brazier could see silver constraints. They were so diminutive in comparison to his muscles they looked like jewellery.

The dwarf stood, arms crossed lazily over his chest while giving them a smile that made Switch’s wolfish grin look pleasant.

Somehow, the *Solace*’s high-security prisoner had escaped his cell.

Epistolar message Fion to Vallorandyl

A telling in Vallorandyl.

The teller is Emries von Cadst, Duke of Ylstgaar, Adjutant to the Fion Throne, and Marshal of the Western Front.

The witness is Vermillies Sidtch, Lord Regent of Ravinica, and Absolver General.

The telling is of the lord regent's good fortune. Of course, this tale is only meant to deceive – meant to force your hand, but your ineptitude in losing Eluthienn has meant we must rely on these scraps, such as they are – this stranger's tale. Lies, much of it surely is, but parts have caught my attention. I voiced my concerns that your spies were too quick to disregard Grindlepeake and your assertions the prince would not hide within Ravinica's borders. I suggest you reinvestigate the city at once for any traces of the prince's presence. The vampire's connection to Eluthienn, however, seems an invention – a misdirection meant to obscure some other truth, for its existence is, at best, questionable. We can only let the tale play out before coming to a conclusion.

The Ecclessiarchal mission this Lyander has been sent on, seems at first foolish, and so improbable, for the Formarian Church are anything but fools. But upon consideration, it may, in fact, be a stroke of genius. If the prince truly was in Grindlepeake, sending two of the unlikeliest individuals, by virtue of their professions, would raise little suspicion among your spies, who they know to be at large in their country. And the attack on the miner could yet hold some truth. Intelligence out of Formaria has been scant, but what little we have gleaned indicates some kind of tumult. But as almost all southern installations we have infiltrated are running reduced transport schedules, it's been impossible to gather information on the centre. Whether this miner is a fabrication or not, we can assume the underground kingdoms face a threat, and as such you will refocus your intelligence operations on the country. Deception this almost certainly is, but one you cannot afford to dismiss Vermillies.

The emperor's initial pleasure at your successful coup is quickly souring at your ineptitude in losing Eluthienn. His favour, you will find, can quickly turn. You will swallow your dislike of this stranger, make no move against him, listen to his tale, and report all he says, and perhaps your future may still hold a shred of promise. The teller is Emries von Cadst, Duke of Ylstgaar. The witness is Vermillies Sidtch, Lord Regent, and no others.

EPISTOLAR MESSAGE VALLORANDYL TO FION

A telling in Fion.

The teller is Vermillies Sidtch, Lord Regent of Ravinica, and Absolver General.

The witness is Emries von Cadst, Duke of Ylstgaar, Adjutant to the Fion Throne, and Marshal of the Western Front.

The telling is of the second night the stranger came before the throne. As before, a visage of death, and with a story only growing in its improbability. The supposed vampire threat he describes is of a scale even the Ecclessius would find impossible to hide. Whispers of "tumult," as you say, and a growing threat, but anything more, anything close to these proportions and we would know of it – of that I am certain. Of that you must see? Even so, this pales in comparison to the supposed "agreement" later made in Thendergaarden. As always, I bow to your superior judgement, but I fail to see where my hand would be forced. The stranger's intent can only be to have us believe Formaria is no threat to Ravinica, and what would that achieve? What I also cannot understand is why this creature would go to such lengths in the tale's fabrication? Why construct such a conceit? I can only voice my doubts – my growing doubts there is any truth at all to what he says, and he is nothing but a trickster, delighting at the lie he sees working on my thoughts.

But as instructed, I have redirected our intelligence to Formaria and Grindlepeake, which I am confident will only reaffirm what my suspicions already tell me. And if what the stranger says of Eluthienn's former location is true, I implore you to see it would have been too well hidden, his time there too brief for them to discover him. As always, my gratitude and unwavering devotion to the emperor endure, his favour and patience providing me strength and succour. I await your wise counsel and instruction upon hearing of the second telling, I now recount.

SEVEN

LYANDER

Lyander took a shaky step off the *Angelus Thorn* and onto the bright grey slabs of Siadon's hangar bay.

It took two days before a ship was close enough to Damoclen to justify his reroute and transfer request. And even then, the *Thorn* needed to deviate significantly from its original transit to pick him up. Before its captain reluctantly changed course, the ship had been bound for Everaux. There, it would unload the two hundred tonnes of ice it was carrying and take on crates of marauder crabs, yellow-backed lampreys, and dire urchins bred in the underground harvesting pools beneath the Kneldierian capital – all of which would be magically imbued to prevent it from spoiling on its journey to the Formarian front line.

Picking up Lyander and dropping him off at Siadon added a day to the *Thorn*'s journey. And the captain – a prickly gnome with a forked blond beard and mistrustful green eyes by the name of Gorlick Gonfowler – had not let him forget it.

To make up as much lost time as possible, Gorlick made his crew work multiple eighteen-hour shifts with just four hours downtime in between. It had been hard to tell who they'd hated more, their captain or himself, who they viewed as the cause of their misfortune.

Lyander couldn't blame them, especially as he'd spent most of the journey nursing a hangover in his cabin, only venturing out to pilfer the vulnerum for numbing draughts and pain antidotes. But just like the war caster's anomancy, none really worked. The bleeding stopped, and he fancied he could see the early signs of new tissue growth. But apart from that, there wasn't much change. It still hurt like black hell, and on top of that, there was a nauseating pain at the front of his head made worse by bright lights. Although that last symptom could have been a result of spending the previous two days getting hammer-beaten drunk with Folgar.

But even feeling as he did, he was thankful for those days. Folgar's seemingly endless supply of strong brown ale had been the only thing keeping the pain in Lyander's hand from becoming unbearable, or the memory of Dracht's death from surfacing too often.

Set up on the bank opposite Damoclen was what Lyander could only describe as a personal brewery. There, Folgar produced several "vintages" and the one he served to Lyander had tasted of yeast, bitter fruit, and fire-roasted nuts, and had been so thick he broke his fasts on it instead of eating.

The ale wasn't the only thing to be thankful for. While Lyander hadn't disclosed the conversation with the Ecclessius or his mission, Folgar could tell he was troubled and took it upon himself to ensure Lyander was distracted. In between the singing, bawdy jokes, and a drunken axe-throwing competition, Folgar plied him with rumours of the lands beyond Formaria.

Most of it had been overblown sailor's talk. A zombie dragon sighted in the Reach. The troll king of Kelej-Orst breeding an army of krakens to fight the Ilvalien fleet. The Ravinican council infiltrated by a male witch with the parts of both a man and a woman. Lyander had nearly spat up his ale at the last one, explaining that the witch could neither be male nor female if they had both sets of genitals.

"Then it makes him both!" Folgar had replied.

"Nay, Folgar," one of his more unruly regulars had cried. "Whenever a mood takes him, he gets to choose!"

The dwarf had reached into his small clothes, fumbled around his groin, and pulled down his breaches. Then Lyander really had spat out his ale. The dwarf had tucked his penis between his legs and proceeded to strut around Damoclen's ramparts, putting on a singsong female voice.

"Whenever he wants it in the rear, he makes it disappear," the dwarf sang to roars of laughter. "But when he wants someone to suck on his spout, he brings it out!" At the last bit, he'd flicked out his penis right next to the head of a fellow soldier, causing the other dwarf to tumble backward in horror and throw his drink everywhere. It had earned more laughter and a thorough dressing down from Folgar.

Lyander found himself smiling at the memory. It had been utterly ridiculous but it had also been some time since he'd shared the company of other soldiers, and Lyander missed it sorely.

And it hadn't all been nonsense. During one of their soberer moments, Folgar repeated a tale he'd heard from no less than three captains: Grindlepeake was turning away river vessels at the Drowned Gate and barring entry to its ports. If Lyander hadn't heard the vampire's message about Eluthienn, he would have scoffed at the tale. Grindlepeake was a port city surrounded by bare earth mountains and miles of swampland. Its survival rested entirely on the merchant ships sailing up and down the Yoinar and across the Amarant Sea. But if the city was harbouring the outlawed prince of Ravinica, there might be some truth in the reports.

According to Folgar's captains, Grindlepeake's self-imposed blockade was grinding trade to a halt from Pontifax to Illigrande. But if that part was true, it hadn't affected Siadon.

Around him, the spire's hangar bay teemed with activity. Soldiers in the red and green liveries of house La'Voline, walked the fortified emplacements lining the bay's interior. Merchant lords and gyre ship captains poured over parchments of inventories and shipment timetables. And officers fought to make themselves heard as they directed trains of carts packed with butchered farm meat, silver river pike, and red eels as long as Lyander was tall. They were loaded onto the gyre ships docked behind him, their access ramps dropped to the bay floor like open mouths, their bright cargo holds lighting up the tunnel walls in an oceanic blue. In his probably still-a-little-drunk state, Lyander thought the whole operation looked like a pod of fat-bellied whales waiting to be fed.

He pulled his eyes from them, feeling the need to get out of the chaos; the constant wafts of raw fish and perspiring bodies made his head worse. And the stuffy heat of the tunnel was starting to make him sweat beneath his cloak and surcoat. Although that, too, could have been the result of two days straight drinking.

He searched the bay for a hex terminal so he

could locate the witch-hunter, finding toward the rear a soldier, probably on sentry duty, standing next to one. He wore a chain vest beneath a spotless crimson surcoat. In its centre, circled in bright gold thread, was an emerald dragon curling around itself. The soldier leant on his pike with the sort of bored look that told Lyander he hadn't seen a fight in a while, and he wasn't expecting to, either. Why would he be? Siadon was far enough south that the Mirrovinjin would have to pass five spires and two vaults before they reached it. And its location at the juncture between the underground and the Pontivar valley made it invaluable for maintaining Formaria's war effort, so it was heavily guarded, meaning it was almost never attacked, which made it a coveted posting for any regiment.

Lyander approached the terminal and the soldier gave him a single, uninterested look and stepped aside. He placed his good hand into the node and made a person location request in his head.

The immediate rush of knowledge was accompanied by an artificial clarity that managed to both eliminate his headache and remind him how rough he was feeling. There was only one witch-hunter in the spire and he was in the aedius, situated in Siadon's upper levels. The lift at the end of the concourse just outside the hangar bay would take him to the top of the installation, and then it would be a short walk. Lyander terminated his request and the throbbing behind his eyes returned.

Having a hangover turned off and on again, he thought as he made his way to the concourse, *is probably a bit like drinking from one of those southern desert oases, only to find out it was all a mirage.*

Even with the crews, the soldiers, and the merchant retinues, Siadon's concourse dwarfed its occupants. Two rows of turquoise-veined pillars reached up to a peaked ceiling and turned the floor and walls a pearly grey. A lift, which could fit a hundred people, occupied the centre and deposited carts and sailors from the lands above.

Lyander turned away from it and banked left between two pillars, where a much smaller chute was cut into the side of the wall. He called a lift, and moments later, the doors opened.

Three white-robed acolytes hurried out as Lyander climbed in. The two remaining people had the sun-bleached skin, braided beards, and painted eyes of Syracuta merchants. Their sable tunics of rich burgundy and gold lace conveyed a wealth that Lyander knew made them attractive customers to Formarian lords and ship's captains. With few natural deposits of their own, Syracuta paid handsomely for both gyre ice and voidstone.

The merchants gave him and his bandaged hand a fleeting glance and continued their conversation, speaking in clipped tones completely unintelligible to Lyander, and accompanied by passionate hand gestures.

For several minutes, he felt the lift rising before it slowed and eventually stopped to let the merchants out. From what he could tell, it then carried him horizontally through the installation only to begin rising again. Before it could gain any real speed, the floor shuddered gently and he came to a stop. When the doors parted, a breeze tasting of wet earth and morning dew swept into the lift, and Lyander was given a full view of the aedius.

The pyramidal structure could fit in a spire-class miner's cargo bay and had been built within a deep scar in the earth. A walkway stretched out before it, connecting the chamber with the rest of the spire. On either side, the walkway dropped away into black nothingness so thick Lyander might scoop it up in his hands. It was a stark contrast to the haze drifting down from Yeggardania's forest floor. The spire was so far underground the light above was little more than an opaque yellow, but as it hit the sides of the chamber, verdant tourmalines and purple azurite permeated the mist. It might have been beautiful, except Lyander's hangover bordered on the unholy.

He forced himself to concentrate on the chamber's triangular portal as he walked across the condensation-slick walkway. Reaching the end, he placed his hand into the portal's node and requested entry. The locks cycled, slowly at first, then sped up. His hand released from the hex and three interlocking triangles pulled apart. He took several steps into the chamber before he heard the triangles click back into place, closing the portal behind him.

What little he could see was lit up by a shaft in one of the sloping walls. Green-tinged light poured onto a Fromryr-made dais in the centre of the chamber where a stone statue of a knight had been erected. It wore a plain surcoat over a primitive style of chain hauberk and full helm. With its left hand it gripped the pommel of a sword, the point resting directly beneath its feet. The other hand rested atop a quartered heater shield leaning gently against its thigh.

Droplets from condensation in the shaft splashed onto the knight's shoulders and ran down its hauberk in rivulets. At its feet, water pooled in the ends of unlit candles and ceremonial bowls, and soaked a dirt-stained banner discarded at the side of the dais, its red cross now a faded brown.

Lyander stepped up to the knight and took a good long look into the helmeted face of his god.

I was happy being your champion and taking everything else along with it, he thought. *But I'll admit, I never really believed. In fact, I never believed anything the Ecclessius said about you. Maybe that's why I am where I am. Or maybe I was right all along?*

A single droplet ran down the knight's visor and splashed onto one of the candles. "I appreciate the thought," he said quietly, looking around the chamber. "But what's done is done; there's no going back now."

He began to think he was in the wrong place when something moved in the corner of the chamber. At first he thought it was an effect of the light, that his still-intoxicated mind was playing tricks on his vision.

He let his eyes adjust.

And he saw it. Tall and lean, its profile little more than a smudge against the darkness. Whatever it was hunched its shoulders and shifted its weight from one leg to the other. Exactly like an animal preparing to pounce on its prey.

Instinctually, Lyander slid his sword from its scabbard – a slow steel whisper, dissonant in the condensation-thick air.

Then something else moved in the opposite corner. Just as tall and just as lean with the same near-black outline as its companion.

Lyander heard himself breathe through his teeth.

Fighting one opponent with a sword meant to be wielded in two hands would be hard enough. Fighting two was futile. But what choice did he have? *I don't think these things are going to be kind enough to just let you back out of the chamber. And even if they did, what are you going to do? Try to open the portal while in a one-handed duel with two opponents?*

"Some divine intervention would be handy right about now," he muttered, glancing at the repentant figure of Redcrosse. Another droplet ran down its visor.

"Yeah," Lyander sighed, picking one of the outlines at random, "I didn't really think it was coming."

He rushed forward, the blade resting on his

shoulder. Two steps out he twisted from his hips and, using the momentum of his body, threw the sword into a sweeping side-arc. The thing lunged with its own sword, aiming for Lyander's neck. He tensed his arm, anticipating the backbite, the jarring that would ride up his wrist as the edge met skull.

But nothing came.

And he knew he was missing, his swing overreaching, his body twisting too far. A thin line of steel emerged in front of his face, his vision blocked, searing pain about to blossom at its touch. Then smoke drifted before his eyes, the blade writhing tendrils, its sting turning to a warm caress. And the rest of the thing was gone, evaporated, the remains a smear of black ash drifting across the floor.

His heart, already hammering so hard it had beaten his hangover into submission, leapt as he realised the thing was a decoy.

He spun, the second shape bounding toward him, and with no time to bring his sword up, he ran the blade forward, praying its midriff lacked anything in the way of armour.

The tip met the thing's sternum and, like its companion, vaporized.

Lyander's mind, now in a heightened state of awareness from the fight, reacted unconsciously, his whole body expecting a third enemy.

Which was coming at him from his left side.

The same size as the others, its movements were animalist, calculated, with a blade – a real blade – held in its hand.

He swung for the throat – a cleave meant to decapitate. But instead of cutting into jugular and cartilage, he connected with thin air, for the man – and he was a man – stopped just short of the point.

"Well," he said, two sorcerous blue eyes staring

down the flat of the blade, "you're quicker than I thought you'd be."

Lyander, panting, and keeping his sword aloft, glanced over either shoulder, making sure this wasn't another trick. The man's mouth, he noticed, curled, caught between amusement and something that looked like derision.

"You're farther away than I thought you'd be," Lyander said, studying the rest of the man's features, now he was confident he wasn't going to be stabbed from behind. High cheekbones sat atop gaunt cheeks, the skin sallow, an almost oiled white making it look unwashed – yellow, even. His hair, long and blond, was pulled into a ponytail and stricken with grease. A prominent brow shadowed his eyes, but neither that nor the shimmering blue of a magic user could hide their arrogance.

"An exorcist with a sense of humour," the man said. "I didn't know that was possible."

"I didn't know witch-hunters could pull tricks like that," Lyander replied, nodding over his shoulder.

"The name's Gabriel," he said, sheathing his sword. "And most can't."

"But you can?" Lyander kept his own where it was.

"A gift. Courtesy of the Church."

"The Church?"

"You know, the one we work for."

It took Lyander a moment to understand what he meant.

"The Church doesn't bequeath anyone below the rank of Admiral," he said. "As a rule."

"Rules change."

"Not the one's set by the Ecclessius. Show me your mark."

He gave Lyander a very pronounced eye roll,

and unlaced his vambrace. The tattoo circling his wrist like a bracelet was etched in Old World numerals and lettering. A unique code identifying each individual witch-hunter, inscribed upon them at birth – or worse, as infants. As a non-magic user, there was no way Lyander could verify it, but it looked like all the others he'd seen and so was the only thing for him to go on.

"Happy?" Gabriel said.

Lyander nodded, putting up his blade.

"Why would the Ecclessius bequeath a witch-hunter?"

"Why does the Ecclessius do anything?" Gabriel asked, as if it was obvious. "Because it wants to."

Unconvinced, Lyander pressed: "Why not abjurancy or evocancy? Symulacrancy can't be very useful for a witch-hunter."

"I wouldn't say that. It's useful for slipping past guards and creating diversions." He smiled. "Sneaking up on foes and making them think you're in one place instead of another. And of course, giving lovers very interesting evenings. Although the whores try and make you pay triple." He shrugged his shoulders as if to say, 'What can you do?'

"I'm sure the Church is very proud," Lyander said, coming to the conclusion he wasn't going to enjoy spending time with this man. *Conceited and condescending; he's the Church personified.*

"Their feelings toward me are decidedly mixed," Gabriel said. "A little like their feelings toward you, it would seem. The infamous Kalbrayeth Lyander, the once beloved First Champion punished with a demotion to exorcist. Only to be tasked with hunting vampires and finding Ravinica's missing prince – an appointment most of us wait a lifetime for, and one well outside your profession's expertise. Why, I wonder, would the Ecclessius do that?"

"Why does the Ecclessius do anything?" Lyander said, noting the displeasure in the way Gabriel said, "outside your profession's expertise." *Unhappy about playing second fiddle to an exorcist in an Aeturnic investigation – can't say I blame him.*

The blue in the witch-hunter's eyes glinted impishly.

"So as the *lead* in this investigation, what does an ancient and supposedly mythical undead have to do with outlawed princes?"

"As the witch-hunter, I thought you'd be able to tell me," Lyander said, and meant it. Nothing about the past few days made sense to him, so he was hoping someone from the Order Abhorrentia might know something about the creatures belonging to the realm that order was tasked with defending against. "Doesn't Mord Gonn have a dusty tome for every creature with fangs?"

"Sure," Gabriel said, snorting. "And the dusty tome on vampires is right in between the dusty tomes on dragons and unicorns – these things aren't supposed to exist. But assuming what you found really was a vampire and it really knew about Ravinica's missing prince, I'd say our new friend, Eluthienn, has made enemies with more than just his own countrymen."

Lyander found that a little obvious. "Most things that crawl out of the Aeturnum aren't looking to make friends," he said.

"Then maybe with the next one, we question it before we kill it."

"You want to try talking to the next one we find, be my guest. I'm sure it'll tell you all it knows about Eluthienn."

The witch-hunter eyed Lyander's bandaged hand, a smile tugging at the corner of his mouth. "Last one didn't want to die peacefully, I take it?"

"Technically, they're already dead. And no, there's nothing peaceful about them."

"How did you do it?"

"I cut it in half with my sword."

Gabriel looked genuinely surprised: "Seems a bit ordinary."

"They don't like crosses, either."

A blond eyebrow rose up the witch-hunter's forehead. "Don't tell me stakes and water blessed by the throne also work?" he said.

"No idea, but if you want to sit one down and find out what it knows about Eluthienn, you'll need to wear a cross."

Gabriel nodded at the statue. "Perhaps what the Ecclessius tells us about our Lord Redcrosse is true, after all."

"Which part?" Lyander asked, not understanding what the witch-hunter meant.

"The part about him being the hero who fought both Immuratic incursions and the Lords of the Eternal Hunt in the Aeturnum. And creating his scions to continue that fight after his death. You know, just his whole story about being the saviour of the Fromryr and the rest of human civilisation."

"And why would that suddenly be true?" Lyander asked, not missing the sarcasm.

"Eluthienn is a direct descendent of Leoncoure Leonette," Gabriel said. "One of the seven scions of Redcrosse, and the one who destroyed the Lord of Undead. You don't think it's a little coincidental that an undead being is looking for that descendent?"

Lyander – who, like most people, believed the tales of Redcrosse and the Lords of the Eternal Hunt were, at best, allegorical and, at worst, complete myth – had missed the connection. But now the witch-hunter said it; it was plain as daylight.

"You think a lone vampire is out to avenge the death of its master?"

The witch-hunter shrugged. "I think Eluthienn will be able to answer that question better than me," he said, and nodded at the portal. "Shall we?"

#

Lyander's horse whinnied, shaking its head back and forth, its shaggy blonde mane fanning outward. He pulled on the reins, trying to steer her to the right, but blind in one eye, she kept drifting to the side she could see from, and toward Gabriel and the mule he was riding.

Every time she came too close, catching the witch-hunter's scent, she nickered and snorted and stamped her hooves. It wasn't uncommon for animals to distrust magic users, but his garron seemed to have a singular fear of the witch-hunter.

Seen in the cold light of day, Lyander could hardly blame the horse. Gabriel wore boiled leathers, reinforced with tight rings of mail on his breast, shoulders, and thighs. A row of wax-hardened pouches – some filled with stoppered vials – lined his belt and the strap across his chest. Everything was a dark brown or polished silver, save for the royal blue pauldrons and vambraces, and the maroon chest strap and sword belt. Lyander thought it looked more like a second skin than functioning armour, and worn by the lean, predatory-looking witch-hunter, it was like riding next to a half-starved mountain lion.

The mule seemed to think so, too, but of all the stable master's horses, it was the least troubled by Gabriel's presence. Looking at its patchy grey coat, bony frame, and white whiskers, Lyander suspected it was simply too old to care.

Pulling his gaze from the horse, Lyander wrapped his reins around the wrist of his wounded hand, and with the other, drew a jam tart from the burlap sack tied to the saddle, and threw it into his mouth. It had been provided by the stable master's wife, who upon seeing how much Lyander was willing to pay for the horses, had scuttled back into her farm house and brought out offal pies, oat cakes, and the tarts.

During the day-and-a-half ride to Grindlepeake's eastern river gate, Lyander ate all of his own share, then most of Gabriel's, who had sniffed at the cakes and tarts before handing them over to Lyander. The only thing he seemed to have a taste for was the offal, which he scooped out of the pie, leaving the pastry for his horse. Lyander wouldn't have guessed the witch-hunter for a picky eater, but he wasn't going to complain; the copious amounts of sugar and pastry was doing his head wonders, and gave him something pleasant to think about while his hand continued its punishment.

He sucked a stray bit of the treacle sweetness from between his teeth, then took the reins from around his wrist and guided the horse to a scree-ridden lip of rock overlooking the Yoinar.

Gabriel pulled up slightly farther down the trail.

"Ten months ago, the Ravinican council deposes their prince, and of all the places to hide, he chooses here?" the witch-hunter said, staring down at the crumbling gate house spanning the neck of the river and guarding the only route from the Yoinar to the Amarant Sea.

Large enough to fit three galleys abreast, the gate house and its iron portcullis was flanked on either bank by stone-cut towers. Attached to the tower on the northern side – their side of the river – was a smaller gatehouse, its heavy wooden doors shut, barring entry from the merchant's road. The opposite tower had been built right into the purple-grey rock of the Daedrimoric mountains, which ranged for miles along the Yoinar and south, farther into Ravinica.

Stretching out from behind the tower was a fortified wall lining the cliffs and providing the perfect vantage over the river. It looked like a colossal stone serpent snaking all the way to Grindlepeake. Lyander, who had lived his entire adult life surrounded by the geometric architecture of Formaria, found the irregularity of the man-made defences strangely comforting.

"It's the perfect place to hide," he said. "And it's the only place he *could* hide."

Gabriel looked up at him. "You know this is Ravinican territory?" he said.

"Run by a pirate who hates that he holds fealty to Vallorandyl. It wouldn't take much for him to offer Eluthienn safe harbour in exchange for his future independence."

"The merchant lords of the archipelagos would have been safer bed fellows. And he wouldn't have been the first prince in exile to run off to Syracuta."

"Hard to take fifteen thousand soldiers with you, though. The lords of Syracuta aren't that accommodating, or that trusting."

"You think Eluthienn still has his army?"

"The only reason the city is locked down is that its playing host to a sizeable force, and Eluthienn doesn't want anyone to know about it."

"You can't keep fifteen thousand soldiers secret for long. And you can't keep them holed up in a city without it turning into chaos."

"Which means he doesn't plan on staying in Grindlepeake much longer."

"You think he's planning a rebellion?"

"What do all exiled princes want?" Lyander

said, turning his horse toward the trail. "Their thrones back."

Farther down, they levelled with the Yoinar's swollen banks, the swirling waters a mud brown from the rainfall and, in parts, overflowing onto the merchant road. The horses laboured through the sludge, and occasionally they were forced around breaches the size of large ponds.

Before the gatehouse, the ground turned to quagmire, the ruts and channels from caravans, boot prints, and animal tracks deep with water. Then the overcast grey blanket above them decided it was time to rain.

"You have a plan for how we get in there?"

"Of course," Lyander said, pulling his hood up and shielding his bandaged hand beneath his cloak.

Two men appeared upon the ramparts – both wore the grey and black surcoats of the Grindlepeake city guard. Lyander could see the mail vests underneath, the dull links at their necks and wrists.

"No further travellers," the one with cropped black hair called down to them. He rested his hands between the crenellations. "Grindlepeake is under quarantine due to an outbreak of Mael's Avarice. Entry to the city is barred to all."

"How convenient," Gabriel said under his breath.

Lyander grunted his agreement.

Mael's Avarice – the sickness caused by exposure to contaminated gyre ice, usually from gyranic devices – was excruciatingly painful, highly contagious, and perfectly treatable. It would rip through a population, usually only fatal to the very old or the very weak. In a city the size of Grindlepeake, it would take local casters a month, two at most, to isolate and treat the sick, giving Eluthienn enough time to . . . *to what? Plan an invasion? Find enough ships to escape with all his forces? A rebellion is the obvious move for a prince in exile but fifteen thousand soldiers can't take Ravinica. They could barely hold one of its regions. Even if he split his force, appearing in multiple places on Ravinica's borders, they'd be surrounded and cut off from one another within a handful of months.*

Eluthienn, from what Lyander knew of the man, was a celebrated commander – a warrior first and prince second. Not the sort to start a war he couldn't win. As he stared up at the tower, the rain pattering his face, his earlier confidence that Grindlepeake was a staging ground dampened, and he was once again reminded that none of this made sense. The truth, therefore, was in all likelihood the best course of action.

"We're Ecclessiarchal emissaries," he called up at the tower. "Representatives sent on behalf of the Fromryian council, here to treat with Eluthienn, prince of Ravinica."

Even at this distance, Lyander could see the man tense, trying to hide his surprise as he decided how to handle the situation. His mouth parted slightly, then his features hardened, lips tightening, brow knitting together. He turned to the soldier next to him, said something Lyander couldn't hear, and pointed down at them. "An escort will see you into the city," he called.

Gabriel pulled closer to him, forcing Lyander to steady his horse.

"Your plan was to tell them exactly who we are and what we're doing here?" he said.

"It was," Lyander replied, keeping his eyes on the gate. They opened and a unit of spear-wielding soldiers in the same black and grey stood waiting for them.

"You didn't think they might have orders to shoot anyone suspicious on sight?"

Lyander hadn't actually considered that.

"I suppose it was possible," he said, nudging his horse forward. But Gabriel grabbed the reins, the proximity causing the horse to shake its head and snort in protest.

"Or lock us in a cell? We could be in a dungeon for months waiting for them to decide what to do with us."

Another possibility, Lyander admitted to himself, trying not to dwell on how bad he was at all this. Not counting his short time as an exorcist, his sole profession involved mainly swinging a sword and shouting orders. To him, sneaking around and using deceit and persuasion was the art of lesser men. *Of men*, he thought, growing annoyed, *like those who stripped me of my title for the sake of politicking and currying favour.*

"I think it's a bit late to worry about that now," Lyander said.

"When the church told me I was to support an exorcist in a delicate Aeturnic investigation, I assumed said exorcist was of such exceptional skill it warranted him being in charge," Gabriel said, with a sort of restrained frustration, so his words wouldn't carry to the tower. "But you've never done anything like this before, have you?"

At that last part, the witch-hunter sounded genuinely surprised and like he might regret the Ecclessius' decision to send him on this mission.

Lyander pulled the reins from the witch-hunter's hands. "Nope," he said, and pushed his horse forward to tramp through the mud.

On the other side of the gate house, the soldiers formed a loose ring around them, the one from the tower pushing his way between them.

"You're on foot from here," he said. "We've a

skiff left to take you up river and there's no room for the beasts."

Lyander and Gabriel dismounted, removing their packs from the saddles as soldiers came forward to take the animals.

"And we'll take those from you," the soldier said, nodding at Lyander's sword while resting a hand on the pommel of his own.

Lyander unstrapped his sword belt and handed it to the man.

"And you," he said to Gabriel. The witch-hunter gave Lyander a hard look before unstrapping his own belt and handing over the slender scabbard, along with a hip knife. "I want those back," he said.

"You will, but only when we say so." He passed the weapons to the man next to him. "Skiff's that way." He pointed down river. "Tarrick and the lads will take you there."

"Thank you," Lyander said.

The man eyed Lyander like he suspected the politeness to be foul play, then said: "Better be quick about it – storm's coming and you don't want to be in the water when it does."

As he left for the tower, Lyander tried to ignore the feeling they were walking into something they might not be able to walk out of.

"Come on," one of the soldiers said, who Lyander assumed was Tarrick. "We don't want to be in the water when the storm comes any more 'an you do."

They took them past a row of empty moorings to a short jetty, protruding into the river like someone's little finger. At the end, a fishing boat bobbed in the water, bumping against the wooden piles. They clambered into it – Lyander and Gabriel first, then the soldiers in the rower's seats, two in front of them and two behind.

As one, they dropped the oars and swept them into the body of the Yoinar. To their right, the cliffs rose, became steeper, their sheer faces dropping straight into the water's edge. To their left, the snaking wall joined with a stocky tower, sat on a bluff like some aged toad. The river grew narrow and they passed beneath the tower and round the bend created by the bluff. It drew to the right and the guard steered along straight river again, this time to where the wall extended downward, all the way to the waterline.

Row upon row of arrow loops looked out from a wall of guaranteed death to the occupants of any ship attempting to pass by. And it wasn't as if they could simply out row the hail of arrows, for the wall met another gate. Built into a rock bridge spanning the river – the gate Lyander knew to be called Mercy's End – was flanked by two rounded towers. Also built into the rock bridge, they formed half-moons with their own rows of arrow loops – six floors from where the defenders could comfortably pick off those below with little fear of taking fire in return.

"It's no fancy Formarian castles like you have in your underground," Tarrick said, raising his voice over the cut and slosh of the waves, "but you'd die all the same trying to take it."

"Formaria doesn't have any castles," Lyander replied. "But you're right, no one in their right mind would attempt to take Grindlepeake by river."

The man's weathered cheeks, sagging from age and covered in a carpet of white stubble, puffed outward as he pulled on the oars. "Oh, a few have attempted it, to be sure," he said. "Didn't get very far, though."

"Oglash Blind Side," Gabriel said.

"What?" Lyander said at the same time as Tarrick said: "Who?"

"Goblin war chief three hundred years ago. One

of the few to unite the clans, or most of them, at least. Thought he could take the city by attacking Grindlepeake on all its fronts. Split his army into four. One part up the river, while another laid siege to the port. Once they'd fought their way through, they'd pick up the other two forces, making their way through the Daedrimoric mountains and the swamps on the northern bank."

Tarrick snorted. "Bet they had fun there."

Gabriel gave the man an annoyed look. Lyander tried to interpret the witch-hunter's odd response but was distracted by the sound of winches turning and iron spokes driving against gear wheels. The portcullis lifted into Mercy's End and they drifted beneath it, droplets soaring from wet grills.

"It was the only place they made it through," Gabriel continued, looking up at the iron teeth now hidden in the gate house. "The clans attacking by river broke on this very gate. Grindlepeake's navy made short work of those being ferried by the Fal'Hannian mercenaries. And those making their way from the south – the bulk of Oglash's forces – were lost in the mountains. Those who did make it to the shoreline were too few and the rest fled or were picked off by Ravinican reinforcements." Gabriel shook his head. "One of the few goblins to bring the clans together and he wasted it on this place," he said.

"Sounds like good ol' goblin stupidity to me," Tarrick said.

"Oh, Blind Side wasn't stupid," Gabriel said. "He knew Grindlepeake could hold out against forces ten, twenty times the number of the defenders, with a near endless food supply from the sea. He wanted a home for the goblin race. He just picked the wrong home, and sent thousands of goblins to their deaths instead."

"Hmm," Tarrick said, as if mulling over a philosophical conundrum. Then said: "So why was he called Blind Side?"

Gabriel pulled his gaze from the river.

"Because he was blind on one side."

"Oh," Tarrick said, as if the simplicity of it was a disappointment. "Well, I never 'eard of him, but it sounds like he did us all a favour."

"I wouldn't be too optimistic," Gabriel said. "There's more where he came from."

"There's maybe one more at best," Lyander chimed in, surprised at Gabriel's claim. "And that goblin has never been able to unite the clans."

"How do you know?" Gabriel asked.

Lyander laughed. "Because I've fought them most of my life and I've never seen more than three war bands working together," he said. "Let alone entire clans. And at any rate, Bork hasn't been seen since he was defeated – by Eluthienn."

At the mention of the prince's name, a dour cast seemed to fall on Tarrick and his men.

"Don't know what you know about the prince. Don't want to know, either. But best you don't go shouting that name around when we get to the city," Tarrick said.

Choosing not to press for more, Lyander simply assumed the obvious: Eluthienn's presence was an open secret in the city and its inhabitants weren't too happy about it.

As if the silence settling on the skiff was an open invitation, the rain began to lash at them, great pellets spattering against their cloaks and creating tiny droplets of splash back as it hit the river. Lyander pulled his cloak tighter around him, shielding his hand from the downpour, and himself against the growing cold.

The river flowed faster now, the rowers doing

little more than keeping the boat in the right direction. A corner rose up before them, another tower built into the rock and looming over the waters below. Two more followed: one on the southern bank, attached to the inner wall, and another on the northern bank, its own impregnable fortress. Then the river straightened, great slabs of grey, green, and white rock to their right, the wall to their left, and ahead, Ghost's Grave – built into a rock bridge like its cousin, Mercy's End, but twice the size, its portcullis hanging over the river like an executioner's axe.

As they approached, Lyander could see its many teeth, like those of some ancient sea creature, slick with green-brown slime, and knotted with ropes of river weed. A salt water breeze wafted toward them as the gate rose, and even with the din of the rain, Lyander could hear the chains clacking rhythmically. On the other side, Grindlepeake struck out of the water. Its walls, twenty times the size of a man, dwarfed the bay surrounding them and even the open sea far off to the west, making the choppy waters look like little more than one large puddle.

In the distance, far behind those walls, the Peake. Three crooked towers rising from a crag, their roofs like pointed mushroom caps, overlooking all the city and out west over the Amarant Sea. Surrounding them, the slate roofs of the old town sloping off in odd directions where the first Lord Grindle made his home. And before them, on an island of its own, the outer bastion – a four-walled fortress of squat towers guarding a single portcullis gate: the river's final defence. If an attacker made it this far, they would have the impossible task of climbing the battlements from ladders raised on the deck of a boat, which would be in flames from the defender's fire arrows and boiling tar, while the waters below became clogged with burning hulls and the dead.

The only option would be to sail past, forced to come within arrow range of the towers or risk grounding on the northern bank's shallows. Then – with whatever was left if the boat wasn't already a flaming wreck or its crew a floating morgue of studded corpses – land in Grindlepeake's northern bay. Once there, assault the fortified docks, its walls overlooking the entire stretch – another impossible task for an attacking force.

Ten thousand Mirrovinjin would be slaughtered trying to take the city. Rakkan, even if they could muster the numbers, would die all the same from death dealt by arrow, bolt, and tar. *For all its unevenness, and how it's built with the natural elements rather than through them, it shows some of us can defend ourselves. That we're not all completely reliant on a technology no one understands.*

The soldiers, rowing harder without the river's current, took them across the bay to the outer island and its squat bastion. They bumped against a stone pier and disembarked, the soldiers first, then Gabriel, followed last by Lyander. The pier became a short walkway leading to the mouth of the bastion that was now being drawn open.

Another unit of soldiers came out to meet them in front of the gate, and Lyander almost did a double take on seeing their uniforms. They wore blue surcoats over chain mail. Two white phoenixes embraced in flight adorned their chests – the colours and insignia of the Ravinican military. *Or in this case, rebel Ravinicans loyal to Eluthienn.*

A woman with blonde hair cut to her shoulders, blue eyes, a scar above her left eyebrow, and a nose broken more than once, stepped forward.

"You were given one order," she said to Tarrick. "*No one enters Grindlepeake* – which of those four words did you not understand?"

The man gave her a withering look.

No love lost between the Grindlepeake city guard and their new guests, it seems.

"We know our orders, Lysana," Tarrick said, "but these two aren't merchants or traders."

Lysana turned to them, hard eyes appraising them.

"We're Formarian emissaries," Lyander said before she could ask. "Here to treat with Prince Eluthienn."

"Prince Eluthienn has been outlawed by the Ravinican council. His whereabouts are unknown. What would give Formaria the notion he's in Grindlepeake?"

"Probably the rebel soldiers standing in front of us," Gabriel said, at which the entire unit seemed to seethe, an angry bristle going from one soldier to another. "Or it could be the piss poor cover story for why Grindlepeake has closed its gates," he continued, before turning to Lyander: "When was the last time you heard of someone actually contracting Mael's Avarice?"

Lyander's experience of diplomacy was limited but he was pretty sure antagonising the other party upon meeting them was exactly how *not* to go about it. "How Formaria knows of the prince's whereabouts," he said, ignoring the witch-hunter, "is best discussed with the prince." Then hoping to de-escalate the tension, he added: "We're here as allies of his majesty."

Lysana studied him, the mix of hostility and distrust still written across her face.

"For now, you'll be held in quarters befitting diplomats of a foreign nation," she said. "And treated as such." Then to Gabriel: "But if you'd like your tongue to remain in your mouth, you'll never use the word *rebel* around us again. Because the way I see it, only one of you needs to do any talking."

The way the witch-hunter grinned said he would

like nothing more than for her to try.

"This way," she said, then nodded for them to follow her.

Their weapons were handed over to the Ravinican soldiers, before Tarrick and his men returned to the skiff, and Lyander and Gabriel were escorted into the bastion. Its four walls surrounded a muddied yard in use as a training ground with the melee pits and an archery range quickly puddling with water. At the opposite end, another portcullis drew open, and they were led onto a fortified bridge, the walls rising on either side to twice Lyander's height. They splashed across the flagstones.

"Want to tell me what in the abyss that was all about?" he said to Gabriel, but quietly enough so only he could hear.

"Just following your lead and being honest with everyone."

"That was an entirely different kind of honesty," Lyander said, trying to keep the annoyance from raising his voice. "From now on, maybe you let me do the talking."

"You are in charge, after all," Gabriel said, eyes straight ahead, but something in his tone made Lyander question whether he meant it. Surely, even if Gabriel was disgruntled about him being in charge, the witch-hunter wouldn't let it sabotage the entire mission? But Lyander found there was no way to answer the question because, so far, Gabriel had demonstrated a mix of irritation and nonchalance that was proving impossible to interpret.

He let the thought slip uneasily to the back of his mind as they neared the end of the bridge where wooden gates bound in iron opened, letting them into the city. Flagstones changed to cobbles and fortified walls gave way to a medley of wattle and daub buildings – the homes, Lyander guessed, of the less wealthy. The cobbled street curved round to the right and rose at a slight incline, rivulets of murky rain water flowing fast between the stones, while the smell of sea salt and raw fish mixed with the pungency of human presence that seemed a mark of all topside cities.

They levelled out, coming onto a straight road heading into the heart of Grindlepeake and providing a view of the old town. Elevated above the city on the naturally formed promontory, it was now shadowed beneath black clouds, a dark vista punctuated by the occasional flash of lightning and crack of thunder.

Lysana quickened the pace and the wattle and daub quickly became purple-grey clay between timber frames, the roofs made from ruddy brown tiles.

The rain sent many people indoors, but even so, to Lyander, the city felt unusually empty. Perhaps it was just the black clouds casting their ominous pall over where they were headed, but Lyander thought the city was on edge, as if the buildings loomed over them, hemming them into narrower and narrower streets.

"You imposed a curfew?" he said, quickening his stride to catch up with Lysana.

The sideward glance told him those weren't the sort of questions she wanted to answer, but seeing that Lyander wasn't going to let up, she said: "At first." She scrunched her face up as the rain grew heavier, then added with what he thought was an awkward look: "For the Mael's Avarice."

Definitely a cover story, then.

"Then what happened?"

She half shrugged, half hunched her shoulders. "We stopped enforcing it, but people still kept to their homes," she said. Because by then, word would have reached them about the disappearance of a prince and his army, and they would have put the whole thing together.

They passed a large square, empty but for a statue of Redcrosse in the centre, as always, fashioned in full plate and helm, his sword raised heroically to the sky.

It dawned on him then: He hadn't seen a single Ravinican solider, other than the six surrounding them. Given Eluthienn had reportedly escaped with fifteen thousand of them, he would expect to see some in the streets. Grindlepeake, although extensively fortified, wasn't a large city.

"What about the army?" he said. "Have they been ordered to stay inside, as well?"

The woman shook her head. "You've asked enough questions. And anyway, we're here."

The street became steeper, the buildings more dispersed. Rising ahead of them: dark grey castle walls made from the purple hued rock native to the nearby mountains. Between the gatehouse, the portcullis was ancient black iron.

A figure in a woollen cloak came out from one of the towers on the other side – two others holding wooden crossbows trailed behind him. Their party came up to the gate, and between the portcullis's latticework, Lyander could make out the blue hem of the Ravinican surcoats beneath the rain cloaks. There *were* others, then, but still too few. *Perhaps Eluthienn doesn't have an army, after all. Or it's not in Grindlepeake.*

"What is it, sergeant?" the one in front said, a thick black beard and large nose jutting out from beneath his hood.

"These two – say they're emissaries from Formaria," Lysana replied.

Lyander watched as the man's mouth curled downward in annoyance. Lysana patted the air in a pacifying gesture and added quickly: "Look, Gyrard, before you say anything, they were given to us by the river guard. We're just handing them over."

"You're making them our problem, you mean," Gyrard, presumably her superior, said.

"We're who we say we are," Lyander said firmly. "My name is Lyander, and this is my colleague, Gabriel. We are Ecclessiarchal representatives, and as diplomats of an allied state, we have a right to an audience with the prince."

"Representatives of Formaria's Church?" Gyrard said. "Not bloody likely. You look like you should be swinging an axe on a battlefield, and he," he pointed at Gabriel, "looks like the sort to poison his blades."

Gabriel shrugged, as if to admit he did look exactly like the sort to poison his blades.

Lyander turned back to the man, trying to hide his frustration. "If we were assassins, we wouldn't walk up to the front gate and ask to be let in."

"Maybe. Maybe not," Gyrard said. "Can't say I've met too many assassins. Still doesn't explain why Formaria would send a party of just two diplomats – two very questionable-looking diplomats, I might add."

To be fair to him, he made a good point.

"Because given the circumstance surrounding the prince," Lyander said, thinking on his feet, "the underground kingdoms felt the need to be discrete in the manner of those diplomats."

"Well, if you ask me, they picked the wrong bloody diplomats."

"And what if they really are who they say they are?" Lysana said.

Lyander turned to her, taken aback by the show of support.

"Don't think that I'm saying you are," she said when she saw Lyander's face. Then to Gyrard: "But if they are, it'll be our hides."

The man chewed the inside of his lip, then yanked the hood from his head, glaring at Lyander. Dark brown eyes watched him from beneath bushy black eyebrows. Looking back, Lyander saw the blotchy purple scar of a magical burn covering part of his cheek, his temple, and the right side of his head where the damage had stripped away the hair and his ear.

"One wrong move and we'll put holes in you," he said.

"That's fair," Lyander said.

Gyrard gave his lip another chew, then called out: "Raise the gate."

He stepped back as the portcullis lifted into the gatehouse and motioned for them to follow. The two others pulled farther apart, placing Lyander and Gabriel into the killing range of their crossbows. Lysana and the other Ravinicans followed behind, their sodden footsteps echoing off the interior walls and the murder holes lining the roof.

On the other side, the buildings were cut brick. Unlike the mostly clay of the city behind them, they were hewn from the same rock as the castle walls with black timber frames around stained glass windows: the homes of the wealthiest in Grindlepeake, the merchant lords, fleet captains, the nobles that there were in such a place, and the families who could trace their lineage back to the settling of the Peake itself, and who remained despite the city's new ruler.

Ahead, the rounded keep of old stone and its three towers was separated from the town by a gully of jagged rock, over which spanned a thin bridge three men abreast would find tight. They crossed and, in the open space, the wind was free to pummel them with all its might. Shoulders hunched, head bent down, Lyander could see the Amarant Sea below, a turmoil of midnight blue raging at the cliff edges.

In the keep, the crackle of the wall sconces mixed with the steady drip of rain water falling from their clothes onto hard flagstones. The sound joined with the wind, which howled as it buffeted the castle walls and was forced down wind tunnels around the keep. In the semi gloom, Lyander thought it sounded like fearful cries. He pushed the thought from his mind and checked his bandages. For the most part, they were still dry.

"We have a healer," Gyrard said, pulling a torch from the wall, "if you want him to check that."

"It wouldn't do much good," Lyander replied. He tried flexing his fingers, which still responded even if the rest of his hand felt like a lump of stone. His hope the pain might lessen quickly diminished on the journey from Siadon. Without the regular intake of Folgar's ale there was nothing to keep it at bay. Piercing stabs still lanced the back of his hand, transcending the wound and clawing up his wrist. He took a deep breath, then let all the air out of his lungs, trying to force calm. The exercise did little more than turn the pain from tight cold incisions to a burning throb. *I'll have to keep the source of the wound secret but who knows, perhaps a Ravinican anomancer will know something a Formarian one doesn't.* "You know, maybe I will see that healer."

"Smart choice. Infirmary is warmer than anywhere else in this damned place."

Gyrard led them around the edge of a hall, a burning hearth on either side, two long tables lining its length, the lord's table facing them at the far end. Behind the lord's seat in the middle was draped the grey banner of Grindlepeake, its giant red Mydradyl shark grinning at them. To either side, the deep blue banners of Ravinica, the twined phoenixes wrapped around each other like they were dancing mid-flight.

Then through a side door and down a spiralling stone staircase. At the bottom, they followed a corridor and down more steps before Gyrard stopped at a door to his right. He banged his fist on it.

"Brasden," he called.

Lyander heard what sounded like a chair scraping against stone floor, and the door swung inward.

The man who opened it wore Ravinican military blue along with the white armlet of his station wrapped around his upper arm and all the way to his shoulder. His grey hair was shorn to the scalp, while his beard covered nearly all of his neck. His eyes, which were kind, were light green, the crow's feet at their edges like a mass of spider's webs.

"We have guests," Gyrard said. "From Formaria," he added. "One needs medical attention, if you can spare the time."

"I have nothing but spare time," Brasden said, the staccato of his accent contrasting with its rich deepness. Lyander would have placed him in southern Ravinica, somewhere close to Celmyr.

The anomancer moved to let them into the room: circular, with a table up against one wall, parchment, ink wells, and an assortment of vials scattered across it. The surgeon's table was off to the left, a seat next to it, a wooden cabinet behind it, a large cot on one side, and a small hearth burning on its right. In the air, the smoky sweetness of herbs mixed with a resin earthiness and burning wood.

"When they're done here," Gyrard said to one of the guards, "bring them to the hall." Then to Lyander: "We'll have rooms prepared for you."

He left and Brasden motioned to the spare chair. Lyander removed his sodden cloak, draped it around the chair and sat. The anomancer dragged the other one over to sit facing him. Gabriel hung his cloak on a hook next to the hearth, and leant against its brick frame, strings of wet blond hair falling over his eyes, a bored look on his face. The guards, stood either side of the door, were tensed and eyeing him like they thought the whole thing a façade. The witch-hunter seemed not to notice, or not to care.

"It's the hand, I take it?" the anomancer asked.

Lyander nodded, unwrapping the bandages.

Brasden took it in one of his own, turning it over and gently probing at the swelling. Lyander grit his teeth so as not to wince.

"So who managed to give you this?"

"More of an it than a who," Lyander replied.

"Makes sense. It's not infected but the hardness of the swelling and the colouring looks gyranic. A monster gave you this?"

He could feel Gabriel's eyes on him, wondering, he supposed, if Lyander was going to keep up the streak of honesty.

He wasn't.

"Aeturnic," he said. "Unclassified, though – I don't know what did it."

Brasden raised an eyebrow at him. "Must have been one hell of a beast," he muttered. He nodded at Gabriel. "Your friend here hasn't got an antitoxin or some sort of nullifier for you?"

"Why would he?" Lyander asked – too flatly.

Brasden laughed. "I know a witch-hunter when I see one."

Gabriel, maintaining the bored look, said: "I left my potion set at home."

"More's the pity," Brasden said, "I can drain the swelling, but if you can't tell me what did this, I'm likely to do more harm than good attempting different spells."

That left Lyander wondering what harm Damoclen's war caster might have done with her attempts to "heal" him.

"Draining the swelling is enough," Lyander said,

thankful Brasden wasn't going to force him to dodge questions about the source of the wound.

The anomancer rose, opened one of the cabinet doors, and pulled out a scalpel and small wooden bowl.

Sitting, he placed them on his knee and took Lyander's hand in both his own, then closed his eyes.

"I thought you said no spells?"

"Just for the pain," Brasden said. "I think you'll need it."

The anomancer shut his eyes again, and Lyander felt a damp warmth spread through his hand, like he'd dipped it in a bath – a feeling he knew all too well.

Brasden released him, his hand visibly unchanged by the magic, then taking the scalpel, made an incision just below his knuckle, drawing downward across the swelling to the size of a fingernail. Inky, bile-like fluid pooled in the cut, then became a fast-flowing trickle filling up the bowl.

Lyander couldn't feel a thing, and while the spell might have removed the pain, it didn't stop the smell. A mix of rot and something acidic, almost like vinegar made him swallow. "That can't be good," he said.

"It's unusual, even for a magical wound," the anomancer agreed, professional enough not to react to the smell. He placed the scalpel on the table, then used both hands to put pressure on the swelling. "But I've smelled worse and seen full recoveries."

When he was done, he wiped away the excess and inspected the hand once more.

"Can you move your fingers?"

Lyander tried, and with the pain numbed by the spell, he was able to curl them over. He was nowhere near clenching them into a fist, but he still felt a tiny glimmer of relief. It was better than his previous attempts, and it was another small sign he might hold a sword again – the type of sword he liked to use, that is.

"Not a bad start," Brasden said. "When did you receive the wound?"

"Nearly three days ago."

"Hmm." Brasden took the scalpel again, and with the soft end probed at the skin around the stitching. "You'll need to keep these in. Another week, at least, by the look of it."

He placed the bowl on the table and stood. Reaching into a different drawer, he pulled out a roll of bandages and a pair of scissors. Cutting it to length, he began wrapping it around Lyander's hand.

"Change these every day, and keep moving the fingers every hour or so. You don't want to break the stitching, but you don't want to let the hand become stiff, either. I've seen magical wounds mortify if left to their own recovery, and you definitely don't want that."

Lyander gave himself a mental reminder to move his fingers as much as possible. "Thank you for this."

"It wasn't like I was busy," Brasden said, tightening the bandage into a knot.

Lyander wanted to ask why, and was trying to phrase the question as nonchalantly as possible when there was a knock on the door.

"Come in," Brasden said, and it swung open.

Gyrard stepped into the room. He looked at Gabriel, his eyes narrowing as he took in the witch-hunter's indifference, then at Lyander, then down at his hand.

"Anything serious?" he asked.

"It shouldn't be," Brasden answered.

"Good because Eluthienn wants to see them now."

#

The wind menaced the tower. It drowned out their footsteps, broke through the cracks between the windows, bit at Lyander's wound despite the fresh bandages.

Sconces lined the walls but they weren't lit – because no one bothered to light them or because they were tired of relighting them, Lyander didn't know. He was forced instead to keep close to Gyrard, who climbed in front with a torch. It provided just enough light to prevent Lyander from tripping on every other step.

As they neared the top, the wind grew to a higher pitch, a keening wail laced with desperation, buffeting the tower with its despair. Lyander, struggling to climb while simultaneously trying to ignore the pain returning to his hand, didn't know how the stones could bear it.

At the very top, light poured from an open doorway, painting the final steps in sun yellows and soft oranges. The light, which danced on the stone steps, seemed to abate the angry storm, for as they came to the landing, the howling lulled. In its place were the muffled sounds of conversation from within the room.

Gyrard stood to the side of the doorway and nodded with his chin for Lyander and Gabriel to enter. They did so and found themselves in a room as wide as the banquet hall below and nearly as long. Its circumference was lined with pillars, each one holding a blazing torch, its light cast onto the dark tiling and into the rafters above. At its centre, the room held a long table, at which Lyander counted thirteen people.

The four nearest on the right, three men and a woman, wore almost entirely black: black sable cloaks over black leather armour, the vambraces and pauldrons inlaid with decorative patterns but still very much black. Their gloves, either resting in their laps or on the table, were also black leather, and while he couldn't see them, Lyander was willing to bet their boots matched the rest. The only colour came from the few links of chain mail visible at their wrists, and the angry purple-red brand seared into each of their necks. Even without it, Lyander would have known them by sight: the mercenary captains of the island city states of Fal'Hannar.

Opposite them, three men wore the unmistakable blue of Ravinican soldiers. The white cloaks with their gold inner lining, draped over their shoulders or over the backs of the chairs, gave them away for officers.

To the right of the mercenaries, two men in long naval jackets, grey with gilded trim and pearl white buttons: the fleet lords of Grindlepeake. And to their right, the lord of Grindlepeake himself: the pirate captain and usurper of the Grindle family home, Vagabor Pent. Like his fellows, he wore a grey navy officer's jacket with gold trim, the only distinction a short plume of shimmering green feathers fixed to its lapel.

The lord of Grindlepeake stared at Lyander with small, suspicious eyes, the irises swimming in a sea of brown, their depths like a storm at sea. To Lyander, they looked like the eyes of a man unfamiliar with the concept of compromise, and stared out from a face tanned from living a life at sea. It was surrounded by long hair pulled into a ponytail the same colour as his eyes, and a beard left to grow over several weeks.

The face of the man opposite – no the face of the elf opposite – looked like it belonged to someone with equal capacity for violence. Shoulder-length black hair pulled back above a prominent nose and jaw line, sculpted with edges full of self-assurance and disdain. They surrounded a cruel mouth, a thin sneering line that looked ready to spill hate and malice at a moment's notice. But it was the maroon red kerchief bound over his right eye that drew Lyander's attention, and the tip of the scar just visible beneath it on his upper cheek.

Next to him, his two companions looked more like what Lyander knew of the elven race: blond haired and fair skinned with high cheekbones to pair with their tipped ears. They all wore a style of light brown gambeson, slimmer than most and with a high collar, worn over a leather cuirass the colour of dulled vermillion. The battle dress, Lyander realised, of the Sorel Tan.

His eyes darted back to the elf with the kerchief and recognition dawned. Worlds ago, Lyander's training included military intelligence briefs and, like all officers of the Fromryian army, he was shown this elf's likeness as a silvery black hex sculpt. In that, Isdria Laanorath, the infamous and bloody Sorel Tan captain, possessed both eyes.

His orders then, as they were now as a member of the Church's military arm, were to capture or kill Laanorath on site. The elf seemed to sense what Lyander was thinking and his thin mouth twisted mockingly. Lyander smiled back, deciding Eluthienn's collaboration with an organisation regarded as terrorists by Formaria was the Ecclessius' problem.

His own problem sat to the elf's right.

At the very end of the table, occupying the lord's seat, could only be Ravinica's outlawed prince. Eluthienn Leonette's face, both rugged and temperate, was strewn with the consequences of war. Faint scars lined the bridge of his nose, one across his right cheek, another licking the edge of his jaw line. His dirty brown hair, long and swept back into braids, was shorn to the skull on either side, like a warrior of the Old World rather than a prince of the new one.

His eyes, Lyander saw, were similar in colour to Gabriel's. But unlike the witch-hunter's and their wells of magical blue, Eluthienn's were lighter, the colour of unrefined ice, the colour of raw power dancing with both cunning and playfulness. Like his generals, he wore Ravinican blues, and on his chest the twined phoenixes circled in white.

The prince stood.

"Come, friends," he called with one arm outstretched invitingly. "The wind is so very loud, but here we are sheltered by the protections of Sadrosil. He calms the storm for us." The rhythmic staccato of Eluthienn's voice was almost singsong in nature. With such slight emphasis on the first syllable of each word and clipped at the last it seemed to roll toward them on invisible currents.

The elf two seats down from the prince spoke: "Who's to say I didn't bring the storm and this little trick is just to impress you of my talents?"

"Ha," Eluthienn laughed. "All sorcerers should have as silvered a tongue as yours, Sadrosil."

One of the Fal'Hannians snorted. Bald and brutish, the man's chalky skin rumpled at the neck, making his brand look like it was floating on curdled milk. "Would we all, then, have to lick your arse, my Prince?" he said, his voice strangely taut and whiny for a man of his appearance.

Eluthienn smiled as if the mercenary was doing nothing more than exchanging pleasantries.

"This is our other high mage, Kuhorro," he said. "A warlock of Fal'Hannar. But his tongue is cruel and black."

"And his talents far less impressive," Sadrosil added. "Or maybe *he'd* be keeping the storm at bay."

"Among strangers, only fools expose their powers," Kuhorro replied.

"Come now," Eluthienn said, still smiling, "or my new guests might think we're not all friends."

"And who are your new guests, Eluthienn?"

Pent asked, his voice as rough as sea salt baked onto hard rock.

"Envoys of Formaria," Eluthienn said, then grinned, looking Lyander straight in the eye. "Representatives of the Church, here at my request."

The lie left Lyander peering at the prince, trying to read his face. *Does he not trust those around him? Given the company he's keeping, I can't blame him. But more likely, I think, Eluthienn doesn't want his new allies to think their location isn't secret. Which means one or more has openly questioned gathering in Grindlepeake.*

But Lyander was given no time to consider who that might be, for Pent continued: "Curios envoys," he said, eyes roaming lazily over Lyander and Gabriel. "Why would Formaria send a member of the Coven, and if my knowledge of Ecclessiarchal insignia is correct, an exorcist of the Order Malignia?"

Eluthienn laughed, a single short hop of a beat, then said: "Not so curious if you know their purpose, as I do, Vagabor. The Ecclessius sends an exorcist and a witch-hunter, for who better to send than those most knowledgeable of evil things? For as I have told you all, the vampire now plagues their lands, and there are few things in this world more evil than the vampire."

Eluthienn looked up at Lyander: "Is that not so, Lyander?"

He met the prince's gaze, trying his best to keep his face impassive, to hide his shock. None of his guessing – his apparently wild guessing – included Eluthienn *knowing* about the creatures hunting him.

"A vampire was found and exterminated within Yeggardania's borders not long ago," he said.

"As I have said." Eluthienn raised his arms, as if to say, 'to all of you.' "And now Formaria has answered my call, for it seeks my aid in ridding its land of the threat."

A game, then, this is what he's playing, one in which Formaria is drawn into whatever plans he's making with this disparate group of cutthroats and traitors. He ought to let the prince play it out, to see where it goes before making a move, but Lyander was never one for games.

"The vampire we captured," he said, feeling Gabriel's eyes on him again, "knew of your whereabouts. It is our understanding that it was hunting you."

Eluthienn's smile was dark, the blue in his eyes glinting malevolently.

"Well, of course they are hunting me," he said. "I am the only one who can return them to the grave."

Lyander opened his mouth to speak but Gabriel beat him to it: "I hate to break it to you, but anyone with a sword can kill these things."

"Yes," Eluthienn acknowledged, shrugging, "you can kill their spawn. But not the one who made them. And while he walks the land, the vampire threat will spread. To every spire, to every cauldron, to every vault. Your world will never be safe."

"And why," Gabriel pressed, his tone making it clear he didn't believe a word Eluthienn was saying, "can only you bring an end to this supposed threat?"

To his generals, Eluthienn said: "Bring in the beast."

Two of them rose, walked toward the end of the room, and exited through the door behind the prince. Moments later, the sound of wheels being drawn across stone floor, and a cage was pushed into the room. Its occupant, bound at the ankles and wrists, an iron mouth clamp covering its entire jaw, was a vampire. Unlike Ameria Forth's mortified corpse, the skin of this creature was deathly pale, save for the dried blackish blue blood around its constraints and its bloodshot red eyes. It wore little but soiled rags and a tangled mass of hair covered so much of its face, the only thing to identify its sex was the muscled calves and wrists.

A tense shroud seemed to settle on those sat at the table, and all eyes turned to the cage.

"Behold," Eluthienn called, throwing an arm out to the vampire like a performer, "the black threat that hangs over this world." He walked to the cage, and brushing aside his cloak, drew his sword from its scabbard.

"And behold, witch-hunter, why only I can slay the maker."

With a flawless thrust and twist of his hip, he ran the blade between the iron bars, piercing the vampire's chest and whatever heart still beat there. The creature's screech, unable to leave its clamped mouth, was a muffled keening quickly turned to a gargled choke. Its eyes, drawn wide by the pain, became demented, trembling in their sockets before rolling back into its skull.

Then the vampire began to collapse in on itself.

First around the sword, the chest cavity giving way, the bone creaking inward before the skin began to turn plum black with internal bleeding. Then the rest of it, its stomach, its neck, its forearms, and down to its thighs, every limb becoming crumpled parchment and staining black. The hair fell from its head, then the head itself grew to the size of an apple, before toppling forward against the iron clamp.

Black abyss, Lyander thought, watching the creature quickly turn into a decaying wreck. *I've watched war casters throw spells at each other for more than half my life, but I've never seen magic like this.* Looking at the faces around the room, it was clear no one else had, either.

"In my veins," the prince said, removing the blade, face flushed, "runs the blood of Leoncoure Leonette, First Hero, protector of the New World." He pointed the blade at Gabriel, black gore dripping from its edge to splash on the tiles. "And slayer of Lokul, the first vampire, and second Lord of the Eternal Hunt." The prince paused, catching his breath. "That is why only I can slay the beast, for my forebear has done it before, and the magic created by the bonds of life and death between those most ancient of foes are ceaseless."

Only the fires crackling in their sconces and the muted calls of the storm could be heard. No one spoke until Lyander did – who in spite of mounting evidence, was not willing to believe everything he was hearing. "Ceaseless they may be," he said, "but Lokul, if such a being ever existed, was slain by Leoncoure Leonette, as you say."

Eluthienn drew a cloth from his pocket and wiped the blood from his sword. "It has been brought back."

Given Dracht's claim that the Lords of the Eternal Hunt were more than myth, Eluthienn's similar belief seemed to shock him less than everyone else in the room. It was the casual assertion with which he claimed one had been *brought back* that shocked Lyander.

"Be reasonable, my Prince," Kuhorro said. "Evidence of the Lords has never been found; they are tales propagated by the Church to justify their rule." He shot Lyander and Gabriel a scornful glance as he said it. "How can you expect us to believe these creatures are the spawn of some fabled monster? What proof do you have?"

"Have I not proved myself at every turn?" Eluthienn said quickly, his tone prickling with anger. "Did I not say the vampires had returned, that they plagued Formaria, that the Church would have representatives treat with us." He brandished his now clean sword: "That I wield the power to defeat them? Have all these things not come to pass?"

Kuhorro held Eluthienn's gaze, the fleshy pink worms that were his lips pressing together, suggesting he might argue. But then he nodded his head slowly: "They have."

"How has Lokul been brought back?" Lyander asked.

"The more appropriate question," Eluthienn said, putting up his blade, "is *who* has brought him back?"

"Then who?"

"Bork," Eluthienn said calmly.

If he wasn't already stunned to silence, Lyander might have laughed. The idea supernatural deities only existing in tales were real was one thing, but the idea a goblin war chief brought one back from the dead, was bordering on the far-fetched. Even with Eluthienn's "magic," this was becoming ridiculous. Apparently, everyone else thought so, too, because a murmur set in around the table: the Sorel Tan whispering among themselves, the mercenaries looking openly astonished. Only the Ravinican officers looked unperturbed by the statement.

"Bork, the fucking Borken," Pent near as growled. "The goblin shit you defeated with a force less than a third the size of his has brought back the vampire king?"

"Bork is a raving lunatic, who thinks leading random ambushes equates to strategy," the Fal'Hannian to Kuhorro's left said, and scoffed. "Bring back a god of the Aeturnum? He can barely bring two tribes together."

"For once," Isdria said, speaking for the first time, "I'm of a mind to concur with the Fal'Hannian. Bork the Borken has spent the last one hundred years conducting failed sieges, botched boarding actions, and sloppy assassination attempts. Blunder after blunder, trying to unite a race, half of which want to kill him, the other half want to torture him first and then kill him. He has neither the power nor the skill to do what you claim he's done."

"I agree," Lyander said. "Bork has made himself a thorn in the side of the underground. But a small thorn. If he had the power or found the power to resurrect Aeturnic beings, Fromryian intelligence would know it."

Isdria's eyes locked onto Lyander's own and he intended to hold the elf's gaze, but Gabriel spoke: "I think you're all forgetting what 'Borken' refers to," he said, over the dissenting voices. "In the goblin tongue, it means 'cunning' – a name given to him by his own race. I wouldn't be so sure of his blunders or of Fromryian intelligence." He looked at Lyander, and for once his face was devoid of humour or mockery.

"Who better to know," Eluthienn said, "than a witch-hunter?"

"And how do *you* know?" Isdria said to Eluthienn, "that Bork is responsible for Lokul's return?"

"Because he told me."

"Told you when?"

"When I captured him at the battle of Osomord."

Kuhorro gave a high-pitched scoff. "And you took him at his word?"

"He had no reason to lie to me."

"And where is Bork now?" Isdria said. "Perhaps he can so easily convince us in the same way he's convinced you."

"That will not be possible," Eluthienn said, "because I let him go."

"Why would you do such a thing?" Lyander asked, hoping to make sense of a story growing more implausible by the second.

"Because that is the bargain we struck. His information for his life. And so far his information has been nothing but the truth. As you have all been witness to."

"And I suppose the goblin also told you where to find the vampire king?"

Eluthienn grinned mischievously at Isdria. "He did," he said, and began to circle the table. "I will seek the vampire king in his lair, destroy him as only I can, and save Formaria from its ruin." He pointed at Lyander. "And in return, Formaria will pledge its might to my cause. And once I sit upon the seat of Vallorandyl, our two nations will be united in common cause, and together we will conquer Fiondagaard."

Lyander's jaw was forming into an involuntary 'O' with every mad word Eluthienn said. He forced it shut.

"I'd like to remind you, Eluthienn," Pent said with such icy control, each word could have been an individual threat. "That we're in the middle of a rebellion, the knowledge of which cannot be kept a secret much longer, and you want to go off on some vampire hunt?"

"And let us imagine," Isdria added quickly, "that you find Lokul, you slay him, and save Formaria from its plight. What's to stop the Ecclessius from reneging on this deal of yours? What's to stop them from simply killing you upon your return?"

"A wise question," Eluthienn said, "but a simple one to answer. Formaria cannot afford to kill me. They cannot afford *not* to fulfil the end of this bargain, for Fion's black hand now rules in Vallorandyl, pulling the strings of its puppet leader. Without a Ravinican king, the Fion emperor will soon rule there openly and Ravinica will become his vassal. What concern is this of Formaria's, you might ask? Why should they care who rules in Vallorandyl? If there is one thing the Fion emperor covets more than Ravinica, it is the wealth and technology of Formaria, and with Ravinica under its command, all is within his grasp. The Ecclessius knows this. And so they will not deny me."

"And you'd like us all to sit here patiently waiting for you? My city, playing host while Ravinica breathes down our necks?" Pent asked.

"No," Eluthienn said, shaking his head. "You will remain here, Vagabor, planning the invasion of Ravinica alongside my generals. The Fal'Hannian's will leave to gather their companies, as the Sorel Tan will leave to gather theirs. They will return here to Grindlepeake, as planned, from where we will launch our great cause. And in the meantime, I will travel to Thendergaarden in the company of the exorcist and the witch-hunter, and there, as is my right, put this bargain before their Ecclessius."

He's mad, Lyander thought as the prince grinned at him. *There's no way the Ecclessius will agree to any of this*. But a quieter voice spoke, one with a worrying level of calm and rationality: *Vampires now exist; there is magic connecting them to Eluthienn's bloodline, and the idea mythical Aeturnic beings are real is becoming increasingly believable. Who's to say the Ecclessius won't agree to this alliance?*

And Lyander was left wondering how he was caught in the middle of it all.

EIGHT

BRAZIER

"Who in the starless black void is this guy?" Switch said, crossbow tucked into her shoulder, eyes trained down its sights.

"High-security prisoner," Freyen answered, her stance mimicking the enginator's. "He was being transported by the Custodians."

"So why isn't he locked in a cell?"

"I think you may have reset the constraining mechanism when you nulled the core."

"Ahh," Switch said, "I'd be more than happy to rectify that error. Zee – permission to put our new friend back in his restraints."

"Permission granted," Brazier said. "Freyen, go with her, and call Axelock and Dalfin up on the way."

The dwarf started chuckling, a low grumble deep in his throat.

"First thing," he said, pointing at Switch, "you

want to use restraints on me, we got to get to know each other first." He smiled at the enginator, then turned his pale grey eyes on Brazier. "Second thing – there's no way I'm going back into that cell."

"Got two repeaters looking right at you that say otherwise," Switch said.

"The third thing," the dwarf said, ignoring the comment, "is if you want to get out of here alive, you're going to need me."

"Not sure how you're coming to that conclusion," Brazier said, and meant it.

"Based on what I've seen so far, I'd put us east of Maw Klioxies and the Hyrulian Gulf. You want to get to Theselan, you need a navigator to make it through both. So with all due respect, *Captain*, I'd say you do need me."

Switch snorted. "If you're a navigator, I'm the Grand Ecclessian."

The dwarf winked at her. "Only one way to find out, sweet cheeks."

"Zee – I've changed my mind, let me drop him out the access hatch instead."

Brazier, his mind still raging with grief, would like to do nothing more than oblige the request. But the kernel of knowledge that he was now in charge wouldn't budge. Something buried deep was cutting through the emotional haze, telling him that making responsible decisions was his job now.

"We can go around Maw Klioxies," he said.

"Hope you brought enough food and water for all of us because that'll take a week in a ship like this. Judging from what I've seen, you didn't plan for that sort of journey."

"We can make it happen," Switch said, "with one less mouth to feed."

"Maybe you can, maybe you can't. You going to

go around the Gulf, too?"

Brazier felt his teeth grinding together. The dwarf was right. Going around would take too long. They neither had the supplies nor, he was betting, did the ship have the ice reserves. And the Navarch needed to be warned. In a week, probably longer, this new enemy could destroy a dozen other ships, attack an installation even. But giving a high-security prisoner control over the ship seemed like a monumentally stupid idea. With an ache that felt like an iron hand crushing his heart, he thought about asking his brother what to do, only to realise, as if all over again, he was dead.

"Get in the pit," he said, not bothering to hide his anger.

"Brazier, he's a high-security prisoner," Freyen said. "We have no idea what he's capable of."

"If he flies us in any direction that isn't Theselan, you both have my permission to kill him." He stared straight at the dwarf as he said it.

The dwarf nodded, grey eyes flat and emotionless. "Sounds like a fair deal." Then he pointed at the space between Freyen and himself: "I don't think we want to hang around."

Brazier looked down at what he was pointing at, his anger and hurt morphing into panic. On the hex display, like before, shade-like beings moved across the tunnel floor. This time, in their direction.

"Blast like that should have killed them all," Switch said.

"Then there's more of them," Brazier said. Then: "Freyen – get the others on board now." To the dwarf: "Get us out of here."

"Name's Matthias," he said, ignoring Switch's crossbow as it followed him round the nav terminal and into the pit. He bent over, and with more care than Brazier would have expected, placed the dead navigator to one side. Removing his boots, he knelt in the hex, spreading his arms out to the side. The hex shifted beneath his open palms, and blue channels flared into life along the walls and ceiling, pulses of power lighting up the deck.

"I hope you're right about this," Switch said, watching the ship come to life.

"If I'm not," Brazier said, quietly, "what I just said still stands."

She nodded at him, then placed a hand into one of the wells.

"Track optimal course. Current location to spire Theselan."

She removed her hand and the well formed into a map, networks of tunnels, then a flat space, shaped like a spear point: the open wound that was the southern tip of Maw Klioxies. Then beyond it, a shallow ravine, the jagged contours riding up on either side of the Hyrulian Gulf. Brazier was trying to find the *Solace* among it all, but the scope was too distant.

Without warning, the hex reformed to a different scale. A line appeared from what was clearly their location and ran past the Maw and the Gulf to the geometric structure that was Theselan.

"You could have just asked me for the map," Matthias said. Brazier couldn't see his face but from the sound of his voice, he thought the dwarf might be smiling.

"Thanks," Brazier said reluctantly, at the same time as he heard Axelock and Dalfin climbing into the fuselage. A moment later, they entered the nav deck, Freyen behind them.

"Zee," Axelock said, his face ashen, his voice thick with grief, "I'm sorry." The dwarf pulled him into an embrace, hard biceps wrapping around his shoulder and under his arm. Brazier, shocked by Axelock's rare show of emotion, took a second to respond. He hugged the old dwarf back. “Thank you, Axelock.”

The dwarf released him, sniffing, clearly trying to hold back angry tears.

“Whatever in the abyss did it,” Dalfin said, almost unrecognisable with such a stern expression, “we’ll come back and give ’em black hell.”

“As touching as all this is,” Matthias said, “we really need to leave.”

Dalfin’s gaze wandered over Brazier’s shoulder. “Who in the abyss is this guy?”

“We’ll explain later,” Brazier said, catching the command well out of the corner of his eye and the shapes almost halfway to the ship. “Matthias – let’s go!”

The ship banked hard, forcing each of them to grab onto the command terminal or the wall handholds.

“Switch,” Brazier said, his voice strained with the effort of keeping himself upright. “Is the ship’s spatial anchor unengaged?”

“Not when I last checked,” she said, her augmented arm clamping her in place next to the terminal.

“By the way,” Matthias said, and this time Brazier was certain the dwarf was smiling, “you should hold on to something.”

“You want to explain why we’re flying unanchored?” he asked.

“You took so long, those things out there were nearly climbing the hull. I needed a little more manoeuvrability.”

“And how,” Switch asked, glaring at the back of Matthias’s head, “did you do that from the nav pit?”

“You don’t need to be an enginator to know about engines.”

Switch looked like she wanted to empty her entire magazine into the dwarf.

"And now they're definitely not climbing the hull," Brazier said. "Perhaps you can reengage it."

A whirring metallic sound, then something intangible he could feel both under his feet and in the air around him, seemed to disperse. Balance reasserted itself. Like the others, he no longer needed to hold on to the ship to keep himself upright.

"So, Zee," Dalfin said, then quickly: "Err, I mean, Captain." The way he said it sounded like he was asking for Brazier's permission to use the title.

"Yeah?"

Dalfin nodded at Matthias. "Who is this guy?"

"High-security prisoner we found on board. As we don't have a navigator; he's now it."

Dalfin nodded slowly, total confusion written across his face.

"And what's the plan?" Axelock asked, eyeing Matthias.

"We get to Theselan and inform the Navarch of the attack on the *Chalice*."

"And do we know what did that? What got the crew? What got . . ." He looked down awkwardly, trailing into silence but Brazier knew what he meant: *What got your brother*.

"We don't," Brazier said, and without thinking placed a hand on Axelock's shoulder, trying to impart strength he himself didn't feel. "But we'll find out."

Axelock gave him a weak smile. "Guessing the same thing happened to this crew?" he asked.

Brazier cast his eyes around the nav deck and over its dead.

"Seems that way. Help me with them. You, too, Dalfin – we'll move them into the fuselage."

He turned to Freyen: "See if you can find yourself any inertial mutagenis in the ship's stores. And anything to cover the crew."

She smiled at him and nodded. As she left, he thought he caught a glimpse of something in those dark brown eyes, something like caring. For one strange second, it made him want to go after her. But he buried the thought. *Your brother is dead, your crew is dead, your ship is gone. You're Captain; time to start acting like it.*

"Switch –"

"I know," she said. "Make sure Matthias here stays on course. If he doesn't, shoot him."

"Don't pretend like you don't want to keep me company," the navigator said.

"Black hell." Switch rolled her eyes. To Matthias: "Do me a favour – make a wrong move."

The navigator chuckled, and the ship dipped its nose, speeding up.

They carried the crew into the fuselage, lining them up along the portside wall. Then they unlocked the prisoners from their constraints and placed them next to the crew. The crew quarters, although almost the size of his entire cabin on the *Chalice*, contained enough bedding to offer them dignity in death. Leaving Axelock and Dalfin to make an inventory of the ship's stores, Brazier stood alone in the fuselage, looking down at the bodies. Indistinguishable under the sheets, he wondered what each of their crimes were, and how much worse Matthias's must have been to require a high-security cell. *Much, much worse*, he decided quickly. *And no amount of charm and smiles can hide that fact.*

"Cap," Freyen called from the nav deck, the shorthand sounding strange directed at him from her mouth. "He wants to ask you something."

Brazier left the dead and stepped onto the nav deck.

"We'll be coming to Klioxies' relative horizon soon," Matthias said, "so we need to go over the terms of our deal."

There was something in the dwarf's voice Brazier did not like.

"We don't throw you back in a cell, you fly us to Theselan. Seems like fairly straight forward terms to me."

"Except in taking you to Theselan, I may as well be throwing myself back in a cell." The dwarf shook his head slowly. "Not going to happen."

"The way I see it, our deal ends when we're at Theselan. What the spire's detachment do with you when we land is your problem."

"Yeah, we're going to have a problem there, too," Matthias said. "I've calculated the ship's reserves against our course. We're going to be short by a league, maybe a league and a half."

Switch gave him a begrudging nod. "I ran the calculations, as well. Ship'll be running on fumes once we've crossed the Gulf."

"Then we send a distress call to Theselan, and they send a ship to come and get us."

Matthias shook his head again. "Like I said, I'm not going back in a cell. We do it that way, there's a good chance that happens."

"And I suppose you have an alternative suggestion?"

"I can point the ship in the right direction. Float her into Theselan's hangar bay. Going to be a rough landing but that's okay for me. Means I can slip away among all the confusion. Also means our deal still stands – I get you to Theselan and you don't get me thrown in a cell."

"You're a high-security criminal – I'm not just letting you get away. Whatever you've done, you can pay for it."

"Was really hoping it wasn't going to go down

like this."

"Cap," Freyen said, leaning in close to him. "A word."

He followed her out into the empty fuselage.

"We don't have a choice," she said firmly. "We have to do what he says."

Brazier felt his brow creasing in confusion. Of everyone, he thought Freyen would share his belief that a criminal, particularly one who required body constraints and sedation, should face the consequences of his crimes.

"Freyen – a high-security prisoner means one of two things: an act of high treason against Formaria, or extreme Aeturnic abilities. Given there wasn't a witch-hunter on board, it's likely to be the former. I'm not letting a traitor walk free."

"You're not going to have a choice. I checked his logs. It's got an admiralty level restriction on it. The only thing it confirmed was his name: Matthias Phaser. And that he's an errant class navigator."

Brazier shook his head, disbelieving. The number of errant class navigators alive at any one time could be counted on two hands. Almost all were human. On rare occasions there might be a gnome. Rarer still were elves. None of them were ever dwarves.

His face must've been giving away his thoughts because Freyen said: "Think about what he did with the engines? When did Jan ever have that much control over the *Chalice*?"

"More reason to make sure we hand him over at Theselan."

Freyen breathed through her nose, an exasperated look on her face. "We can't always do the right thing, Brazier. He's too powerful – the ship is under his control. Even if Switch tried to override the engines, he could just deadlock them, stop her from changing anything."

"Theselan is a major Navarch resupply base," he said, causing Freyen to raise her eyebrows at his unintentionally sharp tone. She couldn't know why, but her comment about *doing the right thing* stung. No, it raked at his chest. He took a breath.

"There will be war casters stationed there. And if there's a gyre star docked, maybe even a contingent. If we just float into Theselan without declaring ourselves, they'll bombard us. We won't make it a league from the spire, let alone crash in its hangar bay."

"We might, if we fly in dark."

"And how can we do that?"

"Between Switch and Matthias, we may be able to reset the ship's core back to how we found it."

"You mean turn off its signature?"

"Exactly."

Brazier rubbed at his beard, trying to picture a hangar bay crew's reaction to seeing the *Solace* falling toward the spire. Without a signature, they'd be reliant on sight alone, by which time it might be too late to blast them out the air. It could work.

"And what if you can't turn off the signature?"

Freyen twirled one of her stray curls between her thumb and forefinger. "I've thought about that, too. We send out a last-minute distress beacon – half a league from the spire. Broadcast that we're out of ice and our long range hex tethering has been corrupted."

"The likelihood of them letting us get within half a league without declaring who we are is slim at best."

"Then let's hope the first plan works."

Brazier rubbed his beard again. The thought of aiding a criminal to escape justice, particularly a potential traitor, warred with the part of his conscience desperate to get to Theselan and warn the Navarch of this new enemy that could destroy gyre ships within minutes.

"Let's hope it does," he said, "because the second one is likely to get us all killed."

She gave him an amused smile and they returned to the nav deck.

"Can you turn the ship's signature back off?" he asked Matthias.

The dwarf tilted his head. "Is that what that was? Thought the engines didn't look quite right."

"Can you do it?" Brazier asked.

His head dropped forward, the index finger on his right hand curling into a single digit claw. "Going to need Switch to work her magic in the engines, but yeah, I should be able to."

Switch regarded Brazier, her coal black eyes cool as voidstone. "Let me guess, we're flying in dark so they don't turn us into floating shrapnel? And then we're letting this one go free."

Brazier nodded.

"You're making the smart choice, Captain," Matthias said. Then: "Freyen, is it? Better pop that IM – we're almost there."

"My favourite part of flying," Freyen said sourly. An aroma of spice and the earthiness of mined ore escaped the vial as Freyen removed the cork. Brazier watched the inertial mutagenis swim against the glass like a molten gold river, specks of white glinting among the silky current.

Draining it in one, she gripped a handhold with an outstretched arm, her jaw tensed, lips pressed tightly together. Beads of sweat formed on her upper lip, and she glared at the nav terminal like she wanted to rip it from the deck.

For dwarves, the spatial and temporal changes in crossing into a Maw were uncomfortable. For the other

Fromryian races, the transition felt like knives running along the fibres of every muscle while a vice constricted the body's internal organs. Or so that was what he was told.

Luckily for them, the effect of the crossing was over as quickly as it came. If it wasn't for the hex display scaling the ship to the size of a dust mite, there would be no way to tell they were in a dimensional space hundreds of times larger than the rest of Formaria. Freyen took a gulp of air and wiped at her mouth.

"Matthias," Brazier said, "what are the scopes telling you?"

"I've got nothing but empty space for ten leagues. Looks like we're alone."

"Good – then you and Switch can work on that signature."

"You're the boss," he said. Brazier very much doubted he meant it.

"Just the job I wanted," Switch said, handing Brazier her crossbow and leaving the nav deck.

Over the next hour, Brazier went through the ship's logs. Part of his mind tethered into the hex network, the other part vaguely aware of Switch and Matthias discussing scalopractic chambers and core mechanics while running different protocols. Even if it didn't sound like listening to a conversation through a stone wall, none of it would make sense.

The logs, he found, were almost entirely restricted. Prisoner information required Navarch script clearance, and only with Freyen's help could he access the ship's history. Watching her bypass the hex protocols made him realise – not for the first time – how little he actually knew about the *Chalice*'s operations officer.

"You're in," her voice said in his head.

The script the ship threw up for him caused his mind to create visual representations – black and grey images the colour of a hex sculpt. At the same time as reading, he saw the *Solace of Iron* flying through tunnels. Then the prisoners in their cells, identification scripts providing names, a classification of their criminality, but the rest restricted behind a blurred wall. The reel jumped to nav reports; the navigator announcing unidentified signals; the single hull-mounted repeater at full sentience; reports its magazines were at seventy percent, then fifty, then thirty. The captain issuing orders to defend the ship; sending an open distress call they were under attack; providing their location; requesting aid. Unexpectedly, it split to a dwarf in the hold, handing out weapons to frantic crew members. Then the eviscerated gnome, alive in the script reel, kneeling in front of the access hatch, a crossbow held in his hands, a determined look in his young eyes.

Brazier's heart sped up. Somewhere outside of himself he could feel his teeth biting into his lower lip. A mix of hope and dread churned in his chest. He was about to see the things that had taken his brother's life.

But there was nothing. One minute the gnome knelt in the fuselage, then blankness. The script turned white and Brazier felt like he was floating in a fog. He pulled his hand from the well, feeling robbed.

"Has this been purged?" he asked Freyen after she removed her hand, as well.

"It feels like a hex purge," she said. "But if that was the case, a purge command would have been registered in the script."

"Then whatever attacked the ship was able to purge the logs?"

She shrugged, shaking her head apologetically.

"Only navigators have the ability to purge a hex network," Brazier said, almost repeating word for word his Navarch academy training.

"Well, it looks like something else has that

ability now, too. But whatever it is didn't do the best job. The script is unstable – as if parts are missing."

"As if whatever did it tried to purge more than they actually could?"

She nodded.

He ran a hand through his hair, staring into the well. The thought that these things could hide their tracks and leave no evidence of themselves caused a pang of despair. He wanted something to hate, something to direct his anger at.

"Are you okay?" Freyen said softly, concern in her eyes.

He nodded quickly. "Just thinking about how we're going to explain this to the Navarch with no evidence," he lied.

Her eyes narrowed ever so slightly, the creases at the corners giving away her scepticism. He was saved from any further explanation by Switch stomping onto the nav deck.

"That was a bitch, but I think we've managed to isolate the signature without effecting the core."

"So we'll be able to fly in dark?" Brazier asked.

"We should."

"Should?"

"We won't know until we try it," Matthias said, as if their lives didn't depend on it working. The casualness did not fill Brazier with confidence.

"Then we also prepare for what happens if it doesn't work. Can you make it look like our hex tethering is corrupted?"

"Yes," Matthias and Freyen said at the same time.

Brazier felt one of his eyebrows rise to his forehead. That was the second time Freyen's skills seemed to extend well beyond the remit of logistical operations.

"We'll do it after we cross the Gulf," she said, her face a mask of impassivity. "We might need it up until then."

"Speaking of," Matthias said, "we're about a league from the horizon wall. Gulf is four leagues after that. Now I know how I'd play this, but I'm guessing you want to talk it over first."

"Talk what over?" Brazier asked.

"If I extend my gyranic range, chance is another ship picks up our signal."

"If you don't, it's almost guaranteed something in that mad soup turns the *Solace* into lunch."

"Wait," Switch said, understanding dawning. "You want to fly blind?" Her jaw dropped with incredulity.

"The Hyrulian Gulf is a witch refuge, goblin ambush site, and crawler breeding ground rolled into one," Freyen added, "and you don't want to look where you're going?"

"And when a Navarch patrol detects us," Matthias said. "What then?"

Brazier turned over the situation in his mind, trying to come up with a solution while simultaneously trying to contain his frustration at the navigator's idiotic obstinacy.

"We just tell them exactly what we are," Freyen said. "If another ship asks, we're prison transport the *Solace of Iron*."

"And the first thing they'll ask for is the captain's identification script," Brazier said. Then, not sure if he needed to make it clearer, added: "Which died with the captain."

Freyen pushed the stray curl behind her ear, biting her lip. "I might be able to get it from the hex network."

They all stared at her; even Matthias turned his

head.

“Well, aren’t you full of surprises,” Switch said. “Care to tell us how you know how to do that?”

Freyen’s jaw tightened and her bat-like ears turned a light shade of rose. “Do you want me to get it or not?” she said.

“We do,” Brazier said.

“This better work,” Matthias said. “I’m not broadcasting myself without a guarantee. No matter our deal.”

Five minutes later, they exited through Klioxies’ west horizon wall. Freyen took a deep breath, tied her curls into a tight bun, and placed both hands into the command terminal’s hex wells. She spent the next thirty minutes with her eyes shut, lids fluttering intermittently, and mouthing instructions, or perhaps commands. Either way they were uninterpretable to Brazier.

“Did you know about this?” Switch asked, leaning against the other side of the nav terminal and watching Freyen.

“You mean did we ask about her hex-breaking skills before she came aboard the *Chalice*?”

Switch arched an eyebrow, lips pressing together, an overall withering look. “I mean did you find out about her background? Maybe some Navarch intel work among all the shipping and logistics?”

“Tee tended to be more concerned with a person’s abilities than where they’d come from.”

In fact, in every interview, his brother seemed to actively avoid asking about a person’s personal history, showing a level of professionalism Brazier always admired.

“Offering a blank slate. How generous.”

“And what would we have found out about you?” Brazier cut back, letting his gaze linger on her augmented arm, before holding her stare. Given he clearly knew very little about Freyen, he wasn't sure why he was defending her privacy so vehemently.

Switch's grin crawled up the sides of her face, revealing rows of pearly white teeth. "Nothing I haven't already told you."

Freyen's shaky exhalation drew his attention away from the enginator.

"It's done," she said. "If we get an identification request, you'll need to put it through to me."

"I hope you're right about this," Matthias said.

On the hex, the outside edge of the Gulf came into view like cliff edges rising from the sea.

Brazier placed his hand into the adjacent well. "Scope at two thirds."

The filaments dissipated then drew together, reforming the display: the Gulf wall the size of his forearm, the *Solace* and its triangular bow and segmented body roughly that of his little finger.

"Almost forgot how hideous this ship is," Switch said.

"Matthias, are you picking anything up?" Brazier asked.

"Nothing but the void."

"Let us know if that changes."

On the hex, the *Solace* crossed the Gulf wall, the black and silver shape floating above a scabrous landscape littered with growths. Then a flat section, a thin body of water cutting through the globular lumps.

Behind it rose swirling limbs, stems as thick as arborealis trunks, the rounded domes of mushroom caps three times the size of the prison transport. Scaled feelers formed tentacle-like pillars, and although the hex never showed the roof of a cavern or tunnel, Brazier knew they reached to its height.

Matthias weaved between it all, and despite the spatial anchor, in a ship this small Brazier's mind kept trying to counterbalance his weight as he watched the *Solace* pull port and starboard on the display.

His brain decoupled from its ancestral conditioning as the hex reformed, the filaments scattering outward and moulding to a smaller scale. Among the chaos of the Gulf, the *Solace* was almost imperceptible.

Then the hex changed again, the landscape undulating, peaks and troughs shrinking and reforming like the waves of a sea storm; it took a moment for Brazier to realise he was watching Matthias probe northwards, seeking farther into the Gulf.

"Thought we weren't trying to broadcast our presence?" Switch said.

When the navigator didn't answer, Brazier looked up. Matthias's neck muscles were working together, perspiration forming at the back of his shaven head, and he kept twitching to the right like he wanted to scratch his ear. Then the rolling sculpt stopped, the display almost indistinguishable from previous regions, except in parts filaments floated in the air forming arbitrary shapes, drifting listlessly. Although most couldn't hold their form, Brazier made out the unmistakable shapes of gyre ships. Six in total, forming a flotilla of what looked like spire-class destroyers.

"How far away?" Brazier asked.

"Three and a half leagues." The navigator's gravelly voice was strained with the effort of projecting his mind.

"Have they seen us?"

"Looks like they're a little too preoccupied, luckily for us."

Brazier watched the ships spit needle-like projectiles into the soup but at what, he couldn't say; the hex was too blurred to make them out.

"What are they engaged with?"

Matthias shook his head. "Too far," was all he could manage.

"This has to be surface interference," Freyen said. "Navarch wouldn't send six destroyers into the Gulf."

As if to prove the point, one of the ships crumbled into nothing, only to reform an inch away, the magical currents spilling down from the Yeggardanian surface either obscuring or imitating the gyranic signal. At this range, it would be impossible for any navigator to know for certain whether what they were seeing was real or a hallucination.

"I'm not counting on it," Matthias said, now growling words rather than speaking. "I'm pulling us south. And make sure you're ready with that identification script. Ship like this isn't outrunning even one of theirs."

"Can we afford that?" Brazier asked.

"We'll have to. Like I said, I'm not going back to a cell."

"I'll be in the engines," Switch said. "See if I can limit the burn this detour is going to cost."

Like wind blowing a sand dune, the hex flattened. Matthias let out a deep breath and it reformed into a rolling sculpt of the *Solace* and its immediate vicinity.

Freyen's hand appeared on Brazier's upper arm. "I'm going to see if there's any mining cable in the hold. For the crew – if this is going to be a rough landing."

Brazier gave her what he hoped was an encouraging smile, then let his eyes wander over the display. After a pause, he asked Matthias: "Any point in asking you what you did to get locked up?"

"Going to make you feel better about letting me go if I feed you some story about wrong place, wrong time?"

At least he's honest about it.

"You're right – don't bother."

There was another pause, the only sound the thrum of the ship under his feet and Matthias's soft breathing.

"For what it's worth, what your brother did –"

Brazier cut in swiftly. "You do not need to go there." Something about a criminal talking about Torquen Veranquis sparked Brazier's anger.

"Every captain's got that responsibility," the navigator continued, anyway. "Not many who'd actually do it."

The hex well nearest Brazier vibrated to the sound of Switch's voice, forcing him to swallow what was about to be a bitter retort.

"Think I've bought us some time in the air," she said, "but it's not much. We'll make it to Theselan's cavern complex but then we're empty."

"Not going to be a problem," the navigator said.

On the hex, their exit from the Gulf looked like a bird leaving a forest's canopies to soar through the gulley of a mountain range. They entered Formaria's tunnel system, a winding route with three right-angled turns before straightening into a cavern shaped like an upside-down helmet. The empty space wrapped around a single bulwark of rock, within which spire Theselan was built.

Then the hex crumbled, leaving nothing but a smooth surface.

"Going to need the power," Matthias said.

Without the visual display, Brazier felt strangely blind.

"And if we need to send a distress beacon?"

"I'll reengage the hex half a league from the spire."

The gyre channels lighting up the nav deck

dimmed to cobalt blue, pockets of shadow forming in the corners, the *Solace's* thrum turning to a purr.

"You might want to tell everyone to hold on to something," Matthias said. "Then I'm shutting down internal tethering."

"Thanks for the warning."

Switch and Freyen came up on either side of him as he sunk his hand into a well.

"Things are going to get pretty rough pretty quick."

"We hear you, boss," Dalfin replied.

He dropped the connection and the hex turned unnaturally still, the silver among the black dulling to a white-grey.

"Five minutes," Matthias said.

Around them, the ship was as quite as if it was docked. So quiet, Brazier imagined he could hear the silence of the tunnels, even feel the blackness closing in without the blistering blue gyre light flooding the bronzite walls.

Beneath his feet, he felt the ship turn, the spatial anchor disengaged, presumably to conserve ice. He felt it turn twice more, then Matthias said: "Entering the spire's cavern space."

Brazier's heart sped up, anxiety building behind his rib cage, waiting to see if Theselan picked up the ship's signature.

"No identification requests," the navigator said. "Looks like we're flying dark."

In front of Brazier, the hex display came to life, the spire rising out of the well like a hand reaching out from the void.

Shaped like an uncut diamond, the flat lines of the Formarian's construction combined with the jagged rock faces. Protruding out around its middle was the eastern hangar bay, an open mouth wide enough for four spire-class gyre stars to berth.

Brazier leaned in, squinting at the sculpt. Theselan, one of the Navarch's primary resupply installations, and its hangar bay was empty.

"Cutting thrust now," Matthias said, and the nav deck grew dark, the channels dying to a near black lapis lazuli. Beneath his feet, the feeling of weightlessness was similar to crossing a horizon wall. On the hex display, the *Solace* arced in a leisurely drift and Brazier gripped the sides of the terminal, watching them fall through the void toward the gaping mouth. He didn't need to see Freyen and Switch to know they were as tense as him.

On the display, the space between the *Solace* and the spire grew smaller and smaller. They were a few inches away, then two, then one, then the ship disappeared, the grey-black insect-like shape merging with the spire. There was a moment of calm, in which Brazier wondered why they were still falling through the air, then it happened.

A deafening thud of solid bronzite meeting the marble hardness of the hanger bay and he was thrown forward against the command terminal, his beard pressed into the hex as both hands lost their grip. A dull screech erupted beneath them, turning to a thunderous metallic roar, like claws scraping along polished rock. He scrambled to find a hold on the terminal's edges but was thrown to the left before he could find a grip.

Instead of flying into Freyen, however, he felt something grasp his gambeson, holding him in place. He peered round to see Switch, her augmented arm locked onto the command terminal, the other griping his shoulder. Brazier was about to offer his thanks when there was a loud crash, the entire nav deck shook, and they were both thrown into the air. At the same time as landing painfully on his shoulder, he felt something angular and hard against his temple, then blackness.

How long the blackness lasted he couldn't tell, but somewhere in the distance, someone was calling his name.

"Zee."

It sounded like someone trying to talk to him while underwater.

"Zee," it said again, this time with more clarity but still like they were in an ocean.

"Captain!" someone else's voice said, much louder; he was no longer underwater. He opened his eyes, vision blurred, the face above him rocking back and forth.

"He's coming around," a female voice said.

The face stopped swaying, and he realised he recognised it.

Another face appeared in his vision. Dark hair, a wide, stern mouth, eyes black as jet.

"What in the black abyss happened?" he said, or maybe slurred.

He pushed himself to sitting, then thought about lying down again when a dizzy pounding blossomed somewhere in his skull.

"No you don't," Freyen said, from somewhere next to him and he could feel her arm keeping him upright.

"Sorry, Zee," Switch said. "I tried to grab you and, err . . . well, I think I must have punched you instead."

"Don't worry about it," Brazier said, running his fingers gently along the side of his head, trying to find where exactly he'd been punched. He found a very pronounced lump just past his temple.

"Axelock, Dalfin?" he managed to ask.

"We're good, boss," Axelock said, from behind him. "Well, mostly."

Brazier turned. Axelock was leaning against the nav deck wall. Dalfin was next to him, a hand to his nose, blood streaming down his gambeson. He winked at Brazier, grinning from ear to ear.

"Wad fun," he said, thickly.

"Matthias?" Brazier asked.

"Gone," Freyen said.

Brazier nodded, then regretted it.

"Alright, let's go. No weapons, though; we don't need to give them any more reason to think we're attacking the spire."

He tried pushing himself to his feet, nearly toppled sideways before Switch and Axelock put an arm under each shoulder.

"I'm fine," he lied.

"You sure you don't want to take a second?" Axelock asked.

"We don't want them to have to force their way in here. Ugly mistakes happen that way."

He let Axelock and Switch guide him out of the nav deck where a bright white light flooded the fuselage, making Brazier's headache feel like he was being bludgeoned between the eyes.

Freyen peered out into the bay, then stepped onto the lip of the hatch. Brazier watched her reach for the thruster arm before she dropped out of his view. Dalfin went next, simply dropping off the edge of the ship. Brazier heard him grunt as he landed. Axelock removed his arm from under Brazier's, then followed – another grunt as he landed.

Switch helped him to the hatch, and Brazier looked down at how far he would need to fall.

"Try and slide down the edge," Axelock called up at him.

"We'll catch dew," Dalfin said through a mouth of blood.

Brazier unceremoniously plonked himself on the hatch's lip, the backs of his calves against the hull. He swallowed hard, trying not to think about what the impact would do to his headache, then pushed himself over the edge.

Axelock caught him before he hit the floor, grunting as they collided, arms wrapping around his middle. He let Brazier try and stand on his own, arms holding him at his sides, like he was holding an infant – for all the stability Brazier felt, he may as well have been.

"C'mon," he said, guiding Brazier from beneath the ship. "Out the way of Switch."

Brazier wobbled forward, one arm on Axelock's shoulder, the other shielding his eyes from the spire's brightness. Behind him, a thud and a grunt as Switch landed on the bay.

"Here's our welcome party," Freyen said.

Brazier removed his hand form his eyes. Soldiers, maybe fourteen in total, spears and shields in hand, chain mail under their surcoats that whipped around their knees as they ran across the smooth slabs. All wore the quartered white and green of house Angelaux.

To their left, Brazier heard doors shift apart and four more soldiers ran onto the bay. White surcoats quartered by a red cross, each knight carried a long blade of naked steel.

Both parties came upon them at the same time, spears levelled and swords at guard.

"My name is Brazier Veranquis, former First Officer of gyre miner the *Chalice of Amaranth*," he said, trying to focus on the soldier directly in front of him to stop his vision from swimming. "We are the last remaining crew following an attack by unknown hostiles."

From among the Angelaux unit, a man with a dark ponytail and a drawn face stepped forward.

"While that might be true, you failed to provide an identification script upon request."

Brazier opened his mouth to explain, but the man held up a hand, cutting him off.

"You're now in the custody of spire Theselan's praefector. You will follow us to the brig." *And without trouble,* his tone seemed to say.

Freyen, Dalfin, Axelock, and Switch all looked at him, waiting for him to tell them what to do. He nodded for them to follow the soldiers.

"The brig, really?" Switch said under her breath as they made their way to the main concourse, loosely circled by their guard.

"At least they didn't blow us out of the sky," Brazier said, now focusing on the spire's tiles. Looking straight ahead, he found, caused his head to spin. "This way we may get a chance to explain ourselves."

"Seems awfuddy quite," Dalfin said, trying – and failing – to keep his voice low.

"You don't need to speak," the ponytailed soldier said.

"If they separate us," Freyen whispered quickly, "what do we say about Matthias?"

Brazier felt a tiny wave of affection for her, and guilt at not anticipating they would all need to agree on a story.

"The truth. We had no option but to let him fly the ship."

"And escape?"

"Not our fault he left before the detachment got here."

"I said, no talking!" the soldier shouted, stepping over to them.

Brazier patted the air with the hand that wasn't

on Axelock's shoulder. "We got it."

#

The brig was only just wider than the corridor outside it: a blue channel running down the ceiling, eight offshoots, four on either side, flowing into each of the cells. Mercifully, there was little need to expend ice on a jail the spire would rarely use, and so the light was a soft, almost regal blue. While Brazier's head still pounded, it meant he was no longer forced to endure waves of dizzying nausea induced by the rest of the spire's near white light.

The soldiers directed them into the cells, one a piece. Once inside, bars the colour of black obsidian and as thick as Brazier's arms slid into place from right to left. Most of the unit left, leaving two guards stood to attention on either side of the door. They stared ahead, eyes fixed on the opposite wall, refusing to look at the prisoners.

A moment later, the brig door shunted open and a man, tall and lean with broad angular shoulders, stepped into the room. He wore the red-quartered surcoat of the Knights Redcrosse, the Laurea, three red-corded braids tied loosely from the back of his shoulder to the front, giving him away as the praefector. He looked at each of them in turn, his thin lips, hidden among a black beard speckled with grey, pursed and turned down at the corners. They matched the look in his eyes, which were dark and scrutinising.

"One of you want to explain how a gyre ship crashed into my hangar bay without being detected?"

"We were forced to turn off its signature," Brazier said, "which we could only do because the core was previously tampered with."

The praefector's mouth parted, the upper lip

curling in anger. Apparently, honesty was not the best course of action.

"I've got multiple reports of hostiles attacking ships all over the southeast quadrant. The only thing their captains can tell me is they are fighting creatures with unidentifiable gyranic signals. And now you five turn up, flying a ship with an unidentified gyre signature. I swear by the abyss that one of you is going to tell me what is going on." He pointed at Freyen. "Take her."

One of the soldiers sunk his hand into the hex terminal next to him, and Freyen's cell opened.

"Hey!" Brazier shouted, pounding on the bars. "We can tell you everything right now!"

"Hey, asshole, I'm the real talkative type," Switch said, looping her metal augment through the bars. "Why don't you take me, too?"

But the praefector ignored them, following Freyen and the guard out of the room.

"Black abyss," Brazier swore, pounding the bars again, then was forced to sit down, the nausea returning.

Dalfin pressed himself up against the bars of his cell. "You want 'o call an abomander down 'ere," he said to the soldier, gesturing at his nose, which was now a mess of clotting blood.

"All war casters have been assigned to ships," the soldier said.

Brazier pushed himself to the cell bars, not trusting himself to stand quite yet. "Navarch doctrine mandates every spire maintains at least one war caster."

The soldier glanced at him quickly, a split second of doubt or even fear before staring straight ahead again.

"You don't leave a spire magically undefended," Switch said, directing the comment at him, even though he couldn't see her.

"Unless there's a greater need in the void,"

Brazier replied, pulling himself very delicately to his feet, "which there usually isn't."

In the corner of the room, the hex terminal gave a single vibration, then reverberated to the sound of a dwarven voice: "Battle stations, battle stations! Spire Theselan is under attack. Hostile forces sighted east hangar bay. All military personnel to report to their crews and regiments. Prepare to defend the spire."

The prison's door slid apart and Freyen was pushed back into the room. Behind, the Angelaux soldier's jaw was tight, his face rigid with intensity – the look of someone who knew they were about to go into a fight.

"What's going on?" Brazier called to the soldier.

He pressed his hand into the hex well and Freyen's cell bars slid open.

"East hangar bay is under attack. You are to remain here until it's over."

"We can help," Brazier said firmly. "Let us out and we can fight."

He gave his head a single shake. "Praefector's orders."

The soldier placed a hand on Freyen's shoulder, guiding her back to her cell. But before they could pass Brazier, a bronze arm darted out from the cell opposite, the fingers wrapping tight around the soldier's neck.

The man gave a choked yell, grabbing at the augment, but Switch yanked hard, pulling him against the bars and placing him in a choke hold. Freyen dashed over, pulling the sword from its scabbard before he could get a hand on it. With the other hand, she felt around his waist and pulled a knife from a hip sheath.

Brazier, his head pressed to the bars, could see the man's face turning blotchy red, then light purple, before darkening to a more worrying shade.

"Switch, you can let him go!"

The soldier slid down the bars, legs sprawled, head slumped to one side, his eyes barely open. Brazier saw two pink-white fingers appear under his jaw.

"He'll be fine," Switch said.

Freyen, her hand in the terminal's well, looked deep in concentration, a single curl dangling over her eyes. Then the bars of his cell pulled to the right. Opposite, the bars on Dalfin's did the same. As one, they all stepped from their confinements.

"Remind me never to fuck with you," Axelock said, staring down at the soldier now splayed half in, half out of Switch's cell.

"Where's the praefector?" Brazier asked.

"East hangar bay. He left me and headed straight there."

"Without sending a direct message to the Ecclessius? He hasn't reported the attack?"

Freyen shook her head. "If he did, he did it after he left me," she said.

Brazier swallowed his queasiness, trying to think through his headache.

"Get to the west hangar bay, find a ship. Wait for me there."

"And where in the murky black abyss are you going?" Switch said. "For a tour of the spire?"

"Yeah, fuck that, boss," Dalfin added. "We stick together."

"This spire is about to be overrun, and from here it's a straight line to Thendergaarden and Formaria proper. The Ecclessius needs to be warned. I'll send an epistolar message, then meet you at the hangar bay."

"You know how to do that?" Freyen asked.

"Torquen told me how."

Switch looked both surprised and impressed. Freyen gave him a hard look before placing her hand back into the well. He watched her mouth the words *west hangar bay* and *epistolar*, her eyelids fluttering, then she removed her hand.

"Okay, I know how to get there." She turned to Brazier: "Epistolar is eight levels above us. Lift at the end of the corridor can take you there."

"One of us should go with you," Axelock said.

"He's right," Freyen added.

Brazier would prefer to know his crew were all together, watching each other's backs, but he didn't think they would accept that.

"Okay, Axelock, you're with me."

"I'm gowin' wid you, too," Dalfin said, trying to sound determined, but sounding slightly ridiculous with the broken nose.

"You, too, Dalfin," Brazier said, and the dwarf smiled. "Okay, let's move."

Freyen handed him the sword, her eyes locking onto his with a quiet intensity. "We'll be waiting."

"I'm counting on it," he said, not sure how to interpret the look.

They piled out of the brig, Switch and Freyen going left; Axelock, Dalfin, and him right, then to the end of the corridor.

In the lift, as its doors closed on them, a hot dread spread from the pit of his stomach as he watched the others dash down a flight of steps and out of sight.

It was the feeling he may never see them again.

NINE
LYANDER

Lyander looked out from man-made ruins unmarked on any map, into a tunnel that shouldn't exist, and upon an army that should be hiding in Grindlepeake.

In the tunnel they overlooked from the ruins, connected to Grindlepeake by a secret passage running beneath the bay and north into Formaria, Eluthienn had hidden his army. Row upon row of blue tents. Every twenty feet or so a blue standard, its white phoenix hidden beneath the crumples. Moving between them were soldiers in blue surcoats, their phoenixes emblazoned on their chests. Amidst the camp were boulders of unrefined ice, blazing with white-blue gyre light. Everywhere was blue and white, just different qualities.

Farther into the tunnel and floating over the edge of the camp, like some alien god sheltering its adopted young, was a gyre ship. Two serpentine bodies formed a streamline hull, contrasting with the orbed midship, and behind three large thrusters, sleek and powerful. The *Gloried Storm*, the Sorel Tan's illegally commandeered cauldron-class cruiser was a ship Lyander knew by reputation alone, and just like its captain, Lyander's orders were to detain the ship on sight. How he would be expected to do that given the circumstances, he didn't know. But he knew he was going to enjoy watching the Ecclessiarchal ministers' faces when he told them it was the Sorel Tan who'd delivered Eluthienn to their door.

"Enchanting, isn't she?" Isdria said, coming up beside him, ruining his good mood. From his brief interaction with the elf, Lyander found him smug, conceited, and self-important. And that was without taking into account the outright sabotage of Formaria's ability to survive.

"Another hunk of bronzite," Lyander said. "Like any other gyre ship."

"Oh, come now, Lyander. We both know she isn't just any other gyre ship."

Out of the corner of his eye, Lyander could see the elf's well-practiced sneer.

"I wonder what the Ecclessius will say when you tell them you had the *Gloried Storm* and its captain within your grasp?"

"I'm a political officer. Detaining terrorists with inflated egos isn't my job."

The elf laughed – a haughty, mirthless sound.

"Of course. Kalbrayeth Lyander, First Champion of the Knights Redcrosse, then an exorcist, and now a diplomat. And before that, a Celmyrian orphan, brought to Formaria by Ecclessiarchal missionaries. You are enjoying a varied life."

Lyander turned to the elf in surprise. There were perhaps four people who knew his past before Formaria, all of them senior officials in the Ecclessius. "I make of a point of knowing potential allies," Isdria said.

Lyander felt his lip curl in anger. "What would give you the idea we could be allies?"

"In this world, the enemy of our enemies so often become our friends."

"And you think I'd join a pack of self-righteous fanatics hell bent on opening the gyre gates and destroying Formaria because I'm no longer First Champion?"

"In the Sorel Tan, we don't shame or abandon the best of us."

Lyander couldn't decide whether he wanted to laugh at the invitation or punch the elf between his oiled lips for even offering it to him.

"Come, Isdria," Eluthienn said, clapping a hand on his shoulder. The prince wore a hooded black cloak over boiled leathers, exchanging his Ravinican military blues for something less conspicuous. "Lyander is far too honourable to turn his back on Formaria, even if it has turned its back on him."

"There is little honour in servitude to a dying regime," Isdria said.

"There's even less in killing its people to further your own ends," Lyander bit back.

"The Ecclessius would have us cowering in the dark for the rest of eternity. Our ends would see the war over and restore the Fromryr as the leaders of this world."

"With you at its head, no doubt?" Gabriel said, standing behind them, his arms crossed.

"I'll die fighting this cause."

"How poetic." Gabriel held a hand over his heart. "I might weep."

"Truly, what would a witch-hunter know about that which is greater than himself when all your kind does is slink around in the dark, hunting shadows between the borders of this world and the next?"

"Friends, friends," Eluthienn said, putting himself in between Isdria and Gabriel, who both looked ready to draw swords. "We are not enemies."

"We're not exactly friends, either," Lyander said, looking pointedly at Isdria as he said it.

"Then let us rectify that mistake," Eluthienn said, gesturing at the path down into the encampment.

Giving them each a dark look, Isdria marched off down it. Shrugging, Gabriel followed, with Lyander and Eluthienn in tow.

"For some time now, I have wanted to meet the great Kalbrayeth Lyander," Eluthienn said, leaning into Lyander as he said it.

Based on every interaction with the prince so far, Lyander assumed this was another game, another play, so Lyander believed not one word of what he was saying, or what he was about to say. "I don't think you had a clue who I was until one of your men told you I was at your door."

Eluthienn gave a melodic laugh.

"You think we haven't heard the tale of the only First Champion in Formaria's history not to die at his post?" The prince cocked an eyebrow at him. "The First Champion stripped of his title for denying a prince so that he may save his fellow soldiers?" Eluthienn asked.

Lyander almost stumbled. "How do you know that?" he said quickly. The Ecclessius, cowing to the Rosantz family influence, buried the truth of Lucretia's fall. Few people knew what really happened.

"I know you chose what was in your heart above mindless obedience to the whims of lesser men. You and I are not so different in this, Lyander."

Great. Another mad fanatic who thinks we can be friends. He was saved from declining an outright invitation to the prince's cause as they entered the camp.

Past the tents were fire pits surrounded by soldiers cooking or cleaning, weapon racks, and even a smithy at work on a turning wheel. The greetings of "My Prince," "Your Highness," from every man or women they passed, or calls of "Hail Ravinica!" from somewhere far off in the camp. Eluthienn answered them all with a smile, the clasp of a hand, a hug and a pat on the back. Well-loved and well-ordered, Lyander noticed. If this army was demoralised from its plight, its officers kept a firm hand on it. Or perhaps these soldiers were true believers, sold on the notion of removing Fiondagaard's so-called *black hand* from Ravinica.

It was so easy, Lyander thought bitterly, *to blindly sell oneself to a cause.*

"They know where you're headed, and why?" he asked as they neared the camp's end.

"They know," Eluthienn said.

"And none of them argued for accompanying you?"

"Many tried. But they have already risked everything for me," Eluthienn said. "I would not ask them to risk more."

Above them now was the *Gloried Storm*'s twin hull, magical currents running through it, creating a gentle buzz and warming the air beneath the ship. An access ramp, dropped to the floor, poured light into the tunnel. They headed toward it.

"Tell me, Lyander, all the models of gyre ships I have seen, have extensions . . ." He seemed to search for the right description. "They are propelled through the air by gyre light external to the ship."

"Thrusters," Lyander said.

"This ship doesn't have them?"

"Capital ships. Anything larger than a spire-class cruiser has enough gyre ice running inside the ship to keep it afloat. They're faster, they burn less power, and it's harder to target with magical barrages if the ice is housed behind a bronzite hull. Nightmare to manoeuvre, though, as you're about to find out."

In the ship, elves in various Sorel Tan uniform stood to attention as Isdria passed, much in the same way they would for the captain of a Navarch vessel. Other than its current crew, Lyander noted, there was little to tell it wasn't a Fromryian ship.

On the nav deck, a large bronzite console containing three hex wells and one larger command display sat behind a navigation pit. The navigator, pale ear tips peeking through lank black hair falling to his lower back, was naked from the waist up and kneeling in what looked like prayer. That picture, too, was just like every other gyre ship in the Fromryian fleet.

To either side of the command terminal, on raised platforms, were two more terminals – a gunnery and tactical officer stationed behind each. Even for Lyander, who found it nigh on impossible to tell an elf's age, thought they looked young.

The two elves behind the command terminal, however, were certainly not. The silver-tongued sorcerer, Sadrosil, stood whispering into the other's ear. Smooth grey hair flowed past his shoulders, an angular face surrounded green eyes, sharp with the certainty of someone half his age, and a mouth used to its commands being obeyed. He leant on a walking stick, the twisted wood of an arborealis, and gave Lyander, Gabriel, and Eluthienn a single glance, revealing absolutely nothing of his thoughts.

"An alliance with the Fromryr, is it, Isdria? Who would have thought?" the old elf said.

"In the making, Traegor."

"And our Ravinican prince is the *maker*, I hear?"

"A bargain will be struck," Eluthienn said. "One

they cannot refuse, and one which is most favourable to the Sorel Tan."

"And to secure this bargain, I presume we're taking you to Thendergaarden. Into the very hands of the Ecclessius?"

"To Theselan," Isdria answered, "where our Fromryian mediators will send word of the prince's arrival via its epistolar."

"Because sending such a message via the *Storm*'s epistolar would implicate us as allies of the prince sooner than the prince would like Formaria to find out?"

"Precisely," Eluthienn said, delivering a cold smile to the elf.

"Not quite the budding alliance just yet, then?"

"Which is why," Isdria said, "we will be dropping them outside of Theselan. They'll make their own way from there."

Lyander, assuming the elf meant a different spire, said: "Theselan sits on a rock island in the middle of a cavern. What do you expect us to do, jump from one side to the other?"

"I expect you to walk," Isdria said, coolly, "from the rock bridge connecting to the island."

"There is no rock bridge," Lyander said.

The elf gave his self-satisfied smirk and said: "Isn't there?" Then to his navigator: "Cerulea, take us out, please."

On the hex, the *Gloried Storm* rose steadily higher in the tunnel, then slipped into the void.

#

"Alignment complete."

The navigator's voice was a ghostly whisper in the near aquatic gloom of the powered-down nav deck.

Running at a tenth sprawl under diminished output made the ship as good as invisible next to the wall of ice it was lining up against. To distinguish the *Storm* from the deposit, a navigator would need to come within half a league – an unlikely occurrence, given the number of secondary and tertiary tunnels between their location and any main transit route.

"Our local space?" Isdria said.

The navigator's head twitched, the fingers of his right hand splayed out as if he was stretching them.

"Quiet. Even the spire is quiet."

"How fortunate for us," Traegor said.

Lyander scratched an itch just beneath his stitching, accidentally clipped said stitching, forcing him to speak through gritted teeth. "How far out are we?"

"Two leagues," Isdria said. "A shuttle will take you within half of that."

"And then?"

"There's a tunnel."

The elf pointed to the cavern wall surrounding Theselan. To Lyander, the slice of rock face his finger hovered in front of looked like all the rest.

"It exits here, where a bridge takes you to the base of Theselan. There, you'll find a stairs cut into the rock. It's a climb."

"Why isn't this showing on the hex?"

Isdria shook his head. "We've never discovered the source of its concealment."

"Nor will we," Traegor said, "given that we can never use it again."

"A worthy sacrifice for something much greater," Isdria replied.

"Captain," the ship's tactical officer said. "Shuttle's ready."

Isdria held Traegor's gaze for a moment longer, then turned to them: "Follow me."

Through the ship and then onto the hangar bay, every elf they passed stood to attention and saluted their captain, but their eyes were all for the three humans. *Do they hope this gambit works? Or did they, like Traegor, see the folly in a foreign prince trying to convince Formaria and the Sorel Tan to join in common cause?*

The shuttle, like most in Formaria, was an insect-like craft, its rounded front end tapering toward the rear with a carapace-like hull and gyre thrusters protruding from four extensions. Its access hatch, a curved door taking up one side of the shuttle and in between two of the thrusters, lifted open.

Isdria stopped before it. He held out an arm for Eluthienn, which the prince took.

"Success in your mission, brother. We'll await you in Grindlepeake."

"You won't be waiting long," Eluthienn said, releasing the elf and stepping onto the shuttle.

Isdria turned to Lyander: "Think on what I said, exorcist."

Without waiting for a reply, the elf gave Gabriel a brief once-over, then marched off across his hanger bay.

"Not even a kiss goodbye," the witch-hunter said. "I'm positively wounded."

Lyander couldn't help but smile, and they both climbed on board.

The copilot, an elf with near silver blonde hair cropped to her neckline, spun a locking wheel on the shuttle's inner wall, and the access hatch fell shut.

The pilot, standing between two waist-high terminals, placed his hands in either hex well when he saw it close. Lyander felt the shuttle lift into the air before its nose dipped and they were propelled forward. A clanging echo told him the *Storm*'s hanger doors were opening, and he felt the shuttle speed up as it entered the void.

Stood in silence, they gripped the ceiling handholds, their weight shifting into a turn as the ship began to bank starboard. It slowed before drawing to a complete stop, and the elf spun the locking wheel. The hatch opened onto a wide landing of black rock, behind which the gyre thrusters' light flooded a cave mouth and the passage behind.

The elf handed each of them a gyre torch, and they stepped off the ship and onto the landing. A loud click as the hatch closed and the shuttle pulled off. Lyander watched as it became little more than four fiery blue discs flying through the air before being swallowed by the black.

He clicked on his torch. Gabriel and Eluthienn did the same, and followed him into the tunnel.

It didn't take long for Lyander – having clipped his shoulders for a third time – to decide the tunnel might be suitable for an elf but it wasn't for him. In places, the space was so tight his scabbard kept scraping along the wall, forcing him to hold the torch awkwardly in his wounded hand while using the other to probe the rock. Both Gabriel and Eluthienn, who were leaner than him by far, seemed to have little problem making it through unscathed. *Or perhaps they're watching me take the hits and know where to avoid.*

Like its entrance, the tunnel exited onto another outcropping. Lyander edged onto it, carefully scanning to find where the rock met empty space. Above them, Theselan was like a cluster of stars in a sky so black Lyander found it suffocating to look at.

He felt the other two step up close behind him.

"The bridge?" Gabriel asked.

Lyander shone his torch ahead of him, the blue landing on a rough surface extending outward. Gabriel and Eluthienn joined theirs and lit up a snaking pathway large enough for two men abreast, climbing through the void like an act of defiance that Lyander knew could only be a feat of Formarian innovation.

"We go slowly," Lyander said.

"No arguments here," Gabriel said.

"You'll be tempted to look up," Lyander said to Eluthienn. "To use the spire as a measure of how far there is left. Do not do that. Not even once."

Eluthienn nodded, and Lyander, holding the torch in his good hand, stepped forward. One foot in front of the other, deliberately and delicately, exactly as if one wrong step could mean his certain death. He heard the others close behind, their own footsteps little more than a shuffle, their torch beams glued to the bridge floor.

The pain in Lyander's hand very quickly reared its head as the intensity with which he was concentrating tensed his entire body. Although, he soon welcomed the growing ache, constantly reminding himself it was preferable to falling off the edge.

He couldn't say for how long they were walking or how far they were along the path. Time seemed to slow, the only evidence of it progressing at all was the perspiration forming at his temples, then his lower back, then under his arms.

He was so deep in concentration – so focused on left foot, right foot – he walked straight into the rock wall ahead of him.

"Black abyss!" he swore as, involuntarily, he reached out his wounded hand to steady himself, and smacked it against the rock.

He felt Eluthienn's hand on his shoulder, stopping him from toppling backward. "Would be a shame to fall now we've made it this far," the prince said.

"Thanks," he said over his shoulder.

Lyander scanned around him, trying as best he could to get his bearings. As it turned out, there was little risk of him falling. The landing was four times the size of its opposite outside the cave exit.

Eluthienn walked up to its edge. "How far down do the tunnels go?" he asked.

"You'd fall for days before you hit anything," Lyander said shakily, checking his hand. It hurt so much he couldn't stop it from trembling. "Weeks in some parts."

"But you'd go insane well before that," Gabriel added. "The mind can't take falling through the black for that long." Then: "Over here."

Lyander looked in the direction the witch-hunter was aiming his torch. Steps rose around the foundation's base. To his relief, they were wide and cut deep into the rock face.

Gabriel climbed, and they followed.

No longer distracted by the need for unwavering concentration, Lyander's wound was free to abuse him every step he took.

"It's true, then, that Formaria's depths match its circumference across the earth?" Eluthienn asked.

"Formaria's boundary extends from Etherlain, north up to the gates of Nexoria, and as far east as the Reach and the Pelothrian mountains," Lyander replied, hearing the strain in his voice as he bit back the pain. "But its tunnels are far, far deeper." Just for something to think about other than his hand, he continued: "Commissioned explorers still find new substructures to this day."

"What do they find?"

"Empty installations, mostly. But very rarely, they'll find a cache."

"A cache?"

"Formarian stockpiles. Some large enough to

contain fleets of ships or whole Constructii regiments. Others so small, they contain only a single fulcrum."

"All of which," Gabriel said, "the Ecclessius would have us believe the Formarians left behind on purpose for the Fromryr to discover and use in its holy wars."

"And is that not so?" Eluthienn asked.

"If you were the Formarians," Gabriel asked, "why would you bury your armies and the fleets to carry them?"

"In case one day, I needed them," Lyander answered for the prince.

Gabriel turned and gave him what he thought might be the witch-hunter's first genuine smile.

"The wealth of this world is vast," Eluthienn said, and something in his tone almost made Lyander turn around to look at him. *Was that envy or greed? Or both, perhaps?*

Gabriel must have heard it, too, for he said: "A wealth owned and controlled by the Ecclessius and the royal houses. And not something they've ever shared, even with their allies."

"They've never had a reason to," Eluthienn said, and Lyander thought the prince's voice was filled with far too much self-assurance.

They climbed in silence the rest of the way, their torches providing the only light, until they neared the spire's lower levels, and their white light shone into the void like the sun bringing the dawn. The stairs levelled out onto another wide landing featuring a single doorway of Formarian design, built into the rock, a hex terminal placed next to it.

Lyander walked over to it, placing his good hand in the filaments, in his mind opening the door. With a torturous groan, like a sleeping beast waking from hibernation, it pulled to the side.

"Guess that hasn't been used in a while," Gabriel said.

The witch-hunter peered into the open doorway and the hewn steps, also of Formarian construction, leading into the spire.

"So what's the plan? We just wonder into Theselan and hope no one notices we came through a secret doorway."

"Pretty much," Lyander said, pushing past him.

The witch-hunter's face was a canvas of disapproval.

The steps, unlit but reflecting the light outside on their smooth surfaces, took them to an octagonal lift, outside of which was another terminal. Lyander requested the lift take them to the epistolar, and in his mind he was shown a route to one of the western concourses, followed by another lift to the epistolar.

"Keep your hood up," he said to Eluthienn. "Theselan is on a major transit route and we need to go via one of its primary levels."

Eluthienn nodded and pulled his cloak tight about himself, then the lift rose into the spire. Purple-grey surfaces danced in front of their eyes, a soft whirring as their speed increased, then diminished as they slowed. Weight returned beneath their feet and the lift's doors parted.

Onto chaos:

Infantry in the quartered white and green of house Angelaux, spear tips glinting as they ran in loosely packed units. Naval crew members in their military blue doublets, some strapping on cuirasses, tightening sword belts to their waists, others carrying leather magazine packs on either shoulder. Among them, the coloured gambesons of mining crews and the robed priests of the Ecclessius, their gowns billowing behind them.

Above the din, officers and sergeants shouted

for their crews, pulling soldiers into formations, directing units to different parts of the spire.

Then, from the hex terminal just outside the lift, as if giving a voice to the frenzied picture in front of them, a dwarf spoke, its words echoing on the concourse's other terminals: "Battle stations, battle stations! Theselan is under attack. Hostile forces sighted east hangar bay. All military personnel to report to their crews and regiments. Prepare to defend the spire!"

"We make for the epistolar as planned," Lyander said. "Then we find a ship."

He dived onto the concourse, the others on his heels.

"Theselan is almost an inner quadrant spire," Gabriel said as they ran. "What would be stupid enough to attack here?"

"Mirrovinjin, if they came this far south."

"There's a Maw and the Hyrulian Gulf in between them and here."

Lyander slowed to let a unit of Knights Redcrosse march across their path, mail clinking under their surcoats, each one carrying a flat-topped great helm under their arm, their sergeant in front, face stern, staring straight ahead.

"Right now, that's not our problem," Lyander said.

Reaching the opposite side of the concourse, Lyander called for a lift to take them to the epistolar. When one finally arrived, they piled into it, the doors closing on the still-manic concourse.

"How does defending a spire work?" Eluthienn asked. "Tactically, I mean."

"Spire command directs units to where they're needed," Lyander said. "They can control lifts and doors, locking attackers in corridors or on different levels. A good praefector can look at a battle over the hex and know which units need reinforcing before even they themselves do, can predict enemy routes of attack, and knows exactly where to counter."

"Sounds impossible to capture a spire."

"It's supposed to be."

They slowed to a stop, the doors parting on a wide intersecting corridor lit by dying blue channels running up into a darkness of indiscernible height. Opposite, the corridor ran past the intersection and up a short flight of steps to a set of large double doors. Great dark grey obelisks, easily three times the height of man, one of which was ajar, gave a glimpse of the shadowy chamber beyond.

Lyander was about to step off the lift when he heard heavy metal clods followed by the steady *twang* and *click* of a repeating crossbow. *Stomp, stomp, stomp, twang* and *click. Stomp, stomp, stomp, twang* and *click.* Then, a sound that cut to his core, full of anguish and evil hunger – a sound he knew all too well: a vampire's monstrous, ear-splitting screech.

From the left corridor, the Constructii came into view. The bronzite machine walked itself backward, a curved blade in its left hand, in place of its right, the heavy repeater crossbow merged at the wrist. It twanged again, the gear wheel, powered by the small gyre cartridge, loaded and cocked the string with interlinking clicks.

Another terrible scream, then, when the humanoid mimicry neared the centre of the intersection. The sound of running and a shape flew toward it.

The Constructii pulled back its blade, bringing it down on the attacker, cutting into its neckline and biting through the shoulder and into its back. The vampire died instantly, legs giving way, body lying still at the Constructii's metal feet. Lyander felt a sense of relief, something that burgeoned into a glimmer of hope upon seeing the monster so easily cut down by one of Formaria's sentinels.

The feeling evaporated the moment four more shapes flew across the corridor, crashing into the construct and tackling it to the ground. Two more dashed around the corner and toward the epistolar's open door.

Lyander drew his sword, but before it was free of its scabbard, Eluthienn had rushed into the corridor.

"Eluthienn!" Lyander shouted, and ran after him, Gabriel just behind.

The prince threw himself at the farthest vampire; Lyander picked the one next to him. Deciding he could worry about his wound later, he tightened both hands around the sword grip. Gritting his teeth as the swelling and the stitching stretched, he brought the blade down on one of the beasts. A former priest, Lyander cut through the robes before crunching through bone and severing an outstretched arm. It leapt to its feet, throwing its head back and shrieking, newly spawned fangs stained red. Spinning toward him, the bloodied stump of its arm drenched its white robes and flung red globes across him and the floor. Before it could do any more, Lyander brought his blade back and thrust it through the vampire's yawning jaw, the steel effortlessly sliding through the back of the throat, beneath the skull, and out the other side.

He pulled back, the blade scratching against fangs, and the creature flopped to the ground.

To his right, Eluthienn, having brought a vampire to its knees, switched to a reverse grip thrust and sunk the blade into the exposed flesh between its shoulder and neck. As in Grindlepeake, the creature cracked and withered, turning to a papery shell before Eluthienn withdrew his sword and the husk fell to the floor and disintegrated. To his left, Gabriel pulled his own sword from the third vampire's stomach, twisting it as he yanked the blade back.

The fourth, straddling the Constructii's chest plate, rained blows upon its masked face, the vampire's clawed hands a bloodied mess from ripping into the solid bronzite.

Lyander moved to the right of their entangled forms and cut down, severing the vampire's head in a single swing – the body crumpling inert, blood pumping from the wound and into the Constructii's dented, lacerated face.

Where a blue torch should have blazed in its left eye socket, there was only beaten bronzite. At the base of its jaw, where the mask met the skull, he could see the glow of gyre light leaking from within its cranium.

The Constructii threw the body to its right, then tried to stand. Lyander stepped back as it toppled toward him, a wheezing metallic groan escaping from behind its mask. It brought itself to one knee, tried to stand again but clattered to its other side.

"Forget it!" Gabriel said. "There's still more of them."

Knowing he was right, Lyander stepped around the bodies, and together they rounded the corner to the epistolar. Up the flight of steps, then all three of them pushed open the great doors and into the chamber.

Ten

Brazier

The bronze husk looked out over the black dunes breaking gently at the edges of the pool: an ancient sentinel watchful over its maker's creation long after those makers were gone. A relic of an alien race, Brazier always thought of them as guardians, as a part of the Fromryr – as cousins, even, especially to the dwarves who were responsible for their maintenance and repair. But looking into the sightless mask refracting the distortions of white light, Brazier knew he was about to step into another world.

"So you know how to do this?" Axelock said.

"More or less," Brazier replied, grateful his nausea had subsided; he would need to concentrate if he was going to get this right.

"Doesn't it kill you if you get it wrong?" Dalfin asked.

"I think that's an exaggerated rumour, told by

the Ecclessius to dissuade people from trying to sneak in and use the Dead Network."

Axelock didn't look convinced. Neither did Dalfin.

Slowly, Brazier walked down the steps and into the pool until the voidstone came to his chest, the black filaments slinking around him as if they were sentient.

"Only tales are told."

Brazier nearly slipped on the bottom of the pool, startled by the voice coming from the face and the rest of the chamber at the same time.

"Err, okay."

"Then tell your story."

"A telling in Thendergaarden," Brazier said, trying to recollect his brother's brief explanation from years before. "I am the teller, Brazier Veranquis, former First Officer of the *Chalice of Amaranth*."

A ripple coursed through the voidstone as if the filaments were briefly paralysed by a shock of lightning, solidifying him in place before releasing him again. *Guess that was the wrong way of saying it.*

"The witness is the Ordained Conglomerate of the Ecclessius," he continued, concentrating hard, not wanting to find out what happened if he got more wrong. "The telling is of Theselan, under attack from an unknown enemy able to cloak its signature – an enemy that proved itself powerful enough to board and kill the crew of the *Chalice of Amaranth* within minutes. In this telling, that same enemy attacked other gyre ships across the quadrant before assaulting Theselan, currently under strength and –"

A spine chilling screech cut through the chamber, sending the white lines into a deranged spin. Brazier turned to the sound's source to see, standing in the shaft of light spilling through the epistolar's open door, a Redcrosse knight. The white surcoat quartered by a red cross – beige gambeson underneath, dark brown sword belt about the waist – was like most knights of the order. But something was wrong – very wrong. Red stains covered the front of the knight's chest, seeping from a neck wound, the flesh gored and flayed, leaving a gaping hole right down to the trachea. An impossible wound for the knight to survive and still stand.

Then Brazier saw the face.

A wraith-like white, its mouth – no, its fangs – awash in blood, its eyes crazed and bloodshot, darting manically between Axelock and Dalfin.

"By the black void!" Axelock said.

The creature tore across the epistolar, a demented gait, arms flying wild as it ran. Axelock brought the sword up just in time, levelling it at its chest and driving forward between its ribs. Impaled on the blade, the thing swung wildly at Axelock, and Brazier heard the dwarf grunt as strings of Axelock's blood sprayed across the floor. It tried to claw at Axelock with its other hand, but Dalfin jumped forward, jamming the knife into the creature's eye. It died (or died again?) slumping on the blade before sliding off the end.

Axelock stumbled backward and Brazier could see slashes running across his chest and upper bicep, cuts so deep they showed white clavicle. The dwarf gritted his teeth, a low growl releasing from his lips as Dalfin tried to steady him.

Then, as if materialising out of the gloom, another of the creatures leapt across the epistolar. The same pale face, the same demented eyes, blood drenching its chest and an arm missing from the wrist down.

"Dalfin!" Brazier cried, trying to warn the dwarf.

But too late. Dalfin turned, bringing the knife up defensively, but the clawed hand, swinging at an impossible speed, was too fast. It ripped into the dwarf's neck, spraying blood, and flinging his throat to splatter on the epistolar floor.

Dalfin dropped to his knees without a sound as Brazier tried to push himself toward the edge of the pool. But the moment he cried the dwarf's name, he was locked in place, the filaments gripping him like a stone cast. They crushed against his chest, binding him so tight he could barely breath.

The creature turned on Axelock, the dwarf struggling to hold the blade in just one hand. And Brazier knew he needed to come to Axelock's aid, knew the dwarf couldn't fight it on his own. But the voidstone held fast, and Brazier watched helplessly, knowing he would be powerless in preventing his friend's death.

"Let's have you, then!" Axelock growled.

But instead of throwing itself at the dwarf, it pulled up short and, for a second, Brazier thought it was just going to stand there and let Axelock run it through with his blade.

But it opened its fang-infested mouth and screamed, a bloodcurdling, sickening sound that sent Brazier's vision reeling and the epistolar's lights frantically scrambling up the walls.

Through eyes swimming with tears, Brazier watched Axelock fall to his knees, the sword dropping from his hands, the dwarf falling face first to the ground, still and utterly lifeless.

"No!" Brazier cried, fighting against the voidstone but the filaments tightened, forcing all the air from his lungs. He gasped, but his chest wouldn't let anything in, the crushing pain enveloping his entire body, and stars formed at the edges of his already blurred vision.

A shape stood above him. Even obscured, he could see the bloody robes, the missing hand. His death loomed and Brazier could feel only one thing. Through the paralysis, through the sickening headache, his anger burned bright. His anger at failing his friends, his anger at his inability to defend himself in these final moments. *Do your worst,* he thought.

But its worst never came.

Instead, something toppled to the ground next to the creature. He heard a soft, wet thud and it crumpled, falling backward. In its place, a towering form wearing a black surcoat quartered by a red cross, and a long, two-handed blade held at its side.

"Who is the teller?" a human's stern voice said. *A voice that could command armies*, Brazier thought hazily. The shape in front of him knelt – a man Brazier could just about make out through the stars now dancing in his eyes.

"Who is the teller?" the man said again.

He was the teller, Brazier realised from somewhere far away.

"Brazier Veranquis," he heard himself wheeze.

"Then say it!" the man shouted at him. The man was desperate, Brazier realised. Desperately trying to help him. "Say: The teller is Brazier Veranquis!"

Brazier repeated the words, his voice barely a whisper.

The encasing around him lessened, the petrifying grip diminishing, and the filaments became sluggish, almost coagulated. Brazier sucked in air, causing the lights in his eyes to go into a frenzy.

The man's voice again: "Now the witness."

Brazier breathed out, and sucked in air again, trying to see who was speaking to him.

"You need to declare the witness," the man said more forcefully.

"The witness is the Ordained Conglomerate," Brazier said weakly.

"And no others."

"And no others," Brazier repeated.

"Alright, get him out of there."

Brazier felt hands on his shoulders, dragging him toward the edge of the pool. Then the hands were under his arms, lifting him up the steps.

Propped up on either side, he stood shakily, a dull ache growing across the whole surface of his body, causing every breath to send shooting pain from his chest down to his toes.

"Lyander," one of them said beside him. Another human voice.

The man in front of him – Lyander, he assumed – turned, and Brazier heard an annoyed growl escape his lips. Two more creatures threw themselves through the open doorway, almost tripping over themselves in their crazed desperation to get into the chamber.

"Hold him," the man to his right said, and he felt an arm disentangle from under and around his shoulder.

Brazier watched as the two men, quite calmly – like they were sculptors walking up to blocks of stone they intended to work on – moved toward the creatures, and swing deadly steel.

The one on the right – neck to toe in boiled leathers and tight links of reinforced mail – stepped lightly, the sword held loosely in his hand like a painter might hold a paint brush. He arced the blade in fluid curves, almost serenely lopping off a hand, dancing out the way of an outstretched arm, slicing into thigh, then cutting through throat with an almost bored, feline grace.

His companion couldn't be more different. Wielding the two handed blade like an executioner, he brought it up high over his head and cleaved down and across, twisting into the cut with a growl. The blow was so forceful it not only ripped a bloody streak across the creature's chest, but flung it to the ground. Standing over it, the man changed to a reverse grip and sunk the blade into the back of its neck.

He glanced at his companion, saw he needed no help, then said: "To the hangar bay, now."

Brazier felt himself pulled forward but he fought against it.

"No!" he croaked, trying to pull away from whoever was holding him up.

But the arm held him strong. "They're gone!" the owner of the arm shouted.

Brazier, unable to release himself from the grip, simply tried to fall beside his companions.

"Gabriel, help me with him!" said the man who refused to let him go.

The other relinked his arm underneath his own.

"There's nothing you can do for them," the man named Gabriel said. His voice was neither kind nor cruel. He was simply making a statement. "They're dead, and you'll be, too, if we don't get out of here now."

Brazier tried to turn as they dragged him across the epistolar, but the effort cost him biting pain in his ribs. He half sobbed, half choked as he was forced to turn away.

"If they're this far into the spire, east hangar bay is likely overrun," the one called Lyander said.

"West hangar bay," Brazier said, forcing the words out. "My crew have a ship." *He hoped.*

"To the west hangar bay, then," Gabriel said.

Half pulled, half stumbling, his feet sometimes dragging across the floor, he was taken from the chamber. His feet felt slack, like flaccid slabs of meat, his calves like solid stone, thighs weak and throbbing, ribs crunching painfully. They ached worse than all the rest combined, but at least they still felt like ribs, unlike his stomach, which seemed to be changing positions with nearby organs.

Through the anger and the anguish of losing his friends and the fear of what might have happened to Freyen and Switch, he was vaguely aware he was in a very bad way. Then somewhere deep in his consciousness was the frightening sense that it might be an irreversibly bad way.

But as his awareness slipped, the thought was forgotten as soon as it came, and suddenly he was in a lift, then the next moment, the doors were parting. Despite his very loose grip on his surroundings, he could tell something was wrong.

He heard the sound of battle. The sickening screeches, dwarves, humans, gnomes, shouting, fighting, dying, steel thuds and clashes, and crossbows twanging.

Through the white stars swimming at the outer edges of his vision, he saw a hangar bay awash in battle: soldiers, knights, and Navarch crews forming irregular units and fighting in lose circles; others pulling into defensive lines, spears in front and crossbows in between, providing a line of retreat for non-military personnel to board the few ships still remaining.

Lining the inner wall, arbalist units fired into the mayhem until one of the creatures flung itself up some side steps and tore into the nearest soldier. Others followed, crashing into one another in their desperation to get at the unit.

Five, six, seven of them, and more, cutting through and overwhelming the arbalists, until in quick succession, bolts hammered into the creatures. At least two simply exploded, blood and limbs spraying up the walls. Others were pinioned in place, the five-foot shafts spearing them through chests, arms, legs. A cheer went up around the bay as the spire-class battle frigate, slipped from its berth, hovered above everything, and unloaded black hell from twelve gyre-fed repeater crossbow turrets.

"Which one is your crew?" Lyander shouted above the fray.

Brazier searched the bay. There were maybe six ships of various class, including a miner, crews and soldiers in defensive circles around their boarding ramps. At the end of one of the docking piers, he saw a ship floating just outside the hangar bay, its ramp dropped to the bay's edge. Standing on it was a gnome's slender form, dark curls falling about her shoulders, a crossbow held firmly in her arms.

"At the end," Brazier said, trying to nod in the ship's direction but sort of just flopped his head forward.

"End of the pier?"

Brazier flopped his head again.

"Let's move," Lyander said, and Brazier was once more half held, half dragged by the two other men.

Past soldiers, crews, and the still forms of the dead, they were at the start of the docking pier when there was a chorus of screeches, like a thousand whetstones drawn down blunted blades. He was turned around to the source of the noise.

Beyond the hangar bay, the lift in the centre of the concourse – large enough to hold a crew of forty – was open. Brazier's heart gave a small leap of joy at the sight of so many soldiers. Reinforcements sent to this side of the spire meant other sections were holding, that Theselan might not be overrun.

But then he saw the ghost white faces, the blood streaked mouths, the bloody torsos, missing limbs, and his heart sunk into his churning insides.

The mass sprang from the lift, racing across the concourse toward the hangar bay. They were joined by more, pouring from other lifts around the concourse.

"Run!" Lyander shouted.

Brazier was heaved around. Then, not bothering

to let him try and walk, he was carried down the pier, his toes occasionally catching on the smooth floor, only for one of the men to grunt and hold him up higher.

Overhead, the turrets strummed at full output, the swish of bolts flying through the air, and the animal howls of their targets, but Brazier knew it wouldn't be enough.

At the end of the pier, he heard Freyen's voice. "Zee!" She ran down the access ramp toward him. "What in the abyss happened?"

"We'll explain once we're out of here," Lyander cut in before Brazier could muster a response.

Freyen ignored him. "Where's Axelock and Dalfin?"

Shaking his head was all Brazier could manage. The mix of sadness and concern in Freyen's eyes almost made him weep.

She reached out a hand to him, but the screeches grew louder, soldiers were shouting, and he could hear the cries of crews scrambling into their ships. There was an almighty *clang,* the sound of bronzite crashing against something hard, then Lyander shouted: "Onboard now!"

Brazier was just able to turn his head as they carried him up the access ramp. Over an arm bound in leather, Brazier watched as the creatures swarmed up the inner wall and leapt out at the frigate. Most failed the jump, missing the ship entirely or crashing off its hull. But some clung fast, clawing their way up the sides, leaving space for others to follow. The last Brazier saw was three of them ripping apart a turret before tearing it wholly from its emplacement. Then he was in the fuselage being lowered into one of the wall seats.

"Do we have a pilot?" he managed to ask.

The voice that responded was low and gravelly and edged with amusement. "We do."

At the other end of the fuselage, half shadowed

in the stair well – the grey orbs that were his eyes glinting like stolen silver – was the convict, Matthias Phaser.

"Glad you could make it, Captain."

ELEVEN

LYANDER

Lyander sat in the fuselage, clutching the wrist of his wounded hand, trying to stop it shaking. But as the adrenaline faded, the reopened wound sent waves of nerve-splintering pain through every fibre of his body. It was so devastating, his imagination bombarded him with images of the hand splitting apart beneath the sodden bandages. Like the tail fin of some sea creature, the two halves flapping in either direction.

He was becoming delusional; a small pocket of his rational mind knew it. But it was as if the pain was purposely trying to break him down, crashing through his physical being until it attacked his very conscious. Wave after wave, and his vision would flicker, like a magical barrage seen from the corner of his eyesight. One moment his hand shaking, the soiled bandages, the other hand gripping the wrist, then a wave of pain and the picture shuddered like it was struggling to hold on to reality.

Breathe he told himself. *Like any other wound, just concentrate on your breathing*. But it wouldn't work, the intensity of battle was almost gone and the pain was free to pummel his mind. Hand, agony, and flash. Hand, agony, and flash. Hand, agony, and the Mirrovinjin parried his thrust with its hooked spear, sending his blade off to the right. But Lyander, a veteran of a hundred battles, knew the technique, knew exactly what the Mirrovinjin would do next. So Lyander followed through, letting his thrust carry him inside the killing range, forcing the Mirrovinjin to throw its spear from one hand to one of its three others, anticipating Lyander's swing with a parry. But he was close enough he could see into the black cavity where its nose should have been. Close enough to see inside the ragged line of flesh cut down the centre of its skull where their necromancers poured Aeturnic energy. Close enough to smell the stench from its yellow teeth. Close enough the parry was ineffective against his cleave, which cut the spear in half before cutting open half the creature's head.

Sweet relish at the combined triumph of outmanoeuvring an enemy and the dull, blunting sensation running up his sword and into his arms. He looked around for another to sustain the feeling but it dissolved as he heard his name shouted in desperation.

"Lyander!"

Through the chaos of battle, among the press of bodies, he heard his name again: "Lyander!"

There were knights in the quartered red surcoats of Redcrosse, and a swarm of Mirrovinjin and their black spears, but he couldn't place the sound's source.

"Lyander, we must fall back!"

He saw Ilian Craid, his shaven head greased with sweat and dirt and blood, trying to push his way through to him. "We must fall back! The prince has ordered all forces to retreat!"

"The prince's forces are supposed to be reinforcing the spire!" Lyander called back.

The knight reached him, out of breath and shaking his head.

"He's gone straight to the command chamber. He's ordered the installation's purge. We must fall back!"

There was anger at the undermining of his command and the stupidity of the decision, then panic that he wouldn't make it to the command centre in time to prevent a calamity, and the early signs of helplessness at the thought of what would happen if he was there too late to stop it.

In his mind, he pictured the units still locked in battle, his friends too far to pull back in time, and the Mirrovinjin who always fought in waves. There would be a secondary force; they would lose the spire.

"We need to stop him!" Lyander shouted back, then pulled himself from the press of bodies.

A hand grabbed his shoulder, trying to pull him around, trying to stop him.

"Lyander, no!"

And he was back in the fuselage; the pain induced memory, over. A hand on his shoulder, grabbing him, shaking him. He looked up and saw a gnome, pointed ears sticking out through dark ringlets of hair. Her face etched with worry, her eyes desperately searching his own.

"What happened to Brazier?" she said. "I need to know what happened in the spire so I can treat him."

Lyander shook his head, trying to recollect if he knew a Brazier. The gnome stepped aside, pointing to a dwarf slumped in a seat on the opposite side of the fuselage. He wore a white reinforced mining gambeson, a dark stain of sweat creating a "V" down the front, and had a fire-red mane of messy hair, half plastered to his forehead with sweat, eyes closed, shallow breaths between parted lips.

"Tell me what happened to him," the gnome said, forcefully and slowly, like she was talking to someone who only vaguely understood the language.

"*Exergis incapacita*," Lyander said.

"What?"

"*Exergis incapacita*," Lyander said with more force. "From voidstone. He needs *vitriolis prevencia*."

To his surprise, the gnome nodded as if she needed no further explanation and dashed up the stairwell. Lyander took a shaky breath, squeezed his eyes shut against the pain, and leant against the fuselage, trying to think about the soft thrum riding through his back instead of the misery shooting from his hand. It didn't really work.

A moment later, there was a soft thud and Lyander opened his eyes to the gnome at the bottom of the stairwell. In one hand, two vials of a turquoise green substance. They sparkled lightly, although that might still be Lyander's questionable vision.

She popped the cork from one of the vials and brought it to the dwarf's lips, holding the back of his head as she slowly poured the vitriolis into his mouth. The dwarf coughed, swallowed hard, his eyes fluttering open before closing again. The gnome waited, then tipped the rest into his mouth for the dwarf to swallow.

She came over to him, handing him the second vial.

"You, as well."

"I don't think it's going to help."

"From the look of you, it's not going to make it any worse, either, so you may as well."

Lyander took the vial in his good hand and she uncorked it for him. He tipped the liquid into his mouth and swallowed in one. There was a tingling coolness at the back of his teeth, followed by a sweet earthiness, like cinnamon mixed with ground rock. The taste rode up the back of his throat and through his nose. He closed his eyes, concentrating on the coolness spreading through his chest.

"I'm Freyen."

He opened his eyes.

"Lyander."

"What happened to those people?"

"Turned."

"Turned into what?"

"Vampires."

Other than a slight furrowing of the brow, the information didn't look like it gave her any more concern than she already felt.

It was then that Lyander realised there was only the three of them in the fuselage. He was certain Gabriel and Eluthienn were the ones to carry the dwarf – Brazier – into the ship.

"Where's Eluthienn?"

"Your friends are on board," Freyen said, in a slight soothing tone. "They're on the nav deck."

Lyander sighed so hard he felt his body mould to the seat.

"Those things, how do you know they're vampires?" Freyen asked.

"It's complicated."

She raised an eyebrow at him. "Has it got something to do with the prince we're currently giving a lift to?"

A perceptive gnome, then, whoever she is. But while he was grateful to be alive, thanks in part to Freyen, he lacked the patience and the will to explain how vampires were connected to Eluthienn, all while trying not to pass out from pain.

"What was your friend doing in the epistolar?" he asked instead. The look on her face told him she knew he was dodging the question and was just choosing to play along.

"Didn't seem like Theselan's praefector had time to get a message to the Ecclessius about what was attacking the spire. Cap went with Axe –" she closed her mouth suddenly. "Went with the others to send that message."

"Well, he did, just about. But I thought you didn't know they were vampires?"

"We didn't. But we know they don't have a recognisable signature, and they can break hex networks."

As if murderous, demented, undead that could make more murderous, demented, undead weren't bad enough, they could also break hex networks. This just gets better and better.

"How do you know they can do that?" he asked.

"Ship we were on was attacked by those things. We didn't know they were vampires because the hex script was purged – right before they breached."

Brazier coughed suddenly, let out a rasping breath, along with a trickle of blood at the corner of his mouth. Freyen sat next to him, wiping it away and then brushed aside one of the ginger strands stuck to his face.

The dwarf needed an anomancer, and quickly, Lyander knew. But instead of causing unnecessary worry, he said: "Your captain did a brave thing back there."

"Seems to run in the family," she said, more to herself than to Lyander.

He thought about asking her what she meant, but he heard heavy footsteps on the stairwell alongside the soft clunk of bronzite on bronzite. A female dwarf emerged. Hair like liquid jet and eyes to match, she was heavyset and broad-shouldered. The set of coveralls and tool belt at her waist was the uniform of any other enginator. Unlike other enginators, however, her white shirt was rolled up at the sleeve, revealing the sort of limb augment usually reserved for high-ranking officials and royalty.

"How's Zee?" she asked.

"Stable," Freyen said, but from the look the two of them shared, they both knew he might not be for much longer.

"Well, it looks like we were the only ship to make it out of Theselan. But we can't know for sure because Matthias refuses to try and contact any other ships."

"Why?" Lyander asked, assuming Matthias was the ship's navigator.

The dwarf turned her eyes in his direction. "Nice to have you back with us," she said. "For a minute there, it looked like you couldn't decide whether you wanted to pass out or throw a fit."

"Maybe a bit of both," Lyander said.

"Well, thanks for bringing back the cap. Looks like it cost you something."

"Yeah," Freyen said. "Thank you."

Lyander shrugged, a little awkward. He couldn't remember the last time someone showed him gratitude. "Don't mention it."

"Switch," the enginator said, holding out her augmented hand.

"Lyander," he said, shaking it. "So why is the navigator refusing to contact other ships?"

"Err, guess he's the shy, quiet type," Switch said. Then quickly: "Says he'll take us outside of Thendergaarden, some cavern he knows that can get us into the city."

Lyander, who never wanted to see another secret

cavern path again, let alone try and cross one, was having none of that.

"We're agents of the Church; he'll take us wherever we say so."

She extended her augment in the nav deck's direction. "Feel free to let him know."

"He's not part of your crew?"

"It's complicated," Freyen said with a wan smile.

Lyander groaned slightly as he stood, cradling his hand. Then, a little unsteady on his feet, he gripped the edge of the stairwell, and slowly, using only his good hand, pulled himself up it. He emerged onto a landing, the nav deck straight ahead. Through its parting doors, he found Gabriel stood with arms crossed, leaning against one of the two tactical terminals, dark rings under his eyes, his skin paler than usual, a light sheen of sweat across his temples. Lyander, who was growing used to the witch-hunter's cavalier invulnerability, was mildly taken aback by the worn-out look. *Seems the battle took it out of both of us*. Although Lyander was willing to bet gold Vidicks he looked worse.

Eluthienn leaned over the command terminal, apparently enthralled by the ship's sculpt and the steadily rolling hex display. Eyes wide, it looked like he was seeing a hex for the first time. *Probably he was,* Lyander thought.

"Your friend tells me you don't want to take us to Thendergaarden," Lyander said.

"More a case of *can't take you* than *don't want to take you*." There was a sort of simmering intensity to the navigator's voice, like listening to the dying embers of burnt charcoal. *Vaguely reminiscent of Bolton,* Lyander thought.

"And why's that?"

"Let's just say I'd like to steer clear of any

authority types. And Thendergaarden, that's got lots of authority types."

It was then that Lyander saw the steel bands around his biceps, thighs, and ankles.

"You're a prisoner?"

"*Former* prisoner, and that's a state of affairs I'd like to maintain."

"We're agents of the Church on a critical mission mandated by the Ordained Conglomerate. The law of the underground guarantees us safe passage to wherever we need to go."

"Like I told your friends here, I can take you point-five of a league from Thendergaarden's outer walls, but that's as close as I'm getting."

A throb rode up his arm and Lyander clenched his teeth, trying to bite back his frustration and not cry out at the same time.

"Fly us into Thendergaarden's primary hangar bay," he said, "and I can guarantee you a full pardon."

He didn't know whether he could make such a thing happen or not. Probably he couldn't. But he wasn't going to spend however long it took traipsing around in the dark while a horde of vampires stormed toward Formaria's second largest vault. And besides, he knew he was going to enjoy watching some snotty cardinal's face when he told them he'd offered a full pardon to what looked like a high-security prisoner.

"Maybe you've got the rank to pull that off. Maybe you don't. Hard to know from where I'm sitting."

"How about you take us to where we want to go," Gabriel said, "and we don't kill you here and now."

"You planning to get to Thendergaarden without a navigator?"

"Here to Thendergaarden is as good as a straight line. I think we could risk that much."

"And you're going to land a battle frigate in one

of the busiest ports in Formaria?"

"Who said anything about landing? We'll send a distress beacon well before we reach the vault and allow ourselves to be boarded."

Gabriel took two steps over to the navigator and drew his sword, placing the point at the back of the dwarf's neck.

"So how about it, would you like to die choking to death on your own blood, or would you like a full and unconditional pardon from the Ordained Conglomerate itself?" The way Gabriel said it, he could have been offering the dwarf the option of cheese or grapes.

"Well, put that way, I think I'll take the pardon," the navigator said, mimicking the conversational tone. "But if your end of the deal isn't upheld," his voice now saturated with deliberate threat, "not even the abyss could hide you from me."

Gabriel put up his steel, returning to slouch against the terminal, looking exhausted. "Sounds fair to me."

"Well, now that's sorted," Lyander said, "I'm going to see if I can find a bunk. Wake me up when we get there or if anything tries to kill us."

#

Lyander laid in semi-wakefulness, drifting into a slumber punctuated with dreams, only to be awoken by his hand, seconds or minutes later. He couldn't tell.

Breathing, he focused on his body's weight against the sheets, trying to let the tiredness win out over the pain. Then he was running. Running through an installation, without terminals or lifts – just an endless maze of polished grey, glossed with purple jasper. He held no sword, wore no armour. He just ran, desperate to get somewhere, desperate to do something so important it made his heart ache with worry and fear. He turned another corner, just like all the rest, and jolted in the cot, eyes opening to a cool, almost metallic blue.

Lying there, the throbbing coursing from his hand, he thought the pain might be lessening. He looked down and saw the bandages were drenched in sweat. As he sat up, feeling his underclothes stick to him, he realised his entire body was sodden.

In the corner of the room, Freyen's voice came from the hex terminal.

"Lyander, we're almost there."

He stood and shuffled over to it, catching a whiff of something like stale onion before realising it was him. *At least in Thendergaarden, I can finally have a bath.*

"I'm on my way up," he said to the hex.

He requested the cabin door open, then made his way to the nav deck. There, he found everyone, including Brazier, surrounding the command terminal.

"How do you feel?" Lyander asked the dwarf.

His face was pale, he looked unsteady on his feet, and Lyander thought he smelled nearly as bad as he did – although it was hard to determine where his stench ended and the dwarf's began.

"Like someone tried to bury me alive in bronzite."

Lyander laughed. "Looked a bit like that before we pulled you out," he said.

The dwarf held out a hand. "My thanks for saving my life."

Lyander grabbed his forearm with his good hand, Brazier's hand wrapping around his forearm in return.

"I'm sorry we didn't get there sooner."

Brazier nodded, smiling weakly. "So am I."

He put out a hand to steady himself on the

command terminal, the other on his stomach, wincing.

"You need an anomancer," Lyander said.

"You're not looking so good yourself, you know."

From the way he felt, Lyander believed him.

"Well, maybe we can both see an anomancer." He nodded at the hex sculpt. "We in range?"

"We are," Matthias said.

"Request a docking approval."

Matthias's head twitched, then the well next to Lyander trembled.

"Tethered," the navigator said.

"This is the battle frigate . . ." Lyander looked around at the others.

"*Ascendant Dawn*," Freyen said.

"*Ascendant Dawn*," Lyander continued. "Legally commandeered by Kalbrayeth Lyander, rank: exorcist, and under orders from the Ordained Conglomerate. We are carrying precious cargo and request an emergency berth at the nearest port."

There was a moment's silence, then a male gnome's voice: "Received exorcist Kalbrayeth Lyander. You're all cleared for entry, south port level two. Welcome home."

The tether dropped.

On the hex, Thendergaarden was like a cluster of diamonds embedded in rock at the centre of a spider's web, seven strands reaching out from the centre, the tunnels leading out into Formaria. Each one was guarded by outer gates, two towers on either side, each one a small spire. Behind them was the "moat," the bottomless cavity between the gates and the inner rock island, upon which the sprawling vault of Thendergaarden was built: a geometric maze of crystalline structures, of which only a tenth was visible on the ship's hex network. The rest existed deep within the island itself, descending for leagues.

Three structures stood out among the rough. Southwest, toward the centre, stood a colossal pyramid, five times the size of the next largest building: the Viatica, the grand Church of the Ecclessius. Northeast, almost as large, was a fortress shaped into a dodecagon and rising into a peak: the Navarch High Command. Lyander watched vault-class ships, half the size of his little finger nail on the hex, zip in and out of the building. A short way east of it, a single tower surrounded by an octagonal ring rose above all the rest. At its height, an orbed chamber: the Observatory of the Navigorum.

Drawing closer to the gates, Thendergaarden proper crumbled, rescaling to show only the two guard towers, the cavern beyond, and a small portion of the vault. Then over the cavern, the towers disintegrated at the edge of the display, and at the other end, the docks materialised. Like gaping mouths, they grew larger and larger. The *Ascendant Dawn* drifted down into one and the hex became a layout of the dock, its piers, the other ships.

There was a light *cu'thunk* and the ship landed. It was followed by another, lighter, *cu'thunk* as the access ramp dropped to the floor.

"Well, that was better than last time," Switch said.

Matthias pulled his boots on and stood opposite the command terminal. "You know, I think you're going to miss me," he said.

The enginator shook her head, a look of utter disbelief playing across her face.

The navigator nodded at Lyander with his chin. "Remember our deal."

Lyander nodded back.

Off the nav deck, down the access ramp, and

onto the hangar bay: twice the size of Theselan's, Lyander counted over fifteen ships berthed, along six docking piers. At the beginning of each, a small tower with a heavy repeater crossbow perched on top. They moved at half-sentience, lazily tracking the flight of each ship as it landed in their pier.

A cohort of Ecclessiarchal guard, perhaps sixteen, wearing pale blue surcoats quartered by a white cross. They flowed over their mail as they marched down the pier toward them. Spear tips glinting under the near white light of the bay, they surrounded a tall dark-skinned human in a white robe and amice, a deep red stole around his shoulders and to his shins, intricate gold thread running through it all. As they drew closer, Lyander saw in place of his eyes a patchwork of pale scar tissue.

"Greetings, Kalbrayeth Lyander," the minister said, turning his empty sockets in his direction. "The Church welcomes you home."

I doubt there's even one Ecclessiarchal member in all of Thendergaarden who welcomes me anywhere, but the Church is nothing if not polite.

"It's good to be home," Lyander said, bowing his head, marginally.

"My name is Olions Moencis, representative of the Ordained Conglomerate. I am to escort you to the Viatica where you will await their summons. But first, among your party is the fugitive Matthias Phaser. He is to be apprehended."

As one, the spears formed into a tight semi-circle, levelling at them.

"The navigator is under my protection," Lyander said, putting out his good hand toward them. "I solicited his services to aid me in my mission in exchange for a full Ecclessiarchal pardon. By the decrees of my order and those set out by the Ordained Conglomerate, I am free to make such an arrangement." *I think.*

Lyander was sure the minister would have raised an eyebrow if both weren't missing. "Your station and order affords you such powers," he said, "but only if the circumstances within which the arrangement was made meet the parameters of the law. The Ordained Conglomerate will be the judge of that. Until that time, Matthias Phaser will remain in our custody."

Two of the guards stepped toward the dwarf, one holding a pair of manacles. Matthias tensed – a ripple of tautness over his biceps, shoulders, and neck – before he breathed angrily through his nostrils, letting them cuff him while his cloudy grey eyes locked onto Lyander's. He wasn't entirely sure of the parameters the minister was referring to, but either way, he could deal with the consequences later. Right now, a high-security prisoner vowing to hunt him down was fairly low on his list of problems.

"Members of my crew need urgent medical assistance," Lyander said, watching them march off. "And we need a meeting with the Conglomerate."

"Members of your crew will be seen by anomancers," the minister said, "but I'm afraid the Ordained Conglomerate is already in session."

"Then that session needs to be interrupted. Theselan has fallen and we –"

"The Church was made aware of the situation by epistolar," the minister cut across him.

"By us," Brazier said, his voice wooden.

"You are Brazier Veranquis?" the minister asked.

The dwarf nodded. At his side, Lyander saw Gabriel shoot a glance at the dwarf, as if he recognised the name.

"Then the Church thanks you for your efforts." Olions turned to Lyander, leaving him wondering what school of magic he must specialise in to see without eyes. "But it remains, the session cannot be interrupted, as they have convened with the Fromryian High Council."

"The royal houses are here?"

"Some of them," the minister said, a hint of annoyance in his voice.

"Good. We escort Eluthienn Leonette, Prince of Ravinica, who holds critical information regarding the ongoing attacks on Formaria. He requests an audience with the High Council, as is his right. I think the council will want to be interrupted for that."

The minister's head turned slowly, the lacerated sockets moving from Lyander to Gabriel, then falling on the prince. He bowed his head. Eluthienn did the same in return.

"The High Council will be made aware of your presence, Your Highness." Then to Lyander: "If you would follow us."

They walked across the bay, beneath rivers of glowing blue, and to one of the lifts. The minister placed his hand into a terminal, eyes fluttering, then said to all of them: "Whoever among your party requires medical attention, please step onto the lift."

Ghostly pale, the rings under his eyes seemingly darker, Brazier stepped forward. He nodded at Lyander as he passed, lips pressed together like he was trying to hold back from crying out.

I know the feeling, friend.

"Until we meet again," Freyen said, giving him a smile.

Then Switch, who punched him affectionately if not somewhat painfully in the arm with her augment: "Take care of yourself, big man."

"Take Brazier Veranquis and his crew to the nearest vulnerum," Olions said to one of the guards.

"They are to be seen by an anomancer immediately and are to remain there until I say otherwise."

To Lyander, gesturing at his hand: "We can take you to an anomancer, as well."

"It can wait."

They passed beneath a series of arches, then onto a wide avenue, much like that of a spire's concourse. It overlooked a series of lower levels alive with the sort of activity only a vault city could have. The blue military doublets of Navarch crews and the red and green liveries of house La'Voline mixed with the regular dress of Thendergaarden's citizenry and the many foreign merchants.

"You can confirm the dwarf you travelled with is Brazier Veranquis, First Officer of the *Chalice of Amaranth*?"

"He sent the epistolar message at great personal risk," Lyander said.

"Just so. We also received a distress signal from his brother shortly before their miner was deliberately overloaded. He and his crew are wanted for questioning."

"I believe their miner was attacked by the same creatures responsible for Theselan. And his crew were instrumental in our mission and bringing the prince to Thendergaarden. I can vouch for them."

"I have no doubt you can. But your advocacy doesn't hold as much weight as it once did, Kalbrayeth Lyander."

Of that, I have no doubt.

They stopped before an open platform and the minister called for a lift using the nearby terminal. Stepping onto it, they rose into the air and above the different levels before entering a chute and its glistening purple-grey walls.

It deposited them before a smaller foyer, a

conjoined chamber, octagonal in shape and twice as large as the lift platform. In similar fashion to a sanctum, bronzite pillars created a magical field in the chamber's centre. Beyond it, on the chamber's opposite side, a pair of Constructii guarded the opening into a hallway. Each one held a two-handed glaive and a short leaf-shaped sword in a scabbard on their hip.

As each of them passed through the magical field, a shimmer rose up beyond the pillars and into the peak. Their gyranic signals, Lyander knew, assessed for any signs of corruption before being admitted audiences with the leaders of the Fromryr.

"Your request will be put to the council. Until then, you will wait here."

The minister and the remaining guard left through the opposite passageway.

"The name Veranquis means something to you?" Lyander asked Gabriel when they were gone.

Gabriel shrugged. "I met his brother some time ago and only briefly," he said.

"The name Veranquis is also known in Vallorandyl," Eluthienn said, surprising Lyander. "The father, Edmerin, was an ambassador to Ravinica. I never met him, but my father had great respect for him."

"*Was* an ambassador?" Lyander asked.

"He was executed for treason," Gabriel said.

"What were the charges?"

"Selling secrets to Formaria's enemies."

Given Torquen's sacrifice and Brazier's recent actions, he wouldn't have thought the father a likely traitor – the opposite, in fact.

His thoughts must've be plain on his face because Eluthienn said: "The news of his execution also came as a shock in Vallorandyl."

"Who truly knows who any of us are," Gabriel said, the playful glimmer returning to his sorcerous blue eyes.

"Spoken like a true witch-hunter," Lyander said.

"Spoken from experience. In particular, experience of those in power."

"Sounds as if you like Fromryr's rulers as much as I do."

Gabriel's smile was a line of chagrin. "The Ecclessius uses us all in its own way," he said.

"And so they are the real power in Formaria?" Eluthienn asked.

Lyander couldn't help but snort a laugh. "In my experience, the power ebbs and flows between the Church and royal families," he said, "but yes, the Fromryr have been fighting a never-ending war for the past one thousand years. The only reason we haven't been defeated is because all four races are so closely united beneath the web of influence the Ecclessius spins."

"My father said as much. He believed the only reason such an enterprise hadn't fallen to infighting and factional politics was because the Ecclessius held all the power."

Lyander understood then what the prince was driving at. "The royal houses have more soldiers, more ships, more Constructii, and more resources, but yes, the Ecclessius holds sway over them all," Lyander said, then added: "Most of the time. If you're looking to convince any member of the High Council, then it is the Grand Ecclessian."

Eluthienn smiled at him. "You would make a good advisor, Lyander. If you're not busy fighting for the Sorel Tan, that is."

"I'd be more concerned about convincing them of your cause than me." Then – and he wasn't entirely sure why he said it but he did: "The Ecclessius serves its own ends, and those ends are to maintain its position of power above all others in Formaria, at all costs."

"If those are their ends, then they will have little choice but to accept my offer."

Before Lyander could say anything else, the minister appeared in the opening. "Lyander, Gabriel. The High Council would like to see you. Alone."

#

Another chamber, a decagon from the number of sides Lyander counted. For each side there were a set of arches, behind which ran a kind of gallery. Its slick grey walls were hidden in semidarkness, blue channels fading to black.

The seating, solid blocks of near purple, were raised on a walled platform circling the chamber. It forced whoever was in its centre to look up to those they were addressing. In this case, it was Lyander and Gabriel in the centre, looking up to nearly every member of the Fromryian High Council.

To Lyander's right were the High Lords of Thendergaarden:

First was Blaeken Rose, Lord Admiral of the Navarch. The dwarf's silvery grey hair and beard flowed over his blue-and-gold trimmed military doublet. Eyes, the colour of green tourmaline, watched Lyander from an implacable face.

On his left was Henselt Braechter, the Lord Marshal of the Knights Redcrosse (and Lyander's former commander) in a red quartered white surcoat. Like the Admiral, a set of Laurea, braided cords signifying military achievements, ran from the top of his shoulder round his arm and to the back of his shoulder. The short dark hair, warrior's jaw line, and sharp nose looked as if they were chiselled from stone and could have been those of any other knight of his order, if it wasn't for the intensity of his pale blue eyes, at once calculating and unsettling. *Although those eyes didn't want to look at me the last time we spoke.* They looked at him now.

To his left was the Lord Huntsman of the Conclave, Anselhelm Vorst: a giant of a man with blond hair like the Admiral's, flowing over his shoulders and the leather bound armour he wore, similar in fashion to Gabriel's, reinforced with rings of mail, except a deep forest green.

Sitting behind them, Priscilla O'Gorn, the First Wizard of the Gyranic Coven. The female gnome wore satin blue robes trimmed with gold. Wrinkled ears pointed out from dark red locks, the same colour as her eyes – her entire eyes, for they lacked sclera or pupil and were all dark iris.

Next to her sat Eklin Stenger, the Royal Emissary of the Navigorum, completely blind, completely bald. The woman's face was angular and pale, giving her the look of a malnourished baby. Robed in black with ornate red hem, she clutched the gold-orbed crozier of her office between fingers thin as petrified twigs.

To Lyander's left were the kings and queens of Formaria's royal houses.

Aymeri La'Voline had short greying hair combed over above a pronounced brow, dark eyes, and solid cheekbones. *A king's face* was what Lyander thought the first time he met him, and it was what he thought now. His dress, however, was anything but. He wore a crimson doublet unbuttoned over a loose cream shirt, making him look more like a petty lord with too much time on his hands than one of the most powerful men in all of Formaria.

On his right was Guiscard Guildain, wearing a light blue doublet with pronounced shoulder boards and ornate cream thread. The king sported a curling moustache and goatee to match the black ringlets falling around his shoulders. His blue eyes seemed to appraise Lyander's worth, as if he was trying to guess his weight in silver.

To Guiscard's right sat the dwarven High King, Lother Dillendwan, enveloped in dark purple robes with sleek black hair falling loose beneath a single band of gold. Featuring a trimmed beard and thick eyebrows, his face was young and surrounded untrusting green eyes.

Next to him was Elspeth Laanorath, the Ilvalien Queen and mother of Isdria Laanorath. Like her dwarven kin, she wore a single gold band around a head of dark curls. But unlike the dwarven king, Elspeth was a tapestry of time. The lines around her mouth and the creases across her forehead were an etching of sorrow and loss – a beauty giving way to grace, and perhaps even now, the twilight of old age. Looking into her deep blue almost purple eyes, Lyander wondered how she would react to the knowledge that her outlawed son was conspiring with the outlawed prince of her country's closest ally.

Behind her, half in shadow and wearing a black and gold doublet beneath flowing black robes, was Varkoneth Rosantz. A perversion of the human form, a body augment encircled his grotesque waist. At once keeping him afloat and extending his life, it required – according to rumour – so much gyranic sorcery, the family bred into slavery its own magic users. Anger coiled in Lyander's belly, causing his hand to throb painfully as he looked up at the bloated creature responsible for stripping him of his position, his purpose, his life.

He bit down both the pain and his emotions, looking at the other responsible party: Sitting directly in front of Lyander and lording it over the rest was the Grand Ecclessian, Cadarrasta Pulance. The gold mitre hat and bright red silk robes, hemmed in expensive cream, failed utterly to distract from his turgid features. His skin, sagging from old age and swollen from the repeated attempts to prolong his life, was covered in blotchy bruising, while his beady brown eyes, surrounded by dark circles, stared hungrily down at Lyander.

Looking up into the seating, Lyander noted the missing members: Marcus Angelaux, King of Pontifax; Caspian Couronne, King of Helispont; Eleanor Fontain, Queen of Taranis; and Maya Yarranstar, Knelderian Queen of Everaux. In their places sat chosen representatives – high-ranking lords and ladies trusted enough to make decisions on their monarch's behalf.

Then, the Grand Ecclessian – who Lyander always thought looked a bit like a petrified potato – opened his mouth and spoke with a wet, pulsating grumble: "Kalbrayeth Lyander, three days ago, you were tasked with investigating the creatures known as vampires and discovering the reason for their pursuit of Eluthienn Leonette, Prince of Ravinica. You were to seek out the prince in Grindlepeake, where you believed him to be, and ascertain his connection, if any, with these creatures. Given the prince's circumstances, you were then to report that information to the Ordained Conglomerate under the utmost secrecy." His jowls gave a tremulous wobble as he enunciated *secrecy*. "And yet we find you brought him here to Thendergaarden, in the company of a known criminal and the son of a convicted traitor. This might have been your chance to repair your reputation, but instead it seems your ineptitude is to become legendary."

As pleasant as the last time we were in this room, Lyander thought bitterly, trying to control his anger.

"We sought out Eluthienn in Grindlepeake and

found him there, as expected. There, he demonstrated his connection to the beasts, or more precisely, he demonstrated his lineage's connection to the vampires. He is a direct descendent of Leoncoure Leonette – the same bloodline that reportedly slew Lokul, the first vampire and maker of those now attacking our ships and installations. It's the prince's belief that because of this ancestral connection, he and he alone can slay the vampire king – an act that in a single blow will destroy every vampire spawn in Formaria. So tell me, Your Eminence, do you still think bringing him here an act of *ineptitude*?"

The Grand Ecclessian leaned forward, eyes peeling to little more than angry brown dots. "What does he want from Formaria for carrying out such an act?"

Of course the Grand Ecclessian knows the prince wants something in return. No acts of kindness, even between supposed allies: a language Pulance speaks fluently.

"He will ask for Formaria's support in reclaiming his throne."

The Grand Ecclessian scoffed, a short gurgling sound at the back of his throat. "Is that all?"

"No. He will also ask that Formaria declare war on Fiondagaard and join Ravinica in its invasion."

"Absurd!" The Grand Ecclessian sat back in his seat, head shaking. "Absurdity!"

"What do you mean he *demonstrated* his lineage's connection?" Priscilla asked.

Lyander turned to face the First Wizard. "He slew one in front of us, my lady. Eluthienn's . . ." he searched for the word, "Eluthienn's *presence* appeared to destroy it both on a physical and a gyranic level."

The Grand Ecclessian's jowls gave another gross tremble.

"You can confirm this, Gabriel? It wasn't a

trick? Something conjured by another sorcerer?"

Gabriel stepped forward. "Lyander's description is accurate. If it was a sorcerous trick, I would have felt it."

"But these beasts can be slain like any other?" Lother asked, and Lyander was surprised to hear such a measured tone from someone who looked so young. "They can be defeated by those not of royal lineage?"

"They can, Your Highness," Lyander said. "But whether Lokul can be slain like any other creature of the Aeturnum, I cannot say."

"And what evidence did he give of Lokul's role in this? What evidence did he give that the being even exists?" Aymeri asked, his voice a steely rumble, his face stern.

"He didn't."

A murmur ran through the council – a timbre of quiet scepticism followed by the sound of gear wheels clicking slowly and the quiet vibration of gyranic propulsion. Varkoneth's bulge shifted out of the shadows, revealing a hairless head of grey folds competing in ugliness with those of the Grand Ecclessian's, the only colour his black eyes and the dark grey lips that moved like coiling sea snakes.

"And how," the King of Thela said in oozy tones that made Lyander's hand ache with hatred, "does Eluthienn know it's this Lord, not some witch spawn of the Aeturnum?"

Lyander held Varkoneth's gaze for several moments before answering. "While in Eluthienn's captivity, Bork told him he resurrected Lokul."

"Bork?"

"Yes, Bork."

"As in Bork the Borken," Priscilla said. "The goblin?"

"The very same."

The Grand Ecclessian turned to the Lord Huntsman of the Conclave, his neck folds moving like sludge. "Could the goblin do this? I thought he was a dullard?"

Anselhelm's blue eyes seemed to ponder the question. Then he answered in a thick, rolling Harothellian accent. "It seems unlikely, but so does the existence of vampires in the first place, and yet here we are."

"Bork the Borken raising mythical undead kings," Guiscard Guildain said in mellifluous tones while twirling his moustache. "We cannot seriously be entertaining this?"

Half a day ago, Lyander would have said the same thing, but experiencing Theselan, seeing so many Fromryr twisted into crazed monsters, and watching a fully operational installation fall so quickly, he was willing to believe just about anything.

"I just watched a full strength detachment overrun and turned into these creatures in less than an hour," Lyander said. "Right now, the idea of Bork raising the king of vampires – and that destroying that king will bring an end to the slaughter – is worth entertaining to me."

"Assuming the Lords are more than just the tales we've been led to believe, who's to say Eluthienn wasn't the one to resurrect this maker, and he's using this to force our allegiance?"

"Precisely that!" the Grand Ecclessian said. "More likely, this is a ruse!"

"Eluthienn's hand in this is certainly more likely than Bork's," Aymeri added.

"And what if it is Eluthienn's doing? And what if it's Bork's?" Elspeth said softly. "No matter our questioning of the prince, the truth is likely to evade us. And so it doesn't change our plight. We have lost contact with nearly twenty ships, and now we have lost an installation that has stood for a thousand years. To face such a threat, we would need to pull vast numbers from the front. Numbers we can scarcely spare. Do we have any choice but to at least consider what the prince will offer?"

Varkoneth's flotation augment droned under the strain of his weight as he turned to the queen. "And let us say we believe all the prince has to tell us – that we believe in this tale about ancient blood lines. Why should we not seek out and capture the vampire king? Bring it here and force Eluthienn's hand, and forget this farce about declaring war on Fiondagaard?"

"And you can tell us where the vampire king is, can you?" Aymeri asked over his shoulder.

"Of course I cannot," Varkoneth waved a hand slovenly in Lyander's direction, "but Eluthienn can."

"Something tells me the prince isn't going to willingly offer up the only thing he has to bargain with," Gabriel said, then added, "Your Highness."

Varkoneth's dark lips formed into a sickly curve. "Who said anything about him being willing?"

"And while you torture the information out of the man this country considers an ally," Aymeri viciously cut across him, "how many more spires will we lose? How many more ships?"

"The king is right," Blaeken said. "Most of our gyre stars are engaged, and during the time it would take to withdraw infantry from the front, we could be looking at an assault here, on Thendergaarden."

"I agree," Henselt said. "While the Mirrovinjin are still licking their wounds from the Heiron campaign, so are we. The front is under strength. Reducing it further would not be wise."

Another murmur, this time, of reluctant consent.

"Then what of his offer of alliance?" Lother

ventured, his gaze settling on each council member in turn. "By all accounts Eluthienn is a commander of some considerable skill. And while disliked in the capital, he's known to have many friends among the Ravinican royal houses. Might this not be an opportunity to strike Fiondagaard? A country openly hostile to many of our people."

"Opportunity or not," Guiscard said. "We risk much allying with who at this stage is but one man – the motives of whom we question."

"Lyander," a voice said, and for a moment he thought he was being addressed by a child before he realised it was Eklin who spoke. "What is your assessment of the prince?"

He's conceited, arrogant, and half mad, Lyander thought, *not unlike most born to positions of power*. But there was also a shrewdness to him; he was courageous, perhaps to the point of recklessness, and he was a skilled mediator despite the rumours of him hating the politics of his own country. Above all, his soldiers gave their loyalty to him freely and in Lyander's experience, soldiers were quick to smell out those undeserving of their position. *Arrogant and mad he might be, but a commander who inspires others to follow him usually speaks of some honour and trustworthiness*.

"The story he's told is far-fetched to the point of being unbelievable, if I hadn't seen the vampires with my own eyes. But he's not a liar. I don't believe his offer to be anything other than what he claims it is."

"And you, Gabriel," Anselhelm asked. "What do you make of Eluthienn?"

Lyander turned to Gabriel, only to find the witch-hunter's blue eyes studying him.

Gabriel looked up at the head of his order. "He can be trusted."

The Grand Ecclessian gurgled with displeasure.

"We will be the judge of that. If there are no objections, we will hear Eluthienn's tale." He surveyed the council with pomposity, head moving from side to side. "Then send him in."

Lyander and Gabriel were guided up steps by one of the Ecclessiarchal aids, taking them to the level behind the seating, beneath the arches of the chamber.

"Why so loyal to our outlawed prince all of a sudden?" Gabriel asked in a whisper.

"Telling the council his offer is sound is hardly loyalty," Lyander whispered back. "You think I'm wrong?"

"I think Eluthienn is weaving schemes so elaborate his plots have plots."

"If you don't think he can be trusted, why not tell the council as much?"

Gabriel shrugged, the corners of his mouth curling like he was remembering something funny. "Well, I couldn't show you up, now could I? We're a team, after all."

Lyander doubted that was the reason, but he couldn't think of any other. As always, the witch-hunter's mood and motives seemed completely arbitrary.

His attention drew back to the chamber as the lull in conversation died and the doors were pulled open. Eluthienn stepped into the centre.

The prince surveyed those in the seats, his eyes resting on Lyander's briefly, and he thought he could see the hint of a smile playing around his mouth.

"You stand before the rulers of the Fromryr," the Grand Ecclessian said. "The High Council of the four races who make up the grand alliance of Formaria. You stand before us, an outlaw of your country and, we are told, with an offer of allegiance."

Eluthienn bowed his head. "Kings and queens of the Fromryr, High Lords of Thendergaarden, protectors of this great realm. I stand before you offering friendship and salvation."

The prince turned slowly, making sure to look upon the faces of every member of the council.

"Our great nations stand upon the precipice. The vampire, the great evil of the Aeturnum, has been loosed upon Formaria by the conniving hand of Bork. And in Vallorandyl, the Fion emperor now rules through its puppets, scheming Ravinica's downfall and its eventual assimilation into the Fiondagaardian empire. Never before have our worlds stood as close to their shared destruction or their fates been so closely intertwined as they are now. For if one falls, so does the other."

Eluthienn paused, then continued.

"By the hour, the vampire multiplies. Its armies grow stronger as yours grow weaker. For every ship you lose, for every installation that falls, for every soldier and citizen it kills, it gains and you lose. While in Ravinica, every day that passes is another day Fiondagaard's blight is left to rot – a rot that, if left to spread, will consume the realm and spread to these very borders, where it will look hungrily upon the technology and wealth of the Fromryr. Only together can we rid the world of the evils that darken our shared horizons. Only together can we triumph. And only together can we claim our shared destinies as the rulers of Aetraya.

"And so I offer you this: I will hunt down the maker of the beasts that desecrate your lands, and as my ancient forebear did before me, and so as only I can, will slay Lokul, second Lord of the Eternal Hunt. And upon my return, together we will reclaim my birthright, cast off the yoke of Fion, and once and for all destroy the empire that has been a black shadow upon our worlds. This I offer to you: friendship, salvation," then turning to the Grand Ecclessian, "power."

Pulance held the prince's gaze, his thoughts

unreadable beneath the folds of flesh.

"Our accord is with Ravinica," Aymeri said, "an accord built on trust and mutual benefit with the Ravinican royal houses over hundreds of years. Your birthright it may be, but you are one man, the last of his line, with no heir."

"Your accord is with royal houses soon to be in Fion's clutches," Eluthienn said, bringing a clenched fist to his chest. "I am Ravinica and I am not alone. Already Grindlepeake pledges itself to my cause, as do the companies of Fal'Hannar, and the Sorel Tan Ilvalien."

"Pirates, mercenaries, and traitors to Formaria," Guiscard said, laughing. "This is the foundation of your rebellion? This is what you would convince us with?"

"I would convince you with the fleet at Grindlepeake's command, the thirteen black companies of Fal'Hannar to sail them, and a truce with the elves that have harried the underground kingdoms for centuries."

"You expect us," Blaeken said slowly, like a wolf building a growl in the back of its throat, "to strike a truce with the Sorel Tan?"

"I expect you to think of your own survival."

The Lord Admiral's eyes dimmed to a smouldering cadmium, but it was Varkoneth who spoke.

"Speaking of our survival, how long would it take you to hunt down this Lord of the Eternal Hunt?"

"His lair is beyond the Pelothrian mountains." The prince waved a hand, a non-committal gesture. "Beyond even the Reach. While my knowledge of gyre ships is limited, I believe that distance would take three days, maybe four."

"Not accounting for the need to refuel and resupply."

Eluthienn shrugged. "Five days, then."

"And so we will also be providing you with a

ship?" Blaeken asked.

"And a crew to command her," Eluthienn said, smiling up at the Lord Admiral. "No larger than the one we arrived here on." He turned to Lyander, expectant.

"A battle frigate," Lyander said. "Spire-class."

"And Lokul," Anselhelm asked, leaning forward and clasping his hands, biceps showing beneath the leather armour. "What makes you think you can defeat him? It took Leoncoure three days in single combat, according to *the story*."

"I do not claim to be Leoncoure himself, master witch-hunter, but nor do I need to be. Lokul is only now reawakened. His state is greatly weakened from ancient wounds and aeons slumber, which is why he sends forth his spawn to do his bidding while he hides in the shadows."

The Lord Huntsman leant back in his seat, looking entirely unconvinced.

"And upon your return," Henselt asked, "how do you expect us to *help* you reclaim your throne?"

"It will be open war or covert guile," Eluthienn said simply. "With the navy and Fal'Hannian companies we can strike fast, owning the seas and then the western coast, drawing their forces and leaving the passages through northern Ravinica free for the Fromryr to march down, taking town after undefended town. But more likely, seeing the Fromryr roused and declaring its support, those houses loyal to my family will flock to our cause. And it will only be a matter of time before the Lords of Vallorandyl remove the traitors within their ranks, welcoming me home."

"Or instead, we are forced to lay siege to Vallorandyl while reinforcements arrive from Fiondagaard," Varkoneth said.

"And what is your alternative?" Eluthienn replied, filling his voice with passion. He gestured around the chamber with his hand: "Is it to wait here, in the darkness, for Ravinica and Fiondagaard to gather its strength and allow them to lay siege to your cities? To whatever is left of your great vaults and cauldrons after the vampire is done ravaging them? Will this be your fate?"

The gears on the king's augment clicked slowly, but Varkoneth said nothing. There was silence in the chamber, until the Grand Ecclessian spoke.

"The Fromryr have stood since the time of Redcrosse, against foes more numerous than the stars. Do not think our ruin is so easily at hand," he said soberly, his voice devoid of the usual rancid contempt. "But it is true our peoples have stood side by side for hundreds of years. Our great houses trace their lineage to Redcrosse. We share the same god, the same forefather, the same border, and often we share the same enemies. And now perhaps we will share the same fate, as well. We will think on these words, Eluthienn Leonette."

The prince bowed to the Grand Ecclessian and the doors opened behind him. He was escorted from the chamber.

More murmuring after he was gone, Priscilla leaning in to whisper something in the Royal Emissary's ear. Aymeri La'Voline conversed earnestly as Guiscard sat aggressively twirling his moustache, and Anselhelm's features grew sterner with every word the king said. The Lord Marshal and the Lord Admiral both nodded their heads in agreement about something. Only Varkoneth was on his own, his slovenly form retired to the shadows.

Then Lyander's gaze met the Grand Ecclessian's. "Keep our guest company," the latter said from across the chamber. "We will call for you when we are decided."

Lyander and Gabriel left the chamber, following

the octagonal hall round to where Eluthienn was waiting in an antechamber.

Hand resting lightly on the pommel of his sword, Gabriel smiled at Eluthienn. “Very . . .” Gabriel searched for the word, “stirring. I do believe you’ve convinced them all.”

“Ha,” Eluthienn laughed. “There was little convincing needed, witch-hunter. They know Formaria’s survival is tied to mine. They will accept this offer. They have no other choice.”

In Grindlepeake, the thought of the Fromryian High Council agreeing to such a pact was laughable. But Lyander was becoming increasingly inclined to agree with the prince; he saw no other choice open to them other than siding with Eluthienn. Engaging in a war with Ravinica, though, would be disastrous for the Fromryr. The numbers aside, the Fromryian armies only ever fought in the close confines of tunnels or installations. Their force organisation was geared to close-quarters fighting supported by a navy, repelling boarding actions on ships, or fighting in specialised units on the Yeggardanian surface. Lyander, who only knew war in Formaria, held back a shudder at the thought of fighting on an open plain.

“The Fromryr have never fought aboveground before. Only the Ilvalien have cavalry, and even they have only ever fought in the forests of Telaj’Itan – never on an open field, against other cavalry.”

Eluthienn smiled, clapping him on the shoulder and squeezing the top of his arm.

“Of course the great Kalbrayeth Lyander is already thinking of the wars to come.” He leant in to Lyander, his blue eyes hard with seriousness, his voice conspiratorial: “Ravinica would need a commander like you. *I* would need a commander like you.”

Lyander stopped himself from rolling his eyes.

"I thought I was going to be your advisor?"

Eluthienn laughed. "Why not both?"

From behind them, the blind minister stepped into the chamber, arms folded under his robes.

"The High Council has made their decision," he said. "They will see you now. All of you."

"Lead on," Eluthienn said, following the minister out of the room.

"Still waiting for my invite," Gabriel said under his breath, causing Lyander to smile.

"There's still time yet," Lyander said.

In the council chamber, he and Gabriel returned to the higher levels. Eluthienn stood in the centre, smiling confidently up at the High Council. To a member, their faces were drawn, affecting either a grim seriousness or a hard-nosed indifference.

"Eluthienn Leonette," the Grand Ecclessian began. "You came before us an outlaw of your country, a prince without a throne, a man wronged and robbed. But now you stand here our friend and ally. We accept your terms: the death of Lokul and the end of this scourge in return for our support and our allegiance. You will be provided with a ship, crew, arms, and armaments for the task at hand. And upon your return, Formaria will prepare itself for war, and as your ally, aid you in reclaiming Ravinica and in the eventual conquest of Fiondagaard."

Eluthienn bowed his head.

"Our great nations will fight and thrive together, bringing an end to the everlasting wars that plague our borders," the prince said. "As it should have always been, from the very dawn of Redcrosse."

The Grand Ecclessian bowed his head in return.

"Tonight you will be our guest. And tomorrow you will leave in the company of those who brought you here." He turned to Lyander. "Kalbrayeth Lyander and the witch-hunter Gabriel will see you to Lokul's lair, fight by your side against any foes, and ensure the fiend's death."

"I suppose that's what I get for hanging around you long enough," Gabriel whispered out of the corner of his mouth. "I wonder who'll be leading the mission, this time?"

"A most excellent choice in companions," Eluthienn said, and nodded up at Lyander – but he only caught it out the corner of his eye. He was staring at the Grand Ecclessian, trying to read into the folds of flesh, trying to interpret the game he was playing. Lyander was as good as expendable in the Church's eyes – the embarrassment they could do without. Sending someone like him meant they didn't care if he returned. Or, Lyander realised, they didn't expect him to.

Did they not believe Eluthienn would succeed? Or did they find his tale too implausible to take seriously?

"Chambers have been prepared for your stay," the Grand Ecclessian said to the prince. "Thendergaarden welcomes you, Prince of Ravinica."

Two priests pushed the doors open. Eluthienn bowed once more, and was escorted from the chamber. Around them, chatter began among the council members as most stood to leave.

"And here I was thinking I was going to miss your dour mood," Gabriel said, his mouth moving into a sly grin. "Looks like there's still a chance for us to become friends yet." He winked at Lyander and stepped down into the pews, moving toward the Lord Huntsman who greeted him with a smile and a hand clasped around the wrist. Lyander, who could expect nothing of the sort, exited the chamber in search of the nearest lift. Tired, hungry, and in a growing amount of pain, he intended to make his way to his order's barracks where a vulnerum, mess hall, and temporary quarters awaited. And that, he decided, allowing himself a small smile, was the order in which he was going to use them.

Several turns down the corridor, though, he was about to place his hand into a lift terminal when Olions appeared at his shoulder.

"The Grand Ecclessian requests your presence, Kalbrayeth Lyander."

Of course he wouldn't be allowed to just slip off and find peace and rest so easily.

"He requests, does he?" Lyander asked, musing on what might happen if he refused. Nothing good, he was sure. The minister's head titled to the side, a look that told Lyander he didn't understand the sarcasm.

"If you would follow me."

Lyander followed him back along the hallway, but rather than returning to the council chamber, they entered a smaller room. Octagonal, like most, it held just four seats. Upon them were the Grand Ecclessian, the Lord Admiral, the Lord Marshal, and Kasteran Mance, the Grand Master of his order, who wore a red quartered black surcoat. It contrasted heavily with his snowy white hair and cropped beard.

"Your Eminence, my lords," Lyander said as the doors closed behind him.

"The Church is impressed with your actions in finding Eluthienn and bringing him here," Henselt said.

"It hasn't gone unnoticed," Kasteran added.

"Indeed," said the Lord Admiral, who sounded distinctly unimpressed. "Yet you travelled in the company of the dwarf Brazier Veranquis, the son of a traitor and the brother of a disgraced gyre star admiral."

"Like attracts like, it would seem," the Grand Ecclessian said, lacing his pudgy fingers together.

"We would know why you solicited Brazier's help," Blaeken said.

Lyander's prior assumption that his connection with Brazier would land him in hot water was coming true. He supposed the son of a traitor couldn't be trusted with the knowledge that the outlawed prince of Ravinica was running around Formaria.

"Soliciting Brazier's help was purely circumstantial – he had a ship and crew, and we needed a way off Theselan." And then, because he knew it would rile Pulance, and because he found he liked Brazier, he said: "His actions in reporting the attack on the spire were nothing short of heroic, and nearly cost him his life. I would recommend him for the Laurea of Honour."

"Recommend?!" the Grand Ecclessian said, jowls trembling with incredulity. "The disgraced exorcist *recommends* does he?!"

"We will judge his actions another time," Henselt said, giving Lyander a reproachful look from beneath his dark brows. "Are we at least satisfied the dwarf's involvement is merely coincidental?"

Lyander thought *coincidental* an odd word to use; he didn't see how or why Brazier would have crossed paths with Eluthienn on purpose.

But the Lord Admiral was nodding, then the Lord Marshal and the Grand Master did the same before finally the Grand Ecclessian followed. Pulance seemed to gather himself, straightening in his seat, the fat at his temples creasing meanly. He said: "The task that now befalls you is of great importance. One in which you cannot fail."

"Bring Eluthienn to Lokul, make sure he slays the vampire king, then return with the prince," Lyander said. *As if it was going to be that easy.*

"No," the Grand Ecclessian snapped. "You won't. The prince cannot be allowed to live."

"Excuse me?"

"You will accompany the prince to Lokul's lair. You will ensure the prince kills the vampire, then, through whatever means available to you at the time, you will kill Eluthienn."

For a moment, Lyander couldn't tell if he was hearing Pulance correctly. When no one spoke, the reality settled in and all the exhaustion of the past three days hit him so hard he could barely feel his hand. *This is why they're sending me.*

"No," he said. "I won't."

The Grand Ecclessian's gaze darkened, his pudgy lips forming into an ugly snarl. "I would remind you your position in this organisation is little more than a kindness," he said. "You wear its colours and call yourself a member because we let you. What little you have left can be taken from you at any time."

"Let me save you the trouble," Lyander snarled back. "I renounce my position in the Church. If you want an assassin, you can find someone else."

Some of the blotches around the Grand Ecclessian's temple grew darker, his lips quivering with rage.

"Six days ago," Henselt said, cutting through the tension, "the First Champion suffered grievous wounds in the tunnels north of Helmharothell. He was brought back to the vault but died shortly after."

Lyander turned to the Lord Marshal. "I'm sorry to hear that." And he was. Toirsten Loet – Lyander's replacement – was a good man. He held no grudge against his appointment to First Champion, and from what Lyander knew of him, he deserved the position. His death came as a shock. He wasn't sure why he was being told, though.

"As are we all. His death is a loss to the Fromryr," Henselt said. "But it means we need to appoint a new First Champion. Carry out this mission, kill Eluthienn, and you will be reinstated as First Champion of the Knights Redcrosse. All the crimes you committed at spire Lucretia will be forgotten. You'll have your life back."

There really was no pain in Lyander's hand anymore; his body was too light. The weight of the words – words said only to him in dreams – stole all the feeling from him. But despite the dreams, he had never let himself believe they could ever come true. He never let himself hope. He saw the Grand Ecclessian's smile, two thin snakes, slick with sick delight, and he knew he'd been right not to. It was a lie; it must be.

I'm being played. It's written plain as a shaft of tunnel light across the Grand Ecclessian's petrified potato of a face.

But as if he could tell what Lyander was thinking, Henselt said: "Agree to carry out this task, and we will announce your promotion publicly to the other members of the Ordained Conglomerate and the Lords of Thendergaarden. It will be made so."

"Although they will not be made aware of the particulars of the task," the Grand Ecclessian added. "Only those in this room can know of what you will do."

"But the pact you arranged with Eluthienn," Lyander said, still not believing what he was being offered. "Supporting his claim to the Ravinican throne is the only way we prevent a Fiondagaardian invasion."

"The Fromryr will not be fighting a war on the planes of Ravinica," the Grand Ecclessian said.

"And when Fiondagaard claims Ravinica, and marches its armies into Formaria, what then?" Lyander said, realising his shock was rapidly turning to anger. Self-serving greed he expected of the Ecclessius, but this was idiocy. Their only chance for survival was being thrown away because the Ecclessius was too narrow minded to see beyond its own needs.

"We are losing this war, Lyander," Henselt said, matching his tone.

"What?"

"We don't have the forces or the resources to commit to a second front," Henselt said, then took a breath, and for a moment Lyander saw beyond the affected rigidity to a man who looked nearly as exhausted as he felt. "We've been locked in a perpetual stalemate with the Mirrovinjin for nearly a thousand years. The balance of power has tipped in one direction or another during that time, but never enough for one of us to gain the upper hand. But that is no longer the case. The Fromryr won the Heiron campaign, but at great cost. We are crippled."

"As are the Mirrovinjin," Lyander said. Something he knew to be true having fought in the campaign and seen the enemy's losses first hand.

But the Lord Marshal shook his head before looking at the Lord Admiral.

"Navarch intelligence shows the Mirrovinjin have recovered far faster than we anticipated," the old dwarf said. "So fast, the Navarch believes the Heiron campaign was a feint, fooling us into committing the bulk of our forces and thereby weakening us for the real assault."

Lyander couldn't decide what stunned him more: the idea of being offered the position of First Champion or the notion the Fromryr could lose to the Mirrovinjin. The perpetual stalemate was such a constant, such a part of their way of life, it was fixed in their minds. That it could be any other way was anathema to Lyander's world view.

"And now with the vampire threat," Henselt continued, "the Navarch is predicting existential losses. If the spread of this infestation grows, then plans will be drawn for a full retreat to major vaults and cauldrons. A levy of the fighting-age populace may even be issued."

"We cannot fight a war against a full-scale Mirrovinjin invasion, the vampires, and against Ravinica," Blaeken said. "This is our only option."

Lyander was unable to speak. Their only option it might be, but this wasn't him. He wasn't an assassin. He fought evil face-to-face with sword in hand, on fair terms. They invaded his home, attacked his people, killed his friends. In return, he stopped them by killing them. There was no more to it than that. But a blade in the back while smiling at the person you pretended was a friend, and after they honoured an agreement, made Lyander feel sick.

Out of the nausea came another image. Like a voice at the back of his mind – quiet at first, then louder. And as the image of himself as the First Champion of Redcrosse formed, the one of him as an assassin lessened. *Who was Eluthienn to him, anyway?* He remembered Gabriel's words: *Even his plots have plots.* The prince was as conniving as those in front of him. *What difference did it make if they were all as deceitful as each other? What was one choice over another when both choices served those who acted solely for their own ends?*

But at the thought of taking the offer, he could feel the stale sweat under his arms and down his back, the puss and blood oozing into his dirty bandages, and the ache in his battle-sore limbs. It was a feeling he rarely felt: weakness and cowardice. The image of himself as First Champion warred with those feelings as he said flatly: "I understand."

"Good," the Grand Ecclessian said slowly. "Very good. Now, in the event the prince fails to kill Lokul, or you fail to find the creature, we need to know where it can be found and understand what connection, if any, there is between Leoncoure Leonette and the

Lord of Undead."

"While Eluthienn may have demonstrated the Leonette connection with the vampire king," Kasteran said, "it may be the case the other scions of Redcrosse also have this connection. And with every royal house in Formaria being direct descendants of those scions, it would give us options in the event this mission fails."

"As such," Pulance added, "an exorcist has been sent to Acheron, where they will use the breach to cross into the Immuratum and consult the Library of the Nine. They will meet you in Teuron on your way to the Pelothrian mountains, to relay this information to you, and to us via epistolar."

Still numb, still lost in his own thoughts, Lyander felt his brow furrow with confusion. Acheron was controlled by a criminal organisation outside of Fromryian jurisdiction. He also couldn't see why a demon library would tell them anything about an Aeturnic being.

"What could the Library of the Nine tell us about Lokul? And how is it an exorcist is able to use that breach? No Fromryr can enter Acheron."

The Grand Ecclessian turned to Kasteran. "Chaos and darkness have warred with one another as much as they've warred with us for dominion over the real world. A fact we scarcely remember, given the paths into the Immuratum have been sundered for aeons. But scripture tells us the demon kin store information about their enemy in the library."

"Scripture?" Lyander asked. "You mean fable?"

"So were the Lords until recently," Henselt said.

"And as for entering Acheron," the Grand Ecclessian said. "We have an agreement with Orpheus Velgar. We are able to use the breach in return for certain judiciary exemptions."

Which does not surprise me one bit, Lyander

thought.

"Eluthienn cannot know about the information from the library or why we have sought it out," Henselt said.

"And how am I supposed to hide that from him?"

"Your colleague will make contact with you in Acheron. Find a reason to separate yourself from the prince, and you and the other exorcist will contact us via the epistolar," Kasteran said.

"Are you clear on the tasks in hand?" the Grand Ecclessian asked, and Lyander was acutely aware he wasn't being asked if he *accepted* the tasks in hand.

Once again, he thought with an agonising throb from his hand, *the Church used him as it pleased.*

"I'm clear," he said. "But I want Brazier Veranquis and his team as my crew. And the navigator, Matthias Phaser, which shouldn't be a problem, as I offered him a full pardon."

Part of him knew it was a childish retort, an angry reaction to being, once again, in thrall to the Ecclessius. But another part realised as he said the words, he *did* want Brazier and the others as his crew. From his brief interaction, he found he liked the dwarf. And his willingness to throw himself into a pit of voidstone when he could have just sailed straight off the spire told Lyander he was someone worth having at his side. Freyen also seemed capable, if somewhat reserved, like she might have something to hide. And the one with the arm, Switch – she also looked like she could handle herself. And just maybe, if he pulled Matthias from whatever cell the Church was holding him in, it might stop the navigator from hunting down Lyander, if he ever returned from this mission.

The blotches along the Grand Ecclessian's face and neck turned dark purple. "What you *want* –" he began, but the Lord Admiral cut across him: "I agree with the Grand Ecclessian. What you want is hardly of concern." He turned to Pulance, his tone, Lyander thought, weighted with meaning: "But given Veranquis's crew and Phaser are already aware of the prince, it may be prudent to send them. We need to limit those who know of Eluthienn's presence, after all."

The Grand Ecclessian's languid flesh creased into a puffy scowl. He leaned forward in his seat, robes crumpling beneath the folds of his fat, his gaze fixed on Lyander.

"So be it," he said. "Brazier Veranquis, his crew, and the navigator are yours."

EPISTOLAR MESSAGE FION TO VALLORANDYL

A telling in Vallorandyl.

The teller is Emries von Cadst, Duke of Ylstgaar, Adjutant to the Fion Throne, and Marshal of the Western Front.

The witness is Vermillies Sidtch, Lord Regent of Ravinica, and Absolver General.

The telling is the patience with which I accommodate your excuses and your lack of insight, Vermillies. If the stranger's account is true, I see no reason to believe the prince was too well hidden. Eluthienn must have been at Grindlepeake some time to convince Pent of the alliance, and to await the arrival of the Sorel Tan and Fal'Hannians. For your benefit, I will keep this oversight from the emperor. And like your excuses, your opinions are of little value to either of us. Your spies failed to find the prince when he was under your very nose, Vermillies, so you will excuse me if I do not trust what you are certain of knowing.

Whether it is the vampire or some other entity, a force weakens Formaria; our informant's information, although limited, corroborates this. The pact between Eluthienn and Formaria, and the Church's planned betrayal, tells me one thing: The stranger wishes us to believe Formaria remains an ally, therefore providing no motive for us to conduct a preemptive invasion: a story it would have us believe because Formaria is so under strength – and so, as the Ecclessius itself admits, it cannot afford a war with a combined Ravinica and Fiondagaard. My guess is, the Church did not plan to betray Eluthienn at all – they only wish us to believe so, for it is becoming clear this stranger has been sent by them. And while the premise resting upon the Leonette bloodline and a Lord of the Aeturnum is grandiose, it is not necessarily untrue. In Fion, such myths are less fable and more warning and so are not as quickly dismissed.

What is clearly true, though, beyond any doubt, is Formaria knows Ravinica will soon be assimilated within the Fiondagaardian Empire. An outcome we knew would happen with the prince's escape – one we expected. But if the Formryian leadership knows, such rumours will spread and act as kindling among Ravinica's royal houses.

You can expect fires, Vermillies. Make sure you put them out. If not, your future truly is doomed. The teller is Emries von Cadst. The witness is Vermillies Sidtch, Lord Regent, and no others.

EPISTOLAR MESSAGE VALLORANDYL TO FION

A telling in Fion.

The teller is Vermillies Sidtch, Lord Regent of Ravinica, and Absolver General.

The witness is Emries von Cadst, Duke of Ylstgaar, Adjutant to the Fion Throne, and Marshal of the Western Front.

The telling is of the third night the stranger came before the throne. The third and final night, concealed as ever, but still, My Duke, I heard the grin through which he told his tale. And after providing its ending, I demanded he give me evidence of the account, for it is conceited and convenient. But he slunk back to the shadows, out of my sight. Any use we might have had from its conclusion is negligible, for all the players are lost or scattered, and finding Lokul's lair to ascertain the veracity would be an impossibility.

Formaria, as you say, is vulnerable, perhaps the most vulnerable it has ever been in all its thousand years. Even with all the technologies they are so unjustly gifted, the Fromryr were unable to stem the tide of this supposed vampire threat on their own. In all matters, I defer to your wisdom, and so what I say next is not intended to invoke your displeasure, but I implore you to consider the possibility this stranger is not sent by Formaria.

Fabricating a tale about betraying Eluthienn and having us believe they are not truly allies of the prince, I can understand, but what good would it do to let us know the country is weakened? If we were to believe it, would it not tempt us into an invasion, to fight in their territory where they will surely bleed us, instead of us them if they were to fight on Ravinica's planes? Or perhaps this is some other party altogether, the entire tale a lie intended to draw us into a conflict with Formaria? Would we not be stretched too thin? Would we then not be vulnerable from other quarters? Once again, I can only recount as accurately as possible the stranger's tale, and trust to your infinite judgement.

Twelve

Brazier

The vulnerum was eight or nine interlinked heptagons, each of their sides radiating an icy white channel meeting in their vaulted peaks. In each, La'Voline anomancers and field medics, wearing quartered red and green surcoats over beige gambesons, attempted to save the dying. Those who were too far gone were attended by black-robed Ecclessiarchal priests, an arborealis cross in one hand, scripture in the other, solemnly delivering last rites.

In the middle of three of the spaces were solid grey blocks, each holding a patient in varying stages of infirmity. On the one in Brazier's field of vision, a piece of black iron was slowly removed from a dwarf's midsection. As the surgeon pulled with a pair of silver tongs, an anomancer stood with her hands directed at the wound. Brazier could just about see the flesh reknitting as the iron retreated.

Standing in the middle of one of the heptagons surrounded by three La'Voline anomancers, he hoped his own wounds were as easy to heal. The sleeves of their gambesons rolled up, their hands forming a sort of butterfly shape, they rotated them slowly, as if moulding a ball out of clay. Eyes closed, they muttered rapidly in an Old World tongue; occasionally one of their eyelids would flutter, a little dance of skin and lashes, but otherwise there was nothing visible to suggest their spells were working.

That didn't mean he couldn't feel it.

Inside his thighs, it felt as if the fibres of his muscles were reforming, like links coming together. A mildly pleasant feeling, he tried to focus on that instead of what was happening around his abdomen. There, he was fairly certain his liver and kidneys were moving back into their correct positions. Wet, squelchy movements, that at once made him hungry, nauseous, and like he needed to vacate his bowls – something he did not want to do with Freyen in the next heptagon.

Pacing in a loose circle, a bored look on her face, it would occasionally flash with annoyance every time she glanced at the far side of the chamber where the Ecclessius guards stood either side of the entrance.

"That's getting a bit annoying," Switch said as Freyen passed her for the fourth time. Sat cross-legged, the contents of her tool belt laid out in front of her, she was using a type of mandrel to tighten the joints on her augment. Or that's what Brazier guessed she was doing.

"So is being held prisoner when you haven't committed a crime," Freyen muttered.

"Maybe our new pal, Lyander, can get us a pardon," Switch said.

Freyen snorted. "Something tells me his pardons don't count for much," she said.

She turned, and as she moved out of the way,

Brazier watched the guard's heads snap around as a man walked up the steps. A head taller than both, his red quartered black surcoat and black gambeson was a stark contrast to those in red, green, and beige. He rested one hand upon the pommel of a sword as long as Brazier was tall, while the other was bandaged and held stiffly at his side. He had dark cropped hair – messy and unwashed – dark eyes surrounded by lines of exhaustion, and a face covered in several weeks' worth of growth. It was all perfectly in keeping with the sort of jaw line made for a man whose only expressions seemed to be grim and grimmer.

Kalbrayeth Lyander looked around until his gaze fell on Brazier, and he made his way across the busy vulnerum, the healers and priests taking one look at his face and moving swiftly out of his way.

The exorcist nodded to Switch and Freyen, then said to Brazier: "You look better."

"You don't," Switch said, looking up at him. Brazier found himself agreeing with her; if anything, he looked worse.

"I'll get the anomancers to take a look at me."

"Might want to ask them to run you a bath while you're at it," Switch said.

The exorcist's hard mouth became a tired smile. "You're not exactly smelling like roses, either," he said.

"Oh, I know. Difference is, I'd like to do something about that but no one's letting us leave."

"I might be able to help."

"Does it involve a pardon?" Freyen asked, an eyebrow raised.

"Have you committed a crime?" Lyander asked, his own brow knitting together.

Switch gave the device she was holding a hard twist, then said: "You tell us. This is the second time we've been imprisoned in less than two days."

Lyander's face softened in understanding.

"The Church was holding you for questioning over your association with Matthias Phaser."

"*Was* holding us?" Freyen asked.

Brazier felt the soft grip all over his body lessen. The anomancers dropped their hands and opened their eyes. The one in front of him ran a hand through her short blonde hair, then massaged one of her wrists with her other.

"We're done here. Your body is healed but go easy over the next few days, especially on anything stronger than ale; your internal organs are still delicate."

I could have told you that, he thought, probing gingerly at his side.

"Would you like us to attend to you now, exorcist?"

"Later."

The anomancer nodded, then all three left to attend other patients.

"So the Church is no longer holding us here?" Brazier asked.

Lyander gave an awkward shrug. "I think that depends."

Switch stretched out her bronzite limb, one of the pistons releasing a light hiss. "Depends on what?"

"On whether you accept the proposal I'm about to put to you."

Lyander looked around the chamber, making sure no one was in earshot.

"Well, don't hold out on us," Switch said. "It's not like we're getting any cleaner just sitting here."

The exorcist gave another weak smile, then said quietly: "As you are now very aware, creatures known as vampires are attacking installations and ships across Formaria, with devastating effect. Their speed and their ability to turn their victims means their spread is going all but uncontested. There is, however, a means of defeating them in a single blow. The vampires are spawned from a single maker – a sort of Aeturnic deity. The man we travelled with – who you know is the prince of Ravinica – knows where to find this maker and is capable of killing it, and in doing so, will destroy the rest. The Ecclessius has tasked me with escorting Eluthienn to the location of this being, and aiding him in its destruction. We need a crew to get us there, so I requested you three."

"We'll do it," Brazier said.

"Whoa there, Captain," Switch said. "You just got your insides put back into place and now you want to go hunting Aeturnic gods?"

"My insides are fine. And if destroying a god is going to kill the things that attacked the *Chalice*, then yeah, I want to go hunt it down."

He could feel Freyen's disapproving eyes on him.

"How does Eluthienn know where to find this maker?" she asked. "And how does he know killing it will kill all the others?"

"That's a long story," Lyander said.

One he looks like he's been over several times, Brazier thought.

"But I can explain it all on the way."

Freyen's dark brown eyes peeled into suspicion, her arms crossing over her chest. "Why us? We're a mining crew, not soldiers."

"The way you got yourselves out of Theselan tells me you're more than just miners. And you have experience with the vampires."

"We have experience of *running away* from the vampires," Switch corrected him.

"Right now, that's more than pretty much everyone else in Formaria."

"Where is it, this maker?" Brazier asked.

The look on the exorcist's face said he was deciding how much to tell them. "Beyond the Pelothrian mountains," he said after a pause.

"We'll need a navigator, then."

"We have one. The Ecclessius has also agreed to honour the pardon I offered Matthias."

Brazier felt his jaw clench. His own father, who he had loved and respected as much as his brother, had been executed as a traitor under circumstances that had never made sense or been explained to him. He could never reconcile it with the respect everyone paid to house Veranquis, and so the notion of "traitor to Formaria" was something he'd never come to terms with. It left him with a strange, queasy shame at the idea of being associated with Matthias, who he suspected had committed crimes against Formaria. It was made worse by the knowledge Matthias was also responsible for saving his life and those of his friends, twice over. *But,* he thought, *if being reminded of your family's past is the cost of stopping these things, of preventing another Chalice, it's a price you'll gladly pay, and you know it.*

"Fine. At least you picked a good pilot," he said.

Freyen turned her disapproving look in his direction before turning it back on Lyander.

"Do we have a choice in this?" she asked.

Lyander shrugged awkwardly. "If you don't come with me, you're held by the Ecclessius for questioning. If you do come with me, there's four hundred gold Vidicks in it for each of you. Half now, half when we're back."

Switch stopped fiddling with a bolt on her arm, and looked up at the exorcist, an eyebrow raised.

"We leave tomorrow," Lyander said. "So I need an answer in the next hour."

"Where will you be?" Brazier asked.

Lyander raised his wounded hand, the bandages stained shades of dark yellow and brown.

"In here," he said, and walked off toward the nearest free anomancer. An aged gnome with a few final strands of grey hair, he held the hand an inch from his eyes before waving over two more healers.

"We just spent the last two days trying to put as much distance between us and the vampires as possible," Switch said, drawing his attention. "And now you want to go hunting down the one who made them?"

"I want to stop these things," Brazier said. "I want to stop them from doing to another crew what they did to my brother and the *Chalice*."

"Zee," Freyen said in a placating tone, "this doesn't feel right. Why would the outlawed prince of Ravinica know where this maker is? And why would he just offer to go and kill it?"

"And why is an exorcist going with him?" Switch added. "Don't get me wrong, Lyander looks like he could kill most things several times over, but didn't he say these things are Aeturnic?"

"Switch is right," Freyen said before Brazier could answer either question. "The Ecclessius is sending an exorcist, an outlawed prince, a criminal, and an addict to fight a vampire king. What does that tell you?"

"An addict?" Brazier and Switch asked at the same time.

Freyen sighed. "When I was looking through the *Dawn*'s stores, trying to find medicine for *you*," she said, as if he'd nearly died on purpose. "I saw Gabriel swallow a vial of something. Whatever it was gave him the sort of shakes people get from tunnel blindness."

Or, Brazier knew, from toxin addictions.

"He is a witch-hunter," Switch ventured. "They take all sorts of stuff."

"To guard against witches or to cross into the

Aeturnum," Freyen said. "Neither of which was happening on the *Dawn*."

To Brazier, it made little difference. "Okay," he said, shrugging. "It's an unconventional crew. So what?"

"So, they're all expendable," Freyen said. "Whatever the Ecclessius has agreed to with Eluthienn, they don't expect him to return, and your brother wouldn't want you to throw your life away."

Something in his stomach squelched uncomfortably as he felt his anger rise. Part of him knew it was just a reaction to being told what his brother would or wouldn't want. Another part of him knew Torquen would agree with Freyen. *But your brother, thanks to you*, he thought with anger, aching regret, and shame, *is not here to agree or disagree with anyone*. "Stopping a vampire horde from taking over Formaria is hardly throwing our lives away," he said.

Freyen pulled one of the curls out of her face, forcing it angrily behind her ear.

"Perhaps," she said. "But we don't have to be the ones to do it."

"And what else are we going to do?" Brazier asked. "Join another crew, and hope it doesn't get attacked like the *Chalice*? Or wait around for the levy? You heard Lyander's words; the vampires aren't being stopped. And if Theselan fell that quickly, other spires will, as well. And when that begins to happen, there will be a levy of all able Fromryr. We'll end up fighting these things no matter what."

"The Ecclessius haven't tried to raise a levy in over four centuries," she said, but there was an edge of doubt in Freyen's voice.

"They put plans in place for one just before the last Heiron campaign ended," Brazier said. "Torquen told me if it had gone on any longer, they would have implemented it. The Ecclessius will do it, if they think it's necessary."

There was silence between the three of them, the only sounds the healer's mutterings and the weak groans of those being healed.

Switch chewed the inside of her lip before looking up at Freyen. "Maybe Zee's right. I'd rather be hunting some daddy vampire than waiting in fear of all his offspring to show up."

"I know you think I'm doing this because of Torquen," Brazier said, trying to keep his voice measured, "and I am, but we have a chance to stop these things."

Freyen twirled a curl between her fingers as she thought, a strange expression on her face as she held Brazier's gaze.

"Okay," she said eventually. "But we're just the crew. We get them there and we get them back. Nothing more."

"I think Lyander has the whole fighting thing covered," Switch said, but Freyen was looking at him expectantly.

"We're just the crew," he said, patting the air with his hands.

Freyen gave a reluctant nod, and Brazier felt a ripple of relief coursing down his body. But there was also an undercurrent to the feeling – something distinctly like the foreshadowing of guilt. Like the guilt he felt at the raw knowledge that it was him who convinced Torquen to respond to the distress beacon. That it was because of him the *Chalice* and almost its entire crew sailed straight to their deaths. *Am I sailing Switch and Freyen to their deaths now?* He ground his teeth, forcing the thought from his mind. This was his chance to make right that wrong; if he didn't take it, he would be living beneath the shadow of guilt for the rest of his life.

"I'll let Lyander know," he said, looking over at

the exorcist encircled by three anomancers, his torn hand raised in front of him, the healers' faces straining with the effort of whatever spell they were casting. "And then we can go spend that gold."

#

The Formarians were a race of war. They built ships, Constructii, and nigh-impenetrable installations. They did not, however, build inns. And so, the oak wood table they all sat around seemed strangely fragile against the hard grey walls and their veins of gyre light. Other tables were scattered around the room, and on one side, barrels that Brazier could have climbed into and had room to spare were suspended from a wooded crossbeam. A selection of smaller casks stood on a bench to the side; a dwarf with grey hair and a dirty apron tied around his waist pulled a stopper from one, and let a short flow of amber liquid pour into a mug.

A woman in a red utility gambeson and trousers placed a silver knorte on the bench and took the mug from the dwarf, carrying it over to a long bench to join what must be the rest of her crew.

At the end of it, next to the steps rising into the street, three dwarves sat on chairs, between them a pipe and tabor, a flute, and a viol. The tabor player beat rhythmically, the sound softened by the flute's whimsy, while both were drawn into a haunting intensity by the viol's depths. Every now and then the pipe's light melody would propel the song along.

"To the *Chalice*," Brazier said, raising his voice over the hum, and lifting his mug into the air.

"To Axelock and Dalfin," Switch said.

"To Axelock and Dalfin," Brazier and Freyen said together, their mugs knocking together, splashing froth into each other's drinks.

Then finally, Brazier added: "To killing vampires."

"May Lyander leave some for the rest of us," Switch said, and drank long, deep gulps. Brazier followed suit, enjoying the rich nuttiness of the Ravinican brown ale. With the Church's gold in their pockets, they were drinking the expensive import instead of the stout earthiness of the mushroom-based beer brewed underground. "What do you think his deal is, anyway? Doesn't look like any exorcist I've ever seen."

"That's because he's not, really," Freyen said. "I looked into his script. Kalbrayeth Lyander used to be a First Champion of the Knights Redcrosse until he lost spire Lucretia to the Mirrovinjin, along with a whole detachment. He was reassigned to the Order Malignia as an exorcist."

"Shit," Switch said. "Thought he looked miserable about something. Probably bored out of his mind."

"Maybe." Freyen shrugged, a doubtful look on her face. "I found other things. Ramovand Rosantz was at Lucretia, as well, at the head of a reinforcing army. But the installation was purged and then Lyander faced a trial over its loss. Ramovand and his father were at the trial."

"That's not unusual," Brazier said after taking a swig of his drink. "Members of royal families often sit as judges on trials. And if Ramovand was there when Lucretia fell, it makes sense for him to be at the trial."

"Lyander calls for reinforcements, those reinforcements arrive, and then he orders the spire purged," Freyen said. "That doesn't make sense."

In the changing tides of battle, decisions were made that made little sense to those fighting in them. But Freyen was right, Brazier couldn't think of a reason for purging a spire after filling it with reinforcements.

"You think Ramovand ordered the purge and the blame was pinned on Lyander?"

Freyen took a mouthful of beer, licking her lips. "If he took the blame before, then the Ecclessius would have no problem sending him on a mission like this."

"Or," Switch said, her augmented elbow resting on the tabletop, a bronze finger in the air. "The Ecclessius is sending its best killer on a mission to go and kill something. Simple as that."

"From what I saw in Theselan, between him and Gabriel, they're sending the right people."

"And us," Freyen asked. "Are we the right people?"

"Little late to back out now," Switch said. "We've spent enough of the Church's gold, and I plan on spending plenty more of it before this night is done." She took another long gulp of ale and wiped her mouth with the back of her real hand. "Now, are you going to tell us why the operations officer of an ice hauler knows how to dig through hex networks?"

Freyen took another lengthy swig before answering. "I'll tell you that right after you tell us how you got that arm," she said.

Switch's grin became wolf-like. "Like I've already said, I was awarded it by the Lord Admiral of the Navarch."

"What's his name?" Brazier asked.

"Who?" Switch asked.

"The Lord Admiral."

"You know," Switch said, her lips pursing and brow furrowing. "The rude bastard never properly introduced himself."

Both Brazier and Freyen laughed, and for a moment he forgot about the *Chalice*, he forgot about hunting down a vampire king, and he forgot about his brother.

#

Later, Switch rose drunkenly from the table and wandered over to two dwarves and a gnome in dark blue military doublets. Whatever line she delivered made the two dwarves roar with laughter and the gnome grin shyly at her over the top of his mug. Switch winked at him, causing his pointed ears to turn red.

"Well, I suppose we could all be dead pretty soon," Freyen said.

"That's not the way this is going to go," Brazier said. "If I can help it."

Freyen turned round in her seat to face him, forearms on the table, leaning forward, her hands clasped around her mug.

"The *Chalice* was not your fault," she said, her brown eyes fixed on his with a kind of melancholic intensity.

"It was me who convinced Torquen to answer the distress beacon," he said, holding her gaze, despite the desire to look anywhere else.

Her eyes softened, a string of curls falling across her face. She didn't seem to notice. "The *Chalice* had a legal and moral obligation to respond to that distress beacon."

Brazier shook his head. "Torquen knew something was off; he knew it was a trap. And it was me who convinced him otherwise. I told him *we're not the sort to just fly on by*."

"Well, Torquen knowing it was a trap sounds like Torquen," Freyen said, "but you know what else sounds like Torquen? A dwarf who gives aid to those who need it. You really think if you weren't there, he would have sailed on? Because I don't."

Freyen was right, but it didn't lessen the

agonising feeling lodged beneath his sternum. It was *his* decision to answer the distress beacon – *his* call. In another world where he was captain, he would have answered that distress beacon without a second thought. And something about that made him feel doubt – fear, even.

"Is that what this is all about?" Freyen asked. "You think killing Lokul is going to make you feel better about sending the *Chalice* into a trap?"

"I think killing Lokul is going to prevent another *Chalice*. And that's why I'm doing it."

Eight mugs of ale in and a glazed film coated his vision, but he could still see the look on Freyen's face – distrust and something that could have been sadness.

"You don't have to come, you know," Brazier said.

She laughed, but there was no real mirth in it. "Don't think the Ecclessius is going to let me off the hook like that. And anyway, who's going to pour medicine down your throat the next time you jump into a pit of voidstone?"

She drained the rest of her ale and stood. "I'll see you in the morning."

And without waiting for a reply, she wove her way between the tables. Watching her gracefully avoid the drunken clientele, Brazier sensed the night could have turned out differently; he wasn't entirely sure how, though.

Finishing his ale, he leant back in his seat, letting the sounds of music and voices wash over him. Then, without a clear idea of exactly what he was doing, he bought another ale and paid for the tankard, as well. Having put away nine of them already, he was only aware, on a subconscious level, of where he was going. And it was only when he reached the vault's edge, as smooth stone lit by a sapphire glow gave way to rock and blackness, that he knew why he was there.

Stumbling up to the very edge, his toe caps less than an inch from the nothingness, he opened the tankard lid with his thumb, and tipped half the contents into the abyss.

"Dream deep in the endless black, brother."

He gulped down the rest in one.

Standing there, gently rocking back and forth, staring into a darkness many believed went on forever, he let himself feel the thing buried since the moment they fled on the *Solace*. It was an ache in his chest, like a mace's blunt force. Except this mace hit a weak point, reopening a wound yet to truly heal. That wound held his parents, and now included his brother. More than that, though, Torquen was also his captain – the person he could turn to for whatever decision needed to be made, who would tell him with a small smile or a slight turn of the head whether that decision was right or wrong. It was like losing two people at the same time and filled the cavity left by the mace with a feeling of unfairness and loneliness so powerful it burned through his drunkenness.

He knew Freyen was right; killing Lokul wouldn't fill that void, wouldn't erase those feelings. But he needed to do it nonetheless.

#

Brazier's hangover felt as if his brain was trying to bludgeon its way out of his skull. Luckily for him, the Navarch High Command's personal hangar bay was lit with just a cross hatch of cool teal blue channels: six straight lines crossing horizontally with another six crossing vertically.

The only ship in the bay, the *Shian Anchorite*, was mercifully powered down, its six thrusters spinning up a soothing lapis lazuli. Any other hangar bay and it would have been the blaring crystal blue of unrefined ice reflected off white-grey surfaces and gleaming near-golden hulls – an effect Brazier was sure would have him throwing up last night's ale.

"You jump in another pit of voidstone since I last saw you?" Lyander said as he joined him at the bottom of the access ramp. Looking markedly better than when they were in the vulnerum, the exorcist wore a chain vest and skirt, and gambeson beneath his surcoat. His hand, although swollen, was no longer bound in soiled bandages. Instead, an ugly line of scar tissue ran from the knuckle down to his wrist.

Lyander caught Brazier looking at it. "Took five anomancers in the end," he said, holding it up. "And only because two of them passed out with the effort. Still hurts like black hell, though."

"Are all vampire wounds that hard to heal?" Freyen asked.

Lyander shrugged. "As we've had no reports of anomancers treating other survivors, we don't know. But for everyone else's sake, I hope I'm just a special case."

Lift doors opened on a chute built into the back wall, and Gabriel and Eluthienn stepped onto the hangar bay. A travel sack in one hand, his sword belt in the other, the witch-hunter sniffed the air as he strolled up to them. "Are we opening a brewery on this little vampire hunt?"

Eluthienn, also carrying a travelling sack, and wearing dark leather armour beneath his black cloak, smiled. "Ravinican brown – good choice."

"As you've all clearly spent a good amount of the Church's gold, I'll assume no one's here to pull out?" Lyander said.

Brazier shook his head, an action he deeply regretted. "No one is pulling out."

"Good," the exorcist said, and with his good hand produced four wooden crosses tied to the end of leather necklaces. "You're going to want to wear these."

"Really?" Switch said, looking at them dubiously.

"They protect against the vampire's vocal attack," Lyander said, and Brazier felt a sorrowful stab deep in his chest at the memory of Axelock dying to a scream. He took one of the crosses and placed it around his neck. Switch and Freyen did the same.

"After you, then," Lyander said, holding out an arm to the ship's access ramp.

On a hex display, Brazier imagined the *Anchorite* would look like the flat of two blades pressed together, tapering at either end, with insect-like limbs sprouting along its middle. The bow, presumably the nav deck, ended in a pair of curved and elongated tips, which as a sculpt would not look unlike pincers. Lining the top of the hull, the bottom, and the sides were six repeater turrets, the bows relaxed, the gear housings silent and absent of gyre light. Even for a battle-frigate, Brazier thought the ship deadly.

Inside, it was like most frigates. The fuselage doubled to accommodate infantry, a stairwell led to her bow and the nav deck, while doors either side of it led into other compartments. At the opposite end, toward the stern, there was a weapons bay with armour and arms lining the walls. There were also chain vests and leather cuirasses, along with swords, axes, and various crossbows, including a body-mounted bolt thrower and several bundles of bolts.

"Nav deck," Lyander said, passing by him. "We need to run through the plan."

"There's a plan?" Gabriel said, passing by him and winking at Brazier, but the exorcist gave no reply.

He followed them up the stairwell and onto a

landing with access doors port and starboard, and a set of heavy double doors to the bow. Lyander walked up to them and pressed his hand into a nearby terminal; a moment later, they opened onto the nav deck. Octagonal in shape, there was a single command terminal in the centre with various wells, and beyond it, the navigation pit.

Matthias stood on the opposite side of the terminal. "Seems we keep doing this," he said, looking at Brazier. "Although I gotta say, you look better than you did last time. Wasn't sure you were going to make it."

"Sorry to disappoint you," Brazier said. The navigator's smile was sly and predatory; *there'll be other opportunities, I'm sure*, it seemed to say. Brazier ignored it, and along with everyone else, took a place around the command terminal.

Lyander placed his hand into one of the nearest depressions and muttered several commands. The display rippled before forming into a map of Formaria.

"Our mission is simple," he said, looking at each of them in turn. "Travel to Lokul's lair, Eluthienn destroys the vampire king, with the aid of Gabriel and myself, and we return the way we came."

He pointed at an installation in the northeast of Formaria. "You will fly us to Teuron, where we will refuel the ship." His finger moved east to a solid wall of hex. "Then you will fly us to the edge of the Pelothrian mountains, where, Eluthienn has informed us, there's a passage leading to Lokul's lair. You'll drop us at a safe distance," he said, looking at Brazier. "Then Eluthienn, Gabriel, and myself will enter, kill Lokul, then come back and get picked up by you. As agreed, you are not expected to engage the maker in its lair, but you are expected to defend the ship, if necessary."

He looked around the command terminal again.

"Any questions?"

"Yes," Freyen said. "What do we know about the location of this lair? And what's the access like from the surrounding tunnels?"

"We don't know any of that," Lyander said.

"What about the structure itself? How long will it take you to get through it?"

"That's something we'll need to assess when we're there."

Freyen's brow creased into a dubious frown. "What about enemy numbers? How heavily defended will it be?" she asked.

"We don't know that, either."

She rubbed at the rings under her eyes, then ran a hand through her curls to pull them out of her face.

"So we're just going to turn up and hope for the best?"

Lyander gave a half shrug, which seemed to mean 'yeah, that's about right.'

Freyen's frown deepened. "Is this how you usually do things?"

"This is grand strategy for Kalbrayeth Lyander," Gabriel said, his tone saturated with sarcasm.

The exorcist gave the witch-hunter a deprecatory glance. "Our information is limited," Lyander said. "So we do what we can with what we've got."

"Have there been any other reports of attacks on installations?" Brazier asked. "Teuron is well north of Theselan but not impossible to get to, especially if you move as fast as a vampire."

"Another miner went dark overnight but no attacks on spires," Lyander said. "But Teuron is a front line installation; a Mirrovinjin presence is likely."

"You mean it's a war zone," Switch said.

"It's also the only safe passage to the part of the Pelothrian mountains we need to get to."

“Okay,” Freyen said, crossing her arms. “So dangerous, followed by more dangerous.”

“Nothing you three can’t handle,” Lyander said, then turned to Matthias: “Let’s get her spun up and ready for launch.”

“I take it you’re the captain now?” the navigator said with a smile.

“I am. Brazier is first officer. So in my absence, you do what he says.”

“Just like old times,” Matthias said, winking at Brazier and kneeling in the nav pit.

“I hope not exactly like old times,” Switch said under her breath.

The *Anchorite*’s thrusters sent a pulsing thrum through the hull and he felt the ship rise into the air before Matthias engaged the spatial anchor, and the weightless feeling dispersed.

“Over to you,” Lyander said to him.

During the next eight hours, Brazier ran through the ship’s systems with Switch and Freyen, and occasionally Matthias.

The first four of those he spent listening to Switch rhapsodize about the *Anchorite*’s engine quality, the perfect upkeep of the coils, and the flow-through rate of the synthesisers. He then spent the following four hours listening to her complain there was nothing to fix. Freyen was almost the same, running a hex diagnostic script against the six repeater turrets, only to find they all tracked and target-locked with near flawless accuracy. She ran other diagnostics with Matthias only to produce the same result; the *Anchorite*’s flight systems ran without fault, and the thrusters responded to his slightest touch.

Eluthienn leant against the command terminal, watching and listening to the whole affair, his impish blue eyes taking it all in as if every second of the conversation was important to him. Occasionally he would ask a question – often so simple, they were what Brazier would expect from a child. But each time he or Freyen responded, he reminded himself there was a whole other world outside of Formaria – no part of which used gyre ships.

"Tell me, Brazier," Eluthienn said after Freyen checked the turrets for a third time. "This ship, it is designed purely for battle?"

"Most are, to be honest with you. But this one in particular, yes."

"Then why do I not see gyre cannons?"

Brazier caught the look of surprise on Freyen's face, and forced his own to be as impassive as possible; it was one of the prince's more basic questions.

"Most ships don't run gyre cannons," he said. "Even for gyre stars, it's too risky. They have an open casing so the converted gyre ice fed through it can be drawn upon and targeted by enemy casters. The dwarves found that out the hard way during the Fennian war. So most ships have their cannons replaced with bolt throwers."

"An open casing?" the prince asked. "Aren't the thrusters also *open*?"

"In a sense," Brazier said. "But there's little power output from the discs; they *draw in* the gyre currents in Formaria, allowing the ship to fly."

The prince made a good show of understanding, then said: "So the cannons are not used at all?"

"Sometimes they're fitted to gyre stars but only in extreme circumstances. Doing so requires a full cadre of war casters. And good war casters, as well, which means pulling them from the front line. The cost and the risk is rarely worth the reward."

"So why would they be used?"

Brazier ran a hand through his hair, thinking.

"Targeted strikes, where significant damage needs to be inflicted straight away, or in the defence of major vaults or cauldrons. They've been used to defend Helmharothell several times."

"And when they're not in use?"

"Locked in secret locations, guarded by small armies of Constructii."

The prince stroked at his beard and moustache. "Ravinica has similar weapons – usually mounted on waggon platforms drawn by horses. They have the same vulnerabilities but they have still been used against Fiondagaardian armies during our wars with one another. Even though for us, they are rare weapons."

"In Formaria," Brazier replied, "a war caster must defend an entire ship or even fleets of ships, in addition to any troops that are deployed, against an enemy whose sorcerers are both plentiful and powerful. On the borders of Ravinica, your mages only need to defend a single war machine against an enemy who I've heard has few sorcerers."

"In Fion, the emperor either kills or enslaves all who demonstrate magical abilities. It's said he fears those with the power, and so keeps them weak."

"Sounds like he's just kneecapping his military."

Eluthienn gave a short laugh. "What Fion lacks in sorcerers they make up for in numbers and brutality. Their population is three times that of Ravinica's, or so we believe. And yet, the country is half the size and sparse in arable land, so it is a cruel place for its people. Their soldiers fair little better – before being sent to our border, they are trained against ogre tribes and troll death cults in the northern and eastern mountains. Those we capture tell us that we are an easy posting."

"If they're stronger, why has Fiondagaard lost every war with Ravinica?" Brazier asked.

"They have not lost," the prince said. "Each has

ended in stalemate, the front line shifting by several miles, perhaps, but neither side has made it beyond Alstgaar or Ylstgaar. What we lack in numbers we make up for in weaponry and mages. What they lack in those, they make up for in numbers. And a thousand years later, here we are still, staring at each other across miles of trenches, neither side gaining the upper hand."

"Until now," Freyen said, confusing Brazier with the comment.

A smile crept up the prince's face, beginning with just the corners of his mouth before reaching his eyes.

"Until now," he said, confusing Brazier even more.

"Why until now?"

"If no side can win a conventional war," Freyen said, "that leaves espionage or political warfare, which might look something like deposing a prince and placing a puppet leader on the throne in his place."

Eluthienn's smile turned into a toothy grin.

"But that prince escaped and wants his throne back," she continued, "so he seeks out the help of a friendly country, and in exchange he offers to help them with the vampire horde overrunning their cities."

Eluthienn began clapping as Brazier felt his jaw dropping. Over the prince's shoulder he could see even Matthias turning his head toward the conversation.

"That would mean a war with Ravinica," Brazier said.

"In some fashion, a war is likely," Eluthienn said.

"And the High Council agreed to this?" Freyen asked.

"Now, would I choose to be here otherwise?"

Behind them, Matthias's chuckle sounded like rocks tumbling down a hill.

"The thought of our alliance amuses you, navigator?" Eluthienn said.

"Brazier, you were in the military, weren't you?" Matthias asked.

"I did my ten years."

"How many times did you fight aboveground?"

"I went straight into the navy – so not once."

"Skipped the infantry – a navy family, then. But even if you'd done your time, how much of that would have been fighting aboveground? And I don't mean clearing bugs off surface installations."

Avoiding the infantry tithe – something only families with political connections could achieve – was usually met with resentment or mockery, but the way Matthias said *a navy family, then* didn't sound like a slight.

"Probably very little," Brazier said.

"You see – that's what I find funny," Matthias said. "Fromryr fighting in open fields, on planes of hills, and in forests where you can see from one end to the other."

"What about Fromryr led and trained by Ravinican officers?"

The navigator chuckled again. "That would be a sight to behold. Luckily for me, I won't be around to see it."

"There's a surprise," Freyen said. "Duty not your thing?"

"It's not my war," Matthias said softly, a hint of bitterness in his voice. "None of this is my war."

"An undead horde taking over Formaria is every Fromryian's war," Brazier said.

"See, that's where you're wrong – I'm not with all of you."

"If that was true, why wait for us in Theselan?"

"Because your enginator was holding a

crossbow to the back of my head." The navigator twisted round, looking at him out of the corner of his vision. "I would have left you there to become undead versions of yourselves along with everyone else."

"At least we know where we stand," Freyen said as the nav deck doors slid apart behind them.

"Zee," Switch said, coming to stand beside him. "This is the most boring ship I've ever been on." She threw a bronzite hand into the air. "Everything works."

"Well, I'm about to make your life a lot more interesting," Matthias said.

"If you're going to suggest we sleep together," Switch said, "I think I'd rather walk blindfolded along the edge of a cavern."

"All our lives are about to get a lot more interesting," the navigator replied, and the command display changed, the tunnel's semi-serpentine shapes crumbling and reforming into the hard lines and angular faces of an installation.

Its west facing lined the edge of a cavern, its hangar bay open to the void while its north, east, and south facings were built into solid rock. At a much higher level, another hangar bay faced eastward. At this level, the north, east, and south facings were surrounded by a large expanse of flat rock, tunnels and passages shooting off from it. Dotted here and there throughout these nearby routes were smaller structures: coves and cradles. Farther south they might be inhabited – small communities protected by a single garrison. But on the front line, Brazier knew they were merely defensive structures, fought over for their strategic value in the never-ending battles between the Fromryr and the Mirrovinjin.

Looking closer, he saw tiny shapes moving in clusters, some on the plane of rock stretching out from the spire, some around the smaller structures, but most were moving through tunnels. One group came together with another along a thin passage, one of its sides dropping away to the void. As the groups merged, they became smaller, the shapes crumbling so only half their number remained.

"They're engaged in multiple skirmishes," Brazier said. "Looks like they're trying to defend passages all around the spire."

"What we're looking at is several hours old," Matthias said. "It's part of a hex broadcast to all ships in the area, warning them the spire is under attack and Mirrovinjin forces are active in the nearby tunnels."

"How far out are we?" Freyen asked.

"Another two hours."

"Tether me to wherever Lyander is," Brazier said.

The nearest well vibrated as if something swam beneath its surface.

"Lyander you're needed on the nav."

"On my way." The exorcist's voice sent a single pulse across the hex before the connection dropped.

A moment later, Brazier heard Lyander pulling himself up the stairwell, then the nav deck doors opened and he came to stand opposite Brazier.

"Teuron?" he asked, eyes roaming across the display.

"Yeah," Brazier said.

"They're fighting in too many places," Lyander said, brow furrowing. "They shouldn't have allowed themselves to be drawn out like that."

"Could've lost communication with one another," Brazier said.

"That would mean the central command structure has broken down, or they've lost war casters and can't send orders to units."

"Or both."

"Or both," Lyander agreed. "Either way, we're landing in that spire."

"While it's engaged in an ongoing siege?" Freyen asked. "If they don't clear the east tunnel, we could be stuck there."

"Or we can be stuck out here. We need to get through Teuron. There's no going around."

"And we don't have the ice to just float outside the spire indefinitely," Switch said. "We'll need to refuel eventually."

Lyander nodded. "The Ecclessius gave us a battleship for this purpose. If we need to use her as one, we will. I want everyone in battle dress. Brazier – I assume you can operate the turrets."

"We both can," Freyen said.

"Good," Lyander said. "Then we're at battle stations from here on out."

Freyen and Switch followed him off the nav deck and down to the weapons bay. Opting for plate over mail, he removed the rock locks from his gambeson, allowing him to tie steel vambraces over his wrists. He slotted his legs into plate grieves and thigh guards, before throwing a chest and back plate over his gambeson, fumbling at the sides to tie it together.

"Here, let me," Freyen said, her fingers brushing against his as she took the lace and began slotting it through the eyelets. Even through the gambeson's heavy padding, he could feel her fingers at his sides, lacing the plate together and tying small bows.

"Now you do me," she said, turning so her back was facing him, her left arm held above her head so he could get at the open side of her cuirass. Stepping behind her, he began fastening the laces through the eyelets running from under her arm to the bottom of her waist, the smell of lilac in her hair a constant reminder of how close he was standing to her. *Not that I need reminding.*

At the final loop, he placed a hand on her back to steady her as he pulled the lacing tight before looping it into a bow.

"Thanks," she said, turning to face him, their faces inches apart. Mail rustling and Switch's annoyed grunts reminded him they weren't alone in the fuselage.

"How in the black void is anyone supposed to wear these things?" she said, half her torso covered in chain mail, one arm flailing at an odd angle while the other seemed to be pinned to her side beneath the vest.

"It's on backward, for a start," Freyen said, going over and pulling the vest up and over Switch's head.

Brazier tightened a sword belt and scabbard around his waist and left them to it, the smell of lilac somehow lingering, even as he pulled himself up the stairwell.

#

"Hasn't changed much," Brazier said.

Lyander grunted – a sort of unenthusiastic grumble in the back of his throat. "They're still fighting in the tunnels," he said, shaking his head.

"And the eastern hangar bay tunnel is still engaged," Brazier added.

At their range, Matthias was able to provide a clearer picture of the battle on the ground. While each individual soldier, Fromryian or Mirrovinjin, were still just nondescript filaments shifting on the surface of the display, Brazier could now make out the battle line outside the hangar bay – or to be more precise, the single snaking line, broken in parts, but still cutting across the tunnel floor.

"Looks like one hell of a fight," Switch said, but Lyander shook his head.

"It's a diversion."

"How do you know that?" Switch asked, squinting at the display, her mouth forming into a puzzled curve.

"Because I've fought in enough battles to know what one looks like."

He pointed at a passage outside a small structure, south of the spire, and at a lower depth. Walls reached up high on either side before the passage rounded left and opened onto a cavern; the passage to its left led all the way up to the flat expanse outside the bay where the main battle took place. Behind the structure, the passage coiled like a worm, eventually leading to a side gate on the spire's south facing. A handful of filaments dotted around the structure could be a small Fromryian group, but from the way they moved, it didn't look like they were fighting anything.

"A second Mirrovinjin battle group will strike there and overwhelm that regiment. The rest of the spire's detachment are too far away to reinforce them."

"Then they should pull back," Switch said.

It was Brazier's turn to shake his head. "The tunnel width is ideal for a shield wall; it's a highly defensible position. And with more soldiers they could carry out a fighting retreat back through that smaller passage to the spire, making the Mirrovinjin pay five for every one of ours."

Brazier moved around the command display to look from a different angle. "But because of its position, it's also an ideal foothold for the enemy. You couldn't fly a ship through that passage, so the Mirrovinjin have a clear run to the spire without fear of taking fire from above."

Brazier saw Lyander's jaw clench, heard the frustrated sigh as he breathed through his teeth.

"Teuron's praefector should be able to see

what's about to happen."

"Well, you can tell him soon enough," Matthias said. "I've got a script identification request from Teuron's spire command."

"Tether it through," Lyander said.

The well next to Switch trembled with the sound of raised voices, some shouting commands, others franticly receiving and relaying orders; then a man's austere voice cut across the commotion: "Unknown craft, this is Teuron spire command. Provide identification script and purpose for your transit."

"Spire command, this is Kalbrayeth Lyander of the battle frigate *Shian Anchorite*. We are on an Ecclessiarchal mission of critical importance and request an immediate berth and refuelling of our ship. Transferring command script and Ecclessiarchal directives now."

The exorcist placed his hand into the adjacent well, his forehead creased in concentration as he relayed the Ecclessiarchal directives before removing his hand again.

"Confirmed, Kalbrayeth Lyander, you are cleared for docking," the man said from the well. "You sure you can't hang around? We could really use a ship like that."

Lyander rubbed the scarring along his wounded hand, the look on his face telling Brazier *hanging around* was exactly what he would like to do. Instead, the exorcist said: "I'm afraid not. Ecclessiarchal orders. Our mission is time-sensitive."

"Understood," the man said, a hint of disappointment in his voice. "Docking crew will look after you from here. Good hunting."

The well flattened, while next to it, the command display resized as the *Anchorite* sailed into Teuron's empty west hanger bay. Unlike those in most other installations, where the bay led onto either a primary or secondary concourse, Teuron's bay extended deep into the spire. At its end, the bay's ceiling opened to a passage so wide it could fit a maw-class gyre star; it rose through the centre of the spire and extended eastward, forming into the east-facing hangar bay.

Matthias set her down toward a wide expanse in the bay's centre, near several refuelling stations where trains of carts ran parallel to the berths. Brazier heard the access ramp drop to the floor and, barring Matthias, they all left the nav deck.

On the bay, a gnome in a red utility gambeson ran over to them. Blond hair sprouting from the centre of his head and messily swept over to one side, there was the waxy sheen to his skin resulting from a day, perhaps even days, without sleep.

"Our ship needs refuelling as quickly as possible," Lyander said to him.

"Well, you'll need to give me a hand," the gnome said, his rolling Harothellian accent strained with tiredness. "There's just me on this side of the spire."

"Where's the rest of the docking crew?" Brazier asked.

"All called in as reserves," he said. "Don't know if you've noticed but the spire is under attack, and badly."

"They left one person managing the bay?" Brazier asked.

"Most ships were called south yesterday, either responding to emergency distress calls or reinforcing fleets under attack. There's not a vessel for twenty leagues." The gnome ran a hand through his hair, sweeping it across to the other side. "Mirrovinjin really picked their moment."

"Are you expecting reinforcements?" Lyander asked.

"Being honest with you, I thought *you* were the reinforcements."

"Where's the praefector?"

The gnome's laugh was colourless. Combined with the visible exhaustion, it sounded somewhere between mania and hopelessness. "Shuttle was ambushed two days ago along with the Fontain commander, two of the spire's war casters, and some exorcist who was also on board, although I don't know why. A rescue force was sent to find them but they ended up being ambushed themselves." He shook his head. "There're regiments fighting in half the tunnels."

"Are you sure there was an exorcist on board?" Lyander asked, an edge to his voice. Only then did the gnome seem to register Lyander's surcoat.

"That's what I heard. I'm sorry."

"Who's the commanding officer here?"

The gnome gave another laugh. "For all I know, it's you."

"How many more war casters does Teuron have?" Lyander pressed.

"Do I look like I've got all the answers, friend?" the gnome said. "I'm the dock officer."

Brazier turned to look at Lyander, only to find him already looking at him, the expression on his face telling him he was thinking exactly the same thing.

"If there're units spread in the tunnels and there're no war casters to contact them –" Brazier said.

"Then there will be no way of withdrawing them to the spire when the second Mirrovinjin force hits," Lyander finished.

"What second Mirrovinjin force?" the gnome asked, but they ignored him.

"We need to round up as many units in the tunnels as we can," Brazier said, but Lyander shook his head.

"*You* need to round up as many units as you can," he said. "That exorcist was supposed to relay information to us from Acheron."

"What information?" Brazier asked.

"That's what we were supposed to find out." Lyander turned to the dock officer: "Are there any shuttles left?"

"A couple in the west hangar bay, but they're pretty beat up."

"Can they fly?"

"They won't drop out the air, but I wouldn't take them into a fight."

"I don't plan on it," Lyander said. Then to Brazier: "Use the *Anchorite* to find any units you can – direct them to that passage. And get a message to whoever is left in the command centre – another Mirrovinjin battle group is on its way." The exorcist turned to Eluthienn, a strange look on his face, as if he was trying to decide what to do with a misbehaving child. "Warn the unit," he said eventually. "But if the Mirrovinjin turn up, stay out of the fight. Do you understand?"

Mild confusion spread across the prince's face before he shrugged, then smiled. "Play the messenger, nothing more."

"Where are you going?" Brazier asked.

Lyander turned to him, grim resolve painted over an already grim face. "Acheron," he said.

Thirteen

Lyander

Lyander and Gabriel were out of the lift the moment its doors parted, striding across the east hangar bay toward two oval-shaped shuttles hovering above landing pads.

Other than the ships, the bay – a mirror of its western counterpart – was empty. No dock crews, no defenders lining the interior walls, no one held in reserve in case the Mirrovinjin broke through and into the spire.

The only movement came from above them. On turrets positioned between the landing pads, the repeaters spun around at full sentience, tracking them as they drew closer, before recognising their gyranic signatures as friendly, and rotating back to the bay's mouth. From there, the din of war rose from the tunnel and into the bay; the ringing steel, the Fromryian battle cries, the howls of the wounded and dying, the Mirrovinjin's guttural screeches, all merged into little more than a distant thunderstorm. To Lyander, who was usually in the middle of that thunderstorm, the sound was oddly nostalgic.

At the landing pad, he placed his good hand into the terminal, requesting the shuttle to release for immediate departure. The terminal confirmed his request and a pulse of white ran along its channels, converging beneath the ship, causing the thrusters to glow a brighter blue. They thrummed gently as they spun up, then the shuttle's door opened with a hiss of escaping air.

"You definitely know how to pilot one of these?" Lyander asked.

"I seem to remember doing it once or twice," the witch-hunter answered, but Lyander didn't think he looked confident.

Gabriel shrugged and stepped on board; moving to the bow, he placed his hands in the chest-high terminals either side of him. The door dropped shut behind Lyander and he held on to one of the rungs above his head. He felt the ship rise, pull away from the landing pad, tilt to the right, then propel forward, out of the hangar bay and, not that he could see it, over the battle below.

As far as he could tell, they continued straight for some time, out into the vast black of eastern Formaria. If he were looking at a hex, he would see a disc the size of an ant and the shape of a ladybug, floating above nothing. Far ahead, a range of cliffs, like a sea wall of the giants, representing the Pelothrian mountain's roots. North was the labyrinth of caverns and tunnels winding toward Nexoria and the home of the Mirrovinjin. South was more tunnels and then the maw.

They were a minnow swimming among the coral of a great black and endless ocean. The ocean was his home, but the thought of defending it brought him no comfort, as it once used to. Could a place be your home if those within it used you as a tool? And when they weren't using you, they shunned you. *But let's be honest, Kalbrayeth, the orphan boy taken from Celmyr was always a tool. Being First Champion just made you the shiniest tool of them all – the status and fame letting you ignore what you really were, the only thing you've ever been: another warrior among millions, sent to fight and die in the Bellum Infinara.*

The ship took a hard bank to its port side, literally shaking Lyander from his thoughts. It righted, juddered in the air, banked portside again, Gabriel's arms tensing like cords of rope, then the ship levelled out, flying straight.

"That you or the ship?" Lyander asked, finding his footing again.

"Forward portside thruster isn't responding well. The propulsion keeps dipping, I think," the witch-hunter said. "Although it could just be me."

"What's the access to Acheron like?" What he meant was: Are there any tight spaces we need to manoeuvre through?

"Open tunnel most of the way. Then it gets interesting."

"Let me know when that happens." Not that Lyander would be able to do much other than cling on with all his might.

"You'll know," Gabriel said, then: "This might be a good time to explain why we're making this little detour – while I can still fly and talk."

He resisted the urge to let go of the handhold and scratch the scarring along the back of his hand; instead, he rubbed it against his sword's hilt. Not really satisfying the itch, all he managed to do was send faint throbs up his wrist. He clenched his jaw against the pain, then answered: "The exorcist who died in the shuttle ambush – he was supposed to bring back information from Acheron about the connection between the Lords and the descendants of Redcrosse – specifically, Lokul and Leoncoure Leonette."

"There're two things in Acheron," Gabriel said. "A highly unpredictable syndicate boss and a breach into the Immuratum, which the highly unpredictable syndicate boss controls. What does either have to do with Aeturnic gods and Redcrosse?"

"The breach leads to the Library of the Nine, which the Church believes has information on both."

"And following our colleague's untimely demise, I assume we will now be searching for that information?"

"Correct."

"And am I also right in assuming we're just going to turn up to Acheron and expect Orpheus Velgar to let us use the breach?"

"An agreement has already been made between him and the Ecclessius," Lyander said, guessing where this was going.

"For one exorcist, who is not you, to cross over," Gabriel said, confirming Lyander's guess. "Velgar's entire reputation is built on taking people he thinks are lying to him and dropping them over the edge of his installation. What do you expect he'll do when the wrong exorcist shows up in tow with a witch-hunter?"

"I expect him to let us use the breach," Lyander said.

"I would find it funny watching you thrown over for demanding that, if I also wasn't going to be thrown over shortly after."

"It would have taken days for the Ecclessius to make a new arrangement with him. Days we don't have."

"And once you've convinced him we're not spies or saboteurs out to bring down his empire, what demon book does the Ecclessius expect us to find?"

"They didn't say," Lyander said, admitting to himself Gabriel was right; he hadn't thought through the particulars of this plan. So far it was: *find a shuttle, get to Acheron.* Exactly how they would find the right book, or even the library, were problems he would solve when they happened.

The witch-hunter sighed. "Everything about this has your name written all over it."

Lyander could see his point. "Have you crossed over before?" he asked, changing the subject.

Gabriel shook his head. "What's it like?"

"No idea – I've never crossed over, either."

The ship juddered briefly before Gabriel regained control. "I thought crossing over was part of every exorcist's training?"

"I don't think they expected me to actually *become* an exorcist."

"But you've exorcised demons? You've conducted liturgical rites?"

"I've killed my share," Lyander said, changing his hands over, and gently wrapping his fingers around the handhold. "And liturgical rites are just something the Church made up."

"The Church just decided to make up some words to convince everyone that saying them would prevent demons from returning to our world?" Gabriel said, laughing, but then: "Actually, that does sound like the Ecclessius."

"If we meet any of the ones I've sent back, we can ask."

"We'll have that opportunity soon enough. We're entering the cavern system."

"I'm guessing this is the interesting part?"

Gabriel nodded. "So let me concentrate."

The shuttle slowed before banking port side, then starboard. It slowed again, and Lyander heard the thruster extensions change position, their thrum becoming almost inaudible as Gabriel reduced speed. His back tensed, his shoulders hunching toward his ears, the ship seemed to crawl along whatever confined space they flew through.

They continued in silence, Gabriel's shoulder or wrist twitching occasionally. Every time it happened, Lyander imagined the ship stopping suddenly before it collided with a wall or edge.

He heard the aft extensions change angle, there was a slight shift in the weight beneath his feet, then he felt the ship rise. Lyander thought they might be through the *interesting* section, but there was a metallic grating that sounded distinctly like a thruster disc scraping against rock, and the ship began to dip starboard.

The grating grew and their angle became steeper before the ship jolted upward, forcing Lyander to steady himself against the wall with his wounded hand.

"We're through," Gabriel said with an exhalation.

"That didn't seem too bad."

"Wait until we try going back that way."

Gabriel eventually brought the ship to a stop, the door lifted open, and Lyander was greeted with a rocky promontory. A landing, littered with boulders and rocks; the ceiling low, it led to a series of rhomboid structures three times the height of a man, reaching up from the ground like giant's claws. Lyander could just about make out the thin channels lining their faces. Devoid of gyre light, the structures hid the path between them in shadow. The only light came from the shuttle's thrusters and a soft white-blue deeper into the cavern, far behind the rhomboid shapes.

"You're sure this is the right place?"

"It's a side entrance," Gabriel said. "Thought there was less chance of being shot on sight this way."

"More chance of being considered spies, though," Lyander said, stepping off the shuttle and onto the hard rock.

The door closed behind them and their footsteps crunched on rocky debris as they made their way to the structures, the enclosed space forming a pocket of warm air. Their way veiled in shadow, the far away light creeping over a distant rock wall, they proceeded slowly, checking each shape they passed.

"Lyander, we're being watched," Gabriel said when they were well into the middle of the rhomboid field. Lyander, who despite being used to Formaria's gloom, saw nothing.

Until he did.

Two bronze-gold discs materialised in the shadows right in front of him. His eyes taking a moment to adjust, he realised they were the oval limbs of crossbows held by dwarves and pointing at his and Gabriel's chests. Steel helmed, with nose and cheek guards, they wore maroon-brown brigandines reinforced with steel studding, over plated grieves and steel-capped boots. Lyander thought they were heavily armoured for criminals before he remembered those criminals lived in a war zone.

"We were expecting only one," a voice said from his left, thick with the huskiness of age.

Lyander turned to see a woman in black robes, and like the crossbows, she seemed to emerge from the shadows. Pulling her hood back, Lyander saw short-cropped hair, pale skin, and dark eyes, surrounded by crow's feet and a mouth and forehead lined with age. "So why are there two?"

"I'm not the best pilot," Lyander said, "so I brought one with me."

He could feel the look Gabriel was giving him.

The woman came closer. A full two heads

shorter than him, she was forced to crane her neck back to look him in the eyes. Then, without seeing it happen, her hand was on his cheek, her fingers cupping his jaw lightly, pushing it to one side, then pulling it to another, as if inspecting. Lyander stared down into her dark eyes, her irises inky black wells.

"Not the best exorcist, either, I would say," the woman said. "He will not like this. But you are here now, and see him you must." Her hand dropped from his face and she nodded with her head toward the light. "Come."

Around them, he heard heavy footfalls as more dwarves came out from behind the rhomboid shapes, flanking Lyander and Gabriel. The structures came to an end before a small passage naturally formed in the face of the cavern wall, only wide enough for two people abreast. They were led along it, walking in single file, the woman little more than a vague outline in front of him.

Out of nowhere, blazing crystal-blue light, then they were on a small landing overlooking the cradle city of Acheron. Built within a small cavern, the city was hemmed in behind a curving wall, its external facing overlooking a naturally forming bay where two cauldron-class frigates floated over the darkness of another cavern far below.

In the far left of the city stood a pyramid, boasting dark grey facades divided into numerous tiers, and atop it perched a colossal crystal, dwarfing the size of a spire-class shuttle threefold. Emitting a radiant white-blue glow, the crystal's hundred facets cast an ethereal light over the entire vicinity, like the Darkenheit moon.

"This way," the woman said, leading them down steps cut into the side of the landing. At a lower level, they joined with the city's wall, the grey slabs built right into the rock. Divided by six towers, they walked beneath open arches straddling the battlements, upon which sat heavy repeaters, each one trained on the bay.

Lyander could hear the noise rising up from the city. Market stalls lined several streets, their vendors and wares hidden beneath dirty beige sheets of canvas. Small units, mostly dwarves in maroon-brown brigandines, their hands on short swords, walking the streets two by two, the stomping of their marching step merging with the merchants conversing with customers.

Farther along, Lyander could see into an open-topped circular building, its sides lined with seating much like the High Council's chamber but much, much larger. Shouts and jeers rose up from the crowd sat or standing in the seats, all of whom stared fixedly on the fight taking place in the arena's centre.

A single Morlett, its leathery skin a pallid grey beneath the pyramid's light – its wide mouth bursting with sharp yellow teeth held in a mouth pulled into a permanent grin – bounced on clawed feet and pawed the earth with its clawed hands. In place of eyes and nose was a sickly grey snout and six red-rimmed and ridged holes, which Lyander knew from experience held a waxy black fluid through which the Morlett sensed the world with extreme acuteness.

It danced around the adolescent Araknor, bobbing from one foot to the other, throwing a clawed hand out to swipe at one of the Araknor's eight limbs. The dire spider jumped back with alarming speed, almost faster than Lyander's vision could capture, the Morlett's claw missing by a hair's breadth, its frustrated cry piercing Lyander's ears, even at this height.

It threw itself forward and the Araknor hopped to its left; they circled, the spider coming back into the centre, where it was just a moment too slow. The Morlett swung again, catching a forelimb before the spider could leap back. Purple-white fluid sprayed across the arena, the limb hanging limp, dragging uselessly in the dirt. But Lyander, having heard the stories from Yeggardanian veterans, knew what was about to happen. The Morlett, believing its enemy weakened, pounced at the Araknor with a wild swipe aimed for the creamy orbs that were its eyes. The Araknor, limping and handicapped, looked as if it could do nothing but take the blow. But in the time it took Lyander to blink, it reared on its hind legs, sprung forward and caught the Morlett's neck between its bone-white mandibles. They snapped together once and cut the Morlett's head clean from its neck, the body falling to the floor, pumping blackish-blue blood from the open wound.

And that, Lyander thought, *is why I hate Yeggardania.*

Those in the crowd either roared with delight or booed their discontent at the outcome. The din grew quieter as they neared the end of the battlements, and the people in the streets grew fewer. They descended a set of steps lining the inner wall, walked down several streets and came to the foot of the pyramid.

Human guards in brigandines and holding spears were posted either side of a portal. Taking one look at the woman, they stood to the side, letting her place her hand into the portal's node. The segments pulled apart and they followed her in, the unit marching behind them. Inside, the air was cool, and the light, provided by a single channel running along the ceiling, was a deep sapphire, flecked with green azurite. It led them straight ahead to a five-sided antechamber, then through the passage beyond, deeper into the pyramid. At what must be the pyramid's core, the passage opened into a square chamber, a foot-high dais in the centre, a portal in the far wall leading into another room.

The dwarf stood on the dais, head bowed, dark

brown hair falling over his shoulders and the long red cloak he wore, the point of his bronzite walking stick resting beneath his feet. His eyes closed and seemingly deep in thought, he was turned away from them, so Lyander could only see his profile.

"The exorcist, master." The woman bowed.

The dwarf mumbled something incoherent, touching a hand to his lips, as if something greatly concerned him. "Two," he said, a rasping wisp of a voice. He proceeded to brush his finger against his lower lip. "Two, is it?" he said, only slightly louder.

Then he rounded on them, turning his ruin of a face in their direction. One side was completely ordinary, like that of any other dwarf his age; its only remarkable feature, the green eye, so bright it could be a gemstone. But the entire right side was a wasted black and grey, feebly clinging to his skull. The skin was so thin in parts, Lyander could see through his cheek, to the molars along the back of his mouth, and into his eye socket – a dark hole of drying flesh. The hair on that side of his head was merely thin wisps of white clinging to flaky flesh – the type of wound, Lyander knew, received from a demon.

"They send two?" he said, the words a snarling rasp as they escaped through his open cheek.

Orpheus stepped toward them, his cane clunking on the floor. It was followed by another metallic *clomp*, then the cane, then another *clomp*. Looking down, Lyander saw both the dwarf's legs were shorn above the knee. In their place, two bronzite augments.

"A plot?" *Clunk*, pause, *clunk, clomp*. "A ruse?!" *Clunk*, pause, *clunk, clomp*. "Have the Ecclessius finally come for me?!" he said, a whiny edge to the coarseness. "Is that it?! They send their spies? They send them slinking through the back of my city?" *Clunk*, pause, *clunk, clomp*, and Orpheus was almost directly in front of Lyander now.

"They think I've spent too long in the dark? Too long on the edges of this world?" he said, his voice so fearful, Lyander thought he might cry, until his mouth curled viciously. "And now they send their agents!" *Clunk*, pause, *clunk, clomp*. "To take me! To take what's left of me!"

"We are here to cross into the Immuratum," Lyander said quickly, thinking the dwarf was about to stab him with his cane. "As agreed by the Church. The witch-hunter is my companion."

"And why," Orpheus said, baring the dead side of his face on Lyander, "do you wish to cross?"

"We seek information in the Library of the Nine."

"You wouldn't lie to me, exorcist?"

"I would not."

"We shall see."

Lyander felt the woman's hand on the nape of his neck, and before he knew what was happening, he was on his knees. The hand, now a vice, a spell freezing him in place, causing his muscles to cramp and spasm. Out of the corner of his eye, he saw Gabriel draw his sword, pointing it at the spell caster, but Lyander held out his arm, palm toward the witch-hunter. Unable to speak with his jaw rammed shut, the muscles twitching violently, he hoped the gesture conveyed his command to stand down.

"What is it the Ecclessius seeks in the library?" Orpheus said. The hold over him lessened, his jaw freed from its clamp but the muscles still tensed, forcing him to speak through gritted teeth.

"Information that may aid Formaria against the vampire threat."

"So it is true," Orpheus said, green eye glinting. "They are burdened with a new enemy. And why does the Ecclessius believe a demon library would hold information about the vampire?"

"They are of the Aeturnum. Enemies of the demon world. The library may tell us how to defeat them."

Orpheus looked at the woman: "Does he tell the truth?"

The grip on Lyander's neck increased tenfold, sending cold stabs of paralysing pain up into the back of his skull and through his head. It forced his mouth open, a silent scream caught in his throat, his eyes widening, staring into dwarf's dead socket.

"He does," the woman said. "But there is more."

"Tell me!" Orpheus said, bringing his face to hover above Lyander's.

The spell lessened, the paralysis receding from around his head and letting him close his mouth. He blinked away tears, a pounding throb blossoming behind his eyes.

"Lokul," Lyander managed to say. "We seek the means of defeating the king of vampires."

Orpheus's single eye grew so wide Lyander wouldn't have been surprised to see it drop from its socket.

"The Lords of the Eternal Hunt," the dwarf said, taking a step back, and bringing a trembling hand to his lips. "The Ecclessius is burdened, indeed." There was a hint of excitement in his voice. "And why should I relieve them of their plight? After all these years of treachery – years spent foiling their many efforts to undermine me, to prevent me from my goal. Why should I, Orpheus Velgar, help them?"

He turned to the guards behind them. "Throw them over the edge!"

"You won't survive!" Lyander tried to shout but his voice was a throaty whisper with the spell still over him.

"What?"

"Plans are being drawn for a full retreat to vaults and cauldrons. If the vampires are left to spread, you will be out here on your own."

The dwarf tipped back his head and laughed – a rattling cackle causing the skin around his cheeks and neck to quiver like parchment in the wind.

"We have always been on our own, exorcist."

"The Fromryr lost twenty ships and a fully operational spire in days. How long do you think you can hold out against such a foe?"

Orpheus looked at the woman with his good eye; pain shot up Lyander's neck and his mind was paralysed once more.

"What he says is true," she said.

The green eye squinted at him, and Lyander could see the doubt creep in. Orpheus bent over him, good eye roaming Lyander's face like the skin might hide a lie, then said: "You may cross, and on your return we shall see if you will swim in the abyss or not."

The woman removed her hand from his neck, the paralysis extinguished from his mind. But the headache remained, and the muscles along the top of his back felt like they might after a day swinging a sword. He rose to his feet, massaging his neck.

Orpheus turned and clomped off toward the end of the chamber.

"Come," the woman said. "The Immuratum awaits."

At the portal, Orpheus placed his hand into the node, and the door split apart. The chamber beyond was pyramidal, its sides running with a patchwork of channels, like a seperium's amber tiling, except these glowed blue. They shone down on the chamber's centre where steps led up to a square dais. Orpheus climbed them, and Lyander and Gabriel followed to find the dais was a pool holding a liquid black substance, glimmering like oil.

"This is no breach," Lyander said.

"A crossing," Orpheus corrected, "made by the Formarians." He touched a finger to his lips, shaking his head. "But who can say why? Who can say why they did anything?"

The woman climbed the steps on the opposite side of the pool, facing them, her hands folded beneath her robes. "Step forward," she said.

Lyander looked at Orpheus, expecting some sort of instruction as to how this would work, but the dwarf was mumbling to himself and shaking his head as if arguing with someone. He caught Lyander looking at him and stopped. Standing on his left and staring at the pool, Lyander could only look into his socket as he spoke: "The skeleton will tell you what to do, but do not trust him. Never trust the dead." The dwarf stepped down from the dais.

Lyander turned to look at Gabriel who, with an eyebrow raised, was giving him what was becoming an increasingly familiar look. The one that said: 'Are we really doing this?'

"We are getting into that pool," Lyander said, then took a careful step into the black liquid. Like an epistolar, steps descended on the other side, but instead of coming to his waist like a voidstone pool, the black substance came only to his shins.

Lyander and Gabriel stood facing one another, a foot apart.

"Don't use our names once we've crossed over," Lyander said. "If something asks for your name, never give it, no matter what."

The witch-hunter nodded.

"And if something gives you its name, never use

it. It's a trick – a spell to bind you to it."

"Sounds like a charming place," Gabriel said. "Now what?" he said to the woman.

"Look toward the sun," she said, nodding at the ceiling.

Gabriel turned back to him, shrugged, and looked up. Lyander did the same, staring into the crystal-blue fire at the pyramid's peak. The light quickly turned to white, then grew brighter and brighter. So bright it filled his vision, blinding him with white. And like staring into the Constructii's eyes in a seperium, he was transfixed, unable to pull his gaze away.

"Exorcist!" Gabriel roared, the witch-hunter's cry so loud and filled with such rare panic, it released him from the white sun.

Around them, a blasted wasteland of barren rock – everything either a deep brown or ruddy green, vast stretches of grey-coloured plains broken up by craggy outcroppings and deep canyons. Wind whipped at the land, howling like a dying animal, throwing up dust and bits of rock, spinning them into man-sized whirlwinds, forcing Lyander to shield his eyes. At what would have been high noon in their world, three suns, each bigger than the last, formed a loose triangle in the sky. The yellow orbs, strangely dimmed as if they were too far away, cast a pasty, vomit-coloured hue across the dying land.

Lyander looked down to find them standing in a pool just like its counterpart in the real world. But instead of holding a viscous liquid, there was cracked white tiling, filled with dust and dirt and crumbled rock.

Like Gabriel, Lyander drew his sword, the pair of them gazing around at the chaos realm known as the Immuratum.

"Over there," Gabriel called over the wind. A hand shielding his eyes, he pointed over Lyander's shoulder.

He turned, and saw the figure in the distance. Standing still as stone, it was only when his eyes adjusted to the haze that Lyander realised the figure was a skeleton.

They stepped out of the pool and down the dais, the gusts thrashing at Lyander's surcoat. Heads down, leaning into the wind, they approached the skeleton carefully, fanning out on either side in case of an unfriendly reaction.

"The Library of the Nine," Lyander shouted. "Where is it?"

The skeleton raised a white hand, pointing off to its left, over hills and into what looked like a ravine. Lyander nodded at Gabriel and they edged around the skeleton in the direction it told them to go.

Keeping one eye on its bone-white form, Lyander thought he saw it smile – a wicked grin that seemed barely able to suppress its glee. *Merely an effect of being a skeleton*, he told himself; *all skulls smiled, after all.* But he remembered Orpheus's warning – *do not trust the dead.* Lyander turned back for a second look to make sure they weren't being misled, but the skeleton was nowhere to be seen. Instead, on the horizon, dark shapes in the air – maybe five, maybe six. Other than their wings, they were too far away to make out their form.

"Come on," Gabriel said, seeing them, too.

They quickened their pace, soon coming upon a path, winding its way through the crags. Every now and then, a dusty blast would throw itself off the top of the rocks, but for the most part, they were protected from the wind. The path opened onto a wide plane, empty of almost anything except the occasional clump of trees, their trunks petrified white, their limbs drooping to the ground.

"The wind," Gabriel said, "it's stopped."

It took Lyander a moment to realise he was right, which made no sense. There was no rock wall or cliff separating them from where they were now from the crags behind them. With no explanation to offer, Lyander said: "We continue."

Across the expanse, the land quickly gave way to dry bedrock, their panting breaths and rapid footsteps cracking in the earth the only sound.

Until Lyander stepped on something hard.

Looking down, he saw a bronze piece of oval metal buried in the dirt.

And then there were more. Some face up, nose and cheek guards sticking in the air, others still attached to white skulls. Then the plane was littered with the debris of war. Broken swords, spear tips, shields, a chest plate – all solid bronzite and scattered among hundreds upon hundreds of skeletal remains. So numerous was it all, they were soon weaving their way around mounds, their progress slowed by avoiding sword edges and cracked helms.

One caught Lyander's eye – a standard protruding from among a pile of skeletons. In place of a banner, metal links held bronzite disks; the phalerae inscribed with an Old World tongue but one Lyander could not understand.

"The Ecclessius should start commissioning explorations into the Immuratum," Gabriel said. "A cache like this would be talked about for decades."

"It would be," Lyander said, "but what you're suggesting is technically heresy."

He saw Gabriel smiling. "Maybe after we've killed Lokul, we can put together a crew. Then come back here, gather it all up, and live as kings for the rest of our days."

Lyander snorted. "Wait until we meet an

Immurati," he said. "That might put you off the idea of coming back."

Gabriel stopped and turned to look behind them, covering his eyes against the suns. "Doesn't look like they're following us."

"Don't be so sure," Lyander said, and pushed on toward the edge of the ancient battlefield. The earth hardened beneath their feet, and walls of rock rose ahead of them, a section split by a deep ravine. With no other obvious route, they headed into it.

The wind returned – a low whistle at first, a breeze that spun up dust around their ankles. But as the ravine narrowed into a passage, it yowled down the wind tunnel, beating at their backs as if propelling them along. Coming to its end, it broke out into a wide expanse, surrounded by crags and cliffs. Among them, the Library of the Nine.

Like no architecture Lyander knew of, its cold metal was a mix of asymmetry and irregularity; the walls contorted with vine-like curves, their buttresses and arches shaped with snaking tendrils. The nine towers, oval rather than circular, were flat topped, and rose as if growing out of the ground. Everything was a hybrid of metal and flesh, formed into what Lyander could only think of as a diseased exoskeleton. With a sense of disquiet, he realised the fluidity of the structure was vaguely reminiscent of Formarian design. But where their creations were hard bronzite or the angular pale grey stone, the building in front of him was something more organic.

"Of course this is where demons keep their books," Gabriel said, and Lyander found himself agreeing.

Steps rose to large doors, cut in the same design as the walls. At their centre, like their might be in a Formarian installation, was a node. Unlike a Formarian installation, however, the node held a fleshy pit; red and raw, it was the colour of a limb stripped of its skin.

Seeing no other means of entry, and assuming it would work in the same way a hex terminal might, Lyander reached his hand out for the pit.

But was stopped by Gabriel's hand clamping around his wrist. "You are guaranteeing yourself malignance," the witch-hunter said.

"If you can see a better way in, I'm all ears." But Gabriel held on to his wrist. "Teuron will have a seperium," Lyander added.

The witch-hunter released him, a dubious look in his eyes.

Lyander sunk his hand into the node, the pit creating a cool, damp bed for his fingers. Instead of the uncomfortable click at the base of his skull, he was assaulted by a wave of nausea rising from his stomach, up the back of his throat, forcing him to swallow his gag. As he did so, the nausea spread through him. His limbs felt weak, his eyes hurt, his mind racked with fog.

Open! he thought before it could get any worse.

The node released him, and the doors shunted apart, pulling into recesses in the walls. Lyander was given a view of a long corridor – the flooring a tapestry of coiling vines, the walls like the inside of a rib cage, and at the end, an opening into a large chamber. From it, a muted light, casting hues of grey and green.

Then he vomited at his feet.

"Yeah," Gabriel said, eyeing the pool of sick. "I think you're going to need that seperium."

Lyander spat, wiped his mouth with the back of his hand, and stepped into the library. Unlike the arid environment outside, the air was moist, while beneath his feet, the vine-like flooring was hard.

Several paces in and the doors slid shut behind them with a soft *thud.* Nearing the end of the corridor, the light lost its grey pallor, becoming steadily whiter, and from inside the chamber came a low moaning.

They stepped cautiously to the opening, swords raised. Inside, it was oval shaped, a large circular portal at the opposite end. On pillars surrounding the chamber, orbs emitted the strange white light; beneath them, Lyander could see what was making the moaning sound.

Alcoves lined the walls – in each, a human being. Their faces to the walls, their arms outstretched, wrists held up in shackles, their skin the grey and black of death. They smelled of sweat, rot, and fear, but the thing making Lyander want to throw up again was the horrific violation done to their backs. Their lungs, removed from their ribcages, were cut like ham into thin slices and arranged on top of their backs, like the pages of a book.

From the roof of the chamber hung a limb-like extension. Pallid grey and green like the rest of the room, it looked like an elongated arm, bent at the elbow, a hand at the end. It swung toward one of the humans, turning the skin flaps with spindly fingers, causing the person to twitch and shiver. Stood in the middle of the chamber was a figure in tattered red robes, the hems fraying and covered in black grime. Bent over what appeared to be a kind of terminal, Lyander guessed the creature operated the limb.

Without moving its legs or back, its head rotated round to face them. Its pasty white skin surrounded a wide mouth, the lips the colour of a rotting corpse. Its eyes, sunken in their sockets, were almost entirely white, save for the black pinprick of a pupil. Over its robes a cross hung upside down around its neck. If Lyander cared about such things, he might have been offended.

“The library requires names. What are yours?” the demon asked, its voice filled with a high-pitched malevolence, both sinister and eerily innocent. Lyander thought it sounded childlike.

"We seek information," Lyander said, stepping forward slowly, conscious of the giant limb hanging overhead. Gabriel stepped over to the right.

The demon's head twitched in his direction, following the witch-hunter's steps. It twitched back to Lyander.

"The library knows my name and so I may use it," the demon said. "It is Hashenut Al'Laykanor."

"We seek the book of the Lords of the Eternal Hunt," Lyander said, ignoring the trick. "We would know how to defeat them."

The demon smiled, the mouth curling up its face too far, the lips parting, showing too many teeth – row upon row of yellow fangs sprouting from black gums.

"All these books can be yours," it said, raising hands hidden beneath its dirty robes. "All you must do is provide your names."

Lyander reached around his neck, removing the cross and holding it up to the demon. "I will use this, Immurati."

The demon's mouth twisted into a snarl before its head flinched and the snarl became a smile. "You seek answers?" it said.

"We do," Lyander replied.

The demon giggled. "Only answers give answers," it said.

Lyander took a deep breath, aware this was likely another trick.

"What answers?" he asked, hesitantly.

"To the riddle."

"And in exchange, you will give us the book?"

"If you answer correctly."

"And if we don't?"

"You become a book." Another giggle.

"Don't say anything," Lyander said to Gabriel.

"A verbal agreement with a demon is a binding pact."

"You mean a spell?"

"Just don't say anything."

Gabriel let out a frustrated breath.

"Let's hear your riddle, demon," Lyander said.

The demon's grin split its face in two and without warning, it floated toward them, the tattered hem brushing along the ground. It stopped in the middle of the chamber.

"One summer, a troupe of travelling performers makes a visit to a king's court. They have heard the king and his family are great lovers of plays and pantomimes, and will always receive performers of any kind," the demon said, still smiling. "For the court, the troupe perform 'The Mask' – the tale of the demon king and the great enemy," it said, its voice taking on an unsettlingly guttural quality, becoming unnaturally deep, as it said: "The false idol." Lyander knew it meant Redcrosse, but would refuse to say the name. Its voice became childlike again, and continued: "The tale of the knight who rises from obscurity, the hero at the demon's slaying. But each night, the ending is different." It giggled, twitching its head from Gabriel to Lyander. "Each night, the mysterious knight is revealed to be a different character from among the cast of players. And night after night, the audience is captivated by who the hero might be. But on the final night, the cast is spent – all among their number have played the hero. So the troupe master says: 'Tonight must be different; this night, we need one among your number to slay the demon king and become the hero. Who among you is worthy; who can tell us how this story ends?'" The demon tittered. "And do you know who stands up?" Another titter, then its mouth grew slack, its voice thick with malevolence: "An exorcist, a witch-hunter, and a prince." The demon grinned, its voice innocent again: "Who did the troupe master choose?"

"That's hardly a riddle," Lyander said, wondering with a sense of apprehension why the demon would select an exorcist, a witch-hunter, *and* a prince. Was it making a reference to Eluthienn? *It can't know who we travel with. It must be a coincidence.*

"Only answers give answers," the demon said.

Lyander decided he could worry about the *coincidence* later; the demon's riddle needed his full attention if he didn't want to spend eternity here. He thought: *The professional demon hunter was the obvious answer, but it felt too obvious.* It felt like he was being goaded into choosing it because he was an exorcist. He couldn't see how it could be the witch-hunter, whose profession was hunting witches not demons. And the prince, whose knowledge of hunting evil was the least of all three, was therefore the least likely. He tried racking his memory for a time when he may have heard "The Mask*"* before, but he'd never been one for frequenting Thendergaarden's auditoriums or theatres. *It must be the exorcist. There was no reason for it to be the prince or the witch-hunter, and every reason the exorcist could be a double bluff.* The more he considered it, the more it made sense – the demon expected him not to choose the obvious answer because it was too obvious. But it didn't make it wrong.

"The troupe master chooses the exor –" he began but stopped himself. He was thinking about this all wrong. The demon's trick was in making him focus on the profession, but the choice didn't depend on the skill in killing demons; it depended on who was most likely to know the end to the tale. He felt himself gripping his sword hard, saw Gabriel tense beside him.

"It's the prince," Lyander said.

"And why not the exorcist?" the demon said quickly, its voice that of a petulant child's. "Surely he knows how the story ends, for among the audience, he is the most knowledgeable of demons – he is the demon slayer."

Lyander felt something building around his chest, like an invisible hand closing around him. He breathed deep, but the hand only grew tighter.

"And why not the witch-hunter?" the demon continued, snapping its head round to Gabriel. "Is he not a worthy choice? He who slays witches and their spawn aplenty? For are there not only a few of my kind left in your world and so what can the exorcist really know of such things?"

"The prince," Lyander growled, straining against the force now causing his ribs to ache. "You said the king and his family were lovers of plays, and so his son would have seen many tales told – more than the exorcist or the witch-hunter. He knows how they all end. He is the worthiest choice."

The demon snarled, and the pressure around Lyander extinguished. It soared back over to the terminal, and the portal ahead of it opened. Like a whirlpool, twisting from the centre, the strange material spun open, revealing another corridor beyond.

"In there is where we will find the book?" Lyander said.

The demon nodded slowly.

"Where in there will we find the book?"

The demon stared at him, impassive.

"You said you would *give us* the book," Lyander said, becoming angry. "You are bound, by your own laws, to tell us exactly where it is."

The demon's mouth twisted into a silent grimace, then said: "Follow it round to your right and into the chamber of the six."

Lyander studied the demon's face, searching for any falsehood in the grin, but found none.

"Let's go," he said to Gabriel, placing the cross back around his neck.

They edged toward the portal, but as they passed the demon, it sniffed the air hungrily. Snapping its head round, its eyes grew impossibly wide, its mouth twisted with hatred.

"I see you, false one," it said, its voice a venomous crackle.

A hand shot up from beneath its robes, pale fingers three times as long as any human's and ending in long black claws, pointing at Gabriel's chest.

Lyander turned to the witch-hunter, who was staring at the demon like he was ready to run it threw with his blade.

"Great deceiver. The trickster," it cackled at him. "I see you; you cannot hide in the Immuratum. You cannot hide from us, he of many forms."

"How rude of me," Gabriel said, almost lazily but with a very clear threat to his tone. "I should have introduced you to them all."

And Lyander watched, utterly perplexed at the exchange, as the witch-hunter split into three. His symulacrums pulled themselves out of their original and surrounded the demon – all perfect copies. The one nearest Lyander stepped forward, its sword readied for a forward thrust. But the demon ignored it, pivoted to one of the others, arm outstretched, and Gabriel – the real Gabriel – was lifted into the air. The symulacrums froze, then shuddered, as if they struggled to hold their form. Gabriel's arms were pinned to his side, his body shaking. The copies sprung back inside of him, then he was thrown across the chamber to crash against the exoskeletal wall.

Oh, black hell! Lyander thought, coming up behind the demon, twisting round at the hip, then decapitating it with a single stroke. Black gore spurted from the neck – an impossible amount, it sprayed upward like a geyser, showering the red robes in the oily black blood. The body flopped forward, the wound continuing to pump all over the chamber floor before slowing to a trickle.

Lyander took two steps toward Gabriel's crumpled form when he realised he was forgetting something. And then it was too late.

The limb extension yanked at his right shin, pulling him into the air and sending him sprawling, face-first, onto the ground. He rolled over, just in time to see the fist come crashing down. He rolled again, dodging it by an inch as it hammered into the floor, leaving a spindly four finger depression. As it retracted, Lyander brought his blade across his body, cutting at the extension's wrist, lopping off the hand. It flailed and spun, like the demon, spurting an unreasonable amount of black blood, soaking the floor, the walls, and Lyander in oily gore.

Then it was gone, retracting into the ceiling orifice, which closed behind it. He wiped at his face, spat, and pushed himself to his knees, then went to check on Gabriel. Slumped against the wall, chin on his chest, the witch-hunter was breathing with laboured heaves. With each exhalation, his body juddered, causing a black shadow to ripple outward before receding back inside, as if the symulacrum was trying to break free. Lyander knelt, taking the witch-hunter's chin in his hands. Gabriel's eyes flickered open.

"On my waist," he croaked.

Lyander looked down at the belt and the many vials held in the wax-hardened pouches. Pulling one out at random, he held it up for Gabriel to see. The turquoise blue liquid swam before his eyes but the witch-hunter shook his head.

Lyander placed it back in the pouch before

picking one containing a dark purple liquid with a lighter, almost orange current coiling through its centre. Gabriel shook his head again, his face now turning pale.

At the far end of the belt, a smaller pouch held a much slimmer vial. Lyander fished it out, holding it up. The substance was like liquid silver, glinting like Inertial Mutagenis might.

"The one," Gabriel grunted.

Lyander popped the cork, held the vial to the witch-hunter's lips and poured slowly. Gabriel's throat moved up and down, draining the entire vial. He coughed, took a long, ragged breath, then leant his head back against the wall, his eyes now able to open beyond a flicker, the symulacrums no longer trying to break free.

"Your cross should have been able to protect you from that," Lyander said.

"I guess you're not the only nonbeliever around here," Gabriel said, breathlessly.

"Pretty sure that's not how it works," Lyander said and, curious at the antidote for demon attacks, sniffed the vial. It was completely odourless, so Lyander held it up to his eye. Among the silver, grey, and white, tiny black particles lined the glass and seemingly moved of their own accord.

"Voidstone?" Lyander asked.

"It's called Veritas," Gabriel said. "The only way my symulacrancy is controlled. The voidstone acts as a binding element, apparently. Stops me from disassociating."

Lyander wasn't exactly sure what *disassociating* meant, but he imagined it was nothing good. *Not an antidote for demon attacks, then.*

"How often do you need to take this?"

"Ohh, only every four days."

"You knew this before accepting the Church's gift?"

The witch-hunter snorted. "You think I would have accepted if I knew the conditions? I thought I was being rewarded. But the Ecclessius were just making a weapon that doesn't stray too far."

"Because the Church controls the flow of voidstone."

"So they control me."

The nonchalance, the cold detachment, and the apparent disinterest in their mission now made sense. What Lyander mistook for pride and arrogance now looked more like bitterness and resentment. *Sound familiar, Kalbrayeth?*

"You're not the only one with a leash around his neck," Gabriel said.

"So what did you do to earn yours?"

"Desperation to prove myself, to be better than others," he said, coughed again, and took a long breath. "I plumbed the depths of Formaria and roved the surface of Yeggardania, out of contact from the Coven for months, even years in my hunt for the worst of all Aeturnic beings. Goblin witches became something of a speciality for me, before becoming high blood shamans – hunting them into the Aeturnum in the hope they would lead me to Bork. I spent a year in that world, only for the goblin king to eluded me at every turn. But it wasn't in vain – I'd gathered more information about the goblins than any other. On my return, I believed the Ecclessius was rewarding me for my efforts, but instead they gave me shackles, preventing me from ranging too far. They were concerned, that even for a witch-hunter, I was spending too long in the realm of darkness."

"Why keep you alive, if they couldn't trust you?" Lyander asked. "The Ecclessius has no qualms about executing its own."

"The Lord Huntsman argued in my favour. And the Ecclessius never kills what it can use. And so here I am, in thrall to the Church, forced to play supporting act to an exorcist in an Aeturnic hunt," Gabriel said, getting to his feet. Looking around the room, he added: "Perhaps that was the right decision after all."

Lyander picked up the witch-hunter's sword and handed it to him. Gabriel's eyes widened with genuine disbelief, and he grinned. Despite the pale exhaustion, a hint of amusement pulled at the corner of his mouth. He was about to say something, but whatever witty comment he was about to make was cut short by the sound of harsh screeches and heavy thuds on the library's roof.

"We need to find that book," Lyander said. "Now."

They stepped around the decapitated corpse, making for the open portal. At the corridor's end, it split into a junction, and as instructed, they followed it round to the right. The murky grey-green cast took on a pallid amber hue as the corridor continued, the coiling channels leading them out onto a walkway, straddling a large oval chamber like a bridge. Its yellow-brown light, seemingly coming from nowhere at all, lit up the room beneath them, revealing what Lyander could only describe as gestation pods. Their sides were formed from a hardened brown sludge, a misty film coating the top. Beneath the surface, human forms laid face down. He realised then, suppressing a shudder, that the bodies and their books would be replaced once their decay became too far gone. Even with all the variously horrific ways to die in Yeggardania, the Immuratum, Lyander decided, was probably worse.

Gabriel gave him a look that told him he was thinking something similar, and they crossed the walkway; ahead of them was another orifice-like portal. Cautiously they approached, and as they drew closer, it slithered apart. Inside, a smaller chamber, rounded and lit from above by a white-green light. Standing in a circle, arms outstretched and stone still, were six bodies black with rot, their lungs carved into open books.

Lyander was about to step inside when a piercing screech filled the air – the sort of sound his instincts associated with jaws, claws, and large successful predators. It echoed through the corridors, coming from far behind them, but it definitely came from within the library.

"I'll hold them off," Gabriel said. "Try not to take too long."

Not needing to be told twice, Lyander picked the nearest "book" and began reading its "page." The writing, carved into the skin, was an obscure Old World tongue – a language he could understand, but he was still forced to lean over the page, trying to make out the writing, much of which was covered in corpse rot.

The sections he could read clearly kept mentioning *Regina Insaniae*. He turned the page, touching it with as little of his finger as he could, and was presented with the image of a woman. Wearing flowing green silk robes trimmed with gold thread, her skin looked as smooth as alabaster, her lips painted red. She might have been beautiful except for her eyes, which looked like glowing pools of fire. Beneath her, the name *Duessa*, and the page over what seemed to be the Mad Queen's various characteristics – words like "hypocrisy" and "falsehood," then a single line: *Her tales come true*. Coming to the conclusion that this was not the right book, he moved on to the one on his left.

As he did so, there was another screech, closer, and broken into two scratching notes – each short and sharp, flowing into one another. *This way*, they seemed to say, and it took Lyander a considerable effort of will to stand with his back to an oncoming enemy and keep reading. *The quicker you read,* he told himself, *the quicker you can get out of here.*

He turned through the book, and like the other, he came across an image in the centre of one of its pages: a figure head to toe in ornate black plate. Like the waves in a sea, the armour was shaped into jagged curves, the pauldrons, toe caps, vambraces, and helm all ending in spikes. Beneath the image, the name *Volkor, Rex Inferis*.

A likely looking candidate, but still not Lokul.

He moved to the next book, and translated the inscription at the top of the page: *The Changeling, Lord of Beasts, Changer of Shapes*. Not the one he was looking for, either, so he moved on to the next, at last thinking this might be the right book. Peering down at the page, he came as close as he was willing, taking shallow inhalations and trying his best not to breathe in the acrid stench of ammonia, bile, and damp earth.

Dominus Immortalis, he began to translate but was stopped by a *tack, tack, tack*, coming from the corridor, then snake-like hissing, so sharp and angry he imagined he could *hear* its venom. *The quicker you get this done…* he told himself again, forcing his feet to stay rooted to the spot.

On the second page, between thin coats of brown slime, he translated: *King of all Undead*. And in the paragraph below it: *The Great Maker*. Then, to confirm it for him, the words in the same paragraph: *Pater Magnificus*.

It took his mind seconds to catch up with the reality, that the *tack, tack, tack*, had stopped and to register the sound of swooshing – once far away, then again, closer, and again, and again, until he turned around, sword ready, half expecting whatever it was to be upon him. Instead, he watched as two webbed wings took up the mouth of the opposite corridor. The body they were attached to was like a giant eel, velvety grey and black, ending in a pointed snout, its teeth bared.

It came soaring down the walkway, jaw wide open and aiming for Gabriel's head. But the witch-hunter stepped lightly to one side, and half crouching, half lunging, he cut the demon from head to tail. Grey innards and black gore poured from the wound, slopping to the ground like offal dropped onto a counter, and the body skidded across the walkway to stop just short of Lyander's feet.

Gabriel winked at him, but his smile receded as the corridor filled with a high-pitched cawing. *The sound of a hunter calling to its pack.*

Lyander turned back to the book, flicking through the pages, scanning paragraphs as quickly as the rot would allow. Like the Mad Queen, the being's characteristics were described over several pages. An architect of plots, it said, describing patience and cunning. A dark sorcerer another paragraph explained, detailing Aeturnic experiments: the turning of the dead, the capturing of souls. And a smaller section with words like *Narrator* and *Fabula*. Most completely unintelligible, the etchings warped by black decay, ended in one phrase: *the teller of tales*. He moved on to the next page, trying to interpret the word *pario,* as three long *caws* echoed far behind him – *the pack answering the hunter's call.*

Willing the images of winged demons clawing their way along the walls and floor from his mind, his blurred memory associated *pario* with *spawn.*

The rest was too detailed though, and he only caught snippets as he scanned: the basic spawn, turned by other recently turned vampires, another requiring the maker, and another called *explorator*. The paragraph fell into decay, and he could translate only three words: *scout*, *venom,* and *claw*.

Realising he was spending too long in a section

he didn't need, he moved on five pages, finding the words *vinculum,* the word for *bond.* And on the opposite page, the word *pario* again. At first, he thought the book now explained the death of all other vampires following Lokul's destruction, but as he continued reading, it was clear, *spawn* also meant *scions*: the scions of Redcrosse.

A tiny thrill ran through him as he realised he was getting closer to the information he needed. But the excitement died as the chamber directly behind him echoed with demonic screeches and the sound of wings. Gabriel released a single, low, *ghuh*, there was the wet slither of rubbery hide parting to cold steel, and the thump of a body hitting the walkway.

More screeches, more grunts and slashes and thumps, and in between, the witch-hunter's laboured breathing.

Telling himself Gabriel could handle it, Lyander forced himself to keep reading, translating the language as fast as he could. Much of it described the battle that took place between Leoncoure and the Lord of Undead. It continued for three pages: where they fought, and the wounds suffered. Then more pages of rot, and the following: a*ncient bonds through wounds afflicted*, another dark smear across the page. Then: *inherited through procreation.* Another smear, lighter and with what looked like pinkish tendrils.

But Lyander gave them little thought, for Gabriel's cry rang through the chamber – a desperate, exhausted sound, causing Lyander to turn.

A demon squirmed, its body pressed against the side of the walkway, wings thrashing uselessly against the low wall, Gabriel's sword protruding from its stomach. With the other hand, the witch-hunter gripped the demon's throat, fighting off the jaws snapping at his head.

With another aching cry, Gabriel dug in his

heels and half pushed, half grappled the thing over the edge of the walkway. There was a crash from below, then nothing.

He can handle it, Lyander told himself, as he turned back to the book, and even in his mind, he could hear the relief in the words.

Picking up where he left off, he found, *the sons and daughters of the scions of the false idol*. Then at the very end of the page, the phrase *destruction assured through bonds of blood*. He tried turning the page, only to find it was the last one. He read the line again, making sure his translation was correct. Then scanning back over the rest, he tried to find anything relating to vampire spawn – words like children, offspring.

Ignoring the sounds of the skirmish, now rising again behind him, he cast his eyes halfway up the opposite page, finding *creation*, then a line down, the word *terminus* along with the phrase *vincula sanguinis*: bonds of blood. He flicked another page and found Lokul himself – or what the demon world depicted as the Lord of Undead. His features were completely hidden beneath the shadow of his hood, and he wore a thin black cloak, so holed and tattered, it was little more than a rag. Lyander could just make out the armour he wore underneath: like his relative, the King of Death, it was all curving black plate and spiked edges. Below the image, the words: *Lokul, The Great Maker*.

Then the sound of wings behind him, so close he was buffeted by the air. Spinning, he gripped his sword in both hands, ready to swing it defensively across his body, only to find Gabriel on his knees in the mouth of the chamber. The winged demon's snaking body curled above him before darting down, its jaw clamping shut over the witch-hunter's head.

For what could only be a tenth of a second, Lyander's heart stopped as he watched Gabriel die. But then the witch-hunter vanished. In his place, wisps of coiling black smoke evaporated into the air.

The demon's head darted from side to side, confused at not finding its prey between its teeth. From behind it, a leaping form: Gabriel, sword held in a reverse grip, plunging the blade downward in a killing blow. It sunk through the demon's head, through its mouth, and out its lower jaw in one clean movement. Its wings twitched, the snake-like body giving a final squirm between Gabriel's feet, then went still.

He pulled his sword from the head and wiped the gore on one of the wings.

"You find what we need?" Gabriel asked, panting.

"I did," Lyander said, letting his heart return to its normal rhythm, before stepping over the body. Another was curled in the middle of the walkway, wings crumpled beneath it, while another draped the banister like a dead fish. In the chamber below, three others were scattered over or between the pods, black blood pooling around them.

They picked their way around them, leaving the walkway, and followed the corridor back around to the larger chamber.

"Any explanation for what's going on there?" Gabriel asked as they entered the room, pointing at the decapitated head with the point of his sword. From the base of its neck, black tendrils about twice the length of Lyander's middle finger writhed and flopped like coiling worms, dripping black sludge across the floor.

"Things don't really die here," Lyander said.

Gabriel pointed behind them with his sword, a questioning look on his face.

"They'll be back too," Lyander said.

"This place is shit."

"No arguments here," Lyander said, and they

crossed the chamber to the corridor leading to the library's exit. Seeing the portal wide open, Lyander gave a silent thanks that he wouldn't need to connect with the network again.

Dashing down the steps, they made their way back to the ravine, both casting looks over their shoulders to make sure none of the winged demons were waiting to ambush them on their way out; none appeared.

Lyander let Gabriel go through the gap first, then gave the library one final look, its nine towers a murky green beneath the yellow suns, their strange faces sinister and timeless – a sight, Lyander expected, that would be etched in his memory. As if by seeing them, the image was burned into his soul. He pushed the thought aside, and ran.

When they exited the ravine, the screeches began in earnest, echoing from behind them.

"If I'd known," Gabriel said, "I'd have killed them more thoroughly."

Lyander was about to tell him it wouldn't have made much difference when a thunderous cawing split the air – so loud, Lyander could almost feel the reverberations.

"Run!" he shouted, not knowing what made the noise but knowing it was nothing good. They bolted across the battle-strewn plane, dashing around or over the skeletal remains, their weapons, and armour. The ground became drier, and they were soon retracing their steps, the boot prints sunken into the cracked earth.

Ahead, the crags rose, the three suns bleaching their tops and turning them yellow verdigris. And the wind was howling. When it began, Lyander couldn't say, but it attacked the tops of the crags like a clawed beast trying to swipe at prey in a rut, and throwing dust and dirt into their eyes. Unable to stop their progress, its howls became infused with anger, turning to desperate wails as it whistled around the peaks and ridges. But it was all drowned out by the symphony of power roaring from behind them, and the beat of wings loud as gyre thrusters.

Something pummelled into his shoulder, the force knocking him from his feet and throwing him to the ground. He landed with a grunt, then turned onto his back, a half-growl on his lips, he prepared to bring his sword up to defend himself, only to realise it was Gabriel on top of him. Over the witch-hunter's shoulder, Lyander watched the end of a giant tail clip the tops of a crag and throw bits of stone down upon them. It slipped behind the rocks and out of his field of vision, a frustrated cry piercing the air.

Two Gabriels sprung from the real Gabriel's back and darted round the crag and in the demon's direction. The witch-hunter pulled himself to his feet, then helped Lyander up as he wiped dust from his eyes. Edging around the rock, he and Gabriel watched as the two symulacrums ran off to the left and away from the stone basin.

Above them, the demon, five times the size of one of its smaller cousins and easily the length of a cauldron-class destroyer, pursued.

"Come on," Lyander said, but Gabriel grabbed his arm, pulling him back.

"Wait," he hissed.

"It's in pursuit," Lyander said. "We can make it to the pool."

"Wait until it dives."

And Lyander watched the demon speed up, its wings beating faster and faster before it tucked them behind its body and dove. Like an arrow, it shot toward the symulacrum on its right.

"Now we go," Gabriel said, pushing him

forward, and the pair sheathed their swords and sprinted toward the pool, heads bowed against the wind. On Lyander's left, he could just about see the demon plummeting along the surface of the earth, its shimmering black hide reflecting the yellow suns. He heard the snap of its jaws as they closed around what he knew would be swirling tendrils, then it was gone from his vision. They jumped over the lip of the pool and skidded to a stop. Facing one another, they looked up as one, staring into one of the demon world's suns.

Behind them, another frustrated screech cracked like peels of thunder, and Lyander's heart raced as his eyes strained against the light. He heard the demon's wings beat the air, bringing it round, turning in their direction – and still the demon sun blinded his eyes. The beating came closer and closer, and Lyander's heart hammered, striking his ribcage like a pickaxe. They were louder now and becoming more frequent, until they stopped altogether and were replaced by the whistling of the wind. Lyander's heart hammered so fast, his body so tense, he felt physically sick with fear. And behind him the swoosh of something streamline-diving through the air, so close he could imagine it coming, jaws wide, teeth a bed of sharpened stakes.

He waited for the crushing blow, to be taken off his feet, to be lifted into the air, teeth sinking into his arms and legs. But there was no sound, just the light of the sun, blinding him. He felt something against his arm and flinched, yanking it backward.

"Lyander, we're back in Acheron."

It was Gabriel's voice, coming from somewhere below him.

"You can stop looking," Gabriel said, causing Lyander to blink.

As if without thinking, he dropped his gaze. Blue light swam in his vision as he looked at the witch-hunter. He blinked again, trying to rid himself of the afterburn.

"So?" Orpheus said, good eye turned toward him.

Lyander rubbed his eyes, then his temples. "Only the blood of Leoncoure can destroy the vampire king – only a son or daughter of his line can stop the spread across Formaria."

"The library told you this?" Orpheus said eagerly.

"*Vincula sanguinis,*" Lyander said. "Through bonds of blood – that is what the book told us."

His green eye glinted with excitement. "And so the High Council must find a child of Leonette," Orpheus said. His eye peeled on Lyander: "Who are they? Who have they found?"

Lyander hesitated, not wanting to reveal the truth, but knowing he couldn't lie. Orpheus stamped his cane, waving at his caster. The woman stepped into the pool, but Lyander put a hand out to stop her.

"Eluthienn," he said. "The High Council have formed an alliance with the outlawed prince of Ravinica. In exchange for killing Lokul, they have pledged Formaria to his cause."

The dwarf's eye grew wide, a finger pulling at his lower lip. "War with Ravinica?"

"Once the vampire king is dead."

"And with the Ecclessius so distracted, I will be free. Free to reach out and take that which I have always desired." The dwarf's voice grew quiet, mumbling as he ran his hand across his lip. "Orpheus Velgar will no longer slink in the shadows, forced to eke out a living on the edge of this world; he will be great, he will be a power, he will be a contender. . ."

The dwarf's hand dropped suddenly, single eye locking onto Lyander as if only just realising others could hear him.

"You're free, Kalbrayeth Lyander. Go back to the Ecclessius, tell them what you've found. Start your war."

His war? he thought as the rapid thuds in his chest subsided. *Will it be my war, if I don't kill Eluthienn? If I let him go, would the prince find a way of retaking Ravinica without Formaria's support? And what then – would Eluthienn turn on those who betrayed him? Would it lead to a Fromryian–Ravinican war?*

Lyander took a tired step out of the pool, thinking that killing the prince might actually be the simpler option. He didn't know if it was the demon network's residue or the shock of nearly being eaten alive, but something sickly churned around in his stomach as he thought about running a blade through Eluthienn's back.

FOURTEEN

BRAZIER

Brazier shovelled the last pile of gyre ice onto the loading tray and watched it hiss and steam before liquefying through the hairline cracks. He wiped sweat from his brow, then pushed the tray into the ship. Three feet wide and a foot deep, it slid slowly against his weight then shut with a *click*.

He hammered his fist against the fuselage, then shouted: "That's the lot!"

It wasn't. As the only ship in the hangar bay, the supply of ice was as good as endless. But a full reserve would take another hour, maybe two – the sort of time, Brazier strongly suspected, they did not have. So they fuelled the ship with just two crates – enough to make runs in the local tunnels and throw a few sharp manoeuvres if it came to it. But Brazier was hoping it wouldn't.

The first thing he and every other cadet learned in the Navarch Academy was gyre ships liked wide, open spaces. They did not like cramped tunnels with narrow passages or tight turns where an ambush could spring from above or below. Unfortunately, from what the hex display showed of Teuron's surroundings, that described exactly what they were about to fly into.

"Got her synthesisers running at max," Switch said as she ambled down the access ramp. "I'll have her purring in no time."

Freyen came from beneath the other side of the fuselage; held in her hand were what looked like glass vials encased in open bronzite shells. She handed the spent coils to Switch, then wiped her hands on a rag.

"That's about all I could find that needs replacing," she said to the enginator.

Switch sighed, looking down at the coils like a mother looking fondly at her child. She turned to Brazier: "What're the chances the Ecclessius will let us keep her after we're done?"

Brazier felt himself blank in confusion. "I think we can keep Freyen," he said.

The laugh was sheer, unencumbered joy, and it took Brazier a split second to realise it belonged to Freyen. The last time he'd heard her laugh like that was in Yeggardania, and he'd almost forgotten what it sounded like.

Switch rolled her eyes at him: "I meant the ship, Zee."

"Right," Brazier said, feeling the heat rising in his cheeks. "I'd say the chances of that are next to none."

"Not if we don't tell the Ecclessius," Matthias said, coming down the access ramp. "Hide the *Anchorite* after completing our mission, find ourselves a shuttle, and tell the Church we lost her in an ambush. They'll be too happy about daddy vampire's death to care."

"Then what?" Brazier asked. "We fly around as blades for hire?"

"Plenty of work for a ship like this," Matthias said. "And I know just where to find it."

"Except then we'd all have to crew her," Switch said, "which means spending more time with you."

Matthias grinned. "I'm not so bad once you get to know me."

But Brazier already knew everything he needed to know. Matthias Phaser was a criminal of the severest kind, and would cut and run with a prize like the *Anchorite* the first chance he got. Under no circumstances could he be left alone with the ship.

"The *Anchorite* goes back to Thendergaarden," Brazier said firmly, looking straight at Matthias.

The grin remained where it was as he said: "Let me know if you change your mind."

A crystal white light blared from inside the ship, showering the navigator before fading as the gyre thrusters gave a light thrum, turning a deeper blue.

"Purring," Switch said happily, then nodded at something over Brazier's shoulder.

He turned to find the dock officer making his way toward them. "Now, this is a long shot," he said, "but if you happen across someone out there who knows how to operate a walker, we have one in the shop."

"Why's it not already out there?" Brazier asked. From the state of the battle, the spire could desperately use it.

The gnome patted the air with his hands. "We only got it repaired just before all my crews were called out. Far as I know, there're not many here who can pilot it."

"I can," Freyen said, and Brazier turned very slowly to face her. "I have an Indomiter class rating."

"Of course you do," Switch said, shaking her head.

Questions like: Why would an operations officers know how to pilot a war walker, why isn't this on your record, and who in the black hell is Freyen Fortigris swirled around his mind. Instead, he said: "We can't fit a war walker in the ship."

"I know; I'll need to meet you at the passage."

"Not happening," Brazier said, and her head dipped by a fraction, looking at him from beneath her brows. "You don't have infantry support," he added quickly, preempting the argument he could see forming.

"I can join with the battle group outside the east hanger bay, and bring some of them with me to the side passage – that way, I've got infantry support and I'm bringing reinforcements."

"To a pass that's about to be overrun by a Mirrovinjin battle group," Switch said.

Freyen pressed her lips together, a serious look on her face. "Then you need to get the rest of the detachment there as quickly as possible."

Brazier wanted to argue; he wanted to use his rank to tell Freyen she wasn't going to pilot the war walker. The problem was, it made sense – a single walker could turn the tide of a battle. He just really didn't want Freyen to be the one to do it.

"Join those outside the east hangar bay, but *wait* for us," he said.

She nodded at him.

"Well now that's settled, I'll take you to her," the dock officer said. "You'll love her – absolutely marvellous." He smiled at Freyen as if he was describing a silk garment, not a war machine with the sole function of dealing death.

He walked around the ship, heading to the north of the bay. "C'mon!" he shouted over his shoulder.

"Give me a hand," Freyen said to Brazier. He nodded and they followed the gnome.

"Took a real beating last time she was out," he said as they crossed the hangar bay. "But I'm from the Helm. Was fixing up walkers before I could read – seriously, pa was an enginator, so I know what I'm doing." He turned to them as he said it. "Even so, her carriage was a challenge. Might need to give it a boot when you want to get out again."

"What happened?" Freyen asked.

"Ahh," the gnome said hesitantly. "Well, a drake ripped the compartment clean off so we needed to replace it." *Which also explained why they didn't have a pilot.*

"The spare we had is for a different class, so it might be a little stiff," he continued, then added: "Will protect you just fine, though."

Three heptagonal portals lined the bay's north wall, seven triangles forming doors large enough for a vault-class lander to fly through with room to spare. The dock officer walked up to a terminal, placed his hand in, and a moment later, the portal on their right opened, its triangles slicing apart.

Stood in the centre of the semi-hexagonal chamber, the war walker was a bipedal tower of solid bronzite. Easily four times Brazier's height and encased in overlapping shell plating over its knees, thighs, up its waist, and from its shoulders and down its arms. Its torso – the pilot's carriage – was like a gilded sarcophagus, curved and heavily plated with a visor through which the pilot could see. Behind the walker, chains with hooks were suspended from gears in the ceiling, and a walkway ran on either side and around its rear to allow enginator crews to access and repair the upper torso, shoulders, and head. Despite seeing others of its sort before, Brazier was still struck by how much it looked like a cross between a giant human and a Constructii.

With the dexterity of all gnomes, the dock officer jumped up on the walker's leg and climbed to the carriage. Planting a boot next to the compartment door, he began yanking on the carriage's handle. After three hard pulls, and a sound like scraping metal desperately in need of oil, the door swung open and he dropped lightly to the ground. Inside, was a compartment with the sort of padding found on ship bulkheads, leather harnesses, and two terminals positioned at waist height.

Freyen pulled herself up the walker, using the plating as handholds and swung into the carriage. Brazier climbed up its leg, using its knee for balance, then strapped the leather foot harnesses over Freyen's boots.

"Thanks," she said.

He pulled himself up to its chest, hanging onto one of the terminals, using the rim of its waist as a foot hold. "As your first officer, I'd like to restate how dangerous I think this is," he said.

"I'm surprised to hear that from someone who likes to jump into pits of voidstone," Freyen said, the playfulness in her voice doing nothing to ease his apprehension.

"That was an unintentional mistake. This is very much intentional."

"I know what I'm doing," she said, strapping the harness across her chest and locking it through the belt buckle.

"Wait for us," he said. "Then maybe after this, you can tell me why you know how to pilot one of these things."

She held his gaze, and Brazier thought he saw her usually intense, bright eyes soften with sadness before they hardened and she placed her hands into the hex terminals on either side of her. Her eyes closed, the lids fluttered, then a sound like gyre thrusters spinning up.

"Maybe I will," she said, and there was a whirring thrum, growing in the bones of the machine, and Brazier felt its thighs shift on the spot, as if flexing. He reached over and pulled the compartment door closed, shoving it into place. Through the visor, all he could see was Freyen, watching him.

"I'll see you soon," he said, and climbed off the walker and backed away.

Stomp, and Freyen stepped the walker forward. Another *stomp*, and she followed with the other leg. Then *stomp, stomp, stomp,* and she was out of the chamber and turned to face them. The walker's hand reached to its hip and took the repeater from its holster. With the other hand, Freyen cocked the gear wheel, then slid the weapon back into the hip grooves. She took it out and slid it back once more. Then did the same with the sword, giving it an arcing cross-cut before tipping the blade to her head in a mock salute. She returned it to its scabbard and strode off toward the end of the bay and the lift that would take her to the battle outside the spire.

#

Brazier watched the walker on the command display, imagining he could hear its metal stomps as Freyen left the east hangar bay and entered the tunnel. Three times the size of any other shapes, he could clearly see her drawing the walker's repeater and firing into the mass. Tendrils of anxiety began to coil around his heart as he watched her walk and shoot, gaining on the battle. With each step, he wished the shape would slow; the thought he was sending her and Switch to their deaths by agreeing to this mission resurfacing, and acted like a toxin steadily pumping out from his chest. *He should have told her to wait in the hangar bay until they arrived with reinforcements. He should have been firmer with her.*

"She'll be fine," Switch said.

"Walker's need infantry support," Brazier said, not looking up at her. "And from the look of what's going on down there, it doesn't look like there's much infantry left."

"Freyen isn't stupid. If she sees things going south, she'll pull back to the spire."

Brazier tried to say "yes" but gave a sort of grunt instead, eyes still on the hex.

"She's also a big girl," Switch said, something in the tone of her voice making him look up. "Can probably handle a lot more than we think she can."

"This is all very moving," Matthias said from the pit, "but I'm picking up units spread out all over the place, and we haven't the ice for all of them."

On the hex, the *Anchorite* sailed above the edge of a cavern pass – the empty void to her port side, the pass below on her starboard. Ahead, the pass rounded to the right, opening out onto a wide plane with three passages shooting off into other tunnels. In the centre of the plane were a handful of shapes, perhaps fifteen in total, stood among a cluster of structures.

The passage on the far left rose at a steady incline, rounding farther left and divided – a pass rising even higher to a cradle, the other pass running below it, leading deeper into more tunnels. A mass of bodies swarmed the cradle, while what was clearly a shield wall held the lower pass.

The second passage splitting off from the plane also rose, then opened onto a narrow ravine, forming a deep 'V' with a smaller passage splitting off from it, snaking round to higher and lower levels. At the foot of the 'V,' where the passage became the ravine, a large

Fromryian unit crowded a small structure, what looked like tens upon tens of tiny mounds spilling out from it. There were other units farther along the ravine and throughout the passage braking off from it – most moving swiftly, hugging the walls as if they expected an attack from above.

The third passage dropped at a sharp decline, spiralling around itself before levelling onto a wide cavern pass extending beyond the edge of the display. Two large Fromryian units, at least fifty soldiers in each, stood in loose formations along the pass, both unengaged.

"Closest unit first," Brazier said. "Set her down on the plane."

Matthias's right hand tilted outward, the filaments in the pit turning like a snake coiling around itself, and the *Anchorite* banked starboard, following the pass round. It declined in altitude, and slowed before landing on the plane. Brazier heard the access ramp open, then he left the nav deck.

He was halfway along the ramp before it finally hit the ground with a metallic *crunch*. Around him, the gyre thrusters spun up grey dust clouds into tiny whirlwinds that grew and collapsed, forcing Brazier to shield his eyes as he stepped onto the plane and out from under the ship. A web of gyre ice twisted along the ceiling, its strands extending down the walls like the branches of a tree and lighting up the plane in bright blue light.

"Have they called back the fleet?" a dwarf shouted above the thrum as he marched toward Brazier. "We were told not to expect air support for another three days."

He wore a battered steel chest plate, pauldrons, and vambraces over a dark blue gambeson. Head shaved, a ginger-brown beard shooting out from his chin, his nose and ears were studded with silver piercings. He cradled a long range repeater in his arms, looking as battered as his armour, the gyre cartridge dulled to a soft azure. The besagew attached to his chest plate told Brazier he was a captain.

"We're the only ship," he said, leaning toward the dwarf so he didn't need to shout. "The southern pass is about to be overrun – we're rounding up reinforcements from this side of the spire."

The captain's lips bunched into a scowl. "Show me," he said, pointing into the *Anchorite*.

Brazier led the captain up the ramp and into the fuselage.

"Chivrin Zolt, Captain of the Taranis fifteenth," the dwarf said, as they walked through the fuselage.

"Brazier Veranquis, First Officer," Brazier said, and was about to say "of the *Chalice of Amaranth"* before remembering he wasn't: "of the *Shian Anchorite*."

"Veranquis?" Chivrin asked. "Related to Torquen Veranquis?"

"His brother," Brazier said, hearing how wooden his voice sounded.

"I knew him during the Heiron campaign," Chivrin said, turning to face him. "He's one hell of a dwarf – I'm glad to know his brother is with us now."

"He was," Brazier said. "Torquen is dead."

Chivrin looked taken aback. "I'm sorry to hear that," he said, sounding it.

Brazier simply nodded, and pulled himself up the stairs; at the top, the nav deck doors shifted open for him.

"Small crew," the captain said, giving the nav deck a quick once-over, eyes lingering on Switch's bronzite augment. "You're not part of Teuron's detachment?"

"We arrived from Thendergaarden," Brazier said and, not wanting to explain further, pointed at the unit both he and Lyander agreed would soon be overrun.

The captain stepped up to the command display, eyes fixing on the southern pass, then onto the main battle taking place outside the spire, then back to the pass. "We're too concentrated on this side of the spire. But we can't withdraw."

"Why not?" Brazier asked; from the hex, there was no reason for so much of the Fromryian detachment to remain here.

The captain pointed at the ravine and its adjacent passages. "All those units there – they're pinned down. A drake – and a big one, from what we've been told." He moved his finger to the mass at the foot of the ravine, and now Brazier understood why they looked like they were huddling beneath the structure. "They've set up a triage camp here with all our wounded." Chivrin's eyes creased at the corners, and he shook his head. "Lot more than I thought there'd be. And we're out of healers." He looked up at Brazier: "Ship like this could get some of them out. You won't get them all in, but you'll get the ones who can't walk."

"If we don't get ripped out of the sky first," Matthias said, leaving the pit to stand on the opposite side of the display. "Heading into a ravine that narrow, landing in the open, they'll rip us open bow to stern."

"And if you don't," Chivrin said, placing both hands on the edge of the display, "they're dead. There're no casters, and if they try and withdraw the wounded back to the spire, they'll be picked off by the drake."

"It's a battle. Fromryr die all the time in battles," the navigator said, as if he was explaining the sun rising in the east and setting in the west. He pointed at the two larger units at the end of the spiralling passage. "Seems to me, we're better off picking up some of them and sending the rest back to the spire."

"Leaving them to die," Chivrin said, pointing angrily at the ravine, and as if death came at its calling, a winged shape appeared from the edge of the display. As long as the *Anchorite*, its tail flicked and swished behind it while its wings beat lazily at the air, and its stubby, horned head was angled down at the passages below. On the hex, the rider was all torso and head, but Brazier could clearly make out the long spear clutched in its hand.

Matthias watched the drake and shrugged. "Just telling you what I'd do."

Brazier's gaze, almost involuntarily, darted from the drake to the war walker, then back to the drake. A tiny war erupted in his mind, broiling with emotions like uncertainty and guilt. The smart decision would be exactly what Matthias suggested: fly to those in the third pass, pick them up, and send the rest back to the spire. Attempting to rescue wounded, sitting in the open with even one drake flying above, was idiocy – no officer would make such a decision. And if they lost the ship, were pinned down in the ravine, Freyen would be on her own.

He felt his jaw grinding together as he thought with an ache in his chest – and not for the first time – that he wished his brother was there. It pulled on his heart with such force, he even glanced up over the terminal, instinct making him look at the empty space next to Matthias where his brother, if alive, might have said maybe three words or simply given him a look, and Brazier would know what was the right thing to do.

He dropped his gaze back to the hex, and something completely unexpected happened; he imagined telling Freyen they'd left dying and wounded just to get back to her. Then her words: *You know what else sounds like Torquen? A dwarf who gives aid to those who need it.* She expected the samc of him – *he* expected the same of him.

"There first," he said, pointing at the two unengaged units in the third pass. "We send them to reinforce the southern passage. Then we collect the wounded from the ravine."

"You've got a real thing for making dumb decisions," Matthias said, his voice thicker, more abrasive than usual, his eyes grey smoke clouds.

"As first officer," Brazier said, "they're my decisions to make, and your orders to follow."

The navigator said nothing, so Brazier turned to Chivrin: "Bring your unit on board; they can reinforce the cove as we take on the wounded."

The dwarf nodded at him, gave Matthias a doubtful look, and left the nav deck.

"Zee," Switch said, "I've been over every inch of this kitten – she won't even break a sweat against one drake. But if things start to get hot, we do not have the ice to engage in aerial combat."

"We land on top of that thing," Brazier said, pointing at the drake, "take it out, then pick up the wounded. One run, that's all."

Switch's scowl was hard as ice: "Good. Because that's all she's going to give you."

Below, the sound of boots marched up the access ramp, voices in the fuselage, the clink of weapons and armour. A hex well vibrated, and Chivrin's voice was loud on the nav deck: "We're good to go."

"Received," Brazier said, and the connection dropped. "You're up," he said to Matthias. The navigator regarded him, turned, and knelt in the pit.

The *Anchorite* rose and shot across the plane, banking lightly to her port side as Matthias guided her down the spiralling passage. She slid from its mouth, then glided across the cavern, at what must be barely ten feet from the floor. The grey and silver shapes representing Fromryian soldiers shifted on the hex, turning, presumably, to face the oncoming ship.

On the other side of the display, Freyen moved to the left flank, to his relief, still only engaging at range. He knew it wouldn't last for long – the Mirrovinjin couldn't let something as deadly as a walker punish their lines without answer. Either they would fall back or, given their advantage on the battlefield, send units to bring her down. *We don't have long*, and with that thought, he made his way down to the fuselage, several members of Chivrin's unit nodding to him as he passed.

There was a mix of gnomes and dwarves, each with a crossbow resting in their lap or between their legs – like their captain, wearing plate armour over dark blue gambesons. The access ramp clicked as it opened, and Chivrin came to stand next to him.

"This'll go easier if I do the talking," he said.

Brazier nodded.

"Got plenty of friends in this detachment – good many of them are in that Ravine," Chivrin said. "You're definitely Torquen Veranquis' brother."

"Won't be easy," Brazier said, uncomfortable at the compliment.

"Didn't say it would be," Chivrin said, his mouth softening with a slight smile. "We're all just doing what we got to do before we meet the abyss." Whether it was his intention or not, Chivrin's words eased the doubt clawing at his insides. *I do need to do this.*

They stepped off the access ramp and into near pitch darkness. Only a single vein of crystal blue ice ran along the cavern wall, miles above them, like a river in the night sky, glinting like star light. It turned the Fontain soldiers' deep red gambesons and the painted red on their curved tower shields a dark purple. They watched Chivrin and Brazier approach in silence, then a man with dark locks and a curved nose, holding his helm under his arm, came marching out to meet them.

"I do hope one of you is about to tell me where the abyss-damned enemy is," the man said, a haughty whine to his voice. Brazier was about to place him in the category of undeserving high born when he saw the purple scar running down his forehead, over his eye, and curving around his cheek.

Experience of at least one battle, then.

"We've been waiting for the Mirrovinjin for half a day," the man finished.

"They're on the other side of the spire," Chivrin said. "South passage. We need your units to fall back to the east hangar bay entrance – reinforce their lines, then move round the side pass and engage the enemy along the southern passage."

The man's eyes darted between Brazier and Chivrin, resting briefly on the dwarf's besagew. "Command is going to leave the northern passages undefended?"

"There's no attack coming here," Chivrin said. "The real assault is on the southern pass. You need to move your units now, lieutenant."

The man's jaw tightened before he – somewhat reluctantly – said, "Yes, sir." He turned to one of his soldiers. "Send word to Kilgrew: East hangar bay tunnel and southern pass are under attack. We are to fall back and reinforce friendly lines."

Chivrin and Brazier made their way back to the *Anchorite*, the clank of shields and armour rising into the cavern as a hundred Fontain soldiers prepared to march. He hoped it would be enough.

In the fuselage, Brazier placed his hand into a terminal and let Matthias know they could leave.

"Tell your unit to strap in," he said to Chivrin.

"We'll engage the drake first, then pick up the wounded."

"Alright, boys and girls," Chivrin called, his voice carrying to the end of the fuselage. "Load up and lock in – we're on for high sprawl manoeuvres."

Shouts of "Yes, sir!" rang out, and they began looping harnesses across their chests, locking themselves into their seats.

Brazier climbed to the nav deck and watched, with a tiny spark of achievement, as the command display showed two units moving swiftly back along the pass, heading for the spiralling passage. Freyen, he saw, was now moving along the rear of the Fontain line, preventing the Mirrovinjin from pulling her into combat. *Smart*, he thought, both impressed and relieved.

"Zee," Switch said. "Drake is on the move – Matthias is going to try and hit it when it comes out of this passage." She pointed at one of the ravine's offshoots, where the drake was mid-dive. It curled its wings under its body, the rider lying flat along its back, its spear aimed at the unit ahead of it.

With ferocious speed, it fell through the air, the long spear connecting with one of the shapes, running it through, lifting it into the air. One arm holding the drake's reins, its other three hoisted the spear into the air; the drake unfurled its wings, beat and rose, and the rider tipped the spear downward, shaking the shaft. The soldier slid off the end, and came crashing down, the filaments representing him or her turning to a mound, indistinct from the passage floor.

"Good plan," Brazier said, eyes on the *Anchorite*. It sped out onto the plane, banked starboard, and headed up the passage. As it rose to the foot of the Ravine, Matthias slowed the ship while letting it climb in altitude. The harried unit began to fall back, running for the passage's mouth. They turned as the drake came in for another pass – as before, flying low, wings curled beneath it, the spear aiming toward them. Several of the shapes threw themselves to the ground, the spear missing its target.

"Come on," Matthias said. "Bring it into the open."

The unit picked themselves up and continued, while the drake looped over itself, wings spanning out, the rider hanging upside down. It twisted round and dived again. Once again, the unit took cover, but the spear found its mark. Farther down the ravine, the *Anchorite* climbed to what Brazier thought must be the hex display's limit, looking like some artificial sun rising over a grey and silver land.

Then Matthias cut the engines. The thruster's constant background drone ceased and a weightlessness settled in his limbs and stomach.

"What are you doing?" he said.

"Trust me," the navigator replied.

"We can't make manoeuvres without our engines."

The drake made another loop, then came diving back at the unit, which was now almost at the mouth of the passage and into the ravine.

"You are going to miss," Brazier said.

"Just trust me," he said again, and the drake flew low, speared a target, and shot out into the ravine. With far more space, the drake banked wide, coming round to its left and down the ravine, toward the *Anchorite*. Well above its flight path, Brazier now knew what the navigator was doing; without the thrusters spitting out gyre light, the ship would be as good as invisible this high up. The drake continued to bank round, almost directly beneath the *Anchorite*, then beat its wings, driving northward up the ravine.

Matthias reengaged the engines, a blaring *hum*

resounding through the ship, and they dove hard. Even with the spatial anchor, it forced Brazier and Switch to lean into the command terminal as the ship followed the drake's path. As the *Anchorite*'s bow crossed over the creature's tail, the repeaters lining the hull erupted in a shower of bolts, each one driving into the drake's serpentine body. It gave an ugly writhe, like a wet rag wrung out, then went limp, wings streaming behind it, as it fell through the air.

Brazier watched it crash to the ground as Matthias pulled the ship to a midair stop, nose pulling up, thrusters angling toward the bow.

"Where did you learn to do that?" Switched asked, barely concealing her amazement.

"Are you trying to tell me you're impressed?"

Switch laughed. "Don't get your hopes up."

"It was a good move," Brazier said. Given it was the truth, he felt Matthias deserved the recognition, regardless of his other feelings toward the navigator.

Matthias craned his neck around. "Are we becoming friends, FO?"

"Don't get your hopes up."

The navigator chuckled and rotated the ship before angling the thrusters behind her, flying back to the ravine's mouth and the make-shift triage camp.

"Set her down just past the cove," Brazier said. He scanned the rest of the map; other than the two units marching up the spiralling passage, it looked much the same as before. "Can we expect any surprises?"

Matthias's head tilted to the right, a finger on his left hand twitching. "Nothing coming our way," he said.

"Our way?" Brazier asked.

"Pretty sure there's a witch heading for the south pass. And she's brought friends."

Brazier let out a deep exhalation. *Just when I thought things were going well.* Outside the spire,

Freyen pulled back behind a shield wall, firing over the top of it at a band of Mirrovinjin about to attempt a charge. It looked like she may have evened the odds which, based on the state of the battle, simply meant the Fromryr weren't facing total slaughter. Their lines were broken; small groups were forming into clusters, pulling together as the Mirrovinjin swarmed like ants around an insect's carcass. *They need the Anchorite there now.*

"We get as many on board as fast as we can," Brazier said to Switch. "In the vulnerum, engines, and magazine bays. Then we're gone."

"You got it, boss," she said, and Matthias slowed the ship, bringing it low over the cove and settling it on a strip of flat rock outside the entrance.

"Let's go," Brazier said.

In the fuselage, Chivrin's unit was already unstrapped and standing – Chivrin himself at the edge of the access ramp. He turned, saw Brazier, and nodded to him. Brazier nodded back as the access ramp opened, and they piled out into the ravine.

The structure was little more than an outpost – what in other countries might be considered a watch tower, a circular, fortified landing built at the edge of the ravine's wall. An entrance sat at the top of a flight of steps, pale grey doors with lines of gyre light around the edge converging in the centre around a node. Built upon rectangular pillars, the structure's roof formed into three triangular blocks, each facing away from the rock wall behind it; gyre channels ran up them and blazed into the dark. Like much of the ancient Formarian's design, they seemed entirely aesthetic.

Around the structure and arranged in rows, wounded and dead Fromryr were lying on stretchers and blankets, their groans becoming audible as the ship's thrusters powered down. Two field medics walked in between the rows, one kneeling to dress bandages, the other simply checking on the wounded, saying words of comfort to the dying.

"Where's Mikolay?" Brazier heard Chivrin call to one of the medics as the rest of his unit formed a perimeter. The gnome, young with a shock of brunet hair, shook his. He leaned into Chivrin and said something Brazier couldn't hear; the captain scowled, then turned to find Brazier and pointed at the cove. Understanding his meaning, Brazier and Switch followed the dwarf through the rows, catching up with him at the foot of the steps.

"Commanding officer is missing," Chivrin said.

"Who's in charge?"

The dwarf shook his head. "Some sergeant," he said, and placed his hand into the node. The doors parted a moment later, and the stench of blood and sweat wafted down toward them, along with the cries of so many wounded.

Most of the floor was taken up with their prone or huddled forms. Only a thin line cut through to the command console in the centre and to the other side of the structure, where a group of Fontain soldiers stood in heated discussion. Using the command console as a substitute medical bed, a medical officer bent over a human – a member of a gyre star crew from the colour of his doublet.

Mouth tight, sweat dripping from his temples, the medic was pulling a broken spear shaft through the man's thigh. A Fontain soldier, a dwarf, and what looked like a member of the wounded man's crew held him down at the shoulders and by his other leg. He screamed through the rag he was biting down on, eyes rolling into the back of his head, then went limp as the medic pulled the shaft free.

Chivrin stepped around the wounded and over to the group at the back of the cove.

"We have to fall back," Brazier heard one of the soldiers say.

"Orders are to hold the ravine," another said.

"That was two days ago," the first soldier replied. "We've had no word from spire command since – we don't even know if we still control Teuron."

"He's right, Igor." It was a woman's voice, weak and spoken through heavy breathing. Only then did Brazier notice the soldier sitting with her back to the wall. The others surrounded her. "We've not heard from Teuron," she continued, then took a breath. "In all likelihood, command structure has broken down and we're on our own. But we can't fall back. Not with drakes in the sky."

"We've dealt with that," Chivrin said as they drew closer. They all turned to look at him, then at Brazier and Switch. "We have a frigate outside, and can take those who can't walk. The rest of you need to fall back on foot with the wounded."

"Move aside, Igor," the woman said, and one of the soldiers made space. Short ginger hair stood out at an odd angle beneath the bloody bandage wrapped around her head, half her face, and under her chin. Her plate armour removed, her gambeson was unbuttoned at the neck, dark stains running down it. More bandages covered her right wrist, and it was only when Brazier looked closer that he saw it was a bloody stump, the hand gone.

"Command sent a ship to come get us?" she asked.

"Not quite," Chivrin said. "Look, the Mirrovinjin are about to make an assault on the southern pass. We've sent back the second and third companies, and we can take as many of your wounded as we can fit in a spire-class frigate. The rest of you are on foot."

"Plenty of us still scattered throughout the

northern passages."

"My unit will wait here for them, and hold the installation."

"Well, aren't you a ray light in the abyss."

Chivrin laughed. "You can thank the FO here – he's the one with the ship."

The woman's eyes slid onto Brazier. "Then you have my thanks, FO," she said, and stood slowly, waving away a hand offered by one of the other soldiers.

"I'd shake your hand," she said, holding up the bloody stump, "but as you can see . . ." She shrugged, then nodded at the medic, who was now strapping a leather belt around the leg, the patient out cold. "Casimir can tell you who to take."

They followed her over to the command console, and now standing over it, Brazier could see there was no hex in the depression. Instead, it was empty and black; inky sludge lining the corners.

"Mirrovinjin corrupted the hex," the sergeant said when she saw Brazier looking at it. "Had to use our helmets to scoop it out."

"They made it in here?" Chivrin asked.

"They took the installation; we forced them out. Cost us most of our company," she said with the sort of grey tone that came from battle exhaustion, watching too many friends die, and knowing it wasn't going to get much better.

"Cas," she said. "Get a frigate to take our wounded – can fit maybe thirty. Tell the captain whose priority and who isn't."

If eyes alone could look relieved, then the medic's surely did. They looked up at Chivrin from within dark purple rings and a face sheened with the waxy sweat of too little sleep. He combed a hand over the growth on his chin. "Does Teuron still have a caster?" he asked.

“Both were lost three days ago,” Brazier said, and he watched the relief evaporate.

“Then take everyone this side of the room who can’t walk,” he said, his voice quiet, then nodded at those on the other side of the line separating the wounded. “They won’t make it without an anomancer.”

“And those outside?” Switch asked.

“Walking wounded,” the medic said. “Mostly.”

“Alright,” the sergeant said, looking around at what remained of her company. “Fight’s not over, so we are double-timing this thing.”

They moved swiftly, using the few stretchers or carrying the wounded under their arms, taking them from their rows in the installation, and making rows down the *Anchorite*’s fuselage. Past those outside the cove, Brazier could feel their eyes flitting from him to the ship to the installation, knowing there wouldn’t be enough room for them, as well.

“Easy, sailor,” Switch said as the man they laid down on the fuselage, then pulled himself into a sitting position, his back against the wall. He unbuttoned his navy doublet, sweat running from his curly blond hair down his pale cheeks.

“That needs to come off,” Switch said, pointing at his leg, which below the knee was red pulp and shards of bone, the shin broken in at least three places, pieces sticking out from among the muscle.

The man – the boy – Brazier saw, seeing how young he was, shook his head, causing a tremble to run down his body. “I’ll wait for the anomancer,” he said with more composure than Brazier would have thought possible, given his situation.

“There’re no casters left in Teuron,” Switch said.

The boy’s lip trembled, a flash of fear in his eyes. If all they needed to do was hold out for a caster, a

Fromryr could put up with almost any amount of suffering. Holding out was a far harder prospect, though, when there was no caster, and the end involved amputation.

"I'll get you something for the pain," Brazier said, and made his way to the front of the fuselage.

In the *Anchorite*'s vulnerum – a heptagonal compartment roughly the size of the nav deck – Brazier moved around one of the three bronzite beds to a circular bronzite disc angled at forty-five degrees and mounted on a kind of pedestal. He placed his hand into the centre of the disc's node and said *Tranquilata* in his mind, and a section of the disc slid open, revealing a ten-degree segment packed with shards of raw gyre ice. Among them, ten bronzite vials. Brazier took one, was about to close the segment, then decided they could restock at Teuron, and took three more – there were others in just as bad shape as the boy. He used the node to close the segment, left the vulnerum, and closed the door behind him, spinning the locking wheel.

Switch knelt next to a female dwarf, lying down, one knee in the air, her face almost entirely covered in bandages. The dwarf's left hand clutched Switch's augment, gripping it hard. Seeing Brazier, the enginator placed her other hand on the dwarf's shoulder, said something in her ear, then stood, coming over to him.

"Her, back there," she said to him, nodding over her shoulder. "And three more at least. The one with a crushed foot and –"

The terminal to the right of the access ramp blurted Matthias's voice, absent of its usual cool: "Brazier, if you're down there, we have a serious problem."

He stepped around Switch, heading for the terminal when there was a shout from outside the ship.

"Drake!"

The unmistakable beat of wings, a cry of "incoming!" and a keening screech. Forgetting the terminal, Brazier ran down the access ramp and onto the ravine floor. The drake plummeted down, clawed feet first, wings pulled tight behind it – then a strangled cry, the crunch of armour and bone, and a wet thud as two members of Chivrin's unit were flattened on impact.

A split-second pause, the Fromryr too stunned to speak, then the *click* and *twang* of repeaters firing at a drake twice the size of the one Matthias shot out of the air. Brazier watched as Chivrin aimed a single shot, found his mark, and fired – a sharp *crack* as the bolt released. Too fast and the ravine too dark to follow its flight, all Brazier could see was the pale, four-limbed shape falling through the air. The Mirrovinjin landed with a thud, a crumbled heap of tangled limbs, and the drake threw back its neck and screeched.

"Get out of here!" Chivrin shouted at Brazier, then bent over his crossbow, winding the bow back with the winch.

"Chivrin!" Brazier shouted back. "Chivrin!" But there wasn't enough time; the captain, still winding the crossbow, looked up too late. The horned head came down like a hammer pummelling iron – the jaws wide, the teeth as long as Brazier's arm. Chivrin put a hand over his eye, like he was shielding himself from the sun, and *snap*. In a single bite, the dwarf was swallowed whole, leaving only his calves, bloody stumps sticking out the top of brown boots. One wobbled slightly before righting and standing still.

Brazier almost fell backward in his attempts to run for the fuselage. He pounded up the access ramp, hearing the *Anchorite*'s repeaters engage, and the drake's piercing screech as they found their mark. *They would be enough*, he told himself, hearing the fear even in his own thoughts. *It was big, but there are few things that can take a broadside from four repeaters and live to tell the tale.*

His hand in the hex, he was shouting even before the connection to the nav deck was made: "Get us out of here!"

Already on it, Matthias said in his mind, and Brazier heard the access ramp closing, the thrusters spinning up. He pulled his hand from the terminal, and watched the ravine floor fall away from them as the ship rose before the access ramp clicked shut. Heart hammering, he let himself breathe out a sigh, let himself start to feel the warm rush of adrenaline-fuelled relief that came from only just escaping certain death.

Like a clawed hand tearing his soul from his body, the feeling was wrenched from his chest the moment the slam hit the *Anchorite*'s hull, sending the ship crashing to the ground. Muted cries from among the wounded, and Brazier fell against the terminal, barely holding himself up. He saw Switch clinging to an overhead handhold as the ship shook; the thrusters fighting against the weight pinning it.

He pushed himself off the terminal, moving along the fuselage, and was thrown forward as the *Anchorite* pitched upward.

He slammed into Switch with an "Oof," the enginator's arm curling around his shoulder to keep him from falling.

"This is becoming a bit of a habit," Switch said as he found his feet.

"Get to the nav," he croaked, only now aware he was winded.

He moved around her, and pulled himself up the stairs as fast as the air in his lungs would allow. Reaching the landing, the thrusters became a pulsating drone, so loud they sounded like they were inside the ship. But there was no way they could be that loud – not through the hull.

Then the heavy hand of realisation dropped from somewhere in his chest, through to the bottom of his stomach, making him spin round. The hole left by the repeater was large enough for Brazier to jump through and not worry about slicing himself on the hull's torn curves.

"Fuck the black void!" Switch said, pulling herself onto the landing and staring at the hole like it personally offended her. "I swear –"

But Brazier never found out what she was going to swear because the drake's horned head smashed through the hole, widening the breach by half, and once more, sent the ship crashing to the ground. Brazier was thrown against the nav deck doors, which opened, and he was sent tumbling backward, rolling over the deck, and smacking the back of his head into the command terminal.

Through the open doors, he saw the drake's grey-white spines, the leathery black skin along its neck; then it thrashed. The ship cavorted one way, then the other, and the drake hissed and shrieked like an animal caught in a snare, its horned head catching on the railing around the landing, the space too tight for it to open its jaw. It twisted its neck round and one eye, a veiny white orb with a slit as black as the void, looked straight at Brazier.

Which meant it didn't see Switch.

She came from the right, almost jumping round, pulling her bronzite arm toward her chin and letting it rip in a straight cross. The augment plunged through the eye like a hot poker running through flesh – up to her wrist, then her elbow, then her bicep. Switch twisted and yanked her arm out, the augment covered in translucent white goo and globs of grey-green matter. The drake's screech was hatred and pain; it writhed manically, like an eel pulled from the water, its weight rocking the ship. It pulled free of the *Anchorite*, several of its spines breaking off against the hole's edges, and they were still.

Switch shook her augment, flinging off eye juice and bits of brains. Shaking her head and scowling so hard Brazier thought the corners of her mouth might meet her jaw line, she stomped onto the nav deck.

"Do you know how hard this thing is to clean?" she said, shaking the arm at Brazier as if the mess running down it was *his* fault.

"I can only imagine," he said, grabbing the edge of the command terminal and pulling himself up.

"Matthias," he said, "how are we looking?"

"Not pretty," he said, a strain in his voice, making it sound as if he was growling. "We've lost a repeater, two more are going to need work, and four of the thrusters are putting out at less than half capacity."

"You forgot the great big fuck-off hole in her hull," Switch said.

"And there's a great big fuck-off hole in her hull," Matthias repeated.

"Can you get us back to Teuron?" Brazier asked.

"It's going to be a rough ride, but I'll get us back there."

Brazier searched the display; the *Anchorite* drifted low along the passage toward the plane, travelling at an angle, not quite nose first. The thruster discs all faced different directions, making Brazier think of broken feet.

"At least I'll have something to fix," Switch said, but Brazier wasn't listening. His gaze fell on the battle outside the east hangar bay. Freyen and what looked like a single unit of Fromryr conducted a fighting retreat, the walker drawing the Mirrovinjin toward it so the unit could make it to the safety of the spire.

"Matthias," he said, not looking up from the

display. “Max sprawl to the east hangar bay.”

FIFTEEN
LYANDER

Lyander sat in one of the shuttle's hard seats, a lancing throb pulsing from the twisted scar across the back of his hand. It shot up his forearm and into his bicep, causing him to grip the seat's armrest with his other hand. In the Immuratum, the pain was nonexistent. Because of the realm's chaotic sorceries or because he'd been so distracted with making it out alive, he didn't know. He did know that right now, however, it hurt like black hell.

But it was a pain he could take, a pain he could *almost* embrace. Flexing the fingers, watching the purple scar pull toward the gap between his middle finger and ring finger, he realised he was grateful. *I can swing a sword in two hands; I can still fight*. And the sheer elation that feeling brought him almost made him forget the pain. Almost.

"So," Gabriel said, as he guided the shuttle out of the cavern complex and back into the wider tunnels.

"Eluthienn was right?"

Lyander gave the fingers another flex, then said: "Eluthienn is telling the truth."

"There might be magical bonds between his blood and Lokul," Gabriel said, and for the first time since knowing him, he sounded like he was speaking with genuine sincerity. "But you'd be a fool to trust him."

"You still think he brought about Lokul's return?"

Gabriel's arm tensed as he turned the shuttle.

"I think lies and the truth are one and the same to Eluthienn Leonette. And he uses whichever is needed to suit his ends."

Lyander massaged his hand, then stopped when it only made the pain worse.

"Even so, the threat of Fiondagaard is real. Without Formaria and Ravinica united, the emperor cannot be stopped. Eluthienn's cause is just."

Gabriel's head twitched to the side, and the terminals released his hands. He came to stand in front of Lyander, holding onto one of the ceiling handles as the shuttle flew on full sentience.

"Is that a good idea?" Lyander asked, nodding at the empty space between the terminals.

Gabriel's eyes were cool blue shards of ice as he looked down at Lyander.

"Eluthienn's cause is just because he wants you to believe it's just," he said, "but he's no better than the ones we already serve. He would use you and send you to die, just as the Ecclessius uses us and sends us to die."

His hand made thinking that much harder, but something about what the witch-hunter said was wrong.

"Then what difference does it make?" he said, conscious Gabriel was unaware of his orders to kill Eluthienn, and so they were having different conversations. "It's only the outcome that matters. Either Formaria stands alone or it stands with Eluthienn's Ravinica."

"And with Eluthienn king, and his neighbours weakened by their wars, what do you think would happen then?"

"Ravinica would be weakened, as well," Lyander said, but in his mind the words rang hollow because he knew if this eventuality came to pass, it would be an Eluthienn betrayed by Formaria sitting upon the Ravinican throne.

"The prince uses others to fight his wars," Gabriel said, shaking his head and returning to pilot the shuttle. "You trust him at your peril, Lyander, and if it is between Eluthienn and the Church, we must choose the Church."

He leant back in his seat and closed his eyes, the pain lessened but still invading his thoughts. Every time he tried to form a coherent thread, his hand sent him a throb, searing the thought, leaving nothing but tendrils of smoky obscurity. He didn't know if he trusted Eluthienn or not – he was certain of that uncertainty. He also didn't know if killing him was the right thing or the wrong thing for Formaria. He was less certain of *that* uncertainty. But he did know that he hated the Ecclessius for ordering him to act as the assassin. He hated them even more for knowing they could offer him his position of First Champion; they could dangle that in front of him, and he might reach out and grab what was offered. He might acquiesce, and remain in their thrall, despite everything —and the way Pulance smirked at him, knowing all of this, as he did indeed later announce the *reward* to the rest of the High Council members.

Just because it distracted him from his hand, he focused on that hatred as they flew in silence, until Gabriel announced they were nearly at Acheron.

Lyander stood, grabbing one of the handholds. "What's it like on the ground?"

Gabriel's head tilted forward slightly before answering: "Doesn't look like it's changed much."

"And the southern side passage?"

"The *Anchorite*'s definitely not there. Looks like they might have had a fight."

"What do you mean, *looks like*?"

"Well, it *looks like* there're fewer of them than when we were on the *Anchorite,* so I'm guessing they had a fight," Gabriel said, but the sarcasm missed Lyander by a mile. He was too busy hoping Eluthienn was among the "fewer" still alive down there. Explaining to the Ecclessius the Prince died in a meaningless spire skirmish before he could carry out the mission would guarantee him expulsion from his Order, maybe even Formaria. *Although it would rid you of all your problems.*

"Set us down in the mouth of the passage."

Gabriel's left hand turned in the well, and the shuttle banked portside, nose dipping as they sped up. It weaved gently back and forth, the thrusters a constant vibration as they propelled the ship forward. They slowed, and he heard the thrusters change position. He felt the ship turn in the air, felt it decline in altitude, and heard the thrusters' propulsion resonate against hard rock before decreasing to a light thrum.

The ship's door swung upward, giving Lyander a view of a small landing surrounded by a wall of dark rock twice his own height. He and Gabriel stepped off the craft, the door closing shut behind them. Then the sound of several pairs of footsteps marching through the dust, the steady clunk of armour, and from around the back of the ship marched four soldiers. Every one of them wore steel plate and helm over gambesons and trousers – the red-maroon of house Fontain. All were breathing heavily, tired looks on their faces, their eyes filled with the sort of intense wildness that lingers after surviving a fight.

The one in front, his bald head slick with perspiration trickling into the stubble dotting his cheeks and down his large nose, looked Lyander and Gabriel up and down with dark eyes. His diamond-shaped besague protected the front of his arm pit. The quartered maroon and yellow of his house held three smaller diamonds identifying him as a sergeant.

"You're with the other one, then?" he said breathlessly, the lilting, rolling *R*s of the Taranis accent barely perceptible beneath the surly tone.

"We are," Lyander said, assuming the *other one* was Eluthienn.

"When he said there'd be reinforcements, I was expected a few more of you," he said, then gestured at them both with a gloved hand, adding: "Not that you two don't look like you can't handle yourselves."

"There's more on the way." *He hoped.*

"Well, we'll take what we can get," the sergeant said. He held out a hand for Lyander to shake: "Tolsten Higglen," he said, "but you can call me Higgs – everyone does."

Lyander took the offered hand: "Lyander. And this is Gabriel."

The sergeant's eyes lingered on the vials and wax pouches. "A witch-hunter?" he asked.

"What gave it away?"

The sergeant smiled, noting the sarcasm. "Think we're going to need you. Our caster says he can detect another magic user. Strong one, as well, apparently."

"You still have a caster?" Lyander asked.

"Barely," Higgs said. "C'mon."

He led them away from the landing, round the rock wall and down toward where the passage opened out onto a much wider tunnel.

"Your pal never gave us his name."

"He's a little shy," Gabriel said.

"Didn't look bloody shy to me. Especially not when he was delimbing that Mirrovinjin." Higgs leaned toward them slightly, as if about to admit something: "If you ask me, he was enjoying himself."

So much for staying out of the fight.

They rounded a large jutting of rock and the passage opened out onto a cavern pass. Nestled between its sheer rock walls, Lyander judged the pass wide enough for twenty soldiers abreast – a tactic the Fontain regiment had evidently deployed. Fifty or sixty soldiers in plate and gambesons stood or knelt in a rough line along the width of the pass. Most with long swords, some with spears or crossbows, they all carried rectangular, curved tower shields with a metal boss at their centre, reinforced with steel bands around the edge. Eluthienn stood among them, talking and laughing, and very much alive. *Looks like I still have all my problems, then.*

A faint blue light fell upon the regiment from the ceiling, where a vein of untapped gyre ice wove through the dark brown rock like a dragon's tail. It ended some one hundred feet in the distance where a smaller passage rounded to the left, and the rest of the pass fell away into the sea of black that was Formaria's void.

In a naturally formed alcove to their right, a Fontain standard stood still in the earth. Around it lay several soldiers on stretchers, most covered entirely with brown blankets, forming a makeshift triage. Off to the side was a small pile of gyre ice. Sitting in front of it, boots planted either side of the translucent blue rocks, was a man in a maroon gambeson, its skirt reaching his shins. Head bowed so far his chin was almost on his chest, his wrists rested on his knees, the sleeves of his gambeson rolled up, revealing blackened, withered hands, the veins glowing gyranic blue. With each breath, the ice at his feet lost a little more of its colour, slowly becoming more like diamonds than magical shards.

"Been like that since the fight," Higgs said.

"What happened?" Gabriel asked.

"Tunnel fiend. Boy saw it climbing up outta the cavern." Higgs nodded in the direction of the void. "Decided to blow it off the edge while he had the chance."

"Brave of him," Gabriel said, sounding impressed.

"Stupid of him, you mean," Higgs said. "Got plenty of crossbows and a nice range to pick it off at. Lad didn't need to do what he did, and now we don't have a caster."

Higgs was right; a caster's primary responsibility was to protect their troops from other magic users, not risk themselves on non-magical opponents. Lyander might not have phrased it as unkindly as Higgs, though; most casters were simply looking out for their fellow soldiers. He suspected the "lad" tried to do just that and bit off more than he could chew.

"I need to talk to him," Lyander said.

Higgs scoffed. "You're welcome to try. Don't know how much you'll get from him, though."

The caster lifted his head as Lyander and Gabriel approached. His combed over, jet-black hair was slick with sweat and plastered to his forehead, his skin a bloodless white with grey shadows creeping down from his angular cheek bones. Vacant eyes stared at the space just over Lyander's shoulder, and he realised the caster's irises were also drained of colour, leaving him at least partially blind. If Lyander was to guess, he was no older than eighteen, which meant in all probability, this was his first and last fight.

"How you feeling?"

"I feel as good as I look," the caster said. "Or as good as I imagine I look – hard to tell now."

Humour, Lyander thought. *At least he still has that.*

"Six bodies lying here – yours isn't one of them. That's what matters."

"Think my fighting days are done, though."

"Plenty of royal households or merchant families would jump at the chance of employing a former war caster."

"Wasn't quite what I imagined for myself," he said. "Not yet, anyway."

"Life never is what we imagine for ourselves."

"I'm sure you're right," the caster said sadly.

"Sergeant told me you detected another magic user?"

The caster nodded. "A Mirrovinjin witch."

"You're sure?"

"I could smell vomit and taste rotting flesh at the back of my throat – that's the exact description they gave us in training." It was also exactly how other casters described sensing a Mirrovinjin witch.

"But it wasn't with the first attack?"

The caster shook his head.

Lyander turned to Higgs. "Whatever you fought off – they were just testing you. There's more to come."

The sergeant's face scrunched in confusion. "The lad received a report about five hours ago," he said. "Mirrovinjin are committed outside the east hangar bay. That's where they're trying to push through."

"That's a distraction," Lyander said. "And now they know for certain this passage is poorly defended."

The sergeant ran a hand over his head, then across his sweaty chin. "We need to fall back to the spire," he said.

"Fall back and you give the Mirrovinjin a staging ground for a larger assault. We defend the passage here until reinforcements arrive."

"Meaning no offense," Higgs said, "but you're not in charge here."

"If we give the Mirrovinjin the advantage, they'll lay siege to the spire uncontested, and force us to pull units from the east hangar bay." Lyander stabbed a finger in the general direction of the spire. "And there's no one to relieve us – all ships have been pulled south."

The muscles around the sergeant's jaw tensed and released as he, almost literally, chewed over Lyander's argument. He ran his hand over his chin again, and opened his mouth to reply with what Lyander thought was going to be agreement when a shout went up from the line.

"Enemy sighted!"

At the end of the pass, pulling themselves over the crest and out of the darkness, came the Mirrovinjin. Wiry, elongated torsos, allowing room for their four arms – a spear between two, a black iron knife in one of the others. Sinewy legs ended in bare feet, hard and blackened by tunnel floors. Their heads were more like naked skulls – the skin sallow, cheeks hollowing, eyes sunken and rimmed in dying black skin. Down their forehead was the terrible ravine that ended in the rotting cavity in the centre of their faces.

Few wore anything more than filthy scraps of leather, bound around their waists and across their chests. Those with armour wore a mismatch of shoulder plates and grieves and vambraces – whatever they could steal and hammer into their own twisted form with overlapping curves and spines and spikes.

"Form up!" screamed Higgs. "Form up!"

The soldiers scrambled, picking up shields,

drawing swords, winding crossbows, and forming a single line three soldiers deep. Lyander and Gabriel ran behind Higgs, following him as he walked down the line.

Wild screeches and trilling war cries came from the end of the pass, and in between the shields and the backs of helms, Lyander could see the Mirrovinjin war band hurtling toward them.

"Crossbows!" Higgs cried, and soldiers shifted to the front. The sergeant stopped, pushed forward to the second row, peered between two sets of shoulders, and waited for the enemy to enter killing range. Lyander followed Higgs, standing next to him. Gabriel positioned himself farther along the line, just behind the third row.

"You are soldiers of Fontain, warriors of the Fromryr!" Higgs bellowed. "A thousand years Formaria has thrown the enemy back into the abyss! You will throw them back now!

As one, the line erupted with the cry: "Formaria! Formaria, Formaria!"

Then, as the Mirrovinjin closed to roughly one hundred feet, Higgs screamed: "Free fire!" The line filled with the twang and click of repeater crossbows. Beyond, harsh cries, stumbling, and bodies crashing to the ground. *Twang, click, twang, click*, and the cries grew closer, the crashing bodies becoming louder.

"Shield wall!" Higgs cried. Those with crossbows pulled back; those with shields and swords closed the gaps, locking together and forming a solid wall; while those in the second and third row created a roof over their heads.

And Lyander could see the Mirrovinjin's bloodshot eyes, their blackened teeth, could hear their rabid snarls, their desperate, frantic panting. Several of their members slowed, turned to their sides, twisted round, and drew back the arm holding the spear. Knowing what was coming, Lyander searched for

Eluthienn, saw him farther along the line to his left, and squarely beneath a shield, then turned back in time to see the arc of spears flying high and come plummeting down. Lyander, taller than most, bent his knees, crouching next to the closest soldier, waiting for the missiles.

There was the sound of successive thuds as they landed, bouncing off shields or deflected by their curves, and then close by, a wet crunch and Lyander's face was splattered with something warm and dripping.

Higgs was lying on his back, the javelin pinning him to the ground through his right eye, his face broken open, the skull cracked apart and leaking red gore.

Of all the things to go wrong at the start of a fight, Lyander thought as other screams went up from along the line, bodies falling backward, black shafts protruding from chests and necks. Several soldiers turned around to see their sergeant lying dead behind them, and before the worst could happen, Lyander cried: "Hold the line!" He drew his sword, again shouting: "Hold the line!"

The Mirrovinjin came crashing toward them, throwing themselves at the shields with heavy thumps and clashes as bodies hit wood, followed by the grunts and growls of soldiers digging in their heels. Then the clang of knife and spear thrusts, followed by the slash and stab of swords darting out from the front line.

Here we go, he thought, and despite the odds stacked against them and the prevailing anxiety about Eluthienn's safety, a familiar surge of nervous excitement coursed through his veins, the kind he always felt moments before the chaos of battle came; he edged backward past the second and third row, out behind the shield wall, waiting.

One Mirrovinjin – which came vaulting out from behind their lines, landing lightly on top of the shield in front of him – snarled at Lyander, drooling from its yellow fangs. Then it sprung from the shield – the spear held in two hands – brought it back over its head, and Lyander threw himself to the side.

His sword arced round, catching the warrior in the abdomen, cutting through stomach muscle as it fell to the ground. It rolled over, clutching its side with three hands, trying to stop its innards from spilling out, its fourth hand trying to drag itself away from Lyander. He was about to finish the creature off when a soft thud came from behind him.

Spinning round, the Mirrovinjin picked itself up from the floor, whirling its spear over its head. A Fontain soldier turned to deliver a backhanded cut across the warrior's neck, but the Mirrovinjin, without even looking, reverse thrust into the soldier's exposed throat. Before the dying man's knees hit the floor, Lyander closed the gap, bringing his sword up and down. The Mirrovinjin deflected with a long black knife while stepping quickly to its right and throwing a fist out from its third arm, catching Lyander under his eye. The blow rocked his head and a stinging pain blossomed around his cheek, but he was only vaguely aware.

Refusing ground, he pushed forward, the pair of them moving parallel with the shield wall's rear. It deflected his second cut, but his third sliced across the top of the Mirrovinjin's left thigh. It stumbled backward, thrusting wildly in an attempt to keep him at bay, but Lyander parried to his right and then drove his sword through its sternum, felt the tip hit the back of the ribs and pulled the blade back. Blackish blue blood spilled from the wound like a spilt inkwell, and the Mirrovinjin hissed weakly, falling to one knee, two hands over the wound, the other two clutching the spear, trying to prop itself up. Lyander stepped forward, brought his blade up high, then down, splitting its head in two down the crack in its skull.

Out of the corner of Lyander's eye, Gabriel and Eluthienn, having also pulled back from the shield wall, stepped away from two Mirrovinjin bodies, both heaped side by side, neither with all its limbs attached. Satisfied the prince wasn't in immediate danger, Lyander assessed the right flank. Behind the shield wall, he watched an arbalist fire her repeater at short range, the bolts studding the Mirrovinjin's chest and stomach, the creature dropping its weapons and stumbling backward. Another caught a Mirrovinjin midair as it flew over the shield wall, the bolts catching it along its thigh and up into its midsection. It crumpled in a heap as it landed, the arbalist drawing a long knife and shoving it into its neck.

On the left flank, the story was the same – mostly dead or dying four-limbed warriors were among the handful of fallen Fontain soldiers. *A weak attempt*, he thought, looking at the enemy's dead. He scanned the shield wall, searching for breaches, sections close to breaking, assuming the Mirrovinjin intended to push through rather than sabotage from behind. *No swells or pockets of desperate fighting – the line holds. This is supposed to be their main thrust,* he thought, *but the Mirrovinjin are just wasting warriors, throwing too few of them to die on a shield wall.*

It was a tactical error – a complete blunder, in fact. But the Mirrovinjin rarely made complete blunders because after a thousand years fighting the Fromryr, their understanding of their enemy was absolute, their tactics against them honed to a razor's edge. They knew exactly how many of their number it would take to defeat any number of Fromryian soldiers, in any number of terrains or under any set of tactical conditions.

Unease flickered to life in his chest, replacing the confusion, and the shadow of a memory danced at the back of his consciousness – the knowledge, built upon years of experience, that the Mirrovinjin fought with cunning.

Then, turning the flicker into a roiling glow of dread, Eluthienn's shout went up from his left: "Lyander!" The prince pointed at something beyond the shield wall. He tried to see through the shifting line of shields and beyond the press of Mirrovinjin bodies to the other side, but saw nothing save the void's black emptiness.

Which, when he looked closer, was moving.

Shapes shifting up and down; the rise and fall of dark silhouettes, and the stamping of marching feet, interspersed with chanting, "Hou, hou, hou."

Lyander, fighting the panic welling within him, pushed his way to the shield wall's second row. Through the press he saw black iron half helms, torsos covered with black iron chest plates, the spaulders protecting their shoulders, and underneath their skin was a leathery pitch black and in parts a wasted dark purple – the colour of ancient beings, made and twisted from dark magic. In their hands were single shards of black iron like butcher's cleavers, or two-handed axes, their edges cut into jagged teeth. Lyander grabbed the nearest soldier, turning him around to face him.

"Get the war caster," he said.

"Sir," the man panted, shaking his head, brown eyes wide beneath his helm, "the war caster can't fight. He's done."

"Just get him!" Lyander pushed the man out of the wall, and he stumbled back, running for the alcove.

A harsh horn, like the last call of a dying animal, sounded from the left flank. The Mirrovinjin brought what looked like a curved femur bone to its lips and blew once more. "Aadoooh!" it called, and the Mirrovinjin fought all the harder, slashing and stabbing at the shield wall, but not necessarily doing more damage. They were acting, Lyander now knew, as a distraction, preventing the Fromryr from bringing their crossbows to bear on the real assault. The horn blew once more, the sound deeper, a single note: "Dhoooh!" it rang, and the Mirrovinjin receded from the wall, pulling back like the tide from cliffs, leaving a line of dead.

"Rakkan!" Lyander shouted. "Form up! Form up!"

The line shifted as soldiers manoeuvred back into position, the sound of shields knocking together, panting breaths, the moans of the wounded, and growing louder, the "Hou, hou, hou."

The last of the Mirrovinjin raced back, and in their place, the Rakkan came. Another horn blew and the uniform rows pulled into two tight wedges – five warriors across and six deep. Aiming for either side of the Fontain centre, the Rakkan's chanting quickened, their march turning into a run.

"Lock shields!" Lyander cried, and corporals down either side of the line repeated his order. Then a hundred *clacks* sounded around him as those in the front line drew together. "Quartet acies!" he shouted and the wall heaved, soldiers pulled in from the flanks, and the line formed into four solid rows. *It won't be enough*, he thought, trying to think through the panic, trying to ignore years of training and experience telling him their chances were next to none, telling him in less than a minute, the entire line would shatter and break.

"Sir," someone said at his shoulder, and Lyander saw two men supporting the war caster between their arms.

Breathing heavily, his sightless eyes only half open, the caster lifted his head from his chin. "What would you have of me?" he said weakly, and Lyander, through the adrenaline and dread, felt a stab of guilt. Ignoring that, too, he said: "You need to break a charge."

Without waiting for a reply, he took the war caster from one of the soldiers supporting him, wrapped his arm beneath the man's shoulder, and pulled him to the front, shouting: "Out the way!"

"I can't see," the war caster said quietly.

"I'll aim you," Lyander said, not sure how exactly he would achieve that. Moving aside two soldiers, he positioned the war caster next to him.

No longer chanting, the Rakkan's only sound were their pounding footfalls and their savage war cries – crazed half snarls and half roars so deep and guttural, they sounded like crashing rocks.

"Two wedges," Lyander said into the war caster's ear. "One directly ahead, the other ten feet to its right!"

The war caster shook his head. "I can't," he said, tears forming in his eyes, his hands shaking. "Anymore, and I'll –"

"If you don't, everyone here is lost!" Lyander cut across him, the Rakkan almost upon them, those in the front rows lifting their shields, preparing to crash into the Fontain line. "You are a war caster of the Fromryr – do your duty!"

The man sniffed, drew a deep breath, then held his arms out in front of him, forming a rough semicircle with his hands. "Show me where."

Lyander turned the war caster by his shoulders, aiming his blackened hands in the direction of the wedge in front. The man began to mouth silent words, and something sparked in the space between his palms, like striking flint. Then another spark, and another, until a writhing mass of yellow light coiled and rotated, growing larger and larger. And Lyander heard the Rakkan's heavy panting, saw the wet glint on their dark armour. Crossbows twanged and clicked along the line, their bolts studding armour, pinging off shields, only occasionally finding dark flesh, and even then their targets seemed to barely notice. An angry cry or a grunt, but they still came.

Then three smoking tendrils erupted from the war caster's hands, spiralling through the air with a swoosh. One swerved to the right, coiled upward, and blew straight into the cavern wall, blasting chunks of rock and dust. Another shot high, flying over the incoming wedge, and fading into the black nothingness beyond.

The third found its mark, shooting straight forward, then dipping just at the right moment, the missile landing squarely in the middle of the wedge, right at the feet of the first line. A deafening blast and bodies, shields, and swords held in hands detached from arms, launched into the air. Blood, gore, and dust rained down upon the remaining Rakkan, and a cheer erupted from the Fontain line. Next to him, the war caster screamed, holding charred and smoking hands in front of his face, the fingers blackened twigs, the skin peeling away from the flesh.

Lyander grabbed him by his shoulders, preventing him from falling to the ground. He turned the man to him in the hope of calming him for another attempt, and looked straight into empty sockets, oozing viscous brown liquid – and Lyander was back in Damoclen. Dracht's hands were in his lap, his brains leaking into his open palms, but in the image, Dracht's blind face looked up at him. *Did my death bring you what you wanted?* he asked softly. And Lyander was back in the tunnel. Staring into the same fleshy sockets, gripping the war caster by his arms. He was frozen in horror, shock paralysing his body as his vision shuddered, and the man was no longer the war caster, but Dracht.

Pale white, bald-headed, and robed in black with

a brown amice, Lyander held his dead friend in his hands, around him, halos of light, bright white stars pooling at the corners of his vision. "Was I worth the sacrifice?" Dracht asked. "Did you get what you wanted?" And the light spilled from his mouth as he spoke, joining with the stars flooding his sight.

Lyander, stunned, a nausea building at the back of his throat, forced himself to blink, to shake his head – and the image away with it. His vision shuddered again, the lights receded, and it was no longer Dracht.

"Get him out of here!" Lyander shouted, pushing the war caster into the arms of another soldier.

Lyander, an almost out-of-body daze settling over his consciousness, hearing the battle around him as if he were underwater, simply stood there. He watched the war caster being carried to the back of the line, and then a woman came into his field of view.

"Sir!" she shouted, and everything came rushing back to him at once – the Rakkan's snarling, their stomping feet, the Fromryian war cries – and the women grabbed him by the shoulder and yanked him toward her.

He spun around in time to see a Rakkan warrior, sword raised, coming straight for him, only for the creature to disappear behind two shields as the wall knitted back together. Splintered thuds as iron crashed against hardened wood, soldiers grunted as they fought to maintain their position, and Lyander was pushed back as the enemy drove against the shield wall. He fell against the shields behind him, his sword arm pinned to his chest by the backs of those in the front row, and the force of the collision. Those behind held their ground, the line swelled, then pushed forward, then back again, knocking hard against a shield, which brought him firmly back into the present. His vision clearing, anger simmered somewhere deep in his stomach as he fought against the press.

"Hold the line!" he cried, his own command fortifying his reeling consciousness, bringing him back to the fight. He forced apart the two soldiers in front of him, drove his sword forward into the brief gap made between their shields. The blade sunk below the plackart's rim and into the Rakkan's stomach. A pig-like squeal, then Lyander saw a fang-filled mouth twist in fear, yellow irises spread wide around the black pupil, and the gap closed.

"Hold the line!" Lyander cried again, and dodged an axe swung over the top of the shield on his right. He was about to answer in kind when multiple pairs of black hands gripped the edges of the shield and pulled, wrenching the attached soldier from the line. A sword came swinging out of nowhere, barely missing Lyander's stomach, lodging itself in the shield on his left. The Rakkan yanked the blade, pulling the shield to the side, and in the opening, an axe came crashing down on the soldier's neck, the head burying deep in the muscle. The soldier screamed, the axe head retreated and he fell, gargling frothy blood.

Lyander was now the front line.

Without a second thought, without even an inkling of doubt about what he was doing, he stepped into the breach, facing off against three, four, five snarling and hissing Rakkan. The pain in his hand was lacerating whips, but dulled by the adrenaline, it simply added fire to his fury, driving strength into his arms, adding speed to his swing. It crashed against an iron blade, throwing it wide, giving Lyander the opportunity to swing against its owner's shield, opening the Rakkan up for a thrust into the throat.

To his right, the axe came hurtling down but he pulled his sword from the other's neck and parried, shaking off the jagged axe head, and stepped forward. With an upward diagonal strike, he lopped off one of the

Rakkan's hands. Following through, he twisted, arcing the blade horizontally and slashing open the Rakkan's cheek, throwing its head backward.

More Rakkan took their place, and from out of the corner of his eye, he saw iron plunging toward his face. He spun, trying to bring his sword up in a high guard to take the blow, but knowing he was too late, he gritted his teeth against the coming impact.

Instead, there was a dull thud as the axe bit into shield. Lyander turned to face another opponent but a second shield appeared on his right, and he felt a hand on his shoulder. He let it draw him back, and the two soldiers withdrew alongside him, reforming the line.

"They've broken through!" a women shouted in his ear. She pointed to a section of the line where black shapes were streaming past Fontain soldiers, fighting desperately to hold their ground. Lyander growled something even he didn't understand, and pushed his way along the rows. Nearing the breach, the sound was like a storm: Fontain soldiers' dying screams; steel and iron clashing; thud upon thud of swords against shields; and the Rakkan's primal snarling.

A shield was ripped from its owner's arm, the soldier booted in the stomach, the force throwing him on his back. Stepping over him, the Rakkan brought its sword up high, then swung down, aiming for a killing blow upon his skull, but Lyander was there, bringing his own sword up to meet the Rakkan's, sending a tremor up his arm. It opened its mouth, bared rows of curved and broken teeth, and screamed with hatred. Lyander threw the sword off, and swung at the Rakkan. It parried, stepping back. Lyander threw another swing, forcing it back another step, and one of its fellows crashed into it, sending it flying to its right and deeper into the Fontain line.

Out of his reach, Lyander used the opportunity

to forward thrust into the other's hip, driving the sword into the pelvis. The Rakkan screamed and crumpled, and Lyander turned, using the momentum to swing at an opponent hacking savagely at a shield, chipping away at the wood. His blade decapitated the Rakkan and blood spurted from the wound.

"Close the breach!" he shouted, grabbing a soldier nearest to him, and pushing him into the gap. "Close the breach!" he shouted again, and was about to pull more soldiers forward but something smashed into his shoulder, throwing him off his feet. He stumbled, trying to keep his balance, and collided with another body. A Fontain arbalist grabbed the front of his surcoat with one hand, fingers clutching at the chain shirt underneath to stop him from tumbling to the ground. He was about to thank her when an axe came swinging from the right side of his vision; he put a hand on her left shoulder, intending to wrench her out of the way but the swing was too quick. Its teeth sunk into her back, biting through the plate, and throwing her against Lyander. Blood spurted from her mouth over the front of his chest. The Rakkan yanked the axe backward and, with its teeth caught in the back plate, pulled the woman with it, flinging her round like a rag doll.

Its weapon stuck in the plate, Lyander dashed forward, cut down and sliced into one of the Rakkan's arms above the elbow, his sword jarring against bone. The Rakkan grunted, let go of the axe, and stumbled back, the arbalist dropping face-first to the floor. Lyander filled the gap with an upward thrust, driving his blade into the Rakkan's armpit. It fell backward, blood leaking from the wound.

Lyander bent down, removed the axe from the arbalist's back and rolled her over. He thought she might still be alive, but the moment he looked into her eyes, something that felt distinctly like a shield rocked his shoulder, sending him flying once more into the press. He landed against a Rakkan's back, sending it to the ground, the collision also sending him into a spin.

A black iron blade came chopping at his shoulder and he deflected it to his side before something hard and flat slammed into his back, propelling him forward. With no other option, he used the momentum to forward thrust, his sword's point ramming straight into the black breast plate of the attacker to his front. Unable to pierce the armour, it simply sent the Rakkan tumbling backward and onto a Fontain soldier's short sword.

Lyander turned to the attacker behind him, raising his sword for a downward thrust and came face-to-face with Gabriel, the would-be assailant dead at his feet.

"Where's Eluthienn?" Lyander shouted above the roaring battle.

Gabriel grabbed Lyander's shoulder, spun him around, and pointed to the centre of the breach – several bodies before where the Fontain line was broken and the enemy poured in. Eluthienn cut bloody swathes through the Rakkan assault, like a dancer threading his way through a dance floor, expertly manoeuvring around the other guests. Except Eluthienn was armed with a long sword, and every time he manoeuvred around a Rakkan, he lopped off a limb, cut a lethal blow across the neck or thigh, or simply parried and moved on.

Lyander resisted the urge to rub his temples. *Of course he of all people would wind up babysitting a maniac prince with a penchant for bloody murder and a complete disregard for his own life. What in the black abyss did he think he was going to achieve? A one-man counter attack?*

As if reading his thoughts, Gabriel shouted: "He's going for the witch!" He pointed to the end of the pass, to where the edge met the void. Standing just before the lip – a black knife in one hand, its other three making various signs and gestures in the air – was a Mirrovinjin in long brown robes. Kneeling at her feet, bound around the ankles, hands tied behind its back, was a dwarf, his naked torso facing the witch.

Lyander grabbed Gabriel's upper arm. "I'll get Eluthienn; you get the witch!" he shouted, and without waiting for an answer, charged into the Rakkan mass.

Barging into a warrior from behind with his shoulder, Lyander ran forward, dodged an incoming blade, before swinging wildly at a black shield, forcing the attacker back as he moved on. Jumping over a dead soldier and his shield, he was forced to a stop as an axe swing came at his head. He sidestepped around the axe-wielding Rakkan while Gabriel came around it and sliced into its lower back. Something crashed into him and, not bothering to see what it was, he let the force throw him forward while swinging at a warrior who parried with its blade. Lyander skirted to its side, throwing a backhanded swing on his way around, clipping the Rakkan on its helm with a clunk.

And Eluthienn was beyond the breach now, his black cloak trailing behind him, blade flashing with every curve and stroke, fighting through to the disordered rear of the Rakkan lines.

Then from his right, Gabriel growled as if straining to hold something off. His blade through a Rakkan's throat, his other hand was holding another attacker's wrist, stopping it from bringing its sword down on his head. Lyander dashed to his aid, slicing into the Rakkan's arm and cutting it near in two. It screamed and dropped the sword, wounded arm hanging limp at its side. Gabriel, in a single movement, withdrew his blade from the other's throat, sending a backhanded cut that sliced across the Rakkan's jaw.

"Thanks for –" he said, but was cut short as his

gaze landed on something over Lyander's shoulder, eyes going wide.

Lyander spun, bringing his sword up in a short guard just in time to catch the Rakkan's blade coming for his throat. The weapons clanged, and Lyander drew his back for a full swing, but the Rakkan grabbed the front of his surcoat and threw its helmed head into his face. The headbutt caught him over his left temple, his head rocking back, hot blood gushing. It blinded him in one eye, and his vision shuddered, white light dancing at the edges, and he was fighting his way to Lucretia's command chamber.

"Lyander!" Ilian Craid called, but Lyander wasn't listening; he was shoving and pushing himself past his fellow knights, then he was running for the spire's northern gate, a triangular portal large enough for a spire-class frigate to fly through, guarded by a squadron of Constructii. Seeing him, they stepped aside, letting him approach the smaller portal at the foot of the larger triangle. Lyander placed his hand into the node and requested entry.

It pulled apart as Ilian caught up with him, out of breath; a hand firmly on his shoulder. "Lyander, there's nothing you can do!"

He turned to shove off the hand and saw Gabriel's blue eyes, inches from his own face and deep with concern. "Lyander!" the witch-hunter shouted, shoving him roughly by the shoulder, and the battle raged around him once more; the constant crash and clang of steel and iron, the fighter's snarls and grunts, the Fontain soldier's indiscernible war cries all merging into a relentless barrage of destruction.

"Go!" Lyander said, shoving Gabriel away. He wiped the blood from his eye, and a painful throb erupted from somewhere above his temple. It beat in time to the throbs coursing from the back of his hand:

throb and *stab, throb* and *stab*, pummelling him. And with each blow from his head, it rocked his vision, each stab from his hand sending white-yellow stars shooting around its edges.

He ground his teeth, clenched his jaw, and the next Rakkan that stepped into his path he roared at as he brought his sword crashing down on its helm. *Crack*, and his blade bit into iron, cutting through the nose guard and deep into flesh, spraying blood and throwing the Rakkan to the ground. Adrenaline and pain fuelling him like a furnace, he couldn't even feel the jarring sensation from hitting armour and bone.

Gabriel ducked an axe from his left, and Lyander barged into the attacker, sending the Rakkan flying, then paced after the witch-hunter. The press thinned. They were leaving the mass fighting through the breach, and were well into the enemy's rear. He could see Eluthienn clearly now, the prince parrying swings from a Rakkan's blade and a Mirrovinjin's spear, forcing him onto his back foot.

He threw off another swing, deflecting the Rakkan's blade to his right, and the Mirrovinjin used the opportunity to plunge the spear into Eluthienn's shoulder. The prince cried out, falling back, and chopping down on the shaft, breaking it in two. With one of its other hands, the Mirrovinjin drew a blade from a hip sheath, and Lyander felt the desperation surging in his veins; the feeling of dread and helplessness that he might be too far away to come to the prince's aid; the frustration and anger at the enemies still in his path.

He arced his sword in a two-handed cross swing at a Rakkan's shield, the impact driving the warrior off its feet and sending a vibrating stab up through his hand with such flaring pain, his entire arm went numb. A white flash blasted his vision, and the pain vanished, replaced with overwhelming anxiety. His breath shortened, his chest became tight. He wouldn't make it to the command chamber in time but he needed to; there was nothing more important than stopping Ramovand Rosantz from condemning Lyander's units to their deaths.

He raced through the spire, blood pounding in his ears, while he ran along shimmering grey corridors, their blue channels casting a sapphire glow. *Nearly there*, he thought. *Just one more corridor and a lift, and he would save everyone.*

He rounded a bend, a long corridor stretching out before him, a single vein running along the ceiling to the lift at the end. Its doors slid apart, shunting as they detracted into the walls, and out stepped Ramovand Rosantz, his personal retinue surrounding him on both sides.

The prince's mane of unkempt black hair falling across his brow turned to shining jet under the gyre channel's light. His skin, which was the sort of pinkish-white Lyander associated with newborn children, was made that much starker against his black cloak and black-dyed leathers. Even from the end of the corridor, he saw the jaw line: haughty, contemptuous, and surrounding a mouth used to talking down to others, used to getting its own way.

Ramovand's deep-set eyes fell on Lyander, and for a moment, the lines around them creased into surprise, then worry, before his mouth turned hard. The pause he took was almost imperceptible, but he couldn't hide the straightening of his back, the squaring of his shoulders as he saw Lyander's rank and insignia.

"Why aren't you with your unit? You were ordered to fall back," Ramovand said, his voice a sonorous baritone, strong and commanding but not quite hiding the doubt, not quite hiding his youth, Lyander realised.

He's still a child – a child in command of armies. It only made Lyander's anger toward him fiercer. "The Mirrovinjin have a secondary war party," he said, walking down the corridor. "And there are still units in the tunnels that won't make it out in time – you need to stop the purge."

"It's already done," Ramovand said, anger lacing his tone. "And you should have thought about your units before you lost this spire, First Champion."

"The spire isn't lost!" Lyander said, his voice rising. "If you purge the installation, the second war party will walk in here and take it uncontested!"

"There is no second war party!" The prince spat the words, and they were drawing close now.

"This is madness!" Lyander shouted back. "Mirrovinjin fight in successive groups. They will take this spire!"

The prince's mouth twitched, eyes flashing with hesitation, and Lyander thought he was going to concede but instead his fist clenched around the hilt of his undrawn sword, and he said: "First Champion, you are relieved of your command and hereby under arrest for defying orders from a royal officer during an ongoing siege."

Lyander drew his sword.

At the sight of naked steel, Ramovand looked that much more the boy, looked that much more a child playing at war.

"Lyander, no!" Ilian said, grabbing his arm but Lyander shrugged him off. The split-second decision was made without thinking; it was the instinctual need to prevent the slaughter of his friends, to protect those he was responsible for – the consequences just a vague grey notion in the back of his mind. Faced with the present crisis, they held no meaning.

Ramovand's retinue – armoured in half plate,

dyed crimson and with the Rosantz Falcon etched on their breasts – drew their own steel, and stepped in front of the prince.

Lyander brought his sword up high, then brought it crashing down against the bodyguard's parry. The clang echoed down the corridor and in his ears, growing louder and louder, becoming many clangs, and crashes and thuds, and cries and screams, and Lyander's downward cut was so powerful the Rakkan's arm buckled, and Lyander's blade sunk into the gap between its pauldron and its neck. It crumpled and Lyander spun, trying to see where he was, to assess the battle.

Blinking through the blood streaked haze, through the sweat pouring from his brow, and against the tremors thrashing at the corners of his eye sight, he saw the breach closed, the Fontain line now only two ragged rows, fighting against greater numbers.

He heard Eluthienn and Gabriel before he saw them, the thwack of steel and grunts behind him. He turned to see a Rakkan warrior. Taller, stronger, more ferocious than any others, its bare chest and arms ripples of sinewy muscle that looked more like steel pleating than living flesh. In place of a helm, and screwed into its lower jaw, it wore an iron hinge shaped into a row of jagged teeth. Wiry lengths of black hair, like a horse's main, flowed messily from the top of its head, the eyes beneath, pools of red, as if the veins were bleeding into the irises. In either hand, it held thin lengths of iron, the blades whirling. One parried the prince's forward thrust, the other knocking aside the witch-hunter's upward arc, both deflecting with inhuman speed – an impossible speed.

Then Lyander saw the black smoke curling out from behind its iron jaw, the tendrils worming their way through the red eyes, its dark purple veins bulging along its arms and up its neck. With the Rakkan's body quickly imbuing with Aeturnic energy, Lyander knew what he would see before his eyes fell on it. The Mirrovinjin witch stood above the dwarf, now slumped on his side, hands and feet still bound behind his back. In one hand, the witch held the dwarf's heart, blood dripping to the floor; between the others, it held the dwarf's intestines, drawing them out of the dwarf's stomach and spinning them between its arms like a spider might spin a web. The witch's eyes didn't leave the Rakkan.

Set on what needed to be done, the focus of a single opponent anchoring his wavering vision, Lyander strode toward the iron jaw, coming up between Eluthienn and Gabriel. The Rakkan parried their swings in quick succession, forcing them back with just the deflection, and in the space now made for him, Lyander brought his sword high and swung it down. It was met with one blade and then the other slapped it aside.

"Get the witch!" Lyander shouted over his shoulder, while keeping his eyes fixed on the iron jaw. He saw Gabriel dart around the side, heading for the Mirrovinjin.

Sword pointed defensively at the Rakkan, Lyander stepped back and to the right so that Eluthienn and he could strike it from opposing angles. "We take it as one!" he shouted at the prince, but Eluthienn, either not hearing, or not caring, charged in, blade swinging.

The Rakkan knocked Eluthienn's swing to the side, then swung with his second sword; the prince leaned back just in time for the blade to miss his face by an inch. A frustrated sigh escaping his lips, Lyander charged, throwing a forward thrust, and was, unbelievably, parried with a single swing. The Rakkan arced its other blade around, forcing Lyander to duck. Eluthienn thrust with his sword, aiming for its chest, but the Rakkan spun back to him, knocking the blade aside, its second sword chopping horizontally for his neck, forcing the prince to parry.

In the moment's pause as Eluthienn tensed against the blow, the Rakkan kicked out, catching the prince in the stomach and sent him sprawling. Then Lyander was on the beast, a two-handed arc swinging across his body, throwing his body round, letting him spin into the momentum, the cut aimed for its neck. The Rakkan turned to him, its neck exposed like a strip of meat hanging from hooks, defenceless against the blade.

And it dropped its chin.

Lyander's sword clashed against the iron jaw, sending ricochets up his blade and into his hands. The Rakkan's head snapped to the side, black eyes rolling, arms splayed out for balance. Disbelief at not cutting its throat merged into quiet elation at the momentary vulnerability. He threw a forward thrust; the Rakkan chopped downward against the attack, knocking Lyander's blade away, but was forced back as it did so.

He pressed, following with a feint, stepping as if to arc his blade, but instead thrust again and, finally, caught the Rakkan in the ribs. It pulled back another step, coughing blood from the wound to its lung, and now Eluthienn was behind it. Together, Lyander and the prince swung with overhand arcs. *Surely*, he thought, *we're about to end this damned fight.*

But the Rakkan spun on the spot, deflecting both blows at the same time, knocking their swords aside – and them back a step.

The advantage was lost; the early flourish of triumph died, and now the blood and sweat was pouring down Lyander's face in such a current, he was spraying it out with each laboured breath. Dead on his feet and half crazed with battle mania, a wave of recklessness he rarely felt in battle spurred him into chancing a shorthand arc. Stepping into the killing range of the Rakkan's swords, he cut downward, aiming for the elbow but instead catching the wrist and slicing so deep he felt steel hit bone.

The Rakkan roared, the sword dropping from its hand, which swung limply from a slither of muscle and skin still keeping it attached to its wrist. Its other arm wide, its sword held out against Eluthienn, Lyander drove his blade between the Rakkan's ribs and deep into its chest. At the feeling of the steel sliding though flesh, triumph quickly became heady relief at the knowledge they would live and the thing trying to take their lives would not.

But instead of dying, it twisted, bringing its other blade up to swing across its body, aiming for Lyander's neck. Trying to pull away from the Rakkan, but knowing he wouldn't be quick enough, he watched the blade arc round, only for it to stop midswing, and drop from the beast's hand. The iron jaw coughed wetly, hot blood spraying Lyander's face, and he looked down to see the point of another blade protruding from the beast's chest, Eluthienn standing behind it.

Black hell, Lyander thought, and even in his mind, the words sounded like they were shaking at the death only just avoided.

Then a hand wrapped itself around the back of Lyander's neck, pulling him down. He tried to resist, tried to fight against the Rakkan's strength, his every thought turned to survival as he tried to pull back from the sword he was about to be impaled on.

Out of nowhere, another blade came swinging down. The hand was cut from its wrist, releasing Lyander like an arrow from a bowstring, and he stumbled back, falling to his knees.

Handless, bleeding from its chest and stomach, the Rakkan did the same, falling face-first in front of him, the iron jaw giving a single *clang* as it hit hard rock. Breathing heavily, one eye drowning in blood, the other swelling shut, Lyander leant against his sword, using it as a crutch while he knelt on the floor. A feeling he barely recognised flooded up from his feet and through his body. It was a strange state of shock at the realisation he was still alive – something he knew from sight because he usually associated it with *other* soldiers. He almost laughed when – almost of its own accord – the thought sprang into his mind: *You're getting too old for this, Kalbrayeth.*

Looking to his left, he assessed the state of the battle. The Fontain line had broken; three pockets of resistance formed loose islands in the mass of black iron and white limbs, like a tide quickly enveloping a shore line. *Brazier, my friend, now would be a very good time to join us with all those reinforcements.*

At the thought, the adrenaline began to fade. Without it, his head and hand joined in a slow rhythmic throbbing: *thump, thump, thump*. Sending successive aches up his arm and down from his temple, the beating grew: *thump, thump, thump*. He could feel it in his chest, the reverberations rocking his body; *thump, thump, thump*.

It was only when he felt it in his thighs, he knew it wasn't the pain from his wounds.

"Lyander," Gabriel said slowly. "Do correct me if I'm wrong, but I believe that is the sound of a skavriin tunnel brawler."

"It's the sound of a skavriin tunnel brawler," Lyander said, and if he wasn't so overwhelmed with exhaustion, he might have felt his heart sink to the bottom of his chest.

Turning his head to the void and the source of the noise, he watched the witch's body, lying among its own dismembered arms and rolls of the dwarf's intestines, vibrate with each *thump, thump, thump*. Instinct was slow to catch up with rational thought; his body ached with bruises and soreness, but his mind told him he should be afraid. He should, right now, be trying to fight off a flood of panic, but all he managed to do, was say: "It's a big one."

As the words left his mouth, a clawed hand appeared from over the lip of the pass's edge. Another appeared next to it, then a hulking black form pulled itself onto the pass, its heavy, clawed feet crushing the witch's body with a crunching squelch. *Almost as if it was a sign of things to come*. But a part of him knew the gallows humour was a bad sign. *You were once the First Champion of the Knights Redcrosse*, he told himself. *Whatever the Ecclessius may have done to you, whatever they may have reduced you to, you are still one of the most dangerous things in this forsaken place – pick yourself up and act like it!*

Even as he stood, it was twice his own height, its body a carving of thick grooves and ridges, the indurate black scaling giving it the appearance of plated armour. The skavriin tunnel brawler threw back its stubby, almost triangular, shark-like head, revealing two rows of teeth not unlike the Rakkan's iron jaw, and roared.

You are still one of the most dangerous things in this place, he told himself again, as panic tried to blossom just south of his sternum.

"We take it together," he said, looking meaningfully at Eluthienn as he said it. "As one."

The prince smiled, then winced as he rubbed his wounded shoulder. "As one," he agreed, and the three of them spread out, moving toward the brawler.

At the sight of the challenge, it let rip another guttural roar – a sound filled with fury and violence, but with the undercurrent of something like delight. *A worthy challenge*, that roar said, but one which it would enjoy because it was likely to win.

The closer they came, the taller the brawler

seemed to become, its scaled hide looking all the more impenetrable, and Lyander found it hard to disagree with its opinion. Unless they brought it to its knees, got around it, managed to drive a sword through its throat, or down through the top of its skull, there would be no victory.

Knowing its death was a remote possibility, it stomped forward confidently – *thump, thump, thump* – and brought a claw back behind its head, ready to swing down on Gabriel. Lyander tensed at his thighs, preparing to dart round to the creature's left and cut into one of its legs, when a high-pitched whistle cut through the air, followed by an explosive *thud.*

The bolt protruded from the brawler's right side, a four-foot shaft embedded between its ribs. A pained roar escaped its mouth, and it brought its claw down on the bolt, snapping it like a twig. Two more slammed into its ribcage, driving the brawler back a step. But like the first, it broke the shafts off, then faced its new assailant.

The war walker strode from out of the side passage, each step a resounding *clunk*, followed by the clacking of overlapping bronzite plate. Nestling the repeater's stock in the shoulder joint, the pilot fired off four more bolts as it moved – two studding the brawler in the arm and thigh, the other two shooting over its shoulder. Less than five strides away, the pilot holstered the repeater on its hip and drew a long, leaf-shaped sword.

Stomp, stomp, stomp as it closed on the brawler, and in response the creature drew its claw back to rake across the walker's chest compartment. Quicker than Lyander thought possible for a hulking tower of bronzite, the pilot sent the blade across its body, slicing at the incoming claw and cutting it off at the wrist. There was an arcane shriek and the brawler swung with its other arm, but too slow. The shaft protruding from above its elbow made the swing sluggish and weak; the pilot slapped it aside with a backhanded cut, then followed through by booting the brawler in its chest. With what must be several tonnes of weight behind it, the bronzite kick landed with a *crack* and sent the brawler flying off the edge of the pass.

Attention fixed on the gargantuan fight, Lyander was only vaguely aware of the rumbling clamour growing to his left. Wiping drying blood from his eye, expecting to see the remainder of the enemy sprinting toward them, his hope dwindling even with the war walker supporting them, he faced the noise. But instead of Rakkan and Mirrovinjin warriors, humans, dwarves, and gnomes streamed from the side passage and into the pass. A disordered assortment of knights, Fontain soldiers, and gyre ship crews, they charged the enemy position like a tidal flood, their war cries a thundering storm, crashing into their lines like headland waves.

The sound rang in Lyander's ears like a tolling bell, the clash of weapons and the Fromryian's shouts rising into a visible gold-white glow, like angelic halos around the fighter's bodies. His vision shuddered, the ringing became pounding in his eardrums, bruising pain shot through his knees as they hit the floor, and the glow grew. Whiter and whiter, it engulfed his vision like a fiery sun hurtling toward him.

Then he knew no more.

Sixteen

Brazier

Lyander's chest rose and fell as if he were sleeping, half his good hand draped over the lip of the bronzite bed, the other resting on his stomach. The parts of his face not covered in swelling were a pallid grey colour, glazed in a coating of perspiration. The swollen parts, below his right cheek and above his right eye, gave his face a lopsided look, as if he'd been born with a disfigurement.

It wasn't helped by the stitching – Brazier's handiwork – which looked like a cracked mosaic, the yellow thread barely holding the flesh together. That, in itself, wasn't a problem; the problem was that neither wound warranted the exorcist's current state. According to the spire's vulnerum, other than mild facial wounds, there was nothing physically wrong with him.

Taking him to the spire's seperium, Gabriel and Eluthienn also discovered he didn't suffer from malignance. And so here he was, in the *Anchorite*'s vulnerum, and still no explanation for why he refused to wake up. Standing either side of him, the looks on the prince's and the witch-hunter's faces were mirrors of Brazier's thoughts: *Why isn't he waking up?* and *He really needs to wake up*.

The vulnerum door pulled apart, and Freyen came to stand around the other side of the bed.

"What's wrong with him?" she asked, wiping her wet curls on a large cloth. She wore a forest green sleeveless shirt and matching trousers tucked into brown boots. Seeing her slender arms, pink from the warm water in the *Anchorite*'s bathing chamber, it was hard to imagine her piloting a war walker and throwing a tunnel brawler off the edge of a pass. *Another puzzle*, Brazier thought. *Not quite as pressing as their current situation, though.*

"We don't know," he said.

"He collapsed after the battle," Gabriel said. "One minute he was cutting apart Rakkan, the next he was on the floor."

Freyen moved to Lyander's head. "Concussion?" she asked.

"We've used salts and poured vigilans down his throat," Brazier said. "If it was concussion, he would have woken up."

"And what if he doesn't?" she asked, meaning: *Do we continue without him?*

"We can't wait around," Brazier said. "Spire command received a hex broadcast during the battle. Reantha has been overrun, and the Navarch High Command is pulling ships from the front to try and retake the spire. No front line installations can expect reinforcements – they were specific about that last part."

"Does Teuron have enough troops to withstand another attack?" she asked.

"No," Brazier said. "There're barely three

regiments to throw together, and without a caster, they can't hold a spire."

Freyen looked at him from beneath her dark curls. "We need to destroy Lokul, then," she said.

"And quickly," he added before remembering why Lyander and Gabriel separated from them in the first place. "Did you find anything in Acheron?" he asked Gabriel.

"Nothing we didn't already know," he said, staring glumly at Lyander.

Eluthienn gave the witch-hunter a quizzical look, but said nothing, and Gabriel seemed too concerned about Lyander to notice.

"Nav deck, then," Brazier said. "Eluthienn – you need to tell us where we're going."

They filed out of the vulnerum, and up the stairwell to the nav deck.

"What happened?" Eluthienn asked, pulling himself onto the landing and looking down at Switch and the various tools and broken bits of bronzite, spread out around her and into the open nav deck. Brazier pointed behind him at the space in the ceiling now covered in fresh sheeting. Around the edges, it still showed marks of the drake's rampage.

"Mirrovinjin drake thought we were an egg it could crack open," Brazier said.

"That was its mistake," Switch said.

Brazier made room for Gabriel as he stepped onto the landing. "Must have been a big one," the witch-hunter said.

"Not big enough," Switch replied.

"You killed it?"

Switch's grin was both triumphant and predatory. "I believe the technical term is 'skull fucking,'" she said.

"If you say so," Gabriel said, giving her an

impressed look.

"How's the big man?" she asked.

"Still out cold," Brazier said. "How's the ship?"

"Not as pretty as she once was, but as we're the only ship in the hangar bay, we pretty much have access to every spare part Teuron has," she said, and waved a hammer toward the stern. "Gave her new thruster discs and fixed her legs. But I'll need a day to replace the repeater, maybe longer."

"We make do without," Brazier said. Down one repeater, the *Anchorite* was still a formidable ship. "We're flying out as soon as you tell us she's ready."

Switch returned the tools to her belt, and pushed herself to her feet. "She's ready," she said, "but don't we want to wait for Lyander to wake up?"

Brazier shook his head. "We're out of time," he said.

"And we can do this without him," Eluthienn added.

"In theory," Gabriel said.

"I'm with the witch-hunter," Matthias said from the end of the nav deck. The navigator's arms were crossed, elbows leaning on the command terminal. "If I was going daddy vampire hunting, Lyander would be the first person I'd invite to the party."

"Could still be time for that yet," Freyen said. She turned to Eluthienn: "How long is it going to take to get to this secret passage of yours?"

The prince smiled. "I'll show you," he said, stepping onto the nav deck and standing by Matthias. The rest of them crowded around the terminal. Eluthienn leaned over to Matthias, waved a hand at the carpet of hex filaments, then said, as if what he was about to ask was highly amusing: "Show me the Pelothrian mountains."

Matthias gave him the sort of look that said he

didn't like being told what to do, then placed a hand into one of the wells. The filaments gathered together, then rose up. On their side of the terminal, a long range of cliffs, spanning north to south and taking up almost all of the display from edge to edge. Westward, extending out from the cliffs were the vast Formarian tunnels and the tip of Maw Kiloxies. Eluthienn, arms crossed over his chest, eyed the display, then shook his head, waving a hand at the terminal. "Too large," he said, then made a gesture with both hands as if he wanted to smooth out the filaments.

"How about you tell me when," Matthias said, then placed his hand back into the well. The hex reformed, then continued to reform, like a stew boiling over a stove, the contours and profiles gathering up and dispersing as it steadily scaled down the landscape.

"There," Eluthienn said suddenly. "Make it a bit bigger."

The hex adjusted, and the prince pointed at a spot on the cliff face that was the Pelothrian mountains. "It's there," he said.

For all Brazier could tell, it was just another sheer mountain edge driving into Formaria's depths.

"How do you know it's there?" he asked.

"Because I was shown on a map like this." What he meant was, he was shown *at a scale* like this, which didn't fill Brazier with confidence.

"If the scale was just a little different, we could be way off," he said. "We could be flying around for months looking for this passage."

"I know what I saw," Eluthienn said. "It's there."

Matthias rescaled the map, focusing in on the supposed tunnel's position. Most of a blank wall filled the display. "How is it hidden?" he asked, eyes still closed.

"How are any of Formaria's passages hidden?" Eluthienn asked, shrugging.

"Pockets of gyre ice can sometimes obscure small passages," Brazier said. "Or surface interference from Yeggardania."

"Either one means sorcery," Matthias said, rescaling the map to the east hangar bay, the *Anchorite* hovering in one of its berths. He pulled his hand from the well, saying: "That's thirteen, maybe fourteen hours' flight."

Brazier looked at Switch: "What're our reserves looking like?"

"Full tank," Switch said. "She's good to go."

"Alright," Brazier said. "We all need to sleep. Matthias – put her on sentience and I'll take first watch with Gabriel. We'll rotate two every four hours. Eluthienn and Freyen, then Matthias and Switch."

Matthias stepped into the pit while everyone but Gabriel left for the crew quarters. "Connect me to spire command," Brazier said, and a moment later the well nearest him rippled.

"*Shian Anchorite* to Teuron actual," he said.

"Actual receiving, *Shian Anchorite*," a women's voice came clear through the hex.

"Requesting departure from the east hangar bay."

"Departure approved," the woman said. "We're sorry to see you leave, *Anchorite*."

"We'd stay if we could," Brazier said.

"Good hunting out there," she said, and the connection dropped.

Matthias guided the ship along the west hangar bay, then up through the spire, before exiting into the east hangar bay. The hex rescaled as the *Anchorite* shot out into the void, the tunnels growing larger and the hangar bay reducing in size.

"Got a straight run for near on six hours," Matthias said, picking himself up from the pit and pulling on his boots. "Should be us and the void the whole way."

He stepped around the command terminal. "But let me know if that turns out not to be true," he said, winking at Brazier as he passed. "I'm starting to enjoy the whole battleship thing."

The nav deck doors slid shut behind him, and Gabriel turned to Brazier. "So," he said. "What is it you wanted to talk about?"

#

The galley was near perfection, Brazier decided, walking across the landing with two tankards of Charok tea: a table and benches, large enough for eight people, surrounded by a cooking top with bronzite heating pads, the conical ice-based recycler, and neat little wall compartments, vaguely reminiscent of a safe within one of Thendergaarden's banks. He'd rummaged through them all, finding, unsurprisingly, they contained mostly mushroom blend rations with various herbs to differentiate one rectangular mushroom 'cake' from another, all packed among shards of ice. And copious amounts of tea.

"So," he said, handing Gabriel one of the tankards, the nav deck quickly filling with the smell of crushed fennel, aniseed, and something citrusy. "What could Orpheus Velgar tell you about vampires?"

"Precious little," Gabriel said, blowing on the tea. His deep blue eyes regarded Brazier, as if contemplating how much or how little to tell him. He shrugged, blew on his tea again, then said: "Orpheus has his own personal breach, leading to a demon library; the Ecclessius believed it held information about Lokul."

Brazier raised his tankard to take a sip of the hot tea but stopped just shy of his chin. Every part of that statement came with a string of questions: *What exactly is a "personal breach"? Why do demons need a library? How could the Ecclessius know what's in it?* But the one he asked was: "Did it?"

"It did," Gabriel said. "Along with one very unfriendly librarian."

"And what was this information?"

"How the ancestral line of Leonette is linked to Lokul. To corroborate Eluthienn's claim."

He saw Brazier looking at him, expectantly.

"The library confirmed it. Only the blood of Leonette can completely destroy the vampire king."

"Why?"

The witch-hunter shrugged. "If Lyander found that out, he didn't mention it," he said, then sipped his tea.

"Why keep this from Eluthienn?"

"I think the Ecclessius felt that if Eluthienn knew the premise of the entire agreement was in doubt, it would signal a lack of trust on behalf of the Church." Gabriel's eyes flashed. "Not the best start to an alliance that intends to take over the known world."

Brazier could see their point. "And if Eluthienn asks you about this information?"

"I assume we tell him the Ecclessius was simply seeking information that might help them fight the spawn."

"You assume?"

"I believe the plan was for the other exorcist to share the information in secret without Eluthienn even knowing."

"Except he does know because Lyander announced it in front of everyone."

"As always with Lyander, it was act first, think

later."

It hadn't escaped Brazier's notice, but he was beginning to think Lyander's reckless, almost impulsive, approach to problem solving was thanks to extreme adaptability and resourcefulness. *Who needs a plan when you're so good at making it up as you go along?* he thought.

Out of nowhere he was hit with a dull ache in the centre of his chest because he knew, with a certainty that was almost instinctual, Lyander was the sort of person his brother would have liked. Then – because he was thinking about his brother, and it was the sort of thing Torquen would have asked – he said: "Why Lyander?"

"Why Lyander what?"

"Why did the Ecclessius charge Lyander with this mission? And why did Lyander accept? He doesn't seem particularly fond of the Church," Brazier, said, then added: "Understandably."

"As far as I can tell, the Church chose Lyander because he was in the wrong place at the right time. And I imagine he accepted out of some vague notion of honour, and misplaced loyalty to Formaria." There was something about the witch-hunter's tone Brazier didn't like; it was the combination of arrogance and mild disinterest with which he spoke.

"And you, Brazier Veranquis," Gabriel asked, clearly unaware of Brazier's thoughts. "Why are you following the prince to the end of the world?"

"Honour," Brazier said. "And loyalty to Formaria."

"Not revenge and guilt?" the witch-hunter asked, a shadow of a smile tugging at one corner of his mouth. "I knew Torquen Veranquis, briefly." The information momentarily stunned Brazier out of his dislike for the man. His brother had never mentioned meeting a witch-hunter. Although, there were many things Torquen had never mentioned.

"Briefly?"

"A chance encounter," Gabriel said. "One neither of us was expecting. I found him highly capable with good judgement, if somewhat taciturn."

"I'm surprised you liked him," Brazier said, growing annoyed again. The witch-hunter spoke with an oiliness that seemed to fill everything he said with mockery. "He was also honourable, and loyal to Formaria."

"Was he?" Gabriel asked, truly smiling now. "I suppose you know all about the Luceron, then?"

"Everyone knows about the Luceron," Brazier said, aware he was glowering at the witch-hunter, and also aware his anger was as much toward Gabriel as it was toward his brother, who had never spoken to him of the *Luceron*'s final, fateful mission, ending in disaster – and also ending Torquen's career in the navy.

As the sole survivor of nearly 180 crew, Brazier saw the pain it brought his brother at the very mention of the ship, and so never asked for details, believing Torquen would one day tell him what happened when he was ready. That day never came.

"I expect very few really know about the Luceron," Gabriel said, "but you are right about one thing – Torquen Veranquis was honourable, in his own way. I am interested to see if you'll live up to him." The witch-hunter's gyranic blue eyes glinted with crystal motes as he handed the tankard back to Brazier. "I need to clean up," he said. "Thank you for the tea."

Watching him leave, Brazier couldn't decide if he was still angry or just confused. *If you'll live up to him* – Brazier wanted to know what he meant by that, but something told him Gabriel would derive enormous pleasure from taunting him with information he may or may not have about Torquen. Instead, he took himself back to the galley, washed the tankards, and forced his thoughts from his brother, to what he was going to do for the next five and a half hours. Briefly, he thought about going to Freyen's cabin under the pretence of 'seeing how she was,' or as her first officer, finally telling her they needed to have the conversation about why she knew how to break hex networks and pilot war walkers.

He dispelled the thought as quickly as it came. If he knew anything about Freyen Fortigris, it was that she would see through those attempts before the words left his mouth. *There would be other opportunities*, he told himself, trying not think of the way she looked at him in the Thendergaarden bar, or the way her fingers brushed against his side as she helped with his breast plate.

To distract himself, he spent a monotonous two hours running diagnostics through the ship's hex networks. But it was hardly necessary, and within the first thirty minutes, he'd made a mental note to tell Switch how good she was at her job. Despite severe structural damage to four of the thruster extensions, the ship was reading them as brand new, the script image projecting something like: *Full range of motion* and *full operational capacity*. All thrusters were putting out at max, with max responsiveness. Even the repaired hull breach was reading as a minor fracture.

Deciding he would find nothing wrong with the ship, he moved on to the backlog of hex communications. The Ecclessius was broadcasting a secure communication to crews and installations, advising that eastern Formaria was under attack from an enemy capable of turning their victims. They were also sharing caster to caster emergency hex communications from those ships lost to the vampire spawn.

This is a rare demonstration of transparency from the Church, Brazier thought, assuming it was so other captains would know what they were facing. There were five in total, so not entirely transparent given the count of lost ships was nearing thirty.

The first detailed an ambush like the one sprung on the *Chalice,* the hex reel showing a vault-class miner opening its bay doors to let a large lander drift into its hangar. The moment the bay doors shut, the lander's side door swung upward, and what looked like a recently turned crew rushed out of it, killing and turning those in the hangar bay before rampaging through the larger ship.

The second, of a mining crew, its hauler powered down while taking on ice, was overrun and boarded within minutes. The third was Theselan, and having been there at the time, he skipped onto the fourth, which was another ambushed gyre miner. *Going for easy targets*, he thought. Or maybe it was just coincidence the vampires were attacking from the south east, the Fromryr's least defended quadrant.

He moved on to the last – a spire-class cruiser. The crew's caster and navigator dead, the captain risking an open broadcast – something few would choose to do, given the possibility of an enemy witch picking up the communication and deciding a downed gyre ship was an easy target. But watching the broadcast, Brazier could understand why.

The cruiser was boarded while navigating a small tunnel complex, the spawn dropping from the tunnel ceiling to land on the hull. Brazier's heart sped up as he watched the vampires race along the ship, tearing open breaches. Despite watching two others just like it, something about this one caused a welling of dread, like a cold hand gripping the underside of his ribcage. It grew tighter and colder as the spawn cut into the magazine compartments, the engines, then tore open the nav deck doors. The captain, a middle-aged woman with cropped hair, instead of fighting for her life, she held her hand in the command well, broadcasting the emergency signal, then provided her script to scuttle the ship. Brazier's heart hammered, anticipating with a degree of gladness the grey fuzz that would engulf his mind's eye as the engines overloaded and the broadcast came to its abrupt end.

But it didn't come.

Instead, from among the wreckage of the doors, out stepped a vampire like no others on the nav deck or anywhere else on the ship. Even through the grey and black script, Brazier could tell the skin of its bald head radiated an ethereal luminescence – white as the moon, black eyes held in two grey-ringed, sunken sockets. Its ears were the combination of a gnome's and an elf's – long and bat-like, but tipped and pulling close around its head. Its mouth seemed unable to hold in its fangs; like some ossified plant's creeping tendrils, they curled out from beneath its lips. Everything else was black plate, from the spiked sabatons on its feet to the spines curving out from its pauldrons, making Brazier think of a torture chamber, and giving him the strange sense of aeons-long suffering and torment.

The unknown vampire, faster than should be possible in such armour, drew a bastard sword as it moved toward the command terminal. Through the veil of mounting horror, Brazier felt an immense and completely unreasonable sense of pride and affection for the captain. She watched the tower of walking death coming toward her, and without even a tremble, stood her ground and finished delivering her command script. But the moment her hand pulled from the hex, the sword cut through her neck, down her collar bone, slicing open her chest, spraying blood and bone. Her body fell onto the command terminal, then slid off, the broadcast ending before it hit the floor.

He was left staring into grey fog, his heartbeat

pounding in his ears. Uncoupling his mind, he removed his hand from the hex, thinking of nothing other than the vampire in black plate. *Was that Lokul? Surely not.* Brazier knew little about Aeturnic beings, and even less about the Lords of the Eternal Hunt, but he assumed the Lord of Undead wouldn't risk itself attacking a single ship – a single ship that, by now it must know could be scuttled, taking everything inside with it. *A lieutenant, then?* One among many, he assumed, who must be directing the newly turned Fromryr. How else could they coordinate attacks on ships and spires? Every spawn Brazier had seen was a rabid animal, barely able to keep itself upright in its desperation to kill.

No, this was one of Lokul's commanders; he was sure of it. And like any organised force, there would be those in the field and those stationed at a command centre. In this case, the vampire's lair. His first thought was he needed to show Lyander, then he remembered the exorcist was out cold, which meant he was in charge. His second thought, a jolt of surprise, was accompanied by mild bewilderment. *He was leading this mission; he was in charge of delivering Eluthienn to the vampire's lair and ensuring the prince killed the beast*. It wasn't the task itself that caused the surprise; it was that he'd slipped into command like he was slipping on a pair of old boots – thinking nothing of it, and at the time, without even knowing he was doing it. Making decisions, he realised, also without thinking: *What would Torquen do*?

His palms pressing lightly against the command terminal, content in the empty nav deck's silence, he listened to the thruster's soft, monotonous, drone. He would inform the crew of the new vampire once they were all awake. Then he would plan their descent into the vampire's lair. For now, he was left with three hours to kill.

Placing his hand back into the hex, he sifted his mind through the remaining broadcasts. Both he and Lyander, it turned out, had been given admiralty-level script access, so he could see series after series of front line battle reports, Mirrovinjin troop estimates, and their movements. After thirty minutes, he knew the picture was bleak. With increasing numbers of reserves pulled from the front, the commander's complaints about a lack of ships quickly turned into outright begging. Infantry were going without aerial support, but more importantly, they lacked the one thing that often turned the tides of battles: manoeuvrability. Units that could have quickly reinforced others were unable to do so in time. More than one detachment found themselves victorious, only to be stranded in a tunnel, forced to hold out for ships that may never come or else risk the dark paths back to installations.

As time passed, the Fromryian strategy became clear. Rather than fight in the open, commanders pulled forces into installations, choosing to risk being besieged rather than lose troops in tunnels. Helmharothell, the capital of the north and the gateway to the Mirrovinjin homeland, was now a bastion for retreating forces and damaged ships. He watched, absentmindedly, the repeating image of gyre stars outside the main gate, as other, smaller, classes streamed into the vault; the sight of so many capital ships was reassuring to Brazier's tired mind.

It was only when he felt a hand on his shoulder that he realised he may have started to drift off, standing upright at the command terminal. Uncoupling his mind, he turned to see Freyen standing next him, eyelids still heavy with sleep.

"Time's up," she said.

He rubbed his eyes, carried himself off the nav deck, and hung his armour on the racks in the bay. In the

Anchorite's bathing chamber, he undressed methodically. The hexagonal room held four compartments, each facing one another, their doors closed. In the centre, a knee-high platform held a circular bronzite tray with cracks along its surface. At its foot, ringing the platform, a depression held a mound of raw gyre ice – a hand shovel wedged among the shards. Brazier threw off his gambeson and trousers in a pile, then peeled off his underclothes, trying not to breathe in the sour musk of dry sweat. Grabbing the shovel, he threw ice onto the tray and watched it hiss and simmer through the cracks. Stepping into one of the compartments, he turned the wall nozzle, and hot water sprayed down from the ceiling jets.

It was too hot. The water turned his skin pink. But something about the heat – how it scalded him, almost burned away the oily grime and the pungent smell – made him feel stronger. He ran a hand through the knots in his hair, down through his beard, letting the water splash onto his face, then onto his neck and down his back. Standing there like that, he let the shower run until the ice ran out.

In his cabin, he dumped his armour and clothes at the foot of his bunk, threw the cloth from around his waist on top of it, then he as good as fell, face-first, onto the sheets. Not bothering to get beneath them, not even bothering to roll over, he let darkness creep over his mind, and he succumbed to a dreamless sleep.

#

He awoke in the same position. Eyes flicking open, his vision horizontal, he looked straight at the terminal in the corner of the room, which rippled to the sound of Matthias's voice.

"Brazier, we're here."

He pushed himself up, feeling both well rested and as if he'd only just fallen asleep. Throwing his legs over the bunk, he stepped over to the terminal.

"I'm on my way," he said, and the connection dropped.

He spun open the locked wall compartment to find four sets of Navarch-issue blue gambesons and black trousers, complete with two pairs of black boots – his size. *Simplicity of the navy*, he thought, dressing.

Everyone looked up from around the command terminal as he stepped onto the nav deck.

"What have we got?" he said, coming to stand between Eluthienn and Switch.

"Exactly what the prince said we'd have," Matthias said, nodding at the hex map. "A passage through the Pelothrian mountains."

At his end of the display, the *Anchorite*, a finger nail-sized cluster of filaments, floated level with an opening so large a vault-class gyre star could fit through it. The opening cut through the mountain range like a mine shaft, straight and narrow, the display image slicing horizontally through the mountains and the top of the passage. They could see it running for roughly two leagues to a large cavern, in the centre of which was what Brazier thought was an installation. Unlike any in the rest of Formaria, it was almost entirely cylindrical – in several places with wide openings that could be hangar bays. To Brazier, it looked like a bucket with holes in it.

"Any ideas on why we can see this now but couldn't earlier?" Brazier asked. In Formaria, the inexplicable rarely came without a threat; he wanted to know what they were about to fly through.

"We're floating directly beneath a cavern complex with an open door to Yeggardania," Matthias said. "Got surface interference pouring through and being sucked into the tunnel – which is why no one can see it.

"Why can we see it now?" Brazier asked.

The navigator placed his hand into a well and the filaments shifted, then continued to shift, those forming the tunnel crumbling, as if the mountain was collapsing in on itself, only to reform into the tunnel again.

"The other sculpt was a still I put together," Matthias said. "And I only managed it because we're sitting right outside."

"The only tunnel the Formarians built leading out of Formaria, and it just happens to be built beneath a surface drift?" Brazier asked, struggling to believe it was a coincidence but not seeing how it could be by design.

A thousand years ago, the Ilvalien and their new human allies fought a war against the Fenn across all of Yeggardania. Victory was only achieved because the Ilvalien war casters and the human technomancers unleashed enough sorcery to permanently alter the forest's fabric of reality, forcing the Fenn to engage the dwarves underground in Formaria, and leading the reptilian race to defeat. But that was thousands of years *after* the tunnel would have been built. The Formarians couldn't know it would be obscured by sorcery from a battle that was yet to take place.

"Could be others like this," Freyen said. "Plenty of places along Formaria's boarder with an opening to Yeggardania."

She was right, but it didn't leave Brazier feeling any happier about the mystery. "Can we move through it?" he asked Matthias.

"Isn't giving the ship any problems," the navigator said. "Might even come in handy."

"How so?" Brazier asked, but it was Freyen who answered.

"Lokul is an Aeturnic being, so we can assume he has magical abilities," she said. "So we can also assume he's going to sense us coming. Especially as the *Anchorite* puts out a gyranic signature the size of a small sun."

"She's a powerful lady," Switch said affectionately.

"The surface interference is likely to hide our approach," Freyen continued. "But once we're in the cavern, Lokul will know we're coming."

It was a problem Brazier had already turned over several times, with no solution. There was just no way they could sneak up on the vampire's lair without a magical being like Lokul seeing them approach. The surface drift was a stroke of luck Brazier hadn't imaged they would receive but as Freyen said, it would make little difference once they left the tunnel.

"So we need to be quick," Brazier said. "Out the tunnel and a rapid descent into the installation."

Freyen fingered one of her curls, lips bunching while she chewed the inside of her cheek.

"There's another way?" Brazier asked, by now recognising Freyen's hesitance about voicing ideas.

"Jan only picked up the vampire's gyranic signature when they started moving," she said.

"Okay," Brazier said slowly, remembering how one minute there was nothing in the tunnel, then the next, the spawn were everywhere. He couldn't see how that would help them, though.

"Their signatures were hidden but they still left an imprint on the hex network, which the *Solace* also picked up. Navarch shared that information with the *Anchorite*. I've been through it and think I've managed to apply the same variations to the *Anchorite*'s signature."

Brazier was fairly certain his mouth was hanging

open. "You just developed a cloaking technology," he said. "Something the Fromryr have been trying to do ever since there have been ships for us to sail in."

A red tint dusted the tops of Freyen's cheeks as she bent forward, letting several curls shield her eyes. "Well," she said, "they didn't have vampires to copy from."

"Vampires or not," Switch said, giving her the same look Brazier assumed was also on his face, "that's still exceptionally impressive."

Freyen smiled at the enginator. "Only works if we're not moving, though," she said.

"So we power down and float toward the installation?" Brazier said.

"In theory," Freyen said. "Coming out of the tunnel, we may just look like stray surface interference. But this has never been tried before, and who knows how powerful a sorcerer Lokul is."

"Let's assume very powerful," Gabriel said, "but it's still the best idea we've got."

"Agreed," Brazier said, then with another idea: "Could this be applied to the *Anchorite*'s hex projection?"

"I could try," Freyen said. "What for?"

"So I can use the ship to project and provide a map of the installation," Matthias said, "without Lokul seeing me do it. Isn't that right, FO?"

"That's right," he said, looking at Freyen.

She pushed the curls behind her ears. "In theory, it might be possible," she said. "I'll need a couple hours."

"Before you do that, there's something you all need to watch," Brazier said, placing his hand into the hex. "Connect to the network." Everyone placed a hand into a nearby well, and he sorted through the broadcasts, providing his admiralty clearance and showing them the script with the black-armoured vampire.

"And I thought regular vampires looked unpleasant," Switch said after the script finished.

"Did you know about this?" Gabriel asked Eluthienn.

The prince shook his head. "This is the first time I've seen one like this," he said.

"Maybe this *is* a regular vampire," Freyen said.

Everyone turned to her. "What do you mean?" Brazier asked.

"What we've seen so far are turned Fromryr – just spawn. This one looks old."

"I'd venture you're right," Gabriel said, a sour look creeping over his face. "I'd also venture there're more of these *actual* vampires in Lokul's lair."

"If I can conceal Matthias's projection," Freyen said, "you'll know where they are before you enter. Gives you the chance to avoid them."

"Assuming you can do that," Gabriel said. "And assuming they don't move."

Freyen crossed her arms. "Or you can go in without knowing where they are," she said. "It's entirely up to you."

Eluthienn leaned over the terminal. "We appreciate your help," he said with a smile.

Gabriel continued to look bored.

As pleasant as he was when he was talking about Lyander, Brazier thought. Then another thought occurred to him: *Is he concerned about Lyander?* Gabriel never struck Brazier as the sentimental type, though. *Perhaps it's the thought of escorting the prince into the vampire's lair without the exorcist.* Empathising, Brazier found he didn't begrudge the witch-hunter his bad mood.

"Matthias," he said. "If you max sprawl to the mouth of the tunnel then drift us down without engines, how long until we're out the other side?"

The navigator's shoulders rose and fell by half an inch. "Two hours," he said. "Give or take."

"Does that give you enough time?" he asked Freyen.

She nodded.

And just maybe, Brazier thought, trying not to think what they'd do if Eluthienn and Gabriel failed, *it would also give Lyander enough time to wake up.*

"Assuming this does work," Switch said, "which I'm sure it will," she added, a bronzite palm held up to Freyen, "we only have a small window where the surface drift conceals us while Matthias builds a layout of the installation."

"Once we're near the tunnel exit, Matthias projects," Brazier said. "If Lokul doesn't pick up his signature, then we drift down into one of the hangar bays. And if he does –"

"– we sprawl like hell down into one of the hangar bays," Matthias finished for him.

"Right." Brazier nodded at him. To everyone else: "Any questions?"

Everyone shook their heads.

He spent most of the next two hours trying to guess where the *Anchorite* was along the churning line that was the tunnel out of Formaria. Every time he thought he saw it, it became another vague block of black-and-silver compound fusing with the rest of the mess. Giving up, he told himself that at least Lokul was unlikely to see them, either.

"It's done," Freyen said. She took a breath, then rubbed her hand, which for the last two hours had been planted in a hex well. "I've applied all the same script readings to the *Anchorite*'s hex projection as I did her signature. I've got no idea if it's going to work, though."

"We'll find out soon enough," Matthias said

from the pit. "We're almost at the exit."

"Let the others know," Brazier said.

Matthias tethered to the fuselage and engines, then Brazier heard Gabriel and Eluthienn climbing the stairwell, shortly followed by Switch.

"Whenever you're ready," Brazier said.

He watched the navigator's head droop, arms relaxing to waist height, the hex pools beneath them churning slowly. Like a rainstorm's final plummeting shower, the hex map flattened. Slowly, it formed the installation. Divided into three levels, a gigantic space ran through all of them: a drum, based on the current scale, large enough for four *Anchorite*s to fit comfortably within its hexagonal walls. Running through it was a hollowed-out walkway, a channel cut into its base to create a kind of duct. Out of the walls, other ducts hung over the drum, like water spouts. Outside of the drum were smaller chambers, the ducts running through them to form connecting passages.

Matthias reformed the hex, the filaments cascading, to show levels farther down. They were presented with cylindrical cavities running the installation's width, large extensions lining the ceiling and walls – the sort of insect-like limbs found in Constructii maintenance chambers but much larger. Brazier could only think they were hanger bays but wouldn't have been able to say what the installation's purpose was; he was certain, however, that nothing else like it existed in Formaria.

The hex changed again, the filaments building up on top of one another, forming the drum, cutting across the installation's second level. As at other levels, a walkway crossed the drum connecting it with corridors and chambers on either side. But in the centre of this walkway, shapes moved. There were a handful more at either end, and he tried to count them but whenever one stood still, the shape crumbled. He guessed thirty in total, but it was impossible to know their true number.

"Well, at least they're all in one place," Gabriel said. No one missed the sarcasm. Gabriel and Eluthienn might be highly proficient in the art of slaughter, but Brazier knew they couldn't take that many. Not all at once, and especially not if they were "vampire lieutenants."

"Is this all of them?" Brazier asked.

"If there're more," Matthias said, as if only half his mind was focused on what he was saying, "then they're not moving a muscle."

"And what about Lokul?" Eluthienn asked, a glint in his eye as he stared down at the map. Brazier thought the glint looked a lot like excitement.

"Centre," Matthias said. "Not moving, but I can tell he's there."

"How do we draw the others away?" Gabriel asked.

"We could try a distraction," Brazier said.

"Maybe using the ship," Freyen said. "Try and draw some of them out of the installation?"

"It's a shipyard," Switch said, staring at the display with an amount of concentration he'd only ever seen when she was looking into an engine.

"A what?" Brazier asked.

"A shipyard," she said again. "The bays are for construction – you can see the manipulator arms," she said, pointing into one of the cavities. "The ducts transport bronzite down through the drum and the antechambers, which cool it, before being used in the bays."

"Gyre ships can be constructed here?" Brazier said, the magnitude of the discovery causing him to momentarily forget the mission.

"If you could find enough bronzite," Switch

said.

"As extraordinary as all this is," Gabriel said, sounding as if he found none of it extraordinary, "it doesn't help our current predicament."

"Actually, it does," Switch said, pointing at one of the ducts with a metal finger. "These are how the bronzite would be transported." The finger moved to where the duct met an antechamber. "The chambers can produce a gyranic shield, blocking off the flow of bronzite – and anything else. We can separate that group into smaller groups."

"How do you know the antechambers can produce a gyranic field?" Gabriel asked.

"The Artificium have theorised about how ships might be constructed for centuries," Switch said. "They need three things: huge amounts of bronzite, a large cooling system, and throughput that can be controlled. Most academics believe the most efficient way of doing that would be through gyranic force."

Gabriel bent over the display to peer at an antechamber. "How can you tell a gyranic shield can be produced here? There's nothing to indicate that," he said.

"There're also no other methods of control," Switch said, and Brazier realised this was the most animated he'd ever seen the enginator. "There're theories about physical barriers, counterbalancing, and moving duct systems, but none of that is evident. So it has to be gyranic shields."

"And presumably those are controlled through the command chamber?" Gabriel asked.

"Control chamber," Switch corrected him.

The display crumbled, the drum and figures washing away. It reformed like waterfalls flowing backward in time, presenting the drum from a level above. Splitting off from it were several chambers, including an elongated room with three large command consoles spread along its centre. Around the edge of the room, facing into the command consoles, were other single-user terminals.

"This what you're looking for?" Matthias said.

"That's the one," Switch said. "You get to that, you control the drum. Black abyss – you control the whole installation."

"Two problems," Gabriel said. "There're only two of us, and it'll need both Eluthienn and me to bring down Lokul." He turned to the prince: "Not to mention the very clear Ecclessiarchal orders not to leave your side once we've found the lair."

"I'm touched," Eluthienn said, "but yes, this does give us a problem."

"One you're going to need to find a solution for quickly," Matthias said. "We're about to find out whether Freyen's hex skills work as well for the ship as they do for me."

"I'll go," Brazier said. "Once enough vampires have left the drum, and you've destroyed Lokul, I'll meet you there. The *Anchorite* then picks us up from inside the drum – it's easily large enough for her." He turned to Gabriel: "What's the second problem?"

"Assuming there are gyranic shields and you can operate them," the witch-hunter said, "what's stopping Lokul from moving with his guard? It's what I'd do if I were him."

"Lokul won't leave that spot," Freyen said. "Take us back to the other sculpt."

Matthias's head twitched and the hex reformed so they all looked down into the drum. Freyen leaned over and pointed at the drum wall. Looking closer, Brazier could see it was lined with nodule-like protrusions.

"Those are its young."

"I know I've made some bold claims about this place," Switch said, "but how in the endless black abyss do you know that?"

"I don't, really," Freyen said, "but have you ever seen Formarian design with . . ." She turned both palms face up, shrugging.

"Rounded lumps?" Brazier suggested.

Freyen nodded at him.

"Those do look horribly like some gestation pods I saw not too long ago," Gabriel said, eyeing the wall like he was looking at a particularly venomous creature on the Yeggardanian surface. "I did hope I'd never have to come across something like that so soon."

"If they see the *Anchorite* heading for the drum, they won't go anywhere," Brazier said. "Matthias – you'll need to wait with the ship in one of the lower construction chambers, or bays, or whatever they are. They'll head toward you, but I'll trap them in the antechambers, making sure they don't cross Eluthienn and Gabriel on their way to the drum." He turned to Eluthienn: "Once I see you engage Lokul on the hex, I'll contact Matthias, and come and meet you there. Then we all get picked up and go home."

"What could possibly go wrong?" Gabriel said, before turning to Brazier: "If you find out there is no shielding," he said, shrugging apologetically at Switch. "But if there isn't, contact us on a terminal and we head back to reformulate this plan."

"Agreed," Brazier said.

The witch-hunter looked him up and down. "I might want to put some armour on, if I were you," he said.

"Not that I plan on fighting any of those things, but I think you're right," Brazier said. "Matthias – how long until we're in the construction bay?"

"Five minutes until I need to turn the engines

back on. Two more until we land."

He nodded – mainly to himself, given the navigator's back was to him – and left the nav deck for the fuselage. Pulling his plate, grieves, and vambraces from the wall, he strapped himself up – first the grieves, then the vambraces. When he turned to pick up the breast and back plate, he found Freyen standing behind him, the armour held out in her hand.

"Need some help?" she said.

"Thanks," he said, realising he hadn't heard her approach.

She lifted the plate over his head and laced up the sides. Unlike the last time she helped him don armour, she was facing him as she did it.

"Lokul is a sorcerer," she said, pulling a knot tight. "And we know vampires can manipulate the hex."

"We know they can break the hex and wipe it," Brazier said, trying to keep his eyes on Freyen's. It was harder than he cared to admit; every time she looped the strap through an eyelet, she leaned into him, her mouth inches from his own.

"Exactly," Freyen said. "That's what we *know* they can do. We don't know what else Lokul may be able to do, how else he might be able to manipulate it."

"What are you saying?" he asked. "You think Lokul has powers that can target me through the hex?"

She sighed as she pulled the last strap tight, and tied the knot.

"I don't know what such a being is capable of," she said, giving him the hard look of Freyen Fortigris, the operations officer. "Just don't die in there."

"I wasn't planning on it," he said, and the hard line of her mouth softened, one corner turning up by a fraction. He reminded himself he was supposed to be concentrating on her eyes when she nodded over her shoulder, and said: "Shall we?"

He followed her back to the nav deck, the whole time wondering whether he should have kissed her. Wondering, with an absurd degree of regret, if that had been his last chance to kiss her. *If you die, you won't be alive to care. But if you live . . . If he lived*, he told himself as the nav deck doors parted, *he would kiss her*; *he would kiss Freyen Fortigris.* With that thought, he stepped up to the command terminal, and watched the *Anchorite* materialise into an actual object.

"Engaging thrusters now," Matthias said, and filaments sprung up from the map, forming the thruster disc's swirling gyre energies. The ship shifted her facing forty-five degrees, then dove for the construction bay.

"Looks like that got their attention," Gabriel said. In the drum, every one of the figures vanished before reforming into angry buzzing shapes. Like a Cicadron nest that knew it was under attack, the vampires knew they were coming.

The display reformed as the *Anchorite* shot through the bay's mouth and sped toward a short landing, halfway up the bay's south wall. Matthias spun the ship in the air, pulling its stern around to face the landing and the corridor beyond.

"That's definitely worked," Switch said. Figures, roughly two thirds of the original group, raced down the walkway and into one of the antechambers. Despite seeing it on the *Chalice* – and in reality, in Theselan – he was still shocked at the speed at which the creatures moved.

"Time to go," Gabriel said, turning and leaving the nav deck. Eluthienn followed, but before he left, he placed a hand on Brazier's shoulder, smiling at him as if they were old friends. "We'll see you soon, Brazier Veranquis," he said.

Brazier watched the doors close on them, perplexed at the familiarity, then watched them appear on the hex – two tall shapes, leaving the fuselage and moving swiftly toward the lift at the end of the corridor.

Matthias pulled away from the landing, propelling the ship farther into the bay, then pulled up outside a second landing. Brazier glanced at the map, seeing the vampires move into a chamber, take a turn, then stream down a corridor.

"We'll see you soon, too," Switch said, but there was no humour in her tone. If anything, it seemed to say: *We better see you soon, too*.

He nodded, and made his way down to the fuselage, down the access ramp, and into an installation, the existence of which, the Fromryr had, up until now, only speculated at. *I very much hope I live to confirm it*, he thought as his heart sped up, his focus narrowed, and his mind became highly aware of the ancient, bloodthirsty beings racing through the installation.

Outside the lift, he placed his hand into the terminal. Guessing Switch was probably right, he requested it to take him directly to the *control chamber* rather than the *command chamber*. He felt the momentary weightlessness as the lift decoupled, then gravity met his shins as it rose, the purple-grey walls glistening as if wet. The lift slowed, stopped, then travelled south horizontally along the upper level. It slowed again, and the doors opened onto the control chamber. Three dark grey command terminals lined the centre in a row. Raised behind them were the smaller, lighter grey terminals. A gyre channel led from the foot of each, crossing the floor, and rising up the wall. They carried on to the ceiling, where they converged in a small depression in the centre, casting bright blue light into every corner of the room.

The walls and floor were bright grey; the hex, shimmering black and grey, and flat as hammered steel; the gyre channels burning a soft azure. *It's as if the*

Formarians disappeared only yesterday, he thought, the room giving him an odd sense of assurance to compete with the growing adrenaline.

He placed his crossbow onto the edge of a command terminal, and sunk his hand into a well, requesting a connection to the *Anchorite*. His mind unshackled from his skull, and he felt himself drifting in fog until Matthias anchored him in place.

I'm in the control chamber, he said.

Received, the navigator replied. *I'll tether an open connection to your location.*

Brazier's mind released from the anchor and he removed his hand from the well, just as the one next to it pulsed. He placed his hand back into the well, and requested a sculpt of the installation's second level, keeping his hand in place and so viewing the image in his mind. It showed him the drum, its antechambers and the corridors and their ducts shooting off from them. More than half the vampire pack was at the end of one corridor, heading toward a lift two chambers away.

With no idea if it would work, he requested *gyranic shield access* in his mind, giving the level and location. The familiar click, and the installation confirmed his control. Riding a wave of relief, he followed the pack's route to another chamber, and once there, he issued the command to *engage shields*. Four hazy, grey walls sprang from the ceiling, blocking the four routes exiting the chamber, providing another wave – this time of both exhilaration and relief. *The plan is going to work; he could control every chamber in the installation. They wouldn't need to fight anyone but Lokul.*

Still mildly elated, he watched one of the vampires move to a terminal in the chamber's corner. He waited for the vampire's request to appear in his mind – the visual and mental acknowledgement of an affirmation, which he would then deny.

But it didn't come.

Instead, the hex confirmed the release of the gyranic shields, and he watched the thin grey haze fizzle into nothing. *That shouldn't be possible*, he thought as the vampires streamed down one of the corridors toward the chamber with a lift. Panic erased his previous feelings as he scrambled to sort through the script in his mind, bringing a shield down as they entered the chamber, then engaging another behind them, trapping them once again. He locked both shields to his command script, then waited, heart a rapid thump in his ears as one of the pack moved to a terminal.

Nothing happened.

The hex gave him no command actions or access requests; whatever they were using the terminal for was completely invisible to his mind's eye.

But the shields remained in place.

Not realising he was holding his breath, the exhalation escaping his lungs came as a shock. He continued to watch the pack – the shapes disappearing and reappearing as they stood still or moved – waiting for something to happen, but for now, they seemed trapped.

Using the reprieve to check for Eluthienn and Gabriel, he requested a track on two moving individuals. The map in his mind raced toward the second level, showing two blurred shapes running down a corridor, heading toward an antechamber containing a lift. Brazier tracked the chute's route, seeing that it would take them to a chamber several corridors down from Lokul's position, just a handful of his guard now surrounding him. And once the vampire king saw the prince and the witch-hunter approaching, it would send that guard to fight them, allowing Brazier to trap the rest of them, as well.

The plan is going to work, he told himself again, as he moved his mind back to check on the larger pack. But as the map refocused on their location, his relief turned to such intense panic, the change in emotion felt like a physical wound. The shields dropped in front of his eyes, and a lift released on the hex network, directed toward the vampire pack's chamber. Caught between reengaging the shields and stopping the lift, he stood stunned for several seconds before his mind, seemingly of its own accord, said: *Halt lift course level two, southern chamber four.*

He watched it come to a stop in the chute, and breathed yet another deep sigh of relief before sending the platform to the other side of the installation.

"Everything alright in there?" he heard Freyen's voice say from far away.

He uncoupled his mind and spoke into the other well: "Vampires' hex commands aren't appearing on the script. I can't know if they're overriding my command script or something else is doing it."

"I'll see what I can do," Freyen said. "Give Matthias access to the chamber's hex logs."

He did so, then returned to the pack; those not standing still he could see pacing around the chamber. One of the group – the one who made the lift request – moved over to the terminal again. Brazier waited for the hex to tell him a platform was moving again, but nothing happened, and a trickle of foreboding began pooling in his gut. *Think*, he thought; *what command could they make without some form of physical change in the spire?*

Stumped for several seconds, it then became so obvious to him he almost kicked the terminal: a tether to another location. It was contacting another vampire. With only one other group to choose from, he sent his mind to the drum, and watched a figure at the end of the walkway, standing next to a terminal just inside the connecting corridor. Any other creature in existence and Brazier would hear the conversation word for word. As it was, he simply stared at a grey shape in the corner of a corridor.

Then it turned around to face him.

In his mind, the hex gave him a field of view, like it always did from a height, angling down at roughly ninety degrees. Impossibly, unbelievably, the grey shape looked up at him, as if it knew Brazier could see it. His heart raced and the pool of foreboding quickly turned into a storm of panic. The shape took a step toward him, then another, and as it did so, it grew larger, then larger still until it was no longer in the room. It was filling his field of vision, and through the panic – now a full-blown thunderstorm – he shouted for his mind to uncouple from the network.

Except it didn't uncouple.

The click at the back of his nasal cavity, the coolness at the back of his throat that came with connecting and disconnecting, never came. Instead, the shape grew – a grey, rectangular blur between his eyes – and whether it was the panic or the figure, something caused lights to dance in the corners of his vision. Like stars twinkling, their crystal-yellow rays enlarged as the shape itself grew. He tried to breathe, to force calm, but as he exhaled, the shape came speeding toward him, engulfing his vision.

Engulfing *him*.

Seventeen

Lyander

Cadarrasta Pulance's girth allowed him to lean forward just far enough so his chin could merge with his neck. "First Champion Kalbrayeth Lyander, you are hereby accused of the murder of three members of the Rosantz royal household guard," the Grand Ecclessian said. "Insubordination, the failure to carry out orders from a royal family member, and above all, the loss of an installation to the great enemy."

Kept in a pitch black cell for a week, the light in the High Council chamber was intolerable. The channels rising up the walls were so crystallised they produced a rainbow-like glare, reflected as if off a diamond's surface. They caused a headache behind his eyes, and bile to rise at the back of his throat. Although both could also be from the magical bonds within which he was bound.

A war caster on either side of him, he was forced

to his knees, hands behind his back, the sorcery a permanent gilded cage around his person. He couldn't move, couldn't speak – couldn't say a word to defend himself.

"Your crimes are indisputable," Pulance continued, his chins wobbling ferociously at the word *indisputable*. "Witnesses, even those of your own unit, confirmed your actions. And as those actions were against a member of a royal bloodline, your right to answer, to plead one way or the other, is forfeit."

In the seats surrounding the Grand Ecclessian, arch-cardinals, none of which Lyander knew, looked down upon him impassively. The only face he recognised – the Lord Marshal of his own order, Henselt Braechter – scowled, looking somewhere over Lyander's shoulder.

In seats higher up sat Varkoneth and Ramovand Rosantz. The father, hands folded over his suspension, feigned dignity, his black lips moulded into affected sincerity. The son to his right, tried to display an aloof contempt, looking down his nose at Lyander, cheek turned away just slightly. But his eyes couldn't hide the embarrassment or the guilt. They were the eyes of a boy who knew he was getting away with something he shouldn't be. And those eyes hated Lyander for it.

He hated the boy back. But it was more than just hatred. It was the blind, arrogant stupidity behind his friend's deaths, the needlessness of them, and the Church's willingness to ignore the crime against so many of their own that caused, instead, a burning sense of injustice. It began with heartache over Lyander's inability to save his fellow soldiers. It morphed into something he recognised as disgust – partly at himself, but mainly because someone like Ramovand could stop him from saving those he was responsible for, that someone as weak and inept as the boy everyone called

"Ramy" could prevent him from saving people he cared for. It morphed again, maintaining its original shape, but was changed by the Church's betrayal – the great, unifying force he was a part of that made him who he was, that *was* who he was, causing a complete loss of self. Anger, heartache, disgust, and betrayal, but it had nothing on what he felt next.

"Your fate is decided, Kalbrayeth Lyander," Pulance said, and Varkoneth's black slugs slid into smug satisfaction. "You are stripped of your rank and title. From this day forth, you are no longer First Champion, or any member of the Knight's Redcrosse. You are appointed to the Order Malignia, whereupon a later date, your new function will be determined."

The bonds holding him moved his legs, forcing him to stand. He raged against them, could feel his jaw tightening, his eyes bulging. It was like he was in sleep paralysis: fully aware but with no control. The inability to speak the truth, to prevent the outcome, for it to be *pre-arranged*, was a white-hot anger that sent the crystallised lights into a tail spin so violent, they blinded him. But still he fought against the bonds, trying to stop them from turning him away from the council, tensing his thighs, his stomach, his biceps, trying to tear himself free of the magic.

And suddenly he was.

His torso flung forward, his arms and shoulders wrenched free of their constraints, and he was staring at a bronzite wall. The crystallised lights danced to the sound of his heartbeat; with each thud in his chest, they pulsed and twirled, twirled and pulsed. And through the spectrum of colour, he realised he could see only part of the wall, as if only one of his eyes worked. He put a hand to his face, and flinched as his fingers brushed against the lump on his cheek. Delicately, he travelled north, feeling the swelling shutting his eye closed, and vaguely remembered a punch, or maybe a headbutt. Pulling his hand from his face, he stared at the scar along the back, the purple ridge like the contours of a mountain winding itself from above his knuckle down to the right side of his wrist. It didn't hurt.

The lights spun in the corners of his vision, refracting the rainbow spectrum like miniature twirling jesters. His head felt dream-like, as if adrift: a boat becalmed at sea. The rest of his body ached, his thighs and shoulders tight, his right arm heavy from lifting his sword, the familiar battle soreness. But from his hand, there was nothing. No bludgeoning pain; no daggers sending his arm aquiver; no lancing throbs running up into his mind and attacking his thoughts. He flexed the fingers, watched the mountain range pull tight, and it was still the same. He had his hand back.

With supreme confidence, he swung his legs off whatever he was sitting on, his feet hit the floor, and he stumbled. A flash of moonbeam yellow and *your fate is decided* slammed into his consciousness, Pulance's ugly face sneering down at him, boiling his blood. Another flash and he was back, the anger receding like the wisps of a forgotten dream, except he couldn't really forget, and the anger remained, as if ready to resurface.

Let's hope that's not permanent.

But he didn't really care. He wouldn't reduce to a quivering wreck after every fight, and that made him feel like himself again. Certainty blended with simmering anger and, not even knowing where he was, he crossed the room, spun open the wheel lock and walked out – into the *Anchorite*'s fuselage, he quickly realised.

Wherever they were, they were hovering, the vibration beneath his feet near as imperceptible, but still causing the lights around his eye to jig merrily. A mildly pleasant sight, he almost smiled. Then he actually did when he saw his sword belt and scabbard hung in the armoury at the end of the fuselage. He walked to it, and even before he tied it around his waist, he knew it would feel good to be there, knew the weight on his left side would feel right. Smiling, he climbed the stairwell, pulled himself onto the landing, and the nav deck doors opened at his presence.

"Brazier, are you there!?" Freyen shouted at the well in front of her. Switch to her right, the enginator's augmented and real hand pressing into the command terminal. She was scowling at the hex as if Brazier's lack of reply was a personal affront.

Broken halos of light surrounded both of them, the semi-circles appearing at their shoulders, their waist, along their arms, shimmering, then dispersing.

"Brazier, please respond!" Freyen said.

"Anything I can help with?" Lyander asked, stepping up to the command terminal. Their heads snapped up to look at him.

"If it isn't the big man," Switch said, grinning at him.

"Thought you were planning on sleeping through the best part," Matthias said from the pit.

"Not a chance," he replied. "What have we got?"

"Brazier is in the installation's control room – we're still tethered but something's happened to him. He's not moving," Freyen said.

Lyander looked down at the command display, saw the chamber and its three large consoles, a dwarf-sized shape, lying on the floor next to one.

"Where's Gabriel and Eluthienn?" he asked.

The whole level dematerialised, and another level rose up. Matthias scoped in on two figures moving quickly down a long corridor. They headed for a large antechamber, walkways spanning it at multiple levels.

Extending eastward from it, another corridor connected it with a chamber so large, it could fit a vault-class frigate. A long walkway spanned its centre, at the middle of which, human-sized shapes moved, then crumbled and reformed as if the composite suffered a hallucination.

Lokul and his guard, Lyander thought, putting two and two together.

"There're more vampires in the installation," Freyen said. "Brazier stopped them from getting to Gabriel and Eluthienn, but somehow they've figured it out – they're headed for the control chamber."

"He stopped them?"

"Installation produces gyranic shielding around the chambers," Switch said. "Should only be able to operate them from the control chamber, but looks like the vampires have figured out another way."

There was a lot in that statement Lyander didn't fully understand but knew he didn't have time to ask for an explanation. "Give me a route to Gabriel's and Eluthienn's location," he said. The western section of the hex crumbled, showing several levels below, and what must be one of the largest hangar bays of all Formarian installations; in it, the *Anchorite* floated outside a short landing.

"Lift outside will take you to where they're going," Matthias said, and Lyander noted the lift chute running up several levels and east, toward the larger chamber.

"Okay, you two get Brazier," Lyander said. "I need to get to Gabriel and Eluthienn." He pointed into the large chamber and the centre of the walkway. "We meet here and –"

"Catch a ride from me," Matthias said. "Way ahead of you."

"So much for not going into the vampire's lair,"

Switch said, and the three of them hurried off the nav deck.

"The vampires in there," Freyen said as they climbed down to the fuselage, "we think they're different."

"Different how?" Lyander asked.

Freyen shook her head, sending halos reverberating into the ether. "Not sure – tougher than the others. More dangerous."

"Just a heads-up," Switch added. "Not that you'll need it."

And with the anger still hot in his veins, he didn't feel like he did, either. If anything, he felt something like anticipation. It was as if he was First Champion again, the nervous excitement of being the best on the battlefield sending a thrill though him, dazzling the lights in his eye. A very small part of his rational mind, like the very quiet voice of sagacity that still existed when blind drunk, recognised he was edging into a kind of euphoria. *You're going to need to keep a handle on that Kalbrayeth*. Whatever *that* was. Right now, though, he needed to get to the prince. He could worry about his mental state after.

"Are you okay?" Freyen asked. "You were out for some time – nothing would wake you."

"Honestly," he said, "I can't remember the last time I felt this good."

"Knew we'd have you back," Switch said, punching him in the arm as she passed him on her way to the armoury bay.

Freyen stood staring at him, concern in her eyes.

"I'm alright, really," Lyander said to her. "Let's go save Brazier and end this."

He stepped onto the open access ramp, then onto the installation's hard grey floor. Drawing his sword, he felt the grip between his closed fist and the steel's weight, like shaking hands with an old friend.

Concentrate on that, he told himself as the stars twinkled at him. *Remember the feel of it; remember how you've used it in a hundred battles – a hundred battles as First Champion of the Knights Redcrosse.*

But as the lift rose, he thought the stars might be laughing at him, their rays reflected off the interior walls, cavorting across his vision. He shook his head, trying to clear the lights away, and *flash*: *From this day forth you are no longer First Champion, or any member of the Knight's Redcrosse*. Rage churned at the back of his clamped mouth, his jaw grinding against the magical bonds. And *flash*: he was stepping out of the lift and into a corridor, a half gasp, half growl breaking out from somewhere in his throat. *I think I might need to fight something*, he thought, gripping his sword that much tighter.

One of the stars sparkled bright, as if to say: *Yes, you do, my friend, and we'd enjoy that very much*. He ignored it, focusing on the corridor ahead. It was formed into a channel, hollowed out like a duct to allow for water or some other substance. It opened onto a hexagonal chamber, empty space either side of the duct, then joined a larger room where the channel was cut into the floor. Overhead was a single vein as wide as his fist and ablaze with so much gyre light, it turned the walls silver.

Reminding himself of the grip, the comfortable weight, he let the blue light soothe his rage, and moved along the channel. In the open chamber, he looked over the edge and saw other ducts running beneath him before moving on. A junction ahead of him, the channels split off at right angles, heading to different chambers. Then: *Clang. Clash. Clatter*. Distant sounds, like a blacksmith's heard from several streets away, steel hitting steel, drifting down from the left-hand channel.

Then, ripping through the muted clamour, a torturous screech, and his stars grew bright at the unmistakable sound of a vampire.

He sprinted down the left channel and headed into a long corridor. At its end, a chamber, in the centre of which, Eluthienn and Gabriel held off against three, four, five attackers, all in curving black plate, like voidstone snow drifts, covering them from the neck down and almost identical to the images he'd seen in the demon library.

Mere seconds of observation told Lyander they were deadly. Something about the way they moved spoke to an experience so ancient it had divorced emotion from the act of killing long ago. If these were matured versions of the spawn, then whatever rage the vampire came into this world with, calcified into an unyielding kind of apathetic hatred.

Somewhere in the back of his mind, a voice filled with warm anticipation was desperate to challenge this new foe. He ran toward the fray, and as he did so, the prince and the witch-hunter were forced back and out of his line of sight, by strikes delivered with a near preternatural awareness. Vampires took their place. One turned to look at Lyander, watching him run down the corridor. Another did the same, then another. All smiling wickedly, their curving bone-white fangs sprouting from beneath pale lips. The one in front stepped forward, opened its jaw, and screamed, lighting up his stars like suns; their radiance ringing in his ears became the sound of his sword against another's. Ramovand's guard faltered against Lyander's attack, the man's brown eyes fearful as his sword dropped too low, and in the space, Lyander cut across his neck, blood spilling from the wound and drowning the falcon on his breast plate.

The other guard parried twice before Lyander's blade sliced across his cheek, opening him from beneath his eye to across his nose, blood and cartilage splattering grey walls. He shouldered the dying man out of his way, desperate to stop Ramovand.

But a third guard was in front of him, and in the narrow corridor Lyander's swing was reduced; his blade smashed to the side, his shoulder crashing into the wall. Lyander ducked, the sword clattering off the wall above his head, and with no room to manoeuvre, no space to swing, he rammed his blade forward into the guard's open mouth. Driving it home, his sword hilt broke teeth; blood drenched his hand, and ran into his mail links. It was a stupid thing to do. There were more guards. He was being surrounded. He was pulling his blade from the man's head. He needed to swing it round to defend himself, and he swung into nothing.

He turned and swung again, assuming the attacker was on his other side, but the blade whistled through the air, and he nearly tripped as the momentum spun him round. He forced himself to a stop, trying to get his bearings, and breathed hard, causing the stars to laugh at him again, rainbows edging along their moonbeam light. And he knew why they were laughing. *Try to save those at Lucretia and condemn yourself*, they said. *Try to save Eluthienn and condemn Formaria*, and they laughed some more. *Try to save yourself*, and they laughed the hardest, *and condemn yourself.*

He squeezed his eye shut, grinding his teeth against the pain the conflict caused him, and *flash*: Varkoneth's lips were sliding over one another with gluttonous satisfaction. *From this day forth, you are no longer First Champion, or any member of the Knight's Redcrosse.* Hatred reemerged and quieted the stars, dampening their brightness as he ran down the duct and into the next chamber. He took a right, following the sounds of battle, down another corridor, opening onto a cavernous antechamber where the duct joined a junction.

Eluthienn and Gabriel held the centre, vampires swarming. Beyond them, straight ahead of Lyander's eyeline, another corridor led out onto the walkway spanning a giant chamber. Standing at the end of the corridor, just before the duct opened onto the chamber was a single figure silhouetted against the light.

Lokul.

Lyander pelted down the corridor, but just as he was about to reach the antechamber, the channel above his head pulsed white and a wall of translucent gyre light filled the corridor from duct to ceiling. He pulled up short, the blue shield swimming as if he was looking through an ocean's surface. Knowing what the result would be, but doing it anyway, he hit the screen with his sword, sending pools of fiery yellow spilling up the gyranic shield. *The control chamber*, he thought with a stab of panic. *It was overrun. Freyen and Switch didn't make it in time*. But then he saw the figure, still silhouetted at the end of the corridor; it stood next to a terminal with its hand in the hex. With cold certainty that cut through his hallucinating vision and made him momentarily forget his hatred, he knew it was Lokul controlling the shield in front of him. *Find another way around*, his racing mind thought, frustrated, *or hope Freyen and Switch can retake control of the shields?*

But both questions vanished as a vampire hurtled into the witch-hunter. Gabriel, seeing it from his periphery, tried to sidestep while slashing but the vampire was too quick; it crashed into him, and together they flew off the edge of the junction, down into the chamber's depths.

"No!" Lyander cried, and stopped himself from thrashing his sword against the gyre gate, helplessness knotting his insides. The feeling took on a toxic quality as he watched Eluthienn become surrounded, then overwhelmed with assailants, missing thrusts and slashes. Links flew from his chain mail as a sword bit into his thigh. More fell from his shoulder as a cut slashed across the top of his arm. Lyander could only watch, holding back blind panic as Eluthienn slowly died from cut after cut.

The prince parried once, twice, then a pale white face appeared in front of Lyander, blocking his view. Seen through the gyre gate, it swam like a watery apparition, the fangs living vines coiling out of its smiling lips, its eyes – entirely black – were abyssal pools, endless as the void.

Then a sound, like the crackles of dying embers, and the gyre gate evaporated, leaving Lyander and the smiling vampire inches from one another. Thanking every bit of training and experience forming his basic instincts, he twisted at the hips, swung, and decapitated the creature. Before the head hit the floor, he was shouldering the body out of the way, and coming up behind the three vampires surrounding Eluthienn. Driving his sword beneath the back plate of the nearest, he felt the blade hit bone and the tip exit the stomach. Pulling hard, he parried an incoming thrust and threw a slash back against the new attacker. Only for the vampire's blade to throw it aside. They clashed once, twice more, before Lyander's sword, intended for the gap above the thigh guard, instead caught the creature's midriff, and clattered off plate armour. The sound of skidding steel dulled his battle euphoria with the sober acknowledgement these things possessed too much strength for the speed at which they moved. It served only to drive Lyander to match their skill with his own. At that very thought, he parried, took one swift step toward the vampire, risking its kill range, and caught the creature across its cheek. He followed with a cut across the thigh, hitting the gap above its knee cap. The vampire stumbled, snarled, its guard going wide, and Lyander kicked out, catching it in the stomach, sending it off the junction's edge.

To his left, a grunt, heavy steel hitting floor, and a screech. The vampire was on its knees, left arm lolling, useless from the elbow down, sword slipping from its fingers. Eluthienn was above it, his backhanded cut slicing across its face, temple to cheek. Black gore sprayed, and the vampire was on its back, its ruined face withered from the Leonette sorcery.

Lyander ran to the junction's edge, searching for Gabriel. Below, in the middle of another duct, a vampire lay sprawled on its back, arms out wide, but there was no sign of the witch-hunter. *Alive, then, probably down one of those other passages, but I think we'll be fighting Lokul on our own.*

"I knew you would be with us," Eluthienn said, his breathing heavy. He leant on his good leg, a hand pressed against the wound to his shoulder; his grin, filled with so much delight, made him look as if nearly dying to vampires was the best thing to happen to him.

The prince raised his wounded arm, grimacing slightly, and placed a hand on Lyander's shoulder. "It was always going to be you and me at the end, Lyander," he said, and the grin met his eyes. "As it will be in the future. The great Kalbrayeth Lyander: You will lead my armies, and together we will fight the evils of this world."

But before Lyander could reply, he heard screeches and howls, the sound of running from the corridor to their left. More vampires appeared, staring down at them from its end.

"Together, then?" Eluthienn said, backing away from him and toward the corridor. He winked at Lyander and turned, moving along the duct and into the corridor.

Lyander's heart was in his throat, his head

snapped around to the figure at the end of the other corridor, its hand still in the hex terminal.

"Eluthienn, stop!" he cried.

But it was too late, the gyre shield came down behind him, the magical blue wall trapping the prince in the corridor. Disbelief took over Eluthienn's usually impish expression as he looked the wall up and down, then through it at Lyander.

With a mix of resignation and cold acceptance, Lyander turned from the prince, and faced the dark figure. The lights – now crystal rainbows in his single eye, their rays ricocheting off the walls – framed the vampire king. But there were no halos around Lokul; it was as if his black silhouette curved the light out from itself, as if it emitted the rays, sending them down the corridor.

The faraway voice told him he was compromised, told him in all probability, he would lose a fight against such a being, especially on his own – especially in his state. But the dominant voice was more pragmatic. It saw the problem in front of it, and knew it needed a solution. All he needed to do was wound the creature, drive it away from the terminal, and give Eluthienn a chance. Thoughts of life and death made as much sense to that voice as the stars made to the abyss.

So Lyander followed the rays to their source – to fight the vampire king.

EIGHTEEN

BRAZIER

Dwen'hiema priests believe the souls of dwarvern dead swim in the abyss for eternity, finding friends, family, and lost loves, forever experiencing the joy and anguish of discovering and departing from one another in an endless dream.

In Brazier's afterlife, he swam straight into Freyen. Initially, that caused him great sadness – it meant she was also dead. But it passed quickly enough, and then he wondered whether souls could kiss. He wanted to try, but she seemed too far away, and try as he might, he couldn't move his soul closer to hers. She was also giving him a strange look, as if she wasn't quite sure what he was doing.

"I'm trying to kiss you," he said, but it came out as: *Ohm tyin kinn 'uo*.

"What did he say?" someone asked, and it sounded a lot like Switch. *That's a shame*, Brazier thought, *I suppose they must all be dead, then. I guess we lost.* And disappointment permeated his soul body. He had led the mission, so he'd let Lyander down. And worst of all, Freyen and Switch were dead because of him. The risk he'd tried to ignore – pretend wasn't really a risk – had happened, and it was his fault. His soul ached at the knowledge. *The priests were right, after all; this is anguish.* The ache in his chest was so strong, so acute, he flinched, curling in on himself.

"Brazier, you're okay," Freyen said. "Just breathe."

He breathed, let out a gasp, and the ache lessened, marginally.

"Deep breaths, that's all," Freyen said. "In and out."

He did as he was told, feeling the air expand his lungs, pushing against his back, and into hard floor. His view filled with Freyen's face, then Switch's appeared next to it, both deeply concerned. In between them, a blue vein crossed a grey ceiling. *Not the abyss, then*, and memory came flooding back. The installation, the vampires, and with a jolt of panic: the hex.

"Don't touch the hex!" he shouted, trying to get to his feet, but his arms weren't working properly. He flapped about like a dying fish, one of his hands catching the side of something hard – the command terminal.

"Brazier, it's okay," Freyen said, placing a hand on his shoulder.

It wasn't okay.

"The hex," he said again, but he felt as if he was waking from sleep. Then simply: "Lokul."

"We know," Switch said. "We know he controls the hex."

Using the command terminal, he pulled himself to his feet.

"How do you know?" he said.

"I opened a gate for Lyander," Freyen said, "but it felt like I was being watched. Then it felt like something was taking over my mind – so I got out of there."

"You're smarter than me, then."

"We all know that," Switch said.

"Where are they now?" Brazier asked, and Switch pointed at the corridor outside the drum.

"Pretty sure that's Lyander – he woke up, by the way – and he's about to fight Lokul." The figure walked down the corridor toward the other grey shape, the one stood next to the terminal.

"He's on his own?"

Switch moved her finger down to the antechamber and over to a connecting corridor, separated by a gate. A single figure stood on the other side – three others at the far end of the corridor. "Think that's either Gabriel or Eluthienn," she said.

"Either?" Brazier asked.

"One of them went over the edge, in the antechamber," Freyen said. "They got up, so looks like they're okay."

"We can't let Lyander fight Lokul on his own," Brazier said.

"It's not ideal," Switch said. "But my money is still on the big man."

Lyander was a one-man army. No doubt about it. That didn't mean Brazier wanted to let him fight – on his own – the being it supposedly took Leoncoure Leonette three days to kill. And either way, Eluthienn still needed to deliver the killing blow, or so he assumed.

"Okay," he said, formulating the plan as quickly as his mind would allow. "We wait for Lyander to distract Lokul, then open the gate for either Gabriel or Eluthienn."

"Don't think we're going to be so lucky," Freyen said, pointing at a corridor not far from them. Six shapes streamed along it, heading for a lift. Brazier followed the chute's route to the control chamber. He guessed one, maybe two minutes, until they were here. He traced a different route for them from a different lift in the control chamber, avoiding the incoming vampires and taking them to one of the duct spouts overhanging the drum.

"Once they start fighting, we open the gate," he said.

"That's going to be cutting it real tight," Switch said.

"There's no other way," Brazier said, watching Lyander head down the corridor toward Lokul, silently imploring the exorcist to move faster. "Lyander can't fight Lokul on his own, and if that's Eluthienn trapped in there, we can only release him from here."

"And once the vampires are in here, they'll have control over the installation," Freyen said.

"Not if we lock the chamber to my command script," Brazier said. "Lokul's the only one who can overpower my commands."

"You're sure about that?" Freyen asked.

"Near enough certain," Brazier said, "but it's not going to matter; by the time they're in here, we'll have the gate open, Eluthienn will be fighting Lokul, and we'll be waiting for Matthias on that duct." He pointed to the overhang.

Freyen gave him the *this is a bad idea* look, but he knew it made sense; they both knew there were no other options. Then out of nowhere, the panic resurfaced, causing his heart to speed up. He looked from Freyen to Switch.

"You left Matthias with the ship?"

"Well, he *is* the only one who can pilot the thing," Switch said.

"It was the only way to get you," Freyen added.

In his head, Brazier cursed himself for needing saving, then cursed again because with Lokul controlling the hex, there was no way to check the *Anchorite*'s location. Matthias might be halfway to Formaria by now.

"We can trust him," Freyen said.

"He also fancies me, remember," Switch said. "He might leave you lot here, but he's going nowhere without me."

Brazier held in an exasperated breath, deciding there wasn't a lot he could do now, and checked the hex. "Think we're about to find out if you really have charmed him," he said.

The shape that could be the prince fought off three others, then the vampire pack climbed into the lift, and Lyander slowed as he came upon the vampire king – who still stood next to the terminal.

Come on, Lyander, do what you do best.

The vampires, now stone-still, were invisible on the hex as the platform sailed through the installation and toward the control chamber.

"Brazier?" Freyen said, unease in her voice.

"We have time," Brazier said. "It's going to happen."

Then it did.

Lyander engaged Lokul: the two figures came together at the end of the corridor, whirling around one another like dancers, closing, then springing apart. One of them, perhaps Lyander, drove the other back, and they moved away from the terminal and onto the walkway. Brazier plunged his hand into a well and requested a tether to the *Anchorite*. His mind floated, and he called: *Matthias, are you there?* No answer. *Matthias?* Again, no answer. *Matt* – Then he was anchored in place.

I'm here, the navigator said lazily. *Didn't know if I'd ever hear your voice again*. The prospect of Brazier's death didn't seem to bother him one way or the other.

We need the Anchorite in the drum, now.

You sure? Everyone's looking a little spread out from what I can see.

We're meeting you there.

You're the boss, Matthias said, and the connection dropped.

Brazier sent his mind back to the internal network, found the gyre gate, and opened it. In his mind's eye, he watched the gate dissolve, saw either Eluthienn or Gabriel disengage from the vampire pack and run for the antechamber. Seeing the opportunity, Brazier reengaged the gate again, trapping the vampires in the corridor.

Brazier, we need to go, Freyen said in his ear, and he moved his mind, seeing the other pack, now almost at the control chamber. He called a platform to the chamber's second lift, locked all three command terminals to his command script, and disconnected.

"Let's go," he said, and picking up his crossbow, they ran to the lift doors, now parting for them. Grey walls glimmered with black and purple as they shot through the installation, travelling down to the next drum level, then across, to the southern duct system. The platform slowed, slotted into the lift chute, and the doors parted. Ahead was a long corridor, dimly lit by a weak vein along the ceiling – pouring through at the end, a blue light, like the depths of an ocean. From within it, a sickly sweet smell, the amalgamation of bodily fluids and rotting flesh, along with the faint, acrid tang of blood.

"Black abyss," Switch said, nose and brow wrinkling. Along with the stench, the faint ringing of steel clashing against steel drifted down the corridor.

"Come on," Brazier said, trying to talk while barely opening his mouth.

They ran toward the sound and the smell, at the end of the corridor, coming to the overhanging duct. Around them, the drum walls were lined with thousands of hardened gestation sacks. Like black flower buds, each one stuck onto a hexagonal tile, lined with gyre light. Below them, the walkway spanning the drum, and from their vantage, they saw the exorcist fight the vampire king.

Lyander was winning.

His cleaves rained down on Lokul's armour, smashing into the black plate, rocking the vampire. A backhand cut hit Lokul's arm, shattering the gold ornamentation curving out from the elbow guard. The vampire spun away, his white hair flowing around him, red eyes enraged, looking out above hollowed cheeks, the skin pale and yellowing, the lips cracked where the fangs jutted from between them.

The exorcist pursued, relentless in his attack, strike after strike forcing the vampire back, until one caught Lokul above his hip, in the gap between his breast plate and his thigh guard. It wasn't deep; it wouldn't kill. But it was enough for the Lord of Undead to flinch, to drop his guard, and leave space for Lyander's thrust. But in that moment, Lyander blanked, as if stunned by a bright light. Face impassive, body momentarily limp, sword arm dropping, as if his mind was somewhere else.

Brazier's heart thudded with such intense panic, it overwhelmed every other sense. He couldn't smell the stench; his vision narrowed on the walkway; he could barely sense Switch and Freyen standing next to him.

But whatever was happening to Lyander, it wouldn't matter, it would be okay because Eluthienn was almost there. Limping, his sword in one hand, the other arm held weakly at his side, but he was almost in the centre of the walkway, coming up behind the pair, and about to aid Lyander.

But it was too late.

Lokul saw the opportunity and, leaning on his unwounded leg, thrust with his blade, driving the sword into Lyander with such force, it broke through the chain mail, and sunk deep into his stomach. The exorcist coughed wetly, the grim set to his jaw now slack with surprise, eyes staring down at the sword as if he couldn't believe it was real. The vampire king withdrew the blade, and Lyander sunk to his knees, a hand over his stomach, before falling to one side. All Brazier could think was how unfair it was; how Lyander was the better fighter; how he shouldn't have lost; how close Eluthienn was; how the prince was, even now, stepping around Lyander's body and swinging his sword against the vampire.

Next to him, Switch raised her crossbow, bringing Brazier out of his trance-like state, but Brazier knocked it aside.

"You could hit Eluthienn from this distance," he said, and not a moment too soon. Their previous wounds seemingly forgotten, the pair whirled, their blades barely seeming to touch, glancing off one another like lightning strikes trying to hit each other out of the sky. Where Lyander was the warrior used to the chaos of battle fields, Eluthienn was the duelist – a master in the art of single combat. But it seemed to offer him little advantage. The pair moved with a blur of precise cuts and thrusts, synchronised as if they were mirror images of the other, the vampire matching the prince's calculated grace with his own.

But the vampire *was* at a disadvantage. While what looked like a wound to Eluthienn's shoulder weakened his attack and lessened his ability to parry, Lokul's thigh made his movements sluggish on the one side. One foot began to drag, he couldn't turn into or away from attacks as quickly as he should, and he became overprotective of the wound as they moved toward the walkway's edge.

Then Eluthienn carried out a level of swordsmanship so masterful, it was a work of art. Their swords met in front of their chests. Eluthienn drove his pommel into the vampire's face, but Lokul blocked the jab. Eluthienn let go of his own grip with his left hand, cupped the vampire's bottom hand, steered the swords around and – by entwining Lokul's wrists – disarmed the vampire. In the same motion, the prince drove his sword under Lokul's armpit and up through his shoulder. The point glinted silver in the drum's blue light, and without so much as a pause, Eluthienn pulled the blood-drenched blade down.

Then Lokul grabbed Eluthienn by his wounded shoulder.

The action, so unexpected, so unlikely at the end, caught the prince off guard. Eluthienn cried out as Lokul's thumb dug into the cut – for a second, paralysing him with pain. And the one second was enough. Lokul threw himself onto Eluthienn, fangs sinking into his neck, a spurt of blood splattering the prince's ear and hair. But whatever happened next, Brazier missed it because a shunt came from the end of the corridor. All three of them turned, seeing the six vampires standing in the lift. One leant its head back and screamed a bloody challenge into the ceiling, then the vampires rushed down the corridor.

Their crossbows were levelled and firing the second they left the lift, bolts flying down the corridor in a rhythmic click and twang. Most pinged and clinked off hard plate, some sunk into cheeks, into necks – one through an eye, the vampire tumbling to the ground, while others smashed its falling body out the way. Then they were all tumbling, falling to their knees; one somersaulting to the floor. Their pearl-white skin turned grey, shrinking in on itself as if being sucked from within their own bodies. Eyes turned to gloop, others rolled out of sockets, the skin so drawn and papery, they were naked skulls. At the end, the closest vampire reached out in their direction, skin falling from its fingers like dead leaves blown from a tree, and the arm fell to the floor.

Back in the drum, Brazier heard Eluthienn let out a short groan. The prince staggered in the centre of the walkway. Lokul, presumably thrown off the edge by the prince, was nowhere to be seen. Eluthienn dropped the vampire's sword, and placed a hand over the bite marks between his shoulder and neck. His face scrunching up at the pain, something at the end of the walkway caught his attention.

Then three things happened at once:

The *Anchorite* plummeted down from the top of the drum, her thrusters an echoing drone as they blasted warm air.

One after the other, then all together, the gestation pods exploded: blackened, withered creatures, coated in brown slime, crawled and fell from the open shells.

And Gabriel emerged from the corridor's shadow.

"Look," Freyen said, pointing at the opposite end of the drum. Another Gabriel appeared along the walkway, the pair of witch-hunters closing on the prince. But Brazier had no time for astonishment; wet thumps came from behind them, a piercing screech, and a blackened vampire child crawled its way toward them along the duct. Switch fired four bolts into its face, each one landing with a crack, and the thing fell still. Others crawled toward them, from their left and right, and down the walls – weakened, pathetic things, falling onto the duct like dying slugs. Freyen and Switch opened fire, but Brazier, a terrible feeling of foreboding curling through his chest, turned to watch the witch-hunter.

"Gabriel?" Eluthienn said, his voice weary, and confused. But even over the *Anchorite*'s thrusters, Brazier could hear the quiver of uncertainty.

"Killing a Lord of the Eternal Hunt," the Gabriel facing Eluthienn called over the noise. "Quite the achievement. Of course, you couldn't have done it without Lyander." Both Gabriels looked down at the exorcist's body with what seemed like genuine sadness. "But did you really think the Ecclessius would agree to such a ludicrous arrangement?" The witch-hunters neared the centre, both drawing swords from scabbards, a flash of coppery green in the eyes of the one facing Brazier, a momentary illusion caused by the light reflected off the *Anchorite*'s hull. "Did you really think they'd let you live? Did you really think *I* would let you live?"

The *Anchorite*'s thruster's reverberated now, sending a current swirling round the drum, and understanding hit Brazier like sunlight breaking the horizon. He adjusted his crossbow to single shot, took aim at the witch-hunter behind Eluthienn, and tried to fire. But the second before he pulled the trigger, a hand wrapped around his ankle, yanking at him, sending the shot high of its intended target.

He looked down, but Freyen was already there, one of her knives sinking into the back of the creature's head. Brazier spun around but knew he was too late. Eluthienn threw a wild, one-handed swing at the Gabriel in front of him, the sword catching the witch-hunter copy across the throat, and he turned to smoking tendrils.

The real Gabriel pulled the dagger from his hip, stepped lightly behind Eluthienn, and slit the prince's throat. Eluthienn covered the wound with a hand, gargled, sprayed blood from his mouth, half stumbled, half turned to face the real Gabriel, and faltered, taking an involuntary step toward the edge of the walkway. He righted himself, but the blood loss was too great. The prince's knees buckled, and he fell sideways off the walkway and into the darkness below.

As if coming out of a dream, the click, twang, and crack of crossbows – and the vampire's screeches – came rushing back to Brazier. The duct was awash with black and slimy corpses, those still clinging to life clawing their way over the mound of dead. And Brazier found they were being forced back to the edge of the lip.

"I'm out!" Switch shouted, and Brazier unclipped a magazine from his belt. He was about to hand it to Switch when Matthias's shout made him look behind them. The *Anchorite* hovered fifteen feet above them, its access ramp open, a length of rope suspended from within the fuselage, Matthias hanging off the edge.

"Jump!" he shouted.

"Go!" Brazier said to Switch, and she tightened her crossbow across her chest, took a step back, and threw herself off the duct, catching the rope with real and augmented hands. She swung in the air, then climbed her way to the ship.

"You're next," Brazier said to Freyen. She strapped up her crossbow, and turned, jumping lightly from the duct and catching the rope, twining it through her legs.

Brazier threw his crossbow over his shoulder, tightened the strap, and stepped back as far as he could. But before he could throw himself at the rope, one of the dying spawn flung itself from the wall and onto one of the *Anchorite*'s thrusters. The creature melted in a sorcerous blaze, its skin liquefying to leave a naked skeleton, then that, too, shattered at the magical force – but not before throwing the thruster angle wide and unbalancing the ship. The *Anchorite* righted itself in the air, but Freyen swung out into the drum, then back toward him.

"Jump!" she shouted, coming toward him, and Brazier did. He threw himself off the duct and caught the rope just above Freyen's head. Their legs tangled as they collided and she grabbed the back of his gambeson, pulling herself close. The ship pulled away from the drum wall, spinning them as they soared over a drop that might go on for leagues. But Brazier knew none of that because Freyen's lips were moving softly against his own.

"Promised myself I'd do that if we lived," she said breathlessly.

"Glad we lived," Brazier said, and her laugh was the light and carefree joy he thought he might be falling in love with. Flying out of the drum, with the vast blackness of the underground appearing around them, Switch pulled them onto the ramp.

"Told Matthias we weren't waiting for Gabriel," Switch said, as the ramp closed behind them and they made their way up the stairwell.

"We're not," Brazier said.

On the nav deck, Matthias placed the *Anchorite* on sentience, and they all stood round the command terminal, watching the ship drift away from the installation.

"Back to Thendergaarden?" Matthias asked.

"No," Brazier said, shaking his head. "The Ecclessius planned to betray Eluthienn. I don't think they were likely to let us walk away with that knowledge." He looked at Switch and Freyen: "I'm sorry," he said. They were all as good as fugitives now, and it was his fault. *But at least they're still alive*, another voice said. It was followed by a shallow ache of sadness at the realisation they weren't *all* alive. Lyander's death, he suspected, would see that ache grow.

Switch shrugged. "Trust me, I've had it worse," she said.

"So have I," Freyen said, giving him a soft smile.

"Where to, then?" Matthias said.

"Wherever we want. It's our ship now," Brazier said, and he returned the navigator's grin.

Epistolar Message Fion to Vallorandyl

A telling in Vallorandyl.

The teller is Emries von Cadst, Duke of Ylstgaar, Adjutant to the Fion Throne, and Marshal of the Western Front.

The witness is Vermillies Sidtch, Lord Regent of Ravinica, and Absolver General.

The telling is of the continued patience I extend to you, Lord Regent. Your lack of reasoning astounds me, given your prior achievements. Or perhaps it is merely my fault for affording your low cunning too much credit. Another party? Who? Celmyr? The Sorel Tan? The Fal'Hannians? There are many who stand to gain from inciting a war between Ravinica and Formaria but none with the resources to capitalise on it.

Now, is the tale grandiose, the teller steeped in self-importance, his ego swelling the further it unfolds?

Certainly. Criminals lording over portals into the Immuratum; ship-building installations on the edge of the world; a Lord of the Eternal Hunt nearly dying to this Lyander, a mortal man in his condition – all preposterous, each new development more unlikely than the last.

We will investigate, at length, and discover where the truth hides. But did Eluthienn die at the hands of the bounty hunter? I think not. I suspect the prince to be at large, or sheltered by Formaria. This stranger and his tale, is deception to mislead us, to send us down false roads. Here are two truths we can be certain of, Lord Regent, and I will set them out for you, as it seems my patience is truly endless.

First: Formaria is weakened, that much we know.

Second: We can be certain it won't be weak for long. The Fromryr have endured against all their foes for such time because of their ability to recover from these kinds of losses. Therefore, a finite opportunity presents itself, one we cannot afford to let slip from our grasp. This tale gives us just one course of action: We will accelerate our plans for the assimilation of Ravinica into Fiondagaard, while also preparing our forces to invade Formaria. These are the emperor's wishes.

The stage is set; the conquest begins.

The teller is Emries von Cadst. The witness is Vermillies Sidtch, and no others.

The End

Glossary

Races

Constructii – Humanoid constructs, presumed built by the Formarians **Dwen'hiema** – Dwarves

Fenn – Reptilian humanoids

Formarians – Unknown, presumed extinct

Goblins – Humanoids, typically green skinned

Humans – Humans

Ilvalien – Elves

Kneldier – Gnomes

Mirrovinjin – Humanoid, typically pale-skinned with four arms

Rakkan – Humanoids, typically black or dark red skinned, sometimes allied to the Mirrovinjin

Skavrii – Large humanoids, typically with black carapace-like skin, allied to the Mirrovinjin

Trolls – Large humanoids, skin colour and features varies

Factions, groups, and orders

Artificium - Order of Enginators

Conclave – Order of Witch-Hunters, Order Abhorrentia

Ecclessius – De facto rulers of the Fromryr, religious organisation

Fal'Hannians – Largest mercenary organisation in Aetraya

Fromryr – Allied races of elves, dwarves, gnomes, and humans inhabiting Formaria

Gyranic Coven – Order of Mages

High Council – The leaders of the Fromryr, made up of monarchs, the High Lords of Thendergaarden and members of the Ordained Conglomerate

High Lords of Thendergaarden – Heads of the Navarch, Navigorum, Gyranic Coven, Conclave, and Knights Redcrosse

Knights Redcrosse – Elite military order of the Ecclessius
Lords of the Eternal Hunt – Aeturnic deities, considered mythical
Navarch – Fromryian navy
Navigorum – Order of Navigators, also refers to nav deck
Ordained Conglomerate – The leaders of the Ecclessius
Sorel Tan – Banished elves dedicated to the restoration of the Gyre Gates, considered terrorists

<u>Chaos and Darkness</u>
Aeturnum – Darkness realm
Immuratum – Chaos realm

Abhorrence – Aeturnic corruption
Malignance – Immuratic corruption

Aeturni – Monster
Immurati – Demon

<u>Gyranic sorcery</u>
Anomancy – Healing
Abjurancy – Defensive
Evocancy – Offensive
Obliquency – Manipulation
Symulacrancy – Imitation

<u>Settlements, structures & features</u>
Cauldron – Second largest settlement
Cradle – Fourth largest settlement
Cove – Smallest settlement
Gyre Gates – Portals to other worlds, all destroyed during the Sundering
Maw – Spatial and temporal space distinct from the rest

of Formaria
Relative horizon – Boundary separating Maws from the rest of Formaria
Spire – Third largest, outpost rather than settlement
Surface drift – Large flows of gyranic sorcery pouring through breaches from Yeggardania
Vault – Largest settlement

<u>Gyre ship classes and type</u>
Ship classes refers to size – Maw, Vault, Cauldron, Spire, Cradle (there is no Cove class)
Ship type refers to function – Gyre Star, Cruiser, Frigate, Destroyer, Miner, Transporter, Lander

<u>Fromryian Royal Houses</u>
Angelaux – Capital: Pontifax
Couronne – Capital: Helispont
Dillendwan – Capital: Thendergaarden
Fontain – Capital: Taranis
Guildain – Capital: Asteron
Laanorath – Capital: Etherlain
La'Voline – Capital: Sephera
Rosantz – Capital: Thela
Yarranstar – Capital: Everaux

About the author

Sam Middleton is a science fiction and fantasy writer. He graduated from the University of Sheffield in 2014 with a Bachelor of Arts degree in English Literature. After graduating he pursued a career in business writing and communications before becoming a freelance writer and author. Find out more about what he's up to, at www.sammiddletonbooks.com

Printed in Dunstable, United Kingdom

71801083R00272